The Roa Science Fiction

Volume 1: From Gilgamesh to Wells

Edited by James Gunn

The Scarecrow Press, Inc.
Lanham, Maryland, and Oxford
2002

SCARECROW PRESS, INC.

Published in the United States of America
by Scarecrow Press, Inc.
A Member of the Rowman & Littlefield Publishing Group
4720 Boston Way, Lanham, Maryland 20706
www.scarecrowpress.com

PO Box 317
Oxford
OX2 9RU, UK

ISBN: 978-0-8108-4414-8
The New American Library edition of this book was cataloged as
LC#77-76965
Scarecrow Press, Inc.

∞™ The paper used in this publication meets the minimum requirements
of American National Standard for Information Sciences—Permanence of
Paper for Printed Library Materials, ANSI/NISO Z39.48-1992.
Manufactured in the United States of America.

To Edgar Allan Poe
Jules Verne,
and H. G. Wells . . .
who got it started

Contents

Introduction — vii

The First Voyage to the Moon — 1
   From *A True Story* — by Lucian of Samosata — 3

Strange Creatures and Far Traveling — 13
   From *The Voyages and Travels of Sir John
Mandeville* — Anonymous — 16

The Good Place That Is No Place — 22
   From *Utopia* — by Thomas More — 25

The New Science and the Old Religion — 31
   From *The City of the Sun* — by Tommaso Campanella — 33

Experience, Experiment, and the Battle for Men's Minds — 42
   From *The New Atlantis* — by Francis Bacon — 44

A New Look at the Heavens and Another Trip to the Moon — 63
   Somnium, or Lunar Astronomy — by Johannes Kepler — 65

Commuting to the Moon — 79
   From *A Voyage to the Moon* — by Cyrano de Bergerac — 81

The Age of Reason and the Voice of Dissent — 87
   From "A Voyage to Laputa" — by Jonathan Swift — 90

Imaginary Voyages in the Other Direction — 119
   From *The Journey to the World Underground* — by
Ludvig Holberg — 122

Visitors from Space   128
   From *Micromegas*—by François Marie Arouet de Voltaire   130

Science and Literature: When Worlds Collide   146
   From *Frankenstein*—by Mary Shelley   149

Science as Symbol   159
   Rappaccini's Daughter—by Nathaniel Hawthorne   162

Anticipations of the Future   186
   Mellonta Tauta—by Edgar Allan Poe   189

Expanding the Vision   201
   The Diamond Lens—by Fitz-James O'Brien   203

The Indispensable Frenchman   224
   From *Twenty Thousand Leagues Under the Sea*   227
   From *Around the Moon*—by Jules Verne   245

Lost Civilizations and Ancient Knowledge   256
   From *She*—by H. Rider Haggard   259

The New Frontier   276
   From *Looking Backward*—by Edward Bellamy   279

New Magazines, New Readers, New Writers   304
   The Damned Thing—by Ambrose Bierce   307

A Flying Start   315
   With the Night Mail—by Rudyard Kipling   318

The Father of Modern Science Fiction   336
   The Star—by H. G. Wells   339

About the Editor   349

Introduction

1

Science fiction is the literature of change. In the first edition of this anthology I called it "the branch of literature that deals with the effects of change on people in the real world as it can be projected into the past, the future, or to distant places. It often concerns itself with scientific or technological change, and it usually involves matters whose importance is greater than the individual or the community; often civilization or the race itself is in danger." But shorter is better. Traditional literature is the literature of continuity, and thus of the past; science fiction is the literature of change, and thus of the present and the future. As the literature of change, science fiction, at its most characteristic, inserts the reader into a world significantly different from the world of present experience because of catastrophic natural events, because of the evolutionary alterations of time, or because of human activities, particularly scientific and technological. Its basic assumptions are that the universe is knowable (though it may never be fully known) and that people are adaptable (that is, they, like everything else, evolve as a consequence of environment and natural selection); science fiction is fundamentally Darwinian and thus could also be called "the literature of the human species."

Science fiction has adopted other fictional modes — the adventure and the romance, for instance — but it is most typical when it deals with ideas worked out in human terms. It is not "the" literature of ideas but surely "a literature of ideas." One touchstone story, Tom Godwin's "The Cold Equations" (*Astounding,* August 1954), takes as its thesis that humanity's romantic notions about how life ought to be have no influence on the inexorable facts ("the cold equations") of the universe. Another Godwin story said, "Machines don't care."

At the hard core of almost every true science-fiction story is an idea — "the quality that makes humanity human is curiosity"; "if people only saw the stars every thousand years, they would not adore but go mad"; "the star that shone over Bethlehem may have been a supernova that destroyed an intelligent race"—and the reader who misses the intellectual level of discourse is missing what more than anything else distinguishes science fiction from other forms of fiction.

The skill of the science-fiction author is evidenced in the way he gives his ideas human form and value. In the process of fictionalizing his ideas, he may develop a structure—a story or plot, if you like—that is indistinguishable from other kinds of fiction. Robert Heinlein, the dean of science-fiction writers, once wrote (*Of Worlds Beyond,* 1947) that there are only three main plots for what he called the human-interest story (as opposed to the gadget story): 1) boy-meets-girl; 2) the Little Tailor; and 3) the-man-who-learned-better. It is for this—the promise that draws a reader into a story and the reward that satisfies him—that we read fiction, and the more we are drawn into a story and care what happens to the characters, the better satisfied we are when the author resolves their situation.

But it is not for this alone that we read science fiction. The best science-fiction stories are those that match manner with matter, story with idea. In "The Cold Equations," for instance, we become concerned about the threat to the girl who stows-away aboard an emergency delivery ship in order to see her brother, who is a member of a small party exploring a frontier planet. The ship has only enough fuel to complete its mission; if the girl remains aboard, the ship will crash on landing, not only killing the girl and the pilot, but also dooming the members of the exploration party, who will not receive the plague serum the ship has been launched to deliver. Those are the cold equations, and the girl goes out the air lock. The reader's concern for the girl is transformed into an intellectual awareness of a higher law than "women and children first"—sentiment is expensive, good intentions are irrelevant, and ignorance is punished as severely as guilt.

James Joyce has defined the "epiphany" of a short story as the flash of recognition that shows the situation in a new light: "its soul, its whatness leaps to us from the vestment of its appearance." In the science-fiction story, the epiphany usually is a revelation not of character but of the relationship of man to his environment, whether man-made or natural, or of man to other men or to other creatures or to his own creations.

2

Thus defined, science fiction could not be written until people began to think in unaccustomed ways. They had, first of all, to think of themselves as a race—not as a tribe or a people or even a nation. Science fiction may contain unconscious cultural or political biases, but there is little tribalism, little rejoicing in the victory over another human group, but rather an implied or overt criticism of the act of war, and there is even less nationalism. Catastrophes, for instance, are catholic; in fact, they usually are placed close to home, as in H. G. Wells's *The War of the Worlds* or John Wyndham's *The Day of the Triffids,* for immediacy of impact if nothing else.

People also had to adopt an open mind about the nature of the universe— its beginning and its end—and the fate of man. Science fiction's religion is skepticism about faith, although there is science fiction about religion, such as Arthur C. Clarke's "The Star" (*Infinity,* November 1955) and James Blish's *A Case of Conscience* (1958; story version, *If,* September 1953). The reasons for this are clear: religion answers all the questions that science fiction wishes to raise, and science fiction written within a religious framework (such as C. S. Lewis' *Perelandra* trilogy) turns into parable.

People also had to discover the future. As long as the future was merely a place where today's activities went on in some eternal cycle, perhaps even spiraling downward from some earlier golden age, a fiction about the future was meaningless. Not until the Industrial Revolution brought to Western peoples the unsettling feeling that tomorrow was going to be markedly different from today did men begin to think about the future, begin to consider choices, such as "Shall I stay here on the farm or go to the new weaving factory opening in Birmingham?" People began to think of the future as a place where they would live, different in degree and perhaps even in kind, a place they might be able to make better lives for themselves if they thought about it and did the right things.

It was no coincidence that Adam Smith's *The Wealth of Nations* was published in 1776 or that Auguste Comte began working on the systematization of sociology about 1830, or that these dates embraced the American and the French revolutions; these were men taking account of change and considering how conditions might be better.

Technological discoveries that had been accumulating since the Renaissance reached a critical mass in the middle of the eighteenth century. With this, and the systematic study of the laws of nature that ran parallel to the Industrial Revolution and later became known as the Age of Science, came the beginnings of science fiction. Inseminated by such new scientific possibilities as electricity and medicine, the gothic novel produced Mary Shelley's *Frankenstein* in 1818; the technology of ballooning and such scientific discoveries as mesmerism, along with the new scientific way of thought, produced the scientific fiction of Nathaniel Hawthorne and Edgar Allan

Poe; Poe, geographic discoveries, and the growing potential of technology produced the *voyages extraordinaires* of Jules Verne; Charles Darwin and his disciple T. H. Huxley and a scientific education produced the scientific romances of H. G. Wells; Poe, Verne, Wells, and the new excitement of electricity and radio produced Hugo Gernsback, and he and the pulp magazines produced *Amazing Stories* in 1926; John W. Campbell and breakthroughs in physics and astronomy and other sciences produced modern science fiction. . . . All this is a familiar story (see *Alternate Worlds*, 1975) that will be incorporated in the headnotes that follow.

Science and technology created social change, and the awareness of social change created science fiction. Technology increased agricultural productivity and offered farmers the opportunity to work only a twelve-hour day in the factory; technology helped create nationalism and provided it with weapons and armies; technology created money (or made it meaningful by spreading it more widely) and provided people with products to spend it on; technology turned raw materials into energy and enhanced man's control over his environment, improved his standard of living, and extended his life span through more healthful conditions and better medicine; technology produced a belief in progress that became a kind of religion for Western man.

Science fiction was the artistic response to the human experience of change. Man began to look ahead to something different and perhaps something better; one way he looked was through a new kind of fiction. John Campbell once said (*Modern Science Fiction*, 1953): "Fiction is simply dreams written out. Science fiction consists of the hopes and dreams and fears (for some dreams are nightmares) of a technically based society."

Man has lived in a technically based society for perhaps a hundred years or so, and although the frame of mind essential to the creation of modern science fiction has developed largely since 1900, the process of invention began long before that. Technology goes back to the discovery of fire and the invention of the wedge, the wheel, the horse collar, the stirrup, the astrolabe, the abacus, and movable type; and science goes back beyond Aristotle, even beyond Democritus, to inquiring minds among the ancient Egyptians, the Chaldeans, and the Chinese.

So, too, back beyond 1900, back beyond 1750, back beyond even the birth of Christ, go the hopes and dreams and fears that ultimately found expression, in a technically based society, as science fiction. In an earlier time, before the future was discovered, much less the concept of progress, men wrote about travel to the distant places of the earth and the wonders that might be found there, even about journeys to other astronomical bodies, particularly the moon, hung out there in the night sky almost near enough to touch; they wrote about the wonders that once were; they speculated about the place of man in the universe. And they incorporated their basic questions and desires into fictional narratives, not into short stories and novels, which had not yet been invented, but into epic poems and plays and tales.

It is this period that this book intends to cover, from *Gilgamesh to Wells*, roughly from 2000 B.C. to A.D. 1900. It will include examples and works that preceded and led up to the contemporary expression of science fiction in magazines and books. In order to understand why science fiction is the way it is today, I think it is important for readers and students of the genre to understand what it has been.

3

Humanity's earliest dreams were to control its environment (by propitiating the gods who controlled—or were—the natural forces of his world), to control other people (by conquering them or by ruling over them, or both), and to live forever. Humanity's greatest fear, after personal death or that of family, was that a particular people would be destroyed, its civilization wiped out, its culture and its history lost.

Humanity's dreams are seldom fulfilled, but its fears are almost always realized. Humanity's heroes—they have been called culture heroes—have been men who were part god, to whom the gods listened, who controlled the elements, who became king, who sought to live forever, and who founded, or saved, the people. All of these elements later found their expression in science fiction.

The earliest written narrative, the first epic, contains almost all of these dreams and fears. *Gilgamesh,* a Babylonian epic poem of about three thousand lines written in cuneiform on twelve tablets, was discovered in scattered fragments over a period of about eighty years beginning in the middle of the nineteenth century and continuing until about 1930. A partial translation was first published in 1872 and the first complete translation in 1900.

The epic begins with a description of Gilgamesh and a recapitulation of his career. Freely translated, the lines run something like this:

He saw everything, to the ends of the earth;
He knew all things and could do all things;

He saw secret things and revealed hidden things;
He brought information about the days before the flood;
He went on a long journey, became weary and worn;
He engraved on a stone table all of his labors;
He built the walls of Uruk, the enclosure,
Of holy Eanna, the sacred temple. . . .

Two-thirds of him is god and one-third of him is man.
None can match the form of his body.

Translate that into modern terms, and you would have something like the novels of Edward Elmer Smith, particularly the *Lensman* series; besides their length, readers had good reason to call Smith's space adventures "epics." One fan press, after World War II, would publish Smith's six-volume *Lensman* series as *The History of Civilization.*

Gilgamesh's concerns are those of science fiction: social (people need a heroic king, but what do people do when a king rules too heavily?) and personal (can man live forever, or, if not, how does he live with the fact of death?). Gilgamesh was not simply a hero; he was part god—the son of a goddess and a high priest—who became king of Uruk. But his exuberance, strength, vigor, and arrogance led him to carry off the maidens and force the young men to work on the city walls and the temple. Finally his subjects called on the gods for relief.

They responded by creating a wild man of incredible strength named Enkidu. Eventually, led by a prostitute, Enkidu came to battle Gilgamesh; after a terrific fight, Gilgamesh was victorious and the two became friends. They went off together to win fame by killing a terrible ogre who guarded a vast cedar forest. With the help of the gods, they succeeded. On their return to Uruk, Ishtar, goddess of love, offered to be Gilgamesh's wife, but he refused. Enraged, she asked her father, Anu, to send the bull of heaven to destroy Gilgamesh, but Enkidu and Gilgamesh killed the bull.

The gods decided that one of them had to die; Enkidu was chosen by lot. Torn by grief at the death of his friend, stricken by the thought that he, too, must die, Gilgamesh went to seek immortality from Utnapishtim, the Babylonian Noah, who was made immortal by the gods. After great difficulties and perils, Gilgamesh finally reached Utnapishtim but learned that only the gods can confer immortality, and why should they choose him?

One hope remained: a thorny plant that grew at the bottom of the sea could rejuvenate old men. Gilgamesh retrieved some, but on his return home, as he was bathing, a serpent ate the plant (and thereby won the power to shed its skin and renew its life). Gilgamesh wept, but eventually he returned to Uruk, having learned to be content with his lot and to rejoice in the work of his hands.

Part of the lesson Gilgamesh learned was given him during his journey by a divine barmaid: "Enjoy your life and make the best of it." There is no immortality; you must make do with what you have.

The epic even contains a bit of technology, not only the weapons with which Gilgamesh and Enkidu do battle but the bricks with which the wall of Uruk is built. When Gilgamesh and Urshanabi (Utnapishtim's boatman) return to Uruk, Gilgamesh says:

> Urshanabi, climb upon the wall of Uruk and walk about;
> Inspect the foundation terrace and examine the brickwork,
> If its brickwork be not of burnt bricks,
> And if the seven wise men did not lay its foundation!

4

Technology plays a more significant part in the Greek myth of Daedalus, a craftsman said to have been taught his art by Athene herself. He took as apprentice his nephew Talos and then killed the boy out of jealousy when he invented the saw, the potter's wheel, and the compass. Daedalus had to flee from Athens and went eventually to Crete.

King Minos welcomed him to Knossos. There Daedalus fathered Icarus, built the maze called the labyrinth for the bullheaded man called the Minotaur (the result of the unnatural coupling of Pasiphaë and Zeus's white bull), and perhaps constructed the bull-headed bronze servant (the first robot?), also named Talos who ran three times a day around the island of Crete, threw rocks at any foreign ships, and destroyed an army of invading Sardinians by turning himself red-hot in a fire and destroying them with his embrace. Other versions say that Talos was a survivor of the bronze race of men who sprang from the ash trees, or that he was forged by Hephaestus in Sardinia and given to Minos by Zeus.

Minos finally learned that his wife's coupling with the white bull had been made possible by Daedalus, who constructed for Pasiphaë a hollow wooden cow in which she placed herself. Minos locked Daedalus and Icarus in the labyrinth; Pasiphaë freed them, and Daedalus fashioned wings out of feathers and wax. The escape, however, ended with Icarus ignoring his father's warning, flying too near the sun, and plunging into the sea (later named the Icaran sea in his honor) when his wings melted.

In some versions Daedalus also is said to have invented sails, built temples, fashioned a lifelike statue of Heracles, and constructed beautiful toys, including jointed dolls. The basic story, however, contains many of the elements of later science fiction: the inventor imprisoned in his own invention, escaping through his ingenuity, and losing someone close to him because of the incautious use of the new technology.

Greek mythology is a rich source of imagery for science fiction, as for literature as a whole. For science fiction, however, it provides a useful tension between great ambitions and their consequences: the heroism of Perseus and his uses of Medusa's head; the capture of the winged horse Pegasus by Bellerophon and his conquest of the Chimera; the adventures of the Argonauts; the misfortune of Midas. But the most science fictional of Greek myths is *The Odyssey.*

Today we make sharp distinctions between the real and the unreal (though such distinctions have come under attack from mystics, absurdists, and fabulists). Science and technology have empowered us to make such distinctions. Their measuring instruments and laboratory techniques, microscopes and telescopes, test tubes and particle accelerators, computers and counters—all the theories and paraphernalia of science encourage us in the illusion that we know what is real and what is not.

Naturalism and realism in fiction have led us to believe, similarly, that we can detect an author's intention to deal with things as they are, to speculate about what might be, or to describe worlds that could not be—to write mundane works (to use the fan term for everything that isn't science fiction or fantasy), science fiction, or fantasy. It seems to many critics (though not to all) that our reaction to a story is significantly affected by the distinction between a fictional world presented to us as an extension of the world we live in and a fictional world that we are told could not exist, though we may be confused when these two worlds are mixed or the distinctions are blurred.

The Babylonians and the Greeks did not have that problem. The real and the unreal flowed together imperceptibly. When one believes that the stars or the gods control human affairs, that storm and drought and good weather are brought by spirits or deities who can be placated by ceremony or sacrifice, that living things can rise spontaneously out of inanimate matter, that even real things are merely poor imitations of some ideal objects existing elsewhere, then the difference between the real and the unreal may be, in every sense of the word, immaterial.

When Odysseus, destined as he knows not to return to Ithaca and his wife, Penelope, for ten long years, makes his epic journey around the Mediterranean, what we take as a strange mixture of superstition, myth, geographic exploration, and natural (and unnatural) history must have seemed all of a piece to Homer's audience, and as real as the battles of *The Iliad.*

Apollodorus speculated that the *Odyssey* was an account of a voyage around Sicily, and Robert Graves, following Samuel Butler, that it was written by a woman; but it may as easily be read as a fictional exploration of the known universe, with speculations about the nature of the unknown that lurks where no man has gone.

The *Odyssey* offers a story about destiny, death, sea-raiding, theft, adventure, and the miraculous; far-traveling, witchcraft, and superstition; and accounts of the strange people who live in the distant places of the world and the strange customs they practice. The fantastic episodes begin with the brief sojourn of Odysseus' ships in the land of the lotus eaters, where his two picked men

> never cared to report, nor to return:
> they longed to stay forever, browsing on
> that native bloom, forgetful of their homeland.

Later Odysseus encountered the Cyclops Polyphemus, was trapped by his curiosity, and escaped by his ingenuity, including the blinding of the Cyclops and giving his name as "Nobody"; received a bag of winds from Aeolus, Warden of the Winds, and had the unfavorable winds released by his men; stayed with the witch Circe after she turned his men back into human form from the pigs they had become; summoned the seer Teiresias from the dead to prophesy for him and conversed with other ghosts; evaded the lure of the Sirens, who promised him foreknowledge of all future happenings; and eluded the monsters Scylla and Charybdis.

Place such a voyage among the stars, and it would evoke what Sam Moskowitz called the sense of wonder. Many a science-fiction writer (and Gene Roddenberry) has done just that.

5

The works of Plato have a different kind of interest—not of form or even of theme but of content. In two of the dialogues, *Timaeus* and *Critias,* he records the earliest account of the lost continent of Atlantis. There are Egyptian parallels. The legend may have a factual background in the destruction of a Minoan civilization by earthquake or volcanic explosion, or both. Or it may be only the kind of myth about a once-flourishing, higher civilization that was destroyed, or disappeared—the sort of thing that still sells books for Erich von Daniken and his imitators.

Plato's story of Atlantis, as told by Critias, describes how the Greek gods portioned out the earth and how Poseidon took the island of Atlantis and settled there his children by a mortal woman. His eldest son, Atlas (who was to bear the heavens on his shoulders as punishment for joining the Titans in their unsuccessful war against the Olympian gods), was king.

As befitted a land established by Poseidon, it was blessed by the sea. The island, larger than Africa and Asia together, lay beyond the Pillars of Heracles; beyond Atlantis, joined by a chain of fruit-bearing islands, was another continent. This was the inspiration for later stories about Atlantis as a once-great civilization located between Europe and the Americas. Mu was the name of a similar island civilization located in the Pacific in more contemporary speculations.

The citizens of Atlantis, according to Critias, cultivated a great central plain and surrounded it with rings of land and sea. They built palaces, baths, racetracks, harbors, and temples, and they made war as far as the western continent and as far east as Egypt and Italy. But greed and cruelty finally overcame them, and the Athenians defeated them single-handedly. At the same time the gods sent a deluge that, in one day and one night, overwhelmed all of Atlantis, burying the harbor and temples under tons of mud and making the sea unnavigable.

The concept that life once was better, or men were wiser or richer or more powerful, or nature was kinder, has exhibited itself in a variety of forms. The Judeo-Christian story of the Garden of Eden followed by man's fall from grace and the Greek myth of the Golden Age are the two best-known versions. Thomas Bulfinch described the Golden Age in his book *Mythology* (1855):

> The world being thus furnished with inhabitants, the first age was an age of innocence and happiness, called the *Golden Age.* Truth and right prevailed, though not enforced by law, nor was there any magistrate to threaten or punish. The forest had not yet been robbed of its trees to furnish timbers for vessels, nor had men built fortifications round their towns. There were no such things as swords, spears, or helmets. The earth brought forth all things necessary for man, without his labor in ploughing or sowing. Perpetual spring reigned, flowers sprang up without seed, the rivers flowed with milk and wine, and yellow honey distilled from the oaks.
>
> Then succeeded the *Silver Age,* inferior to the golden, but better than that of brass. Jupiter shortened the spring, and divided the year into seasons. Then, first, men had to endure the extremes of heat and cold, and houses became

necessary. Caves were the first dwellings, and leafy coverts of the woods, and huts woven of twigs. Crops would no longer grow without planting. The farmer was obliged to sow the seed, and the toiling ox to draw the plough.

Next came the *Brazen Age,* more savage of temper and readier to the strife of arms, yet not altogether wicked. The hardest and worst was the *Iron Age.* Crime burst in like a flood; modesty, truth, and honor fled. In their places came fraud and cunning, violence, and the wicked love of gain. The seamen spread sails to the wind, and the trees were torn from the mountains to serve for keels to ships, and vex the face of ocean. The earth, which till now had been cultivated in common, began to be divided off into possessions. Men were not satisfied with what the surface produced, but must dig into its bowels, and draw forth from thence the ores of metals. Mischievous *iron,* and more mischievous *gold,* were produced. War sprang up, using both as weapons; the guest was not safe in his friend's house; and sons-in-law and fathers-in-law, brothers and sisters, husbands and wives, could not trust one another. Sons wished their fathers dead, that they might come to the inheritance; family love lay prostrate. The earth was wet with slaughter, and the gods abandoned it, one by one, till Astraea alone was left, and finally she also took her departure.

The concept of fallen man or the Golden Age is the opposite of the concept of progress, the concept that man's condition is improvable and is, in fact, steadily improving through his own efforts. The possibility of progress was suggested in the utopian vision that first found expression in Plato's *Republic.* In this dialogue Plato constructs a model state planned not for the benefit of any one citizen but for the good of all.

"Our aim in founding the State," says Socrates, Plato's spokesman, "was not the disproportionate happiness of any one class, but the greatest happiness of the whole."

Plato's Republic was not distinguished by its happiness. In order to make it work, each individual had to be relatively miserable and completely content with his condition and his situation; otherwise the state would be disorderly, and when the state is disorderly, all citizens suffer.

All the citizens of Plato's Republic had to belong to one of three social classes: worker, soldier, or guardian. Each citizen had to know his place, perform his job, and be content. No one could possess gold or silver, and thus grow rich. The state raised the children, assigned their roles, and regulated all economic and social activities. Because the state would be firm and strong, the citizens of the state would be happy.

Later writers would imagine other utopias—the word was invented by Sir Thomas More in 1516, by combining two Greek words to mean "no place"—where man at last would find perfect happiness.

6

Satire always has been a different matter.

Satire offers criticisms of society, using humor and wit, so that humanity or human institutions may be improved. It depends on the reader's recognition of the difference between reality and fantasy. Satire presents real people or real institutions in a fantasy setting or fantastically exaggerated; the reader or audience must transfer the qualities from the fantastic to the real, and in that transference his appreciation resides.

Thus the Greek tragedies of Aeschylus, Sophocles, and Euripides were considered to deal dramatically with reality, with real historical personages; certain dramatic license was permitted for emphasis or reinterpretation. The civic religious nature of the drama allowed little room for fantasy.

The comedies of Aristophanes, however, clearly could be fantastic, and their departure from reality had to be recognized by the audience if they were to succeed. In *The Clouds,* for instance, Aristophanes satirized the sophistic system of education that was leading Athenians to argue for victory, not truth; to make a bad cause triumph over the right. To personify these traits, Aristophanes put Socrates in a basket hanging between heaven and earth.

In *The Birds,* Aristophanes caricatured the schemes and ambitions of the Athenian expedition against Sicily by describing how two elderly Athenians went to live with the birds, persuaded the birds to build an enormous wall in the Mid-Air between men and gods so that no sacrifices could reach the gods, and starved the gods into submission. In *The Frogs,* Dionysus, patron of the drama, visited Hades to obtain the release of Euripides in order to reinvigorate Greek tragedy, but in a literary contest Aeschylus won over Euripides and was released by Pluto to return with Dionysus.

Let me be clear: I am not claiming that any of these examples is science fiction. No true science fiction was written prior to Mary Shelley's *Frankenstein* in 1818, and perhaps not until Jules Verne's *Journey to the Center of the Earth* in 1864. Nor do I claim that they exist in any special paternal relationship to science fiction; in a sense they are the parents of all Western literature. What I do claim for them is some of the same kind of qualities that later science fiction would possess, and one must trace a kind of literary ancestry or claim that science fiction was created, implausibly, without parents or precedents.

These examples have science-fictional interest as treatment of ideas that might have developed as science fiction under different conditions; they represent a continuing line of literary interest that eventually, when the conditions were right, became science fiction; and the intellectual concerns they reflect were influential on later science fiction.

The First Voyage to the Moon

The first extended narrative that has enough of the qualities of science fiction to be included in this anthology is "A True Story" by Lucian of Samosata.

The days of the battling Greek states had been ended by the successes of Rome. Rome had conquered the world and brought peace, plenty, efficiency, engineering, a concern for material values, and time for contemplation.

Edward Gibbon began his *Decline and Fall of the Roman Empire* with the statement:

> In the second century of the Christian Aera, the empire of Rome comprehended the fairest part of the earth, and the most civilized portion of mankind. The frontiers of that extensive monarchy were guaranteed by ancient renown and disciplined valor. The gentle, but powerful, influence of laws and manners had gradually cemented the union of the provinces. Their peaceful inhabitants enjoyed and abused the advantages of wealth and luxury. . . .

Under Roman rule men had opportunity to make money, to get ahead, to see their children get ahead, and to enjoy the longest period of peace in Western history. Every major city had a university; many citizens listened to lectures or to soap-box orators.

In this period Lucian was born in Samosata, a remote town of the empire, on the Euphrates in Syria. He was a poor boy. He was apprenticed as a stonemason but took off for Ionia, learned Greek, steeped himself in Greek literature, mastered public speaking, became a lawyer but soon became a traveling lecturer in Greece, Italy, and Gaul, held a government professorship in Gaul, settled in Athens, became a satirical writer, returned to lecturing, and as an old man accepted an appointment from the Emperor Commodus to a well-paying government job in Egypt.

Lucian wrote two satirical stories about a trip to the moon. In the first, "Icaromennipus," a philosopher bent on proving that the earth is round flies to the moon with one wing from a vulture and one from an eagle. Lucian's more ambitious work is "A True Story." It was written between A.D. 165

and 175, in Lucian's most creative period. It belongs to that kind of narrative that would later be called a tall tale. It satirizes, and in places parodies, Homer (going Odysseus one better by sailing not just around the Mediterranean but to the moon), Herodotus, Xenophon, Thucydides, and other authors whose works have been lost, such as Iambulus.

Lucian's sailing ship is no spaceship. His adventurers have no intention of going to the moon, and Lucian's purpose is not to make such a journey credible or to speculate about what we might find if we could really make the journey. He was writing satire. But a sailing ship is not that much different from Poe's balloon or Verne's cannon shell, and the story probably was read (or listened to) largely for its adventure and its inventiveness.

"A True Story" inspired a long chain of literary descendants, including Kepler, Godwin, Cyrano de Bergerac, Swift, Voltaire, and Poe.

From A True Story

BY LUCIAN OF SAMOSATA
TRANSLATED BY LIONEL CASSON

No athlete or body-building enthusiast thinks only of exercising and being in condition. He thinks also of relaxing when the occasion calls for it and, as a matter of fact, he considers this the most important part of training. In my opinion the same holds for book enthusiasts: after poring over a lot of serious works, they ought give the mind a rest to get it into even better shape for the next workout. The most suitable way for them to spend the interval is with light, pleasant reading which, instead of merely entertaining, furnishes some intellectual fare as well—and this I think they'll agree is true of the present work.

It is a work that will appeal to them not only because of the exotic subject matter, the amusing plot, and the way I've told all sorts of lies with an absolutely straight face, but because I've included comic allusions to all our noted poets, historians, and philosophers of old who have written so many fabulous tall stories. I don't need to name names: you'll recognize them yourselves as you read along. Ctesias of Cnidus, the son of Ctesiochus, has written things about India and the Indians that he neither saw himself nor heard from anyone who had any respect for the truth. Iambulus has written a lot of unbelievable stuff about the ocean; everyone knows he made it all up, yet, for all that, he has put together an amusing account. Lots of other writers have shown a preference for the same technique: under the guise of reporting their travels abroad they spin yarns of huge monsters, savage tribes, and strange ways of life. The arch-exponent of, and model for, this sort of tomfoolery is Homer's Odysseus telling the court of Alcinous about a bag with the winds in it, one-eyed giants, cannibals, savages, even many-headed monsters and magic drugs that change shipmates into swine—with one such story after another he had those simple-minded Phaeacians goggle-eyed.

Now, I've read all the practitioners of this art and I've never been very hard on them for not telling the truth—not when I see how common this failing is even among those who profess to be writing philosophy. What I have wondered at, though, is the way they're convinced they can write pure fable and get away with it. Since I'm vain enough myself to want to leave something behind to posterity and since I have nothing true to record—I never had any experiences worth talking about—in order not to be the only writer without a stake in the right to make up tall tales, I, too, have turned to lying—but a much more honest lying than all the others. The one and only truth you'll hear from me is that I am lying; by frankly admitting that there isn't a word of truth in what I say, I feel I'm avoiding the possibility of attack from any quarter.

Well, then, I'm writing about things I neither saw nor heard of from another soul, things which don't exist and couldn't possibly exist. So all readers beware: don't believe any of it.

Some time ago I set out on a voyage from the Straits of Gibraltar. A favorable breeze carried me into the Atlantic Ocean, and I was on my way. The basic reasons for the trip were my intellectual curiosity, my thirst for novelty, and the desire to find out what formed the farther border of the ocean and what peoples lived there. I had consequently put aboard a large stock of provisions and plenty of water and had taken on as crew fifty acquaintances who shared my interests; I had also laid in a good supply of weapons, induced—by the offer of a handsome salary—the best navigator available to go along, and had our vessel, a fast brig, made shipshape for a long and hard stay at sea

For a day and a night we sailed before a wind that was favorable but not strong enough to carry us out of sight of land. At dawn of the following day, however, the wind made up, the sea began to run, and the sky grew dark. There wasn't even time to take in sail; we gave up and let the ship scud before the gale. For the next seventy-nine days we were driven along by a furious storm. Suddenly, on the eightieth, the sun broke through and we saw, fairly near, a hilly island covered with forest. The sound of the surf was not too loud; by now the storm had mostly subsided. We made for the shore, disembarked, and for hours just lay on the ground, a natural thing to do after such a long ordeal.

Finally we got up and decided that thirty of us would stand by to guard the ship while I took the other twenty to reconnoiter the island. We had advanced about a third of a mile through thick forest when we came upon a bronze shaft. It was inscribed in Greek, and the legend, dim and worn, read: "This marks the spot reached by Heracles and Dionysus." And, pressed in the rock nearby, were two sets of footprints, one a hundred feet long, the other somewhat less. I figured the smaller were Dionysus' and the larger Heracles'. We paid our respects and pushed on.

We hadn't proceeded very far when we came upon a river, not of water, but of wine, which had the very same taste as our vintage Chian. The stream was so wide and deep that in places it was actually navigable. In view of such tangible evidence of a visit from Dionysus I was now much more inclined to believe the inscription on the shaft. I decided to track down the source of the river and walked upstream. Here I found no signs of any spring but, instead, a large number of enormous vines full of grapes. The roots of each were oozing drops of clear white wine, and these formed the river. Under the surface we could see a good many wine-colored fish which, it turned out, also tasted like wine; in fact, we got drunk on some that we caught and ate. (Naturally, when we cut them open we found them full of dregs.) Later, having given the matter some thought, we mixed them with fresh-water fish and thus made our sea-food cocktails less potent.

After fording the river at a narrow point, we came upon vines of a fabulous type. The part growing out of the ground, the stalk proper, was well set up and thick. But the part above that was a perfect replica of a female body from hips to head, looking somewhat like Daphne in those paintings where she's shown turning into a tree as Apollo lays his hands on her. The women had branches bearing clusters of grapes growing out of the tips of their fingers and, instead of hair, actual shoots with leaves and grapes. They called out to welcome us as we came up, some in Lydian, some in Indian, but most in Greek. They also started kissing us on the lips, and everyone they did this to immediately became drunk and began to reel. We weren't able to pick the grapes because, as we pulled them off, the women would cry out in pain. They were burning with desire to have intercourse with us. Two of my men tried it—and couldn't be pried loose: they were held fast by the penis; it had grown into, become grafted onto, the vines. Soon the pair became entwined in a network of tendrils, sprouted shoots from their fingers, and looked as if even they were ready to bear fruit. We abandoned them and fled back to the ship, where we gave the men who had stayed behind a report of everything, including the vinous intercourse of their two shipmates.

We then broke out the water jars, watered up—and also wined up from the river—and, after spending the night on the beach, sailed off at dawn before a moderate wind. Around noon, when the island had dropped out of sight, a typhoon suddenly hit us. It spun the ship around and lifted it about thirty miles high in the air. But, before it could let us drop back into the water, as we hung suspended in the sky, a wind filled our sails and carried us along. For seven days and nights we sailed the air. On the eighth we sighted a large land mass like an island in the sky. It was round and, illuminated by some immense light, shone brightly. We put in there, anchored, and disembarked, and, upon reconnoitering the countryside, found it was inhabited and under cultivation. During the day we could see no other land about but, when night came on, we saw a good many other islands the color of fire, some bigger than ours and some smaller. Below was another land mass with cities, rivers, seas, forests, and mountains; we guessed it was our own earth.

I decided to push farther inland. En route we ran into what is called locally the Buzzard Cavalry and were taken captive. Now the Buzzard Cavalry is made up of men who ride on buzzard back; they use birds the way we do horses. Their buzzards, you see, are enormous creatures, mostly three-headed; to give you an idea of their size I need only point out that any one of their wing feathers is longer and thicker than the mast on a big cargo vessel. This Buzzard Cavalry has orders to run patrol flights over the countryside and bring before the king any aliens they find. So we were arrested and brought before him. He looked us over and, guessing from the way we were dressed, said, "You are Greek, gentlemen?" We nodded. Then he said, "How did you get here with all that air to cross?" We told him our whole story and he, in turn, told us all about himself. His name was Endymion and he, too, had come from earth: some time in the past he had been snatched up in his sleep, brought here, and made king of the place.

He explained to us that the land we were in was what appeared to people on earth as the moon. He told us, however, not to worry or be apprehensive, that we were in no danger, and that we would be given everything we needed. "Once I win this war I'm involved in against the people living on the sun," he added, "you can stay here with me and live happily ever after." We asked him who his enemies were and how the disagreement had come about. "Phaëthon," he told us, "is king of the people living on the sun—the sun, you see, is inhabited just like the moon—and he's been at war with us for a long while. It all started this way. Some time ago I got the idea of collecting the poorest among my subjects and sending them out to found a colony on the Morning Star, which is completely bare and uninhabited. Phaëthon out of spite called out his Ant Cavalry and intercepted the expedition before it had gone halfway. We were beaten—we were no match for his forces at the time—and turned back. Now I want to take the offensive again and establish my colony. If you're willing, come, join our army. I'll supply each of your men with one buzzard from the royal stables plus a complete outfit. We leave tomorrow."

"If that's what you want, why, of course," I replied.

We stayed the night with him as his guests. At the crack of dawn his lookouts reported that the enemy was approaching, and we rose and took our positions. Endymion had 100,000 troops, not counting supply corps, engineers, infantry, and contingents from foreign allies. Of the 100,000, 80,000 were Buzzard Cavalry and 20,000 Saladbird Cavalry. The saladbird is an enormous bird covered all over with salad greens instead of feathers;

its wings look exactly like lettuce leaves. Alongside these were units of Peashooters and Garlickeers. He also had some allied forces from the Big Dipper: 30,000 Fleaborne Bowmen and 50,000 Windrunners. The Fleaborne Bowmen are mounted on huge fleas hence the name—each as big as twelve elephants. The Windrunners, though ground forces, are able to fly through the air without wings. This is the way they do it: they wear shirts that go down to their feet; by pulling these up through the belt and letting them belly before the wind like sails, they're carried along the way a boat would be. In battle they serve for the most part as mobile infantry. There was talk that 70,000 Ostrich-Acorns and 50,000 Crane Cavalry were expected from the stars over Cappadocia, but they never showed up so I didn't see them and, consequently, haven't dared to describe what they're like—the fabulous things I heard about them are unbelievable.

So much for the make-up of Endymion's army. The equipment was standard throughout: a helmet made from a bean (enormous, tough beans are grown there), a breastplate of overlapping lupine husks (since the husks of the lupines are very hard, like horn, they are made into armor by being stitched together), and a sword and shield of the Greek type.

At the appropriate moment Endymion drew up his forces for battle. The Buzzard Cavalry together with the king and his elite guard (including us) were on the right, the Saladbird Cavalry on the left, and, in the center, the cavalry units from the foreign allies, each disposed as it chose. The infantry, numbering about 60,000,000, he positioned as follows. He ordered the local spiders—they are numerous and big, any one of them larger by far than the average Aegean island—to span the air between the moon and the Morning Star with a web; as soon as they finished, he stationed the infantry on the plain so formed, with General Nightly Goodday and two others in command.

On the enemy side the Ant Cavalry with Phaëthon in command formed the left wing. This army uses enormous winged beasts similar to our ants in every respect except size, for the largest can run upwards of two hundred feet in length. The mount as well as the rider fights, principally by using its feelers. Their number was reportedly 50,000. On the right wing were the Aerognats, bowmen astride huge gnats, also 50,000 in number, and, behind them, the Aerojumpers. These, although light-armed infantrymen, are especially dangerous because they have slings that fire elephantine radishes capable of inflicting in whomever they hit a gangrenous wound which spells instant death; rumor has it these missiles are tipped with mallow juice. On the Aerojumpers' flank were 10,000 Stalk-and-Mushroomeers, heavy-armed troops for hand-to-hand combat, so called because they use mushrooms for shields and asparagus stalks for spears. Nearby were 5,000

Dog-Acorns, dog-faced men who fought mounted on winged acorns; they
had been sent by the inhabitants of Sirius. According to reports, Phaëthon
had other allies who were late—the Cloud-Centaurs and a detachment of
slingers he had summoned from the Milky Way. The Cloud-Centaurs arrived after the battle had been decided. (How I wish they hadn't gotten
there at all!) The slingers never showed up, and I've heard say that
Phaëthon was so angry he subsequently laid their country waste with fire.

Such was the make-up of the force attacking us. The standards were raised;
donkeys—the substitute in these armies for trumpeters—brayed the charge on
both sides; the lines clashed, and the battle was on. The sun's left immediately
fled without waiting to engage our Buzzard Cavalry; we pursued, slaughtering
as we galloped. Their right, however, overpowered our left, and the Aerognats
gave chase all the way to where our infantry was drawn up. The infantry came
to the rescue, and the Aerognats, well aware that their left had been defeated,
gave way and ran. The retreat turned into a full-scale rout: our men killed or
captured huge numbers. Streams of blood spilled over the clouds, drenching
them and turning them the scarlet color they take on at sunset. Quite a lot
dripped down on earth—which makes me wonder whether something similar
hadn't occurred centuries ago and Homer simply jumped to the conclusion it
was Zeus sending down a shower of blood to honor Sarpedon's death.

As soon as we returned from the pursuit we erected two monuments, one
on the cobwebs to commemorate the infantry battle, the other on the clouds
for the air battle. Before we had finished, our lookouts reported the approach
of the Cloud-Centaurs, the forces which were to have joined Phaëthon before the battle. Sure enough, they came into view, an absolutely incredible
sight: each was a combination of man and winged horse, the human part as
tall as the upper half of the Colossus of Rhodes and the equine as big as a
large cargo vessel. I won't put down their number; it was so great I'm afraid
no one will believe it. Sagittarius, the archer from the Zodiac, was in command. When they realized their allies had been defeated, they sent word to
Phaëthon to return to the attack and, lining up in battle formation, charged.
The Moonmen who, because of the chase and subsequent search for plun-
der, had broken ranks and scattered all over, were routed to a man; the king
himself was pursued to the walls of his capital, and most of his birds were
killed. After tearing down our two monuments, the Cloud-Centaurs overran
the entire plain woven by the spiders and, in the process, took me and two
of my shipmates prisoner. When Phaëthon arrived on the scene, monuments
were again erected—this time for his side.

The very same day we were carried off to the sun, our hands tied behind
our backs with a strip of cobweb. The enemy decided against laying siege;

instead, on the way back they set up a barricade in mid-air, a double wall of cloud, which cut the moon off completely from the sun's light. The moon consequently went into total eclipse and remained in the grip of perpetual night. Greatly upset, Endymion sent a message to the Sunmen imploring them to tear down the structure and not force his subjects to live their lives in pitch-darkness. He said he was ready to submit to taxation, furnish military aid when required, and enter into a nonaggression pact, and he volunteered to supply hostages to guarantee performance. Phaëthon and his people held two referendums: in the first they were as bitter as ever, but in the second they changed their minds and agreed to a treaty of peace worded thus:

> The Sunmen and their allies hereby agree to a treaty of peace with the Moonmen and their allies on the following terms:
>
> > The Sunmen shall tear down the barricade they erected, shall here-after never make war on the moon, and shall return all prisoners at a ran-som to be determined for each;
> > the Moonmen shall grant autonomy to all other stars and shall not bear arms against the sun;
> > each party shall render aid to the other in the event of aggression by a third party;
> > the king of the Moonmen shall pay to the king of the Sunmen an an-nual levy of 10,000 jars of dew and provide 10,000 hostages from his own subjects;
> > both parties shall co-operate in founding the colony on the Morning Star; interested nationals of any other country may take part;
> > this treaty shall be inscribed on a tablet of silver and gold to be erected in mid-air at the common frontier.
>
> > > Sworn to by
> > > Firestone
> > > Heater
> > > Burns
> > >   for the sun;
> > > Nighting
> > > Moony
> > > Allbright
> > >   for the moon.

Peace was made on these terms, and the moment it took effect the wall was torn down and the prisoners, including us, released. When we arrived back on the moon, our shipmates and Endymion himself came out a little way to meet us and welcomed us with tears in their eyes. Endymion asked us to stay on and take part in founding the colony, promising to give me his own son in marriage (there are no women on the moon). I was not to be persuaded and requested instead to be sent back down to the ocean. When he realized my mind was made up he let us go after a week's entertainment as his guests.

I want to describe the strange, new phenomena I observed during this stay on the moon.

The first is that males and not females do the child-bearing. Marriage is with males, and there isn't even a word for "woman." Men under twenty-five are the wives, men over, the husbands. The embryo is carried not in the belly but in the calf. Once conception takes place, the calf swells up; after a due period of time it is cut open and the child, not yet alive, extracted. Life is induced by placing the child, mouth wide open, toward the wind. It's my opinion that the Greek word for calf, which literally means "belly of the leg," came to us from the moon, since there the calf and not the belly serves as the region of gestation.

I shall now describe a second phenomenon which is even stranger, namely the race called "tree people." The procreation of tree people is as follows. A man's right testicle is cut off and planted in the ground. This produces a huge tree of flesh with a trunk like a penis. It has branches and leaves and, as fruit, bears eighteen-inch acorns. When ripe, these are gathered, the shells cracked open, and men are hatched from them.

Moonmen have artificial penises, generally of ivory but, in the case of the poor, of wood; these enable them to have intercourse when they mount their mates.

They never die of old age but dissolve and turn into air, like smoke.

The diet is the same for everyone: frog. Every time they light a fire they grill frogs on the coals because there's such a plentiful supply of these creatures flying about. While the cooking goes on, people seat themselves in a circle around the fire as if at a table and have a banquet sniffing in the smoke that's given off. Frogs provide their food; for drink they compress air in a cup to produce a liquid resembling dew.

They don't urinate or defecate. They have no rectal orifice so, instead of the anus, boys offer for intercourse the hollow of the knee above the calf, since there's an opening there. A bald pate or no hair at all is considered a mark of beauty: they can't stand men who wear their hair long. (Among the inhabitants of the comets, on the other hand, the opposite is true, as some natives who were visiting the moon informed me.) They do, however, wear beards which grow a little above the knee. Their feet terminate in a single toe, and they have no toenails. Above the rump grows a cabbage which hangs down like a tail; it's always ripe and doesn't break off even when they fall on their backs.

Their nasal discharge is a very bitter honey. When they work or exercise they sweat milk from every pore; by adding a few drops of the honey, they can curdle this into cheese. They make oil not from olives but onions, a rich grade that smells as sweet as myrrh. Their vines, which are plentiful, are a water-producing variety since the grapes are a form of hailstone; it's my theory that, when the wind blows and shakes the vines, the clusters burst and this produces hail on earth.

They use the belly as a pocket, putting into it whatever they need to carry with them, for it can be opened and closed. No liver is visible inside, only a rough, furry lining; infants consequently snuggle in there during cold weather.

The wealthy wear clothes of flexible glass and the poor of woven copper. The country is rich in copper; it's worked the way we work wool, by being soaked in water.

I am going to describe the kind of eyes they have, though I hesitate to do so since you're sure to think I'm lying. They have removable eyes: whenever they want they take them out and keep them safe until they need them; then they put them back and have sight again. Many who have lost their own borrow other people's, and some men, all well-to-do of course, own a good supply of spares. Everybody has ears of plane-tree leaves except the men hatched from acorns; theirs are of wood.

Another marvel I saw was in the royal palace. Here there is an enormous mirror suspended over a rather shallow well. If you stand in the well, you hear everything said on earth; if you look at the mirror, you see each city and nation as clearly as if you were standing over it. When I took a look, I saw my own homeland and my house and family; I can't say for sure whether they saw me.

Any person who doesn't believe that all this is so need only go there himself. He'll quickly discover I'm telling the truth.

When the time came, we bid farewell to the king and his court, embarked, and set off. Endymion gave me as a goodby gift two glass and five copper shirts and a suit of lupinehusk armor, all of which I left behind in the whale. He also sent a thousand of the Buzzard Cavalry to escort us for the first fifty miles. On the way we passed a number of other countries but didn't stop till we came to the Morning Star, which we found in the course of being colonized. Here we disembarked and took on water. Boarding ship again, we entered the Zodiac and passed the sun close to port, almost touching the shore. We didn't land, although my men were very anxious to, because the wind was foul. We could see, however, that the countryside was green and fertile, well-watered, and full of good things. The Cloud-Centaurs, who are in Phaëthon's pay, spotted us and came after our ship but, on learning we were protected by the treaty, turned back. Our Buzzard Cavalry escort had left us earlier.

We continued sailing that night and the next day and, toward evening, when we had already begun the slant down to earth, arrived at Lampville. This city is located in mid-air halfway between the Pleiades and the Hyades, at a much lower altitude than the Zodiac. On going ashore, we found no humans but only great numbers of lamps scurrying about or lounging around the main square and the waterfront. Most were small, the lower classes as it were; a few, the rich and influential, were conspicuously bright. The lamps had each their own house and bracket, bore names the way we do, and were capable of speech (we heard them talking). They did us no harm but actually offered hospitality; we, however, were afraid, and not one of us had the courage to accept their invitations to dine or spend the night. Downtown they have a city hall where the mayor, sitting in judgment all night, calls up each lamp by name. Those who don't answer are considered deserters and receive the death penalty, namely snuffing out. We stood around watching the proceedings, listening to the lamps defend themselves and submit their reasons for being late. At one point I recognized my own lamp. I spoke to it and asked how things were back home, and it gave me a full account.

We stayed the night there and the following day raised sail and set off again. By this time we were down among the clouds. We sighted Cloud-cuckooland and wondered about it but couldn't put in because of an unfavorable wind. We did receive word, however, that Jay Crow was on the throne. I was minded how people had foolishly been skeptical of what the playwright Aristophanes had written; he was a wise man who told the truth. Two days later we could see the ocean clearly. No land was visible except, of course, the islands in the air, and these now had a fiery bright aspect. On the third day, toward noon, the wind slackened off to a gentle breeze, and we landed on the surface of the sea. The moment we touched water we went hysterical with joy; we celebrated as best we could under the circumstances and then jumped overboard for a swim since the day was calm and the sea smooth. . . .

Strange Creatures and Far Traveling

Like the Roman gods, much of Roman literature seemed to follow Greek models, for example the *Aeneid,* the Latin *Odyssey,* by Vergil (70–19 B.C.). Aeneas was a mythical Trojan prince who fled with his followers from the fall of Troy and made his way around the Mediterranean to Italy, where his descendants founded Rome. The epic contains a celebrated episode in which Aeneas descends into the underworld to consult with his dead father, Anchises, which inspired Dante's *Divine Comedy.*

Elements of the fantastic continued to be represented in Roman narratives of various kinds. One example is *The Golden Ass,* or *Metamorphoses* of Apuleius (A.D. second century), in which the hero is changed into a donkey and experiences various misadventures. *Gilgamesh* and the *Odyssey* were prototypical travel stories. Herodotus (c. 480–425 B.C.), the Greek "father of history," carried on the tradition, describing not only his authentic travels but also fabled countries that lay beyond the realm of human experience and their strange inhabitants: the Ethiopians, who lived beyond the mountains at the source of the Nile; the Sycthians, who lived beyond the Euxine Sea; and the Hyperboreans, who lived at the back of the North Wind.

These classical fancies would be adopted by later fantasy writers, particularly the heroic fantasy school created by Robert E. Howard. Howard introduced *Conan the Conqueror* with the following epigraph attributed to "The Nemedian Chronicles":

> *Know, oh prince, that between the years when the oceans drank Atlantis and the gleaming cities, and the years of the rise of the Sons of Aryas, there was an age undreamt of, when shining kingdoms lay spread across the world like blue mantles beneath the stars—Nemedia, Ophir, Brythunia, Hyperborea, Zamara with its dark-haired women and towers of spider-haunted mystery, Zingara with its chivalry, Koth that bordered on the pastoral Shem, Stygia with its shadow-guarded tombs, Hyrkania whose riders wore steel and silk and gold. But the proudest kingdom, of the world was Aquilonia, reigning supreme in the dreaming west. Hither came Conan, the Cimmerian, black-haired,*

sullen-eyed, sword in hand, a thief, a reaver, a slayer, with gigantic melan-cholics and gigantic mirth, to tread the jeweled thrones of the Earth under his sandaled feet.

In another sense, the Ethiopians, the Scythians, the Hyperboreans were aliens—strange creatures, not quite human, fascinating but possibly dangerous, who live in places hard to find and difficult to reach. The Romans picked up the old Greek stories and added their own embellishments. Their storytellers described the Fortunate Isles, where there were men with elastic bones and bifurcated tongues; the island of Panchaia, where incense grew; the valley of Ismaus, where the feet of wild men turned inward; Albania, where albinos lived; a place inhabited by hermaphrodites. And they told of the Arimaspi, who passed their lives fighting for gold with griffins in the dark; of the Psyllians, whose bodies were poisonous to snakes; of a race of fascinators who used enchanted words; of women who killed with their eyes. . . .

Some of the fascination of the alien would be taken over by later science fiction as authors dealt with the possibilities of other ways of existence, other ways of behaving, other ways of appearing. To that would be added a more important consideration: how will humanity relate to aliens, and how will they and humanity interact? The sense of wonder eventually gives way before the wonder of sense.

After the fall of Rome, literary concerns were lost in the general concern for staying alive; the only significant literary effort was to preserve and copy classical manuscripts. But oral literature was reborn, chiefly in the form of epics about the deeds of heroes, such as the eighth-century *Beowulf* and the twelfth-century *Nibelungenlied* or the French romance cycle of Charlemagne typified by the *Song of Roland*. The twelfth century also provided the first great literary treatment of the Arthurian romances by Chrétien de Troyes, and of Parzival by Wolfram von Eschenbach. Most of these stories involved dangerous journeys, battles with other men and with monsters or dragons, and sometimes a quest for something transcendent; these elements too would be reflected in later science fiction.

Meanwhile, in the developing Arabic civilization that gave Europe much of its mathematical knowledge, other kinds of legends were being accumulated that would not be translated into English until the nineteenth century under the title of *The Thousand and One Nights,* or *The Arabian Nights.* From them later writers would get the fantasy stories of Ali Baba, Aladdin and his magic lantern, and Sindbad and his fabulous voyages, flying carpets, rocs, and all.

Dante (1265–1321) summed up the medieval Christian attitude toward the natural and the supernatural in his great work, *The Divine Comedy* (c. 1307–1321), in which Vergil escorts the poet on a tour of the Inferno and Purgatorio, and Beatrice escorts him through Heaven. Meanwhile the small world of Europe was suddenly expanded by the return of Marco Polo from China to Venice in 1295, with information about a fantastic civilization to the east, as rich and almost as strange as any imagined in the Greek and Roman travel stories.

In the fourteenth century Boccaccio (1313–1375) wrote his *Tales* and then, after the outbreak of the Black Death in Europe, his *Decameron,* and the great travel book of the late Middle Ages, *The Voiage and Travaille of Sir John Mandeville,* became popular all over Europe.

Ostensibly the account of the travels of one Sir John Mandeville (or Maundeville), Kt., but probably a collection of old and new travel stories put together by an anonymous compiler, the book is subtitled, "which treateth of the way to Hierusalem; and of marvayles of Inde, with other ilands and countryes." One of the earliest editions in English contained the following information:

> *Here begynneth the book of John Maundeville, Knyght of Ingelond, that was y bore in the toun of Seynt Albons, and travelide aboute in the world in manye diverse contreis to se mervailes and customes of countreis, and diversiteis of folkys and diverse shap of men, and of beistis, and all the mervaill that he say he wrot and tellith in this book. . . .*

The sample that follows illustrates the appeal of the book and the manner in which fact and fancy are mingled.

From The Voyages and Travels of Sir John Mandeville

CHAPTER XVIII

OF THE PALACE OF THE KING OF THIS ISLE OF JAVA—
OF THE TREES THAT BEAR MEAL, HONEY, WINE, AND
VENOM; AND OF OTHER WONDERS AND CUSTOMS, IN THE
ISLES THEREABOUTS

Beside the isle I have spoken of, there is another great isle called Sumobor, the king of which is very mighty. The people of that isle made marks in their faces with a hot iron, both men and women, as a mark of great nobility, to be known from other people; for they hold themselves most noble and most worthy of all the world. They have war always with the people that go all naked. Fast beside is another rich isle called Beteinga. And there are many other isles thereabout.

Fast beside that isle, to pass by sea, is a great isle and extensive country, called Java, which is near two thousand miles in circuit. And the king of that country is a very great lord, rich and mighty, having under him seven other kings of seven other surrounding isles. This isle is well inhabited, and in it grow all kinds of spices more plentifully than in any other country, as ginger, cloves, canel, sedewalle, nutmegs, and maces. And know well that the nutmeg bears the maces; for right as the nut of the hazel hath a husk in which the nut is inclosed till it be ripe, so it is of the nutmeg and of the maces. Many other spices and many other goods grow in that isle; for of all things there is plenty, except wine. Gold and silver are very plentiful.

The king of that country has a very noble and wonderful palace, and richer than any in the world; for all the steps leading to halls and chambers are alternately of gold and silver; and the pavements of halls and chambers are squares of gold and silver; and all the walls within are covered with gold and silver in thin plates; in which plates are inlaid stories and battles of knights, the crowns and circles about whose heads are made of precious stones and rich and great pearls. And the halls and the chambers of the palace are all covered within with gold and silver, so that no man would believe the richness of that palace unless he had seen it. And know well that the king of that isle is so mighty, that he hath many times overcome that great chan of Cathay in battle, who is the greatest emperor under the firmament, either beyond the sea or on this side; for they have often had war between them, because the great chan would oblige him to hold his land of him; but the other at all times defendeth himself well against him.

After that isle is another large isle, called Pathan, which is a great kingdom, full of fair cities and towns. In that land grow trees that bear meal, of which men make good bread, white, and of good savour; and it seemeth as it were of wheat, but it is not quite of such savour. And there are other trees that bear good and sweet honey; and others that bear poison, against which there is no medicine but one; and that is to take their own leaves, and stamp them and mix them with water, and then drink it, for no medicine will avail. The Jews had sent for some of this poison by one of their friends, to poison all Christendom, as I have heard them say in their confession before dying; but, thanked be Almighty God, they failed of their purpose, although they caused a great mortality of people. And there are other trees that bear excellent wine.

And if you like to hear how the meal comes out of the trees, men hew the trees with a hatchet, all about the foot, till the bark be separated in many parts; and then comes out a thick liquor, which they receive in vessels, and dry it in the sun; and then carry it to a mill to grind, and it becomes fair and white meal; and the honey, and the wine, and the poison, are drawn out of other trees in the same manner, and put in vessels to keep. In that isle is a dead sea, or lake, that has no bottom; and if anything fall into it, it will never come up again. In that lake grow reeds, which they call Thaby, that are thirty fathoms long; and of these reeds they make fair houses. And there are other reeds, not so long, that grow near the land, and have roots full a quarter of a furlong or more long, at the knots of which roots precious stones are found that have great virtues; for he who carries any of them upon him may not be hurt by iron or steel; and therefore they who have those stones on them fight very boldly both on sea and land; and, therefore, when their enemies are aware of this, they shoot at them arrows and darts without iron or steel, and so hurt and slay them. And also of those reeds they make houses and ships, and other things, as we here make houses and ships of oak, or of any other trees. And let no man think that I am joking, for I have seen these reeds with my own eyes many times, lying upon the river of that lake, of which twenty of our fellows might not lift up or bear one to the earth.

Beyond this isle men go by sea to another rich isle, called Calonak, the king of which has as many wives as he will; for he makes search through the country for the fairest maidens that may be found, who are brought before him, and he taketh one one night, and another another, and so forth in succession; so that he hath a thousand wives or more. Thus the king has many children, sometimes a hundred, sometimes two hundred, and sometimes more. He hath also as many as fourteen thousand elephants, or more, which are brought up amongst his serfs in all his towns. And in case he has war with any of the kings around him, he causes certain men of arms to go up into wooden castles, which are set upon the elephants' backs, to fight against their enemies; and so do other kings thereabouts; and they call the elephants *warkes.*

And in that isle there is a great wonder; for all kinds of fish that are there in the sea come once a year, one kind after the other, to the coast of that isle in so great a multitude that a man can see hardly anything but fish; and there they remain three days; and every man of the country takes as many of them as he likes. And that kind of fish, after the third day, departs and goes into the sea. And after them come another multitude of fish of another kind, and do in the same manner as the first did another three days; and so on with the other kinds, till all the divers kinds of fishes have been there, and men have taken what they like of them. And no man knows the cause; but they of the country say that it is to do reverence to their king, who is the most worthy king in the world, as they say, because he fulfils the commandment of God to Adam and Eve, "Increase and multiply, and fill the earth"; and because he multiplies so the world with children, therefore God sends him the fishes of divers kinds, to take at his will, for him and all his people; and thus all the fishes of the sea come to do him homage as the most noble and excellent king of the world, and that is best beloved of God, as they say.

There are also in that country a kind of snails, so great that many persons may lodge in their shells, as men would do in a little house. And there are other snails that are very great, but not so huge as the other, of which, and of great white serpents with black heads, that are as great as a man's thigh, and some less, they make royal meats for the king and other great lords. And if a man who is married die in that country, they bury his wife alive with him, for they say that it is right that she make him company in the other world, as she did in this.

From that country they go by the Sea of Ocean, by an isle called Caffolos; the natives of which, when their friends are sick, hang them on trees, and say that it is better that birds, which are angels of God, eat them, than the foul worms of the earth. Then we come to another isle, the inhabitants of which are of full cursed kind, for they breed great dogs, and teach them to strangle their friends, when they are sick, for they will not let them die of natural death; for they say that they should suffer great pain if they abide to die by themselves, as nature would; and, when they are thus strangled, they eat their flesh as though it were venison.

Afterwards men go by many isles by sea to an isle called Milk, where are very cursed people; for they delight in nothing more than to fight and slay men; and they drink most gladly man's blood, which they call Dieu. And the more men that a man may slay, the more worship he hath amongst them. And thence they go by sea, from isle to isle, to an isle called Tracoda, the inhabitants of which are as beasts, and unreasonable, and dwell in caves which they make in the earth, for they have not sense to make houses. And when they see any man passing through their countries they hide them in their caves. And they eat flesh of serpents, and they speak nought, but hiss, as serpents do.

After that isle, men go by the Sea of Ocean, by many isles, to a great and fair isle called Nacumera, which is in circuit more than a thousand miles. And all the men and women of that isle have dogs' heads; and they are reasonable and of good understanding, except that they worship an ox for their god. And also every man of them beareth an ox of gold or silver on his forehead, in token that they love well their god. And they go all naked, except a little clout, and are large men and warlike, having a great target that covers all the body, and a spear in their hand to fight with. And if they take any man in battle they eat him. The king is rich and powerful, and very devout after his law; and he has about his neck three hundred orient pearls, knotted, as paternosters are here of amber. And as we say our Pater Noster and Ave Maria, counting the paternosters right, so this king says every day devoutly three hundred prayers to his god, before he eats; and he beareth also about his neck an orient ruby, noble and fine, which is a foot in length, and five fingers large.

And when they choose their king, they give him that ruby to carry in his hand, and so they lead him riding all about the city. And that ruby he shall bear always about his neck; for if he had not that ruby upon him they would not hold him for king. The chan of Cathay has greatly coveted that ruby, but he might never have it, neither for war, nor for any manner of goods. This king is so righteous and equitable in his judgments, that men may go safely through all his country, and bear with them what they like, and no man shall be bold enough to rob them.

Hence men go to another isle called Silha, which is full eight hundred miles in circuit. In that land is much waste, for it is so full of serpents, dragons, and cockodrills, that no man dare dwell there. These cockodrills are serpents, yellow and rayed above, having four feet, and short thighs, and great nails like claws; and some are five fathoms in length, and some of six, eight, or even ten; and when they go by places that are gravelly, it appears as if men had drawn a great tree through the gravelly place. And there are also many wild beasts, especially elephants.

In that isle is a great mountain, in the midst of which is a large lake in a full fair plain, and there is great plenty of water. And they of the country say that Adam and Eve wept on that mount a hundred years, when they were driven out of Paradise. And that water, they say, is of their tears; for so much water they wept, that made the aforesaid lake. And at the bottom of that lake are found many precious stones and great pearls. In that lake grow many reeds and great canes, and there within are many cockodrills and serpents, and great water leeches. And the king of that country, once every year, gives leave to poor men to go into the lake to gather precious stones and pearls, by way of alms, for the love of God, that made Adam. To guard against the vermin, they anoint their arms, thighs, and legs with an ointment made of a thing called limons, which is a kind of fruit like small pease, and then they have no dread of cockodrills, or other venomous things. This water runs, flowing and ebbing, by a side of the mountain; and in that river men find precious stones and pearls, in great abundance. And the people of that isle say commonly, that the serpents and wild beasts of the country, will do no harm to any foreigner that enters that country, but only to men that are born there.

CHAPTER XIX

HOW MEN KNOW BY AN IDOL IF THE SICK SHALL DIE OR NOT—OF PEOPLE OF DIVERS SHAPES, AND MARVELLOUSLY DISFIGURED; AND OF THE MONKS THAT GIVE THEIR RELIEF TO BABOONS, APES, MONKEYS, AND TO OTHER BEASTS

From that isle, in going by sea towards the south, is another great isle, called Dondun, in which are people of wicked kinds, so that the father eats the son, the son the father, the husband the wife, and the wife the husband. And if it so befall that the father or mother or any of their friends are sick, the son goes to the priest of their law, and prays him to ask the idol if his father or mother or friend shall die; and then the priest and the son go before the idol, and kneel full devoutly, and ask of the idol; and if the devil that is within answer that he shall live, they keep him well; and if he say that he shall die, then the priest and the son go with the wife of him that is sick, and they put their hands upon his mouth and stop his breath, and so kill him. And after that, they chop all the body in small pieces, and pray all his friends to come and eat; and they send for all the minstrels of the country and make a solemn feast. And when they have eaten the flesh, they take the bones and bury them, and sing and make great melody.

The king of this isle is a great and powerful lord, and has under him fifty-four great isles, which give tribute to him; and in every one of these isles is a king crowned, all obedient to that king. In one of these isles are people of great stature, like giants, hideous to look upon; and they have but one eye, which is in the middle of the forehead; and they eat nothing but raw flesh and fish. And in another isle towards the south dwell people of foul stature and cursed nature, who have no heads, but their eyes are in their shoulders. . . .

The Good Place That Is No Place

Chaucer (c. 1340–1400) wrote his *Canterbury Tales* about 1387 and Malory his *Morte d'Arthur* in 1469. They were the last of the great works of the Middle Ages. Both had elements of the fantastic and the supernatural; both were expressions of a world view that demanded a necessary role for the supernatural. Even before Chaucer, however, indications already were accumulating that this particular world, with its system of obligations and responsibilities, its hierarchies and its divine intervention, was coming apart.

The Renaissance began in Italy about the beginning of the fourteenth century, a century in which gunpowder was introduced into Europe and initiated the process of turning warriors into soldiers. In England the portent was Roger Bacon (c. 1214–c. 1294), a Franciscan friar who espoused the virtues of natural science, experiment, and direct observation in a period when ignorance was valued more highly than knowledge. Saint Augustine (354–430) wrote, "Nothing is to be accepted save on the authority of Scripture, since greater is that authority than all powers of the human mind." The only historical novel about Roger Bacon, *Doctor Mirabalis* (1964, revised 1973), was written by science fiction author James Blish.

Bacon quarreled with many prominent people, was accused of magic and astrology, and was thrown into prison in 1277, where he remained for fifteen years. On his deathbed he is reputed to have said, "I repent of having given myself so much trouble to destroy ignorance." But his vision of a future of human accomplishment was like a foreshadowing of science fiction in the Middle Ages, and would largely come true. In one famous letter, he predicted:

> It is possible that great ships and sea-going vessels shall be made which can be guided by one man and will move with greater swiftness than if they were full of oarsmen.
>
> It is possible that a car shall be made which will move with inestimable speed, and the motion will be without the help of any living creature. . . .
>
> It is possible that a device for flying shall be made such that a man sitting in the middle of it and turning a crank shall cause artificial wings to beat the air after the manner of a bird's flight. . . .

It is possible also easily to make an instrument by which a single man may violently pull a thousand men toward himself in spite of opposition, or other things which are tractable.

It is possible also that devices can be made whereby, without bodily danger, a man may walk on the bottom of the sea or of a river. . . .

Infinite other things can be made, as bridges over rivers without columns or supports, and machines, and unheard-of engines.

Between the writing of *The Canterbury Tales* and *Morte d'Arthur* came the invention of the Gutenberg press; it would begin the process of popularizing literature, by making inexpensive copies available to the general public, that would be completed in the nineteenth century by the development of general literacy. Making literature easily accessible also vulgarized it, in the sense that the ability of large numbers of the populace to buy books led to the writing of books for them. Many critics believe that the novel was invented by and produced for the new middle class that arose in the eighteenth century.

In 1492 Columbus made the first of his world-shaping voyages to the Americas, and Western Europe's concept of the world was changed—not merely from flat to round but in scope and image. In the new lands that were being discovered and explored were peoples and creatures as strange and as wonderful as any imagined in the medieval travel books, as much wealth as in Cathay and the fabulous kingdom of Prester John, and more land and rivers and mountains and forests than European man could ever explore.

From this point on, the isolated places of the world where authors would locate their adventures or their better societies would be undiscovered islands—until the process of exploration would leave no places of the world unexplored. Lost civilizations could still be imagined in Africa or at the poles as late as the 1930s (the 1950s in film), but even in the early part of the twentieth century authors were beginning to look toward the planets and other stars for new islands in the sky.

Rabelais (c. 1495–1553), a Benedictine monk and scholar, criticized society in two important satirical romances with major elements of the fantastic and the grotesque, *Pantagruel* (1532) and *Gargantua* (1534), and gave his name to a kind of ribald humor that would later be called Rabelaisian.

A few years earlier a work more important in the history of science fiction was created by a scholar and lawyer, a humanist who became a member of Parliament and later Lord Chancellor of England under King Henry VIII, was unable to approve the king's divorce from Catherine of Aragon, and was executed. His story was dramatized on stage and in film in recent years under the title of A *Man for All Seasons*. Between 1514 and 1516 Sir

Thomas More (1478–1535) wrote a story about a perfect society, placed the society on a distant island, and named the island and the story *Utopia.* He invented the word, combining the Greek words "ou" meaning "not" and "topos" meaning "place."

Utopia means "no place," but because it describes a better way of organizing society, the word has come to mean "the good place" or "the beautiful place" as well—the good place that is no place, an irony implicit in every utopian vision. The irony, of course, is in part the result of narrative necessity: the utopia must be located in a place that is distant and nearly inaccessible or the reader would have heard of it before and its obvious virtues might have been adopted.

Although More was inspired by the philosophy of Plato and the accounts of travelers like Amerigo Vespucci (1507), his semifictionalized narrative was the start of a new way of organizing and dramatizing an author's ideas about how to improve human conditions. More's *Utopia* had many successors: Campanella's *The City of the Sun* (1623); Francis Bacon's *The New Atlantis* (1624); Swift's *Gulliver's Travels* (1726), which also provided a starting point for the anti-utopia or "bad place"; Butler's *Erewhon* (1872); Bellamy's *Looking Backward* (1888); and Wells's *The New Utopia* and many of his other novels. Because science fiction is in large part a social fiction, the utopia and the anti-utopia, or dystopia, have been a persistent theme in science fiction down to the present.

As man began to change his own way of life, the possibility of changing it for the better became inescapable, as well, eventually, as the possibility that consciously or unconsciously he might change it for the worse. The more interesting part of *Utopia,* Book II, is narrated to More in Antwerp by Raphael Hythloday, a seaman who, according to More, accompanied Vespucci on his first three voyages and was left behind, at his own request, on the fourth. He set out on a journey of exploration with his companions and eventually reached the island of Utopia.

From Utopia

BY THOMAS MORE

BOOK II

The island of Utopia is in the middle two hundred miles broad, and holds almost at the same breadth over a great part of it; but it grows narrower towards both ends. Its figure is not unlike a crescent: between its horns, the sea comes in eleven miles broad, and spreads itself into a great bay, which is environed with land to the compass of about five hundred miles, and is well secured from winds. In this bay there is no great current, the whole coast is, as it were, one continued harbour, which gives all that live in the island great convenience for mutual commerce; but the entry into the bay, occasioned by rocks on the one hand, and shallows on the other, is very dangerous. In the middle of it there is one single rock which appears above water, and may therefore be easily avoided, and on the top of it there is a tower in which a garrison is kept, the other rocks lie under water, and are very dangerous. The channel is known only to the natives, so that if any stranger should enter into the bay, without one of their pilots, he would run great danger of shipwreck; for even they themselves could not pass it safe if some marks that are on the coast did not direct their way; and if these should be but a little shifted, any fleet that might come against them, how great soever it were, would be certainly lost. On the other side of the island there are likewise many harbours; and the coast is so fortified, both by nature and art, that a small number of men can hinder the descent of a great army. But they report (and there remains good marks of it to make it credible) that this was no island at first, but a part of the continent. Utopus that conquered it (whose name it still carries, for Abraxa was its first-name) brought the rude and uncivilized inhabitants into such a good government, and to that measure of politeness, that they now far excel all the rest of mankind; having soon subdued them, he designed to separate them from the continent, and to bring the sea quite round them. To accomplish this, he ordered a deep channel to be dug fifteen miles long; and that the natives might not think he treated them like slaves, he not only forced the inhabitants, but also his own soldiers, to labour in carrying it on. As he set a vast number of men to work, he beyond all men's expectations brought it to a speedy conclusion. And his neighbours who at first laughed at the folly of the undertaking, no sooner saw it brought to perfection, than they were struck with admiration and terror.

There are fifty-four cities in the island, all large and well built: the manners, customs, and laws of which are the same, and they are all contrived as near in the same manner as the ground on which they stand will allow. The nearest lie at least twenty-four miles' distance from one another, and the most remote are not so far distant, but that a man can go on foot in one day from it, to that which lies next it. Every city sends three of their wisest senators once a year to Amaurot, to consult about their common concerns; for that is chief town of the island, being situated near the centre of it, so that it is the most convenient place for their assemblies. The jurisdiction of every city extends at least twenty miles: and where the towns lie wider, they have much more ground: no town desires to enlarge its bounds, for the people consider themselves rather as tenants than landlords. They have built over all the country, farmhouses for husbandmen, which are well contrived, and are furnished with all things necessary for country labour. Inhabitants are sent by turns from the cities to dwell in them; no country family has fewer than forty men and women in it, besides two slaves. There is a master and a mistress set over every family; and over thirty families there is a magistrate. Every year twenty of this family come back to the town, after they have stayed two years in the country; and in their room there are other twenty sent from the town, that they may learn country work from those that have been already one year in the country, as they must teach those that come to them the next from the town. By this means such as dwell in those country farms are never ignorant of agriculture, and so commit no errors, which might otherwise be fatal, and bring them under a scarcity of corn. But though there is every year such a shifting of the husbandmen, to prevent any man being forced against his will to follow that hard course of life too long; yet many among them take such pleasure in it, that they desire leave to continue in it many years. These husbandmen till the ground, breed cattle, hew wood, and convey it to the towns, either by land or water, as is most convenient. They breed an infinite multitude of chickens in a very curious manner; for the hens do not sit and hatch them, but vast number of eggs are laid in a gentle and equal heat, in order to be hatched, and they are no sooner out of the shell, and able to stir about, but they seem to consider those that feed them as their mothers, and follow them as other chicken do the hen that hatched them. They breed very few horses, but those they have are full of mettle, and are kept only for exercising their youth in the art of sitting and riding them; for they do not put them to any work, either of ploughing or carriage, in which they employ oxen; for though their horses are stronger, yet they find oxen can hold out longer; and as they are not subject to so many diseases, so they are kept upon a less charge, and with less trouble; and even when they are so worn out, that they are no more fit for labour, they are good meat at last. They sow no corn, but that which is to be their bread; for they drink either wine, cyder, or perry, and often water, sometimes boiled with honey or liquorice, with which they abound; and though they know exactly how much corn will serve every town, and all that tract of country which belongs to it, yet they sow much more, and breed more cattle than are necessary for their consumption; and they give that overplus of which they make no use to their neighbours. When they want anything in the country which it does not produce, they fetch that from the town, without carrying anything in exchange for it. And the magistrates of the town take care to see it given them; for they meet generally in the town once a month, upon a festival day. When the time of harvest comes, the magistrates in the country send to those in the towns, and let them know how many hands they will need for reaping the harvest; and the number they call for being sent to them, they commonly dispatch it all in one day. . . .

Thus have I described to you, as particularly as I could, the constitution of that commonwealth, which I do not only think the best in the world, but indeed the only commonwealth that truly deserves that name. In all other places it is visible, that while people talk of a commonwealth, every man only seeks his own wealth; but there, where no man has any property, all men zealously pursue the good of the public: and, indeed, it is no wonder to see men act so differently; for in other commonwealths, every man knows that unless he provides for himself, how flourishing soever the commonwealth may be, he must die of hunger; so that he sees the necessity of preferring his own concerns to the public; but in Utopia, where every man has a right to everything, they all know that if care is taken to keep the public stores full, no private man can want anything; for among them there is no unequal distribution, so that no man is poor, none in necessity; and though no man has anything, yet they are all rich; for what can make a man so rich as to lead a serene and cheerful life, free from anxieties; neither apprehending want himself, nor voiced with the endless complaints of his wife? He is not afraid of the misery of his children, nor is he contriving how to raise a portion for his daughters, but is secure in this, that both he and his wife, his children and grandchildren, to as many generations as he can fancy, will all live both plentifully and happily; since among them there is no less care taken of those who were once engaged in labour, but grow afterwards unable to follow it, than there is elsewhere of these that continue still employed. I would gladly hear any man compare the justice that is among them with that of all other nations; among whom, may I perish, if I see anything that looks either like justice or equity: for what justice is there in this, that a nobleman, a goldsmith, a banker, or any other man, that either does nothing at all, or at best is employed in things that are of no use to the public, should live in great luxury and splendour, upon what is so ill acquired; and a mean man, a carter, a smith, or a ploughman, that works harder even than the beasts themselves, and is employed in labours so necessary, that no commonwealth could hold out a year without them, can only earn so poor a livelihood, and must lead so miserable a life, that the condition of the beasts is much better than theirs? For as the beasts do not work so constantly, so they feed almost as well, and with more pleasure; and have no anxiety about what is to come, whilst these men are depressed by a barren and fruitless employment, and tormented with the apprehensions of want in their old age; since that which they get by their daily labour does but maintain them at present, and is consumed as fast as it comes in, there is no overplus left to lay up for old age.

Is not that government both unjust and ungrateful, that is so prodigal of its favours to those that are called gentlemen, or goldsmiths, or such others who are idle, or live either by flattery, or by contriving the arts of vain pleasure; and on the other hand, takes no care of those of a meaner sort, such as ploughmen, colliers, and smiths, without whom it could not subsist? But after the public has reaped all the advantage of their service, and they come to be oppressed with age, sickness, and want, all their labours and the good they have done is forgotten; and all the recompense given them is that they are left to die in great misery. The richer sort are often endeavouring to bring the hire of labourers lower, not only by their fraudulent practices, but by the laws which they procure to be made to that effect; so that though it is a thing most unjust in itself, to give such small rewards to those who deserve so well of the public, yet they have given those hardships the name and colour of justice, by procuring laws to be made for regulating them.

Therefore I must say that, as I hope for mercy, I can have no other notion of all the other governments that I see or know, than that they are a conspiracy of the rich, who on pretence of managing the public only pursue their private ends, and devise all the ways and arts they can find out; first, that they may, without danger, preserve all that they have so ill acquired, and then that they may engage the poor to toil and labour for them at as low rates as possible, and oppress them as much as they please. And if they can but prevail to get these contrivances established by the show of public authority, which is considered as the representative of the whole people, then they are accounted laws. Yet these wicked men after they have, by a most insatiable covetousness, divided that among themselves with which all the rest might have been well supplied, are far from that happiness that is enjoyed among the Utopians: for the use as well as the desire of money being extinguished, much anxiety and great occasions of mischief is cut off with it. And who does not see that the frauds, thefts, robberies, quarrels, tumults, contentions, seditions, murders, treacheries, and witchcrafts, which are indeed rather punished than restrained by the severities of law, would all fall off, if money were not any more valued by the world? Men's fears, solicitudes, cares, labours, and watchings, would all perish in the same moment with the value of money: even poverty itself, for the relief of which money seems most necessary, would fall. But, in order to the apprehending this aright, take one instance.

Consider any year that has been so unfruitful that many thousands have died of hunger; and yet if at the end of that year a survey was made of the granaries of all the rich men that have hoarded up the corn, it would be found that there was enough among them to have prevented all that consumption of men that perished in misery; and that if it had been distributed among them, none would have felt the terrible effects of that scarcity; so easy a thing would it be to supply all the necessities of life, if that blessed thing called money, which is pretended to be invented for procuring them, was not really the only thing that obstructed their being procured!

I do not doubt but rich men are sensible of this, and that they well know how much a greater happiness it is to want nothing necessary than to abound in many superfluities, and to be rescued out of so much misery than to abound with so much wealth; and I cannot think but the sense of every man's interest, added to the authority of Christ's commands, who as He was infinitely wise, knew what was best, and was not less good in discovering it to us, would have drawn all the world over to the laws of the Utopians, if pride, that plague of human nature, that source of so much misery, did not hinder it; for this vice does not measure happiness so much by its own conveniences as by the miseries of others; and would not be satisfied with being thought a goddess, if none were left that were miserable, over whom she might insult. Pride thinks its own happiness shines the brighter by comparing it with the misfortunes of other persons; that by displaying its own wealth, they may feel their poverty the more sensibly. This is that infernal serpent that creeps into the breasts of mortals, and possesses them too much to be easily drawn out; and therefore I am glad that the Utopians have fallen upon this form of government, in which I wish that all the world could be so wise as to imitate them; for they have indeed laid down such a scheme and foundation of policy, that as men live happily under it, so it is like to be of great continuance; for they having rooted out of the minds of their people all the seeds both of ambition and faction, there is no danger of any commotion at home; which alone has been the ruin of many states, that seemed otherwise to be well secured; but as long as they live in peace at home, and are governed by such good laws, envy of all their neighbouring princes, who have often though in vain attempted their ruin, will never be able to put their state into any commotion or disorder.

When Raphael had thus made an end of speaking, though many things occurred to me, both concerning the manners and laws of that people, that seemed very absurd, as well as their way of making war, as in their notions of religion and divine matters; together with several other particulars, but chiefly what seemed the foundation of all the rest, their living in common, without the use of money, by which all nobility, magnificence, splendour, and majesty, which, according to the common opinion, are the true ornaments of a nation, would be quite taken away; yet since I perceived that Raphael was weary, and was not sure whether he could easily bear contradiction, remembering that he had taken notice of some who seemed to think they were bound in honour to support the credit of their own wisdom, by finding out something to censure in all other men's inventions, besides their own; I only commended their constitution, and the account he had given of it in general; and so taking him by the hand, carried him to supper, and told him I would find out some other time for examining this subject more particularly, and for discoursing more copiously upon it; and indeed I shall be glad to embrace an opportunity of doing it. In the meanwhile, though it must be confessed that he is both a very learned man, and a person who has obtained a great knowledge of the world, I cannot perfectly agree to everything he has related; however, there are many things in the Commonwealth of Utopia that I rather wish, than hope, to see followed in our governments.

The New Science and the Old Religion

The year after the completion of *Utopia,* Martin Luther nailed his ninety-five theses on the door of the castle church at Wittenberg and launched the Protestant Reformation. But other innovations may have been equally revolutionary: the invention of the rifle, Copernicus' discoveries in celestial mechanics culminating in his announcement that the earth revolved around the sun, Georg Agricola's classification of minerals, Mercator's scientific mapmaking, Lee's knitting machine, Galileo's laws of motion, Jansen's microscope, Gilbert's studies of magnetism, Lippershey's telescope, Kepler's laws of planetary motion, Napier's logarithms, and Descartes' analytical geometry.

Scientific discoveries began to reach a critical mass in which one would set off another, and technology not only was suggesting its ability to change humanity's existence but also was providing the basic data by which science would change humanity's image of itself and its position in the universe. Humanity's world expanded in both directions, into the very small and out to the stars, and the place of humanity was greatly reduced by comparison.

Scale and the means by which humanity measures it have always been important to science fiction.

In literature, Ludovico Ariosto (1474–1533) wrote what has been called the greatest Renaissance poem, *Orlando Furioso,* whose final version was published in 1532. In this epic treatment of the Roland story, Astolpho goes to the moon in the same chariot that carried off Elijah, so that he might find Orlando's lost wits; for the moon has cities and towns and everything lost on earth. And in 1605 Miguel de Cervantes (1547–1616) published *Don Quixote,* which not only has some claim on the title of the world's first novel but also, in its treatment of the realistic consequences of living in a fantasy world, has some relevance in the literary history of science fiction.

But the important science-fiction-related works of the times were still utopian. The author of one was a Dominican monk named Tommaso Campanella (1568–1639), an Italian philosopher and poet who insisted on the preeminence of faith although his work emphasized rationality, science, and a concern for the condition of humanity here on earth. As a result of differences with the rulers of southern Italy (who were Spanish), he spent twenty-eight years of his life in prison, and wrote many of his eighty-eight books while imprisoned (as Cervantes is said to have planned *Don Quixote*), including *Civitas Solis, idea republicae Platonica* (1623). *The City of the Sun* is in the form of a dialogue between a grandmaster of the Knights Hospitaliers and his guest, a Genoese sea captain.

From The City of the Sun

BY TOMMASO CAMPANELLA

G. M. Prithee, now, tell me what happened to you during that voyage?

Capt. I have already told you how I wandered over the whole earth. In the course of my journeying I came to Taprobane, and was compelled to go ashore at a place, where through fear of the inhabitants I remained in a wood. When I stepped out of this I found myself on a large plain immediately under the equator.

G. M. And what befell you here?

Capt. I came upon a large crowd of men and armed women, many of whom did not understand our language, and they conducted me forthwith to the City of the Sun.

G. M. Tell me after what plan this city is built and how it is governed?

Capt. The greater part of the city is built upon a high hill, which rises from an extensive plain, but several of its circles extend for some distance beyond the base of the hill, which is of such a size that the diameter of the city is upwards of two miles, so that its circumference becomes about seven. On account of the humped shape of the mountain, however, the diameter of the city is really more than if it were built on a plain.

It is divided into seven rings or huge circles named from the seven planets, and the way from one to the other of these is by four streets and through four gates, that look towards the four points of the compass. Furthermore, it is so built that if the first circle were stormed, it would of necessity entail a double amount of energy to storm the second; still more to storm the third; and in each succeeding case the strength and energy would have to be doubled; so that he who wishes to capture that city must, as it were, storm it seven times. For my own part, however, I think that not even the first wall could be occupied, so thick are the earthworks and so well fortified is it with breastworks, towers, guns and ditches.

When I had been taken through the northern gate (which is shut with an iron door so wrought that it can be raised and let down, and locked in easily and strongly, its projections running into the grooves of the thick posts by a marvellous device), I saw a level space seventy paces wide between the first and second walls. From hence can be seen large palaces all joined to the wall of the second circuit, in such a manner as to appear all one palace. Arches run on a level with the middle height of the palaces, and are continued round the whole ring. There are galleries for promenading upon these arches, which are supported from beneath by thick and well-shaped columns, enclosing arcades like peristyles, or cloisters of an abbey.

But the palaces have no entrances from below, except on the inner or concave partition, from which one enters directly to the lower parts of the building. The higher parts, however, are reached by flights of marble steps, which lead to galleries for promenading on the inside similar to those on the outside. From these one enters the higher rooms, which are very beautiful, and have windows on the concave and convex partitions. These rooms are divided from one another by richly decorated walls. The convex or outer wall of the ring is about eight spans thick; the concave, three; the intermediate walls are one, or perhaps one and a half. Leaving this circle one gets to the second plain, which is nearly three paces narrower than the first. Then the first wall of the second ring is seen adorned above and below with similar galleries for walking, and there is on the inside of it another interior wall enclosing palaces. It has also similar peristyles supported by columns in the lower part, but above are excellent pictures, round the ways into the upper houses. And so on afterwards through similar spaces and double walls, enclosing palaces, and adorned with galleries for walking, extending along their outer side, and supported by columns, till the last circuit is reached, the way being still over a level plain.

But when the two gates, that is to say, those of the outmost and the inmost walls, have been passed, one mounts by means of steps so formed that an ascent is scarcely discernible, since it proceeds in a slanting direction, and the steps succeed one another at almost imperceptible heights. On the top of the hill is a rather spacious plain, and in the midst of this there rises a temple built with wondrous art.

G. M. Tell on, I pray you! Tell on! I am dying to hear more.

Capt. The temple is built in the form of a circle; it is not girt with walls, but stands upon thick columns, beautifully grouped. A very large dome, built with great care in the centre or pole, contains another small vault as it were rising out of it, and in this is a spiracle, which is right over the altar. There is but one altar in the middle of the temple, and this is hedged round by columns. The temple itself is on a space of more than three hundred and fifty paces. Without it, arches measuring about eight paces extend from the heads of the columns outwards, whence other columns rise about three paces from the thick, strong and erect wall. Between these and the former columns there are galleries for walking, with beautiful pavements, and in the recess of the wall, which is adorned with numerous large doors, there are immovable seats, placed as it were between the inside columns, supporting the temple. Portable chairs are not wanting, many and well adorned. Nothing is seen over the altar but a large globe, upon which the heavenly bodies are painted, and another globe upon which there is a representation of the earth. Furthermore, in the vault of the dome there can be discerned representations of all the stars of heaven from the first to the sixth magnitude, with their proper names and power to influence terrestrial things marked in three little verses for each. There are the poles and greater and lesser circles according to the right latitude of the place, but these are not perfect because there is no wall below. They seem, too, to be made in their relation to the globes on the altar. The pavement of the temple is bright with precious stones. Its seven golden lamps hang always burning, and these bear the names of the seven planets.

At the top of the building several small and beautiful cells surround the small dome, and behind the level space above the bands or arches of the exterior and interior columns there are many cells, both small and large, where the priests and religious officers dwell to the number of forty-nine.

A revolving flag projects from the smaller dome, and this shows in what quarter the wind is. The flag is marked with figures up to thirty-six, and the priests know what sort of year the different kinds of winds bring and what will be the changes of weather on land and sea. Furthermore, under the flag a book is always kept written with letters of gold.

G. M. I pray you, worthy hero, explain to me their whole system of government; for I am anxious to hear it.

Capt. The great ruler among them is a priest whom they call by the name HOH, though we should call him Metaphysic. He is head over all, in temporal and spiritual matters, and all business and lawsuits are settled by him, as the supreme authority. Three princes of equal power—viz., Pon, Sin and Mor—assist him, and these in our tongue we should call POWER, WISDOM and LOVE. To POWER belongs the care of all matters relating to war and peace. He attends to the military arts, and next to HOH, he is ruler in every affair of a warlike nature. He governs the military magistrates and the soldiers, and has the management of the munitions, the fortifications, the storming of places, the implements of war, the armories, the smiths and workmen connected with matters of this sort.

But WISDOM is the ruler of the liberal arts, of mechanics, of all sciences with their magistrates and doctors, and of the discipline of the schools. As many doctors as there are, are under his control. There is one doctor who is called Astrologus; a second, Cosmographus; a third, Arithmeticus; a fourth, Geometra; a fifth, Historiographus; a sixth, Poeta; a seventh, Logicus; an eighth, Rhetor; a ninth, Grammaticus; a tenth, Medicus; an eleventh, Physiologus; a twelfth, Politicus; a thirteenth, Moralis. They have but one book, which they call Wisdom, and in it all the science are written with conciseness and marvellous fluency of expression. This they read to the people after the custom of the Pythagoreans. It is Wisdom who causes the exterior and interior, the higher and lower walls of the city to be adorned with the finest pictures, and to have all the sciences painted upon them in an admirable manner. On the walls of the temple and on the dome, which is let down when the priest gives an address, lest the sounds of his voice, being scattered, should fly away from his audience, there are pictures of stars in their different magnitudes, with the powers and motions of each, expressed separately in three little verses.

On the interior wall of the first circuit all the mathematical figures are conspicuously painted—figures more in number than Archimedes or Euclid discovered, marked symmetrically, and with the explanation of them neatly written and contained each in a little verse. There are definitions and propositions, &c. &c. On the exterior convex wall is first an immense drawing of the whole earth, given at one view. Following upon this, there are tablets setting forth for every separate country the customs both public and private, the laws, the origins and the power of the inhabitants; and the alphabets the different people use can be seen above that of the City of the Sun.

On the inside of the second circuit, that is to say of the second ring of buildings, paintings of all kinds of precious and common stones, of minerals and metals, are seen; and a little piece of the metal itself is also there with an apposite explanation in two small verses for each metal or stone. On the outside are marked all the seas, rivers, lakes and streams which are on the face of the earth; as are also the wines and the oils and the different liquids, with the sources from which the last are extracted, their qualities and strength. There are also vessels built into the wall above the arches, and these are full of liquids from one to three hundred years old, which cure all diseases. Hail and snow, storms and thunder, and whatever else takes place in the air, are represented with suitable figures and little verses. The inhabitants even have the art of representing in stone all the phenomena of the air, such as the wind, rain, thunder, the rainbow, &c.

On the interior of the third circuit all the different families of trees and herbs are depicted, and there is a live specimen of each plant in earthenware vessels placed upon the outer partition of the arches. With the specimens there are explanations as to where they were first found, what are their powers and natures, and resemblances to celestial things and to metals: to parts of the human body and to things in the sea, and also as to their uses in medicine, &c. On the exterior wall are all the races of fish, found in rivers, lakes and seas, and their habits and values, and ways of breeding, training and living, the purposes for which they exist in the world, and their uses to man. Further, their resemblances to celestial and terrestrial things, produced both by nature and art, are so given that I was astonished when I saw a fish which was like a bishop, one like a chain, another like a garment, a fourth like a nail, a fifth like a star, and others like images of those things existing among us, the relation in each case being completely manifest. There are sea-urchins to be seen, and the purple shell-fish and mussels; and whatever the watery world possesses worthy of being known is there fully shown in marvellous characters of painting and drawing.

On the fourth interior wall all the different kinds of birds are painted, with their natures, sizes, customs, colours, manner of living, &c; and the only real phœnix is possessed by the inhabitants of this city. On the exterior are shown all the races of creeping animals, serpents, dragons and worms; the insects, the flies, gnats, beetles, &c., in their different states, strength, venoms and uses, and a great deal more than you or I can think of.

On the fifth interior they have all the larger animals of the earth, as many in number as would astonish you. We indeed know not the thousandth part of them, for on the exterior wall also a great many of immense size are also portrayed. To be sure, of horses alone, how great a number of breeds there is and how beautiful are the forms there cleverly displayed!

On the sixth interior are painted all the mechanical arts, with the several instruments for each and their manner of use among different nations. Alongside the dignity of such is placed, and their several inventors are named. But on the exterior all the inventors in science, in warfare, and in law are represented. There I saw Moses, Osiris, Jupiter, Mercury, Lycurgus, Pompilius, Pythagoras, Zamolxis, Solon, Charondas, Phoroneus, with very many others. They even have Mahomet, whom nevertheless they hate as a false and sordid legislator. In the most dignified position I saw a representation of Jesus Christ and of the twelve Apostles, whom they consider very worthy and hold to be great. Of the representations of men, I perceived Cæsar, Alexander, Pyrrhus and Hannibal in the highest place; and other very renowned heroes in peace and war, especially Roman heroes, were painted in lower positions, under the galleries. And when I asked with astonishment whence they had obtained our history, they told me that among them there was a knowledge of all languages, and that by perseverance they continually send explorers and ambassadors over the whole earth, who learn thoroughly the customs, forces, rule and histories of the nations, bad and good alike. These they apply all to their own republic, and with this they are well pleased. I learnt that cannon and typography were invented by the Chinese before we knew of them. There are magistrates, who announce the meaning of the pictures, and boys are accustomed to learn all the sciences, without toil and as if for pleasure; but in the way of history only until they are ten years old.

LOVE is foremost in attending to the charge of the race. He sees that men and women are so joined together, that they bring forth the best offspring. Indeed, they laugh at us who exhibit a studious care for our breed of horses and dogs, but neglect the breeding of human beings. Thus the education of the children is under his rule. So also is the medicine that is sold, the sowing and collecting of fruits of the earth and of trees, agriculture, pasturage, the preparations for the months, the cooking arrangements, and whatever has any reference to food, clothing, and the intercourse of the sexes. LOVE himself is ruler, but there are many male and female magistrates dedicated to these arts.

Metaphysic then with these three rulers manage all the above-named matters, and even by himself alone nothing is done; all business is discharged by the four together, but in whatever Metaphysic inclines to the rest are sure to agree.

G. M. Tell me, please, of the magistrates, their services and duties, of the education and mode of living, whether the government is a monarchy, a republic, or an aristocracy.

Capt. This race of men came there from India, flying from the sword of the Magi, a race of plunderers and tyrants who laid waste their country, and they determined to lead a philosophic life in fellowship with one another. Although the community of wives is not instituted among the other inhabitants of their province, among them it is in use after this manner. All things are common with them, and their dispensation is by the authority of the magistrates. Arts and honours and pleasures are common, and are held in such a manner that no one can appropriate anything to himself.

They say that all private property is acquired and improved for the reason that each one of us by himself has his own home and wife and children. From this self-love springs. For when we raise a son to riches and dignities, and leave an heir to much wealth, we become either ready to grasp at the property of the state, if in any case fear should be removed from the power which belongs to riches and rank; or avaricious, crafty, and hypocritical, if any one is of slender purse, little strength, and mean ancestry. But when we have taken away self-love, there remains only love for the state.

G. M. Under such circumstances no one will be willing to labour, while he expects others to work, on the fruit of whose labours he can live, as Aristotle argues against Plato.

Capt. I do not know how to deal with that argument, but I declare to you that they burn with so great a love for their fatherland, as I could scarcely have believed possible; and indeed with much more than the histories tell us belonged to the Romans, who fell willingly for their country, inasmuch as they have to a greater extent surrendered their private property. I think truly that the friars and monks and clergy of our country, if they were not weakened by love for their kindred and friends, or by the ambition to rise to higher dignities, would be less fond of property, and more imbued with a spirit of charity towards all, as it was in the time of the Apostles, and is now in a great many cases.

G. M. St. Augustine may say that, but I say that among this race of men, friendship is worth nothing; since they have not the chance of conferring mutual benefits on one another.

Capt. Nay, indeed. For it is worth the trouble to see that no one can receive gifts from another. Whatever is necessary they have, they receive it from the community, and the magistrate takes care that no one receives more than he deserves. Yet nothing necessary is denied to any one. Friendship is recognized among them in war, in infirmity, in the art contests, by which means they aid one another mutually by teaching. Sometimes they improve themselves mutually with praises, with conversation, with actions and out of the things they need. All those of the same age call one another brothers. They call all over twenty-two years of age, fathers; those who are less than twenty-two are named sons. Moreover, the magistrates govern well, so that no one in the fraternity can do injury to another.

G. M. And how?

Capt. As many names of virtues as there are amongst us, so many magistrates there are among them. There is a magistrate who is named Magnanimity, another Fortitude, a third Chastity, a fourth Liberality, a fifth Criminal and Civil Justice, a sixth Comfort, a seventh Truth, an eighth Kindness, a tenth Gratitude, an eleventh Cheerfulness, a twelfth Exercise, a thirteenth Sobriety, &c. They are elected to duties of that kind, each one to that duty for excellence in which he is known from boyhood to be most suitable. Wherefore among them neither robbery nor clever murders, nor lewdness, incest, adultery, or other crimes of which we accuse one another, can be found. They accuse themselves of ingratitude and malignity when any one denies a lawful satisfaction to another, of indolence, of sadness, of anger, of scurrility, of slander, and of lying, which curseful thing they thoroughly hate. Accused persons undergoing punishment are deprived of the common table, and other honours, until the judge thinks that they agree with their correction. . . .

They divide the seasons according to the revolution of the sun, and not of the stars, and they observe yearly by how much time one precedes the other. They hold that the sun approaches nearer and nearer, and therefore by ever-lessening circles reaches the tropics and the equator every year a little sooner. They measure months by the course of the moon, years by that of the sun. They praise Ptolemy, admire Copernicus, but place Aristarchus and Philolaus before him. They take great pains in endeavouring to understand the construction of the world, and whether or not it will perish, and at what time. They believe that the true oracle of Jesus Christ is by the signs in the sun, in the moon, and in the stars, which signs do not thus appear to many of us foolish ones. Therefore they wait for the renewing of the age, and perchance for its end. They say that it is very doubtful whether the world was made from nothing, or from the ruins of other worlds, or from chaos, but they certainly think that it was made, and did not exist from eternity. Therefore they disbelieve in Aristotle, whom they consider a logician and not a philosopher. From analogies, they can draw many arguments against the eternity of the world. The sun and the stars they, so to speak, regard as the living representatives and signs of God, as the temples and holy living altars, and they honour but do not worship them. Beyond all other things they venerate the sun, but they consider no created thing worthy the adoration of worship. This they give to God alone, and thus they serve Him, that they may not come into the power of a tyrant and fall into misery by undergoing punishment by creatures of revenge. They contemplate and know God under the image of the Sun, and they call it the sign of God, His face and living image, by means of which light, heat, life, and the making of all things good and bad proceeds. Therefore they have built an altar like to the Sun in shape, and the priests praise God in the sun and in the stars, as it were His altars, and in the heavens, His temple as it were; and they pray to good angels, who are, so to speak, the intercessors living in the stars, their strong abodes. For God long since set signs of their beauty in heaven, and of His glory in the Sun. They say there is but one heaven, and that the planets move and rise of themselves when they approach the sun or are in conjunction with it.

They assert two principles of the physics of things below, namely, that the Sun is the father, and the Earth the mother; the air is an impure part of the heavens; all fire is derived from the sun. The sea is the sweat of earth, or the fluid of earth combusted, and fused within its bowels; but is the bond of union between air and earth, as the blood is of the spirit and flesh of animals. The world is a great animal, and we live within it as worms live within us. Therefore we do not belong to the system of stars, sun, and earth, but to God only; for in respect to them which seek only to amplify themselves, we are born and live by chance; but in respect to God, whose instruments we are, we are formed by prescience and design, and for a high end. Therefore we are bound to no Father but God, and receive all things from Him. They hold as beyond question the immortality of souls, and that these associate with good angels after death, or with bad angels, according as they have likened themselves in this life to either. For all things seek their like. They differ little from us as to places of reward and punishment. They are in doubt whether there are other worlds beyond ours, and account it madness to say there is nothing. Nonentity is incompatible with the infinite entity of God. They lay down two principles of metaphysics, entity which is the highest God, and nothingness which is the defect of entity. Evil and sin come from the propensity to nothingness; the sin having its cause not efficient, but in deficiency. Deficiency is, they say, of power, wisdom or will. Sin they place in the last of these three, because he who knows and has the power to do good is bound also to have the will, for will arises out of them. They worship God in Trinity, saying God is the Supreme Power, whence proceeds the highest Wisdom, which is the same with God, and from these comes Love, which is both Power and Wisdom; but they do not distinguish persons by name, as in our Christian law, which has not been revealed to them. This religion, when its abuses have been removed, will be the future mistress of the world, as great theologians teach and hope. Therefore Spain found the New World (though its first discoverer, Columbus, greatest of heroes, was a Genoese), that all nations should be gathered under one law. We know not what we do, but God knows, whose instruments we are. They sought new regions for lust of gold and riches, but God works to a higher end. The sun strives to burn up the earth, not to produce plants and men, but God guides the battle to great issues. His the praise, to Him the glory!

G. M. Oh, if you knew what our astrologers say of the coming age, and of our age, that has in it more history within a hundred years than all the world had in four thousand years before! Of the wonderful invention of printing and guns, and the use of the magnet, and how it all comes of Mercury, Mars, the Moon, and the Scorpion!

Capt. Ah, well! God gives all in His good time. They astrologize too much.

Experience, Experiment, and the
Battle for Men's Minds

The battle for human understanding that had been waged by Roger Bacon in the thirteenth century still was in progress by the seventeenth century when another Bacon set out to destroy old errors and establish a new system of understanding based on observation and experiment.

Francis Bacon (1561–1626) studied law, entered the legal bureaucracy under Queen Elizabeth, and rose to the peak of his profession (like his utopian predecessor, Thomas More), becoming Lord Chancellor under James I. After three years, however, he was accused of taking bribes, confessed to corruption and neglect, and spent his last five years in retirement.

His success in the realm of ideas was more lasting. Empiricism, the philosophical doctrine that all knowledge comes from experience, was not a new concept with Bacon; the sixteenth-century Swiss alchemist Paracelsus already had stressed the importance of empiricism in contrast to a dependence on the authority of Galen and other classical physicians. Bacon's contribution was an emphasis on controlled and repeated experiments, carefully coordinated, and directed and focused by theory.

In his *Novum Organum* (1620), or *The New Instrument of Learning,* Bacon set out to completely reconstruct human learning, first attacking those ideas that delude, mislead, and bewilder humanity, which he called Idols, and then setting forth his own way to truth. *The New Atlantis* (1627) is his never-completed utopian vision of an island where the scientific method has been perfected, laboratories have been built to explore natural phenomena, and the discoveries of science have been turned to the service of a better life for the people, though the scientists assume the responsibility for deciding which discoveries are released and which are kept secret.

The high point of *The New Atlantis* is the description of Salomon's House (or Solomon, who was reputed to have been the wisest man of antiquity). It sounds very much like a modern research university, and the pursuits laid out for it seem like a scientific prospectus for the next three centuries. Perhaps because Bacon's vision of a helpful science was unsullied by political theory, his concepts were more quickly implemented than that of the social scientists. Within thirty years, the Philosophical Society was formed in England for the study of natural phenomena and the discussion of scientific data and theory; in 1662, this was chartered as the Royal Society, a scientific organization that still exists and still is involved in the original goals set forth by Bacon.

Bacon has been called the father of the scientific method.

From The New Atlantis

BY FRANCIS BACON

We sailed from Peru, where we had continued by the space of one whole year, for China and Japan, by the South Sea, taking with us victuals for twelve months; and had good winds from the east, though soft and weak, for five months' space and more. But then the wind came about, and settled in the west for many days, so as we could make little or no way, and were sometimes in purpose to turn back. But then again there arose strong and great winds from the south, with a point east; which carried us up, for all that we could do, towards the north: by which time our victuals failed us, though we had made good spare of them. So that finding ourselves, in the midst of the greatest wilderness of waters in the world, without victual, we gave ourselves for lost men, and prepared for death. Yet we did lift up our hearts and voices to God above, who showeth His wonders in the deep; beseeching Him of his mercy, that as in the beginning He discovered the face of the deep, and brought forth dry land, so He would now discover land to us, that we might not perish. And it came to pass, that the next day about evening we saw within a keening before us, towards the north, as it were thick clouds, which did put us in some hope of land: knowing how that part of the South Sea was utterly unknown: and might have islands or continents, that hitherto were not come to light. Wherefore we bent our course thither, where we saw the appearance of land, all that night: and in the dawning of next day, we might plainly discern that it was a land flat to our sight, and full of boscage, which made it show the more dark. And after an hour and a half's sailing, we entered into a good haven, being the port of a fair city. Not great indeed, but well built, and that gave a pleasant view from the sea. And we thinking every minute long till we were on land, came close to the shore and offered to land. But straightways we saw divers of the people, with bastons in their hands, as it were forbidding us to land: yet without any cries or fierceness, but only as warning us off, by signs that they made. Whereupon being not a little discomfited, we were advising with ourselves what we should do. During which time there made forth to us a small boat, with about eight persons in it, whereof one of them had in his hand a tipstaff of a yellow cane, tipped at both ends with blue, who made aboard our ship, without any show of distrust at all. And when he saw one of our number present himself somewhat afore the rest, he drew forth a little scroll of parchment (somewhat yellower than our parchment, and shining like the leaves of writing tables, but otherwise soft and flexible), and delivered it to our foremost man. In which scroll were written in ancient Hebrew, and in ancient Greek, and in good Latin of the school, and in Spanish these words: "Land ye not, none of you, and provide to be gone from this coast within sixteen days, except you have further time given you; meanwhile, if you want fresh water, or victual, or help for your sick, or that your ship needeth repair, write down your wants, and you shall have that which belongeth to mercy." This scroll was signed with a stamp of cherubim's wings, not spread, but hanging downwards; and by them a cross. This being delivered, the officer returned, and left only a servant with us to receive our answer. Consulting hereupon amongst ourselves, we were much perplexed. The denial of landing, and hasty warning us away, troubled us much: on the other side, to find that the people had languages, and were so full of humanity, did comfort us not a little. And above all, the sign of the cross to that instrument, was to us a great rejoicing, and as it were a certain presage of good. Our answer was in the Spanish tongue, "That for our ship, it was well; for we had rather met with calms and contrary winds, than any tempests. For our sick, they were many, and in very ill case; so that if they were not permitted to land, they ran in danger of their lives." Our other wants we set down in particular, adding, "That we had some little store of merchandise, which if it pleased them to deal for, it might supply our wants, without being chargeable unto them." We offered some reward in pistolets unto the servant, and a piece of crimson velvet to be presented to the officer; but the servants took them not, nor would scarce look upon them; and so left us, and went back in another little boat which was sent for him.

About three hours after we had despatched our answer there came towards us a person (as it seemed) of a place. He had on him a gown with wide sleeves, of a kind of water chamolet, of an excellent azure colour, far more glossy than ours: his under apparel was green, and so was his hat, being in the form of a turban, daintily made, and not so huge as the Turkish turbans; and the locks of his hair came down below the brims of it. A reverend man was he to behold. He came in a boat, gilt in some part of it, with four persons more only in that boat; and was followed by another boat, wherein were some twenty. When he was come within a flight-shot of our ship, signs were made to us that we should send forth some to meet him upon the water, which we presently did in our ship-boat, sending the principal man amongst us save one, and four of our number with him. When we were come within six yards of their boat, they called to us to stay, and not to approach farther, which we did. And thereupon the man, whom I before described, stood up, and with a loud voice in Spanish, asked, "Are ye Christians?" We answered, "We were"; fearing the less, because of the cross we had seen in the subscription. At which answer the said person lift up his right hand towards heaven, and drew it softly to his mouth (which is the gesture they use, when they thank God), and then said: "If ye will swear, all of you; by the merits of the Saviour, that ye are no pirates; nor have shed blood, lawfully nor unlawfully, within forty days past; you may have license to come on land." We said, "We were all ready to take that oath." Whereupon one of those that were with him, being (as it seemed) a notary, made an entry of this act. Which done, another of the attendants of the great person, which was with him in the same boat, after his lord had spoken a little to him, said aloud: "My lord would have you know, that it is not of pride, or greatness, that he cometh not aboard your ship: but for that, in your answer, you declare that you have many sick amongst you, he was warned by the conservator of health of the city that he should keep a distance." We bowed ourselves towards him, and answered: "We were his humble servants; and accounted for great honour and singular humanity towards us, that which was already done: but hoped well, that the nature of the sickness of our men was not infectious." So he returned; and a while after came the notary to us aboard our ship; holding in his hand a fruit of that country, like an orange, but of colour between orange-tawny and scarlet: which cast a most excellent odour. He used it (as it seemed) for a preservative against infection. He gave us our oath, "By the name of Jesus, and His merits": and after told us, that the next day by six of the clock in the morning, we should be sent to, and brought to the strangers' house (so he called it), where we should be accommodated of things, both for our whole and for our sick. So he left us; and when we offered him some pistolets, he smiling, said, "He must not be twice paid for one labour": meaning (as I take it) that he had salary sufficient of the state for his service. For (as I after learned) they call an officer that taketh rewards twice-paid.

The next morning early, there came to us the same officer that came to us at first with his cane, and told us: "He came to conduct us to the strangers' house: and that he had prevented the hour, because we might have the whole day before us for our business. For (said he) if you will follow my advice, there shall first go with me some few of you, and see the place, and how it may be made convenient for you: and then you may send for your sick, and the rest of your number, which ye will bring on land." We thanked him, and said, "That his care which he took of desolate strangers, God would reward." And so six of us went on land with him; and when we were on land, he went before us, and turned to us, and said, "He was but our servant, and our guide." He led us through three fair streets; and all the way we went there were gathered some people on both sides, standing in a row; but in so civil a fashion, as if it had been, not to wonder at us, but to welcome us; and divers of them, as we passed by them, put their arms a little abroad, which is their gesture when they bid any welcome. The strangers' house is a fair and spacious house, built of brick, of somewhat a bluer colour than our brick; and with handsome windows, some of glass, some of a kind of cambric oiled. He brought us first into a fair parlour above stairs, and then asked us, "What number of persons we were? and how many sick?" We answered, "We were in all (sick and whole) one and fifty persons, whereof our sick were seventeen." He desired us to have patience a little, and to stay till he came back to us, which was about an hour after; and then he led us to see the chambers which were provided for us, being in number nineteen. They having cast it (as it seemeth) that four of those chambers, which were better than the rest, might receive four of the principal men of our company; and lodge them alone by themselves; and the other fifteen chambers were to lodge us, two and two together. The chambers were handsome and cheerful chambers, and furnished civilly. Then he led us to a long gallery, like a dorture, where he showed us all along the one side (for the other side was but wall and window) seventeen cells, very neat ones, having partitions of cedar wood. Which gallery and cells, being in all forty (many more than we needed), were instituted as an infirmary for sick persons. And he told us withal, that as any of our sick waxed well, he might be removed from his cell to a chamber: for which purpose there were set forth ten spare chambers, besides the number we spake of before. This done, he brought us back to the parlour, and lifting up his cane a little (as they do when they give any charge or command), said to us, "Ye are to know that the custom of the land requireth, that after this day and to-morrow (which we give you for removing your people from your ship), you are to keep within doors for three days. But let it not trouble you, nor do not think yourselves restrained, but rather left to your rest and ease. You shall want nothing; and there are six of our people appointed to attend you for any business you may have abroad." We gave him thanks with all affection and respect, and said, "God surely is manifested in this land." We offered him also twenty pistolets; but he smiled, and only said: "What? Twice paid!" And so he left us. Soon after our dinner was served in; which was right good viands, both for bread and meat: better than any collegiate diet that I have known in Europe. We had also drink of three sorts, all wholesome and good; wine of the grape; a drink of grain, such as is with us our ale, but more clear; and a kind of cider made of a fruit of that country; a wonderful pleasing and refreshing drink. Besides, there were brought in to us great store of those scarlet oranges for our sick; which (they said) were an assured remedy for sickness taken at sea. There was given us also a box of small grey or whitish pills, which they wished our sick should take, one of the pills every night before sleep; which (they said) would hasten their recovery. The next day, after that our trouble of carriage and removing of our men and goods out of our ship was somewhat settled and quiet, I thought good to call our company together, and when they were assembled, said unto them, "My dear friends, let us know ourselves, and how it standeth with us. We are men cast on land, as Jonas was out of the whale's belly, when we were as buried in the deep; and now we are on land, we are but between death and life, for we are beyond both the old world and the new; and whether ever we shall see Europe, God only knoweth. It is a kind of miracle hath brought us hither, and it must be little less that shall bring us hence. Therefore in regard of our deliverance past, and our danger present and to come, let us look up to God, and every man reform his own ways. Besides we are come here amongst a Christian people, full of piety and humanity. Let us not bring that confusion of face upon ourselves, as to show our vices or unworthiness before them. Yet there is more, for they have by commandment (though in form of courtesy) cloistered us within these walls for three days; who knoweth whether it be not to take some taste of our manners and conditions? And if they find them bad, to banish us straightways; if good, to give us further time. For these men that they have given us for attendance, may withal have an eye upon us. Therefore, for God's love, and as we love the weal of our souls and bodies, let us so behave ourselves, as we may be at peace with God, and may find grace in the eyes of this people." Our company with one voice thanked me for my good admonition, and promised me to live soberly and civilly, and without giving any the least occasion of offence. So we spent our three days joyfully, and without care, in expectation what would be done with us when they were expired. During which time, we had every hour joy of the amendment of our sick, who thought themselves cast into some divine pool of healing, they mended so kindly and so fast.

The morrow after our three days were past, there came to us a new man, that we had not seen before, clothed in blue as the former was, save that his turban was white with a small red cross on the top. He had also a tippet of fine linen. At his coming in, he did bend to us a little, and put his arms abroad. We of our parts saluted him in a very lowly and submissive manner; as looking that from him we should receive sentence of life or death.

He desired to speak with some few of us. Whereupon six of us only stayed, and the rest avoided the room. He said, "I am by office governor of this house of strangers, and by vocation I am a Christian priest; and therefore am come to you, to offer you my service, both as strangers, and chiefly as Christians. Some things I may tell you, which I think you will not be unwilling to hear. The state hath given you license to stay on land for the space of six weeks: and let it not trouble you, if your occasions ask further time, for the law in this point is not precise; and I do not doubt, but myself shall be able to obtain for you such further time as shall be convenient. Ye shall also understand, that the strangers' house is at this time rich, and much aforehand; for it hath laid up revenue these thirty-seven years: for so long it is since any stranger arrived in this part; and therefore take ye no care; the state will defray you all the time you stay. Neither shall you stay one day the less for that. As for any merchandise you have brought, ye shall be well used, and have your return, either in merchandise or in gold and silver: for to us it is all one. And if you have any other request to make, hide it not; for ye shall find we will not make your countenance to fall by the answer ye shall receive. Only this I must tell you, that none of you must go above a karan (that is with them a mile and a half) from the walls of the city, without special leave." We answered, after we had looked a while upon one another, admiring this gracious and parent-like usage, that we could not tell what to say, for we wanted words to express our thanks; and his noble free offers left us nothing to ask. It seemed to us, that we had before us a picture of our salvation in heaven; for we that were a while since in the jaws of death, were now brought into a place where we found nothing but consolations. For the commandment laid upon us, we would not fail to obey it, though it was impossible but our hearts should be inflamed to tread further upon this happy and holy ground. We added, that our tongues should first cleave to the roofs of our mouths, ere we should forget, either this reverend person, or this whole nation, in our prayers. We also most humbly besought him to accept of us as his true servants, by as just a right as ever men on earth were bounden; laying and presenting both our persons and all we had at his feet. He said, he was a priest, and looked for a priest's reward; which was our brotherly love, and the good of our souls and bodies. So he went from us, not without tears of tenderness in his eyes, and left us also confused with joy and kindness, saying amongst ourselves, that we were come into a land of angels, which did appear to us daily, and prevent us with comforts, which we thought not of, much less expected.

The next day, about ten of the clock, the governor came to us again, and after salutations, said familiarly, that he was come to visit us; and called for a chair, and sat him down; and we being some ten of us (the rest were of the meaner sort, or else gone abroad), sat down with him; and when we were set, he began thus: "We of this island of Bensalem (for so they called it in their language) have this: that by means of our solitary situation, and of the laws of secrecy, which we have for our travellers, and our rare admission of strangers; we know well most part of the habitable world, and are ourselves unknown. Therefore because he that knoweth least is fittest to ask questions, it is more reason, for the entertainment of the time, that ye ask me questions, than that I ask you." We answered, that we humbly thanked him, that he would give us leave so to do. And that we conceived by the taste we had already, that there was no worldly thing on earth more worthy to be known than the state of that happy land. But above all (we said) since that we were met from the several ends of the world, and hoped assuredly that we should meet one day in the kingdom of heaven (for that we were both parts Christians), we desired to know (in respect that land was so remote, and so divided by vast and unknown seas from the land where our Saviour walked on earth) who was the apostle of that nation, and how it was converted to the faith? It appeared in his face, that he took great contentment in this our question; he said, "Ye knit my heart to you, by asking this question in the first place: for it showeth that you first seek the kingdom of heaven: and I shall gladly, and briefly, satisfy your demand.

"About twenty years after the ascension of our Saviour it came to pass, that there was seen by the people of Renfusa (a city upon the eastern coast of our island, within sight, the night was cloudy and calm}, as it might be some mile in the sea, a great pillar of light; not sharp, but in form of a column, or cylinder, rising from the sea, a great way up towards heaven; and on the top of it was seen a large cross of light, more bright and resplendent than the body of the pillar. Upon which so strange a spectacle, the people of the city gathered apace together upon the sands, to wonder; and so after put themselves into a number of small boats to go nearer to this marvellous sight. But when the boats were come within about sixty yards of the pillar, they found themselves all bound, and could go no further, yet so as they might move to go about, but might not approach nearer; so as the boats stood all as in a theatre, beholding this light, as an heavenly sign. It so fell out, that there was in one of the boats one of the wise men of the Society of Salomon's House; which house or college, my good brethren, is the very eye of this kingdom, who having a while attentively and devoutly viewed and contemplated this pillar and cross, fell down upon his face; and then raised himself upon his knees, and lifting up his hands to heaven, made his prayers in this manner:

"'Lord God of heaven and earth; thou hast vouchsafed of thy grace, to those of our order to know thy works of creation, and true secrets of them; and to discern (as far as appertaineth to the generations of men) between divine miracles, works of Nature, works of art and impostures, and illusions of all sorts. I do here acknowledge and testify before this people, that the thing we now see before our eyes, is thy finger, and a true miracle. And forasmuch as we learn in our books, that thou never workest miracles, but to a divine and excellent end (for the laws of Nature are thine own laws, and thou exceedest them not but upon great cause), we most humbly beseech thee to prosper this great sign, and to give us the interpretation and use of it in mercy; which thou dost in some part secretly promise, by sending it unto us.'

"When he had made his prayer, he presently found the boat he was in movable and unbound; whereas all the rest remained still fast; and taking that for an assurance of leave to approach, he caused the boat to be softly and with silence rowed towards the pillar; but ere he came near it, the pillar and cross of light broke up, and cast itself abroad, as it were into a firmament of many stars, which also vanished soon after, and there was nothing left to be seen but a small ark, or chest of cedar, dry and not wet at all with water, though it swam; and in the fore-end of it, which was towards him, grew a small green branch of palm; and when the wise man had taken it with all reverence into his boat, it opened of itself, and there were found in it a book and a letter, both written in fine parchment, and wrapped in sindons of linen. The book contained all the canonical books of the Old and New Testament, according as you have them (for we know well what the churches with you receive), and the Apocalypse itself; and some other books of the New Testament, which were not at that time written, were nevertheless in the book. And for the letter, it was in these words:

"'I Bartholomew, a servant of the Highest, and apostle of Jesus Christ, was warned by an angel that appeared to me in a vision of glory, that I should commit this ark to the floods of the sea. Therefore I do testify and declare unto that people where God shall ordain this ark to come to land, that in the same day is come unto them salvation and peace, and goodwill from the Father, and from the Lord Jesus.'

"There was also in both these writings, as well the book as the letter, wrought a great miracle, conform to that of the apostles, in the original gift of tongues. For there being at that time, in this land, Hebrews, Persians, and Indians, besides the natives, every one read upon the book and letter, as if they had been written in his own language. And thus was this land saved from infidelity (as the remain of the old world was from water) by an ark,

through the apostolical and miraculous evangelism of St. Bartholomew."
And here he paused, and a messenger came, and called him forth from us.
So this was all that passed in that conference.

The next day, the same governor came again to us, immediately after dinner, and excused himself, saying, "That the day before he was called from
us somewhat abruptly, but now he would make us amends, and spend time
with us, if we held his company and conference agreeable." We answered,
that we held it so agreeable and pleasing to us, as we forgot both dangers
past, and fears to come, for the time we heard him speak; and that we
thought an hour spent with him was worth years of our former life. He
bowed himself a little to us, and after we were set again, he said, "Well, the
questions are on your part." One of our number said, after a little pause, that
there was a matter we were no less desirous to know than fearful to ask, lest
we might presume too far. But encouraged by his rare humanity towards us
(that could scarce think ourselves strangers, being his vowed and professed
servants), we would take the hardness to propound it; humbly beseeching
him, if he thought it not fit to be answered, that he would pardon it, though
he rejected it. We said, we well observed those his words, which he formerly spake, that this happy island, where we now stood, was known to
few, and yet knew most of the nations of the world, which we found to be
true, considering they had the languages of Europe, and knew much of our
state and business; and yet we in Europe (notwithstanding all the remote
discoveries and navigations of this last age) never heard any of the least
inkling or glimpse of this island. . . .

"There reigned in this island, about 1,900 years ago, a king, whose memory of all others we most adore; not superstitiously, but as a divine instrument, though a mortal man: his name was Salomona; and we esteem him as
the lawgiver of our nation. This king had a large heart, inscrutable for good;
and was wholly bent to make his kingdom and people happy. He therefore
taking into consideration how sufficient and substantive this land was, to
maintain itself without any aid at all of the foreigner; being 5,000 miles in
circuit, and of rare fertility of soil, in the greatest part thereof; and finding
also the shipping of this country might be plentifully set on work, both by
fishing and by transportations from port to port, and likewise by sailing unto
some small islands that are not far from us, and are under the crown and laws
of this state; and recalling into his memory the happy and flourishing estate
wherein this land then was, so as it might be a thousand ways altered to the
worse, but scarce any one way to the better; though nothing wanted to his
noble and heroical intentions, but only (as far as human foresight might
reach) to give perpetuity to that which was in his time so happily estab-

lished, therefore amongst his other fundamental laws of this kingdom he did
ordain the interdicts and prohibitions which we have touching entrance of
strangers; which at that time (though it was after the calamity of America)
was frequent; doubting novelties and commixture of manners. It is true, the
like law against the admission of strangers without license is an ancient law
in the kingdom of China, and yet continued in use. But there it is a poor
thing; and hath made them a curious, ignorant, fearful foolish nation. But
our lawgiver made his law of another temper. For first, he hath preserved all
points of humanity, in taking order and making provision for the relief of
strangers distressed; whereof you have tasted." At which speech (as reason
was) we all rose up, and bowed ourselves. He went on: "That king also still
desiring to join humanity and policy together; and thinking it against humanity, to detain strangers here against their wills; and against policy, that
they should return, and discover their knowledge of this estate, he took this
course; he did ordain, that of the strangers that should be permitted to land,
as many at all times might depart as many as would; but as many as would
stay, should have very good conditions, and means to live from the state.
Wherein he saw so far, that now in so many ages since the prohibition, we
have memory not of one ship that ever returned, and but of thirteen persons
only, at several times, that chose to return in our bottoms. What those few
that returned may have reported abroad, I know not. But you must think,
whatsoever they have said, could be taken where they came but for a dream.
Now for our travelling from hence into parts abroad, our lawgiver thought
fit altogether to restrain it. So is it not in China. For the Chinese sail where
they will, or can; which showeth, that their law of keeping out strangers is a
law of pusillanimity and fear. But this restraint of ours hath one only exception, which is admirable; preserving the good which cometh by communicating with strangers, and avoiding the hurt: and I will now open it to you.
And here I shall seem a little to digress, but you will by-and-by find it per-
tinent. Ye shall understand, my dear friends, that amongst the excellent acts
of that king, one above all hath the pre-eminence. It was the erection and institution of an order, or society, which we call Salomon's House; the noblest
foundation, as we think, that ever was upon the earth, and the lantern of this
kingdom. It is dedicated to the study of the works and creatures of God.
Some think it beareth the founder's name a little corrupted, as if it should be
Solomon's House. But the records write it as it is spoken. So as I take it to
be denominate of the king of Hebrews, which is famous with you, and no
strangers to us; for we have some parts of his works which with you are lost;
namely, that natural history which he wrote of all plants, from the cedar of
Libanus to the moss that groweth out of the wall; and of all things that have

life and motion. This maketh me think that our king finding himself to sym-
bolize, in many things, with that king of the Hebrews, which lived many
years before him, honoured him with the title of this foundation. And I am
rather induced to be of this opinion, for that I find in ancient records, this order or society is sometimes called Solomon's House, and sometimes the
College of the Six Days' Works; whereby I am satisfied that our excellent
king had learned from the Hebrews that God had created the world, and all
that therein is, within six days: and therefore he instituted that house, for the
finding out of the true nature of all things, whereby God might have the
more glory in the workmanship of them, and men the more fruit in their use
of them, did give it also that second name. But now to come to our present
purpose. When the king had forbidden to all his people navigation into any
part that was not under his crown, he made nevertheless this ordinance: that
every twelve years there should be set forth out of this kingdom, two ships,
appointed to several voyages; that in either of these ships there should be a
mission of three of the fellows or brethren of Salomon's House, whose er-
rand was only to give us knowledge of the affairs and state of those countries to which they were designed; and especially of the sciences, arts, manufactures, and inventions of all the world; and withal to bring unto us books,
instruments, and patterns in every kind: that the ships, after they had landed
the brethren, should return; and that the brethren should stay abroad till the
new mission, the ships are not otherwise fraught than with store of victuals,
and good quantity of treasure to remain with the brethren, for the buying of
such things, and rewarding of such persons, as they should think fit. Now for
me to tell you how the vulgar sort of mariners are contained from being discovered at land, and how they that must be put on shore for any time, colour
themselves under the names of other nations, and to what places these voyages have been designed; and what places of rendezvous are appointed for
the new missions, and the like circumstances of the practice, I may not do it,
neither is it much to your desire. But thus you see we maintain a trade, not
for gold, silver, or jewels, nor for silks, nor for spices, nor any other com-
modity of matter; but only for God's first creature, which was light; to have
light, I say, of the growth of all parts of the world." . . .

Three days after the Jew came to me again, and said, "Ye are happy men;
for the father of Salomon's House taketh knowledge of your being here,
and commanded me to tell you, that he would admit all your company to
his presence, and have private conference with one of you, that ye shall
choose; and for this hath appointed the next day after tomorrow. And because he meaneth to give you his blessing, he hath appointed it in the
forenoon." We came at our day and hour, and I was chosen by my fellows

for the private access. We found him in a fair chamber, richly hanged, and carpeted under foot, without any degrees to the state; he was set upon a low throne richly adorned, and a rich cloth of state over his head of blue satin embroidered. He was alone, save that he had two pages of honour, on either hand one, finely attired in white. His under garments were the like that we saw him wear in the chariot; but instead of his gown, he had on him a mantle with a cape, of the same fine black, fastened about him. When we came in, as we were taught, we bowed low at our first entrance; and when we were come near his chair, he stood up, holding forth his hand ungloved, and in posture of blessing; and we every one of us stooped down, and kissed the end of his tippet. That done, the rest departed, and I remained. Then he warned the pages forth of the room, and caused me to sit down beside him, and spake to me thus in the Spanish tongue:

"God bless thee, my son; I will give thee the greatest jewel I have. For I will impart unto thee, for the love of God and men, a relation of the true state of Salomon's House. Son, to make you know the true state of Salomon's House, I will keep this order. First, I will set forth unto you the end of our foundation. Secondly, the preparations and instruments we have for our works. Thirdly, the several employments and functions whereto our fellows are assigned. And fourthly, the ordinances and rites which we observe.

"The end of our foundation is the knowledge of causes, and secret motions of things; and the enlarging of the bounds of human empire, to the effecting of all things possible.

"The preparations and instruments are these. We have large and deep caves of several depths; the deepest are sunk 600 fathoms; and some of them are digged and made under great hills and mountains; so that if you reckon together the depth of the hill, and the depth of the cave, they are, some of them, above three miles deep. For we find that the depth of an hill, and the depth of a cave from the flat, is the same thing; both remote alike from the sun and heaven's beams, and from the open air. These caves we call the lower region. And we use them for all coagulations, indurations, refrigerations, and conservations of bodies. We use them likewise for the imitation of natural mines and the producing also of new artificial metals, by compositions and materials which we use and lay there for many years. We use them also sometimes (which may seem strange) for curing of some diseases, and for prolongation of life, in some hermits that choose to live there, well accommodated of all things necessary, and indeed live very long; by whom also we learn many things.

"We have burials in several earths, where we put divers cements, as the Chinese do their porcelain. But we have them in greater variety, and some of them more fine. We also have great variety of composts and soils, for the making of the earth fruitful.

"We have high towers, the highest about half a mile in height, and some of them likewise set upon high mountains, so that the vantage of the hill with the tower, is in the highest of them three miles at least. And these places we call the upper region, account the air between the high places and the low, as a middle region. We use these towers, according to their several heights and situations, for insulation, refrigeration, conservation, and for the view of divers meteors—as winds, rain, snow, hail; and some of the fiery meteors also. And upon them, in some places, are dwellings of hermits, whom we visit sometimes, and instruct what to observe.

"We have great lakes, both salt and fresh, whereof we have use for the fish and fowl. We use them also for burials of some natural bodies, for we find a difference in things buried in earth, or in air below the earth, and things buried in water. We have also pools, of which some do strain fresh water out of salt, and others by art do turn fresh water into salt. We have also some rocks in the midst of the sea, and some bays upon the shore for some works, wherein is required the air and vapour of the sea. We have likewise violent streams and cataracts, which serve us for many motions; and likewise engines for multiplying and enforcing of winds to set also on divers motions.

"We have also a number of artificial wells and fountains, made in imitation of the natural sources and baths, as tincted upon vitriol, sulphur, steel, brass, lead, nitre, and other minerals; and again, we have little wells for infusions of many things, where the waters take the virtue quicker and better than in vessels or basins. And amongst them we have a water, which we call water of Paradise, being by that we do it made very sovereign for health and prolongation of life.

"We have also great and spacious houses, where we imitate and demonstrate meteor—as snow, hail, rain, some artificial rains of bodies, and not of water, thunders, lightnings; also generations of bodies in air—as frogs, flies, and divers others.

"We have also certain chambers, which we call chambers of health, where we qualify the air as we think good and proper for the cure of divers diseases, and preservation of health.

"We have also fair and large baths, of several mixtures, for the cure of diseases, and the restoring of man's body from arefaction; and others for the confirming of it in strength of sinews, vital parts, and the very juice and substance of the body.

"We have also large and various orchards and gardens, wherein we do not so much respect beauty as variety of ground and soil, proper for divers trees and herbs, and some very spacious, where trees and berries are set, whereof we make divers kinds of drinks, besides the vineyards. In these we practice likewise all conclusions of grafting, and inoculating, as well of wild-trees as fruit-trees, which produceth many effects. And we make by art, in the same orchards and gardens, trees and flowers, to come earlier or later than their seasons, and to come up and bear more speedily than by their natural course they do. We make them also by art greater much than their nature; and their fruit greater and sweeter, and of differing taste, smell, colour, and figure, from their nature. And many of them we so order, as that they become of medicinal use.

"We have also means to make divers plants rise by mixtures of earths without seeds, and likewise to make divers new plants, differing from the vulgar, and to make one tree or plant turn into another.

"We have also parks, and enclosures of all sorts, of beasts and birds; which we use not only for view or rareness, but likewise for dissections and trials, that thereby may take light what may be wrought upon the body of man. Wherein we find many strange effects: as continuing life in them, though divers parts, which you account vital, be perished and taken forth; resuscitating of some that seem dead in appearance, and the like. We try also all poisons, and other medicines upon them, as well of chirurgery as physic. By art likewise we make them greater or smaller than their kind is, and contrariwise dwarf them and stay their growth; we make them more fruitful and bearing than their kind is, and contrariwise barren and not generative. Also we make them differ in colour, shape, activity, many ways. We find means to make commixtures and copulations of divers kinds, which have produced many new kinds, and them not barren, as the general opinion is. We make a number of kinds of serpents, worms, flies, fishes of putrefaction, whereof some are advanced (in effect) to be perfect creatures, like beasts or birds, and have sexes, and do propagate. Neither do we this by chance, but we know beforehand of what matter and commixture, what kind of those creatures will arise.

"We have also particular pools where we make trials upon fishes, as we have said before of beasts and birds.

"We have also places for breed and generation of those kinds of worms and flies which are of special use; such as are with you your silkworms and bees.

"I will not hold you long with recounting of our brewhouses, bake-houses, and kitchens, where are made divers drinks, breads, and meats, rare and of special effects. Wines we have of grapes, and drinks of other juice, of fruits, of grains, and of roots, and of mixtures with honey, sugar, manna, and fruits dried and decocted; also of the tears or wounding of trees, and of the pulp of canes. And these drinks are of several ages, some to the age or last of forty years. We have drinks also brewed with several herbs, and roots, and spices; yea, with several fleshes, and white-meats; whereof some of the drinks are such as they are in effect meat and drink both, so that divers, especially in age, do desire to live with them with little or no meat or bread. And above all we strive to have drinks of extreme thin parts, to insinuate into the body, and yet without all biting, sharpness, or fretting; insomuch as some of them put upon the back of your hand, will with a little stay pass through to the palm, and yet taste mild to the mouth. We have also waters, which we ripen in that fashion, as they become nourishing, so that they are indeed excellent drinks, and many will use no other. Bread we have of several grains, roots, and kernels; yea, and some of flesh, and fish, dried; with divers kinds of leavings and seasonings; so that some do extremely move appetites, some do nourish so, as divers do live of them, without any other meat, who live very long. So for meats, we have some of them so beaten, and made tender, and mortified, yet without all corrupting, as a weak heat of the stomach will turn them into good chilus, as well as a strong heat would meat otherwise prepared. We have some meats also and bread, and drinks, which taken by men, enable them to fast long after; and some other, that used make the very flesh of men's bodies sensibly more hard and tough, and their strength far greater than otherwise it would be.

"We have dispensatories or shops of medicines; wherein you may easily think, if we have such variety of plants, and living creatures, more than you have in Europe (for we know what you have), the simples, drugs, and ingredients of medicines, must likewise be in so much the greater variety. We have them likewise of divers ages, and long fermentations. And for their preparations, we have not only all manner of exquisite distillations and separations, and especially by gentle heats, and percolations through divers strainers, yea, and substances; but also exact forms of composition, whereby they incorporate almost as they were natural simples.

"We have also divers mechanical arts, which you have not; and stuffs made by them, as papers, linen, silks, tissues, dainty works of feathers of wonderful lustre, excellent dyes, and many others, and shops likewise as well for such as are not brought into vulgar use amongst us, as for those that are. For you must know, that of the things before recited, many of them are grown into use throughout the kingdom, but yet, if they did flow from our invention, we have of them also for patterns and principals.

"We have also furnaces of great diversities, and that keep great diversity of heats; fierce and quick, strong and constant, soft and mild, blown, quiet, dry, moist, and the like. But above all we have heats, in imitation of the sun's and heavenly bodies' heats, that pass divers inequalities, and as it were orbs, progresses, and returns whereby we produce admirable effects. Besides, we have heats of dungs, and of bellies and maws of living creatures and of their bloods and bodies, and of hays and herbs laid up moist, of lime unquenched, and such like. Instruments also which generate heat only by motion. And farther, places for strong insulations; and again, places under the earth, which by nature or art yield heat. These divers heats we use, as the nature of the operation which we intend requireth.

"We have also perspective-houses, where we make demonstrations of all lights and radiations, and of all colours; and out of things uncoloured and transparent, we can represent unto you all several colours, not in rainbows, as it is in gems and prisms, but of themselves single. We represent also all multiplications of light, which we carry to great distance, and make so sharp, as to discern small points and lines. Also all colourations of light: all delusions and deceits of the sight, in figures, magnitudes, motions, colours; all demonstrations of shadows. We find also divers means, yet unknown to you, of producing of light, originally from divers bodies. We procure means of seeing objects afar off, as in the heaven and remote places; and represent things near as afar off, and things afar off as near; making feigned distances. We have also helps for the sight far above spectacles and glasses in use; we have also glasses and means to see small and minute bodies, perfectly and distinctly; as the shapes and colours of small flies and worms, grains, and flaws in gems which cannot otherwise be seen, observations in urine and blood not otherwise to be seen. We make artificial rainbows, halos, and circles about light. We represent also all manner of reflections, refractions, and multiplications of visual beams of objects.

"We have also precious stones, of all kinds, many of them of great beauty and to you unknown; crystals likewise, and glasses of divers kind; and amongst them some of metals vitrificated, and other materials, besides those of which you make glass. Also a number of fossils, and imperfect minerals, which you have not. Likewise loadstones of prodigious virtue: and other rare stones, both natural and artificial.

"We have also sound-houses, where we practice and demonstrate all sounds and their generation. We have harmony which you have not, of quarter-sounds and lesser slides of sounds. Divers instruments of music likewise to you unknown, some sweeter than any you have; with bells and rings that are dainty and sweet. We represent small sounds as great and deep, likewise great sounds, extenuate and sharp; we make divers tremblings and warblings of sounds, which in their original are entire. We represent and imitate all articulate sounds and letters, and the voices and notes of beasts and birds. We have certain helps, which set to the ear do further the hearing greatly; we have also divers strange and artificial echoes, reflecting the voice many times, and as it were tossing it; and some that give back the voice louder than it came, some shriller and some deeper; yea, some rendering the voice, differing in the letters or articulate sound from that they receive. We have all means to convey sounds in trunks and pipes, in strange lines and distances.

"We have also perfume-houses, wherewith we join also practices of taste. We multiply smells which may seem strange: we imitate smells, making all smells to breathe out of other mixtures than those that give them. We make divers imitations of taste likewise, so that they will deceive any man's taste. And in this house we contain also a confiture-house, where we make all sweetmeats, dry and moist, and divers pleasant wines, milks, broths, and salads, far in greater variety than you have.

"We have also engine-houses, where are prepared engines and instruments for all sorts of motions. There we imitate and practice to make swifter motions than any you have, either out of your muskets or any engine that you have; and to make them and multiply them more easily and with small force by wheels and other means, and to make them stronger and more violent than yours are, exceeding your greatest cannons and basilisks. We represent also ordnance and instruments of war and engines of all kinds; and likewise new mixtures and compositions of gunpowder, wild-fires burning in water and unquenchable, also fire-works of all variety, both for pleasure and use. We imitate also heights of birds; we have some degrees of flying in the air. We have ships and boats for going under water and brooking of seas, also swimming-girdles and supporters. We have divers curious clocks and other like motions of return, and some perpetual motions. We imitate also motions of living creatures by images of men, beasts, birds, fishes, and serpents; we have also a great number of other various motions, strange for equality, fineness and subtilty.

"We have also a mathematical-house, where are represented all instruments, as well of geometry as astronomy, exquisitely made.

"We have also houses of deceits of the senses, where we represent all manner of feats of juggling, false apparitions, impostures and illusions, and their fallacies. And surely you will easily believe that we, that have so many things truly natural which induce admiration, could in a world of particulars deceive the senses if we would disguise those things, and labour to make them more miraculous. But we do hate all impostures and lies, insomuch as we have severely forbidden it to all our fellows, under pain of ignominy and fines, that they do not show any natural work or thing adorned or swelling, but only pure as it is, and without all affectation of strangeness.

"These are, my son, the riches of Salomon's House.

"For the several employments and offices of our fellows, we have twelve that sail into foreign countries under the names of other nations (for our own we conceal), who bring us the books and abstracts, and patterns of experiments of all other parts. These we call Merchants of Light.

"We have three that collect the experiments which are in all books. These we call Depredators.

"We have three that collect the experiments of all mechanical arts, and also of liberal sciences, and also of practices which are not brought into arts. These we call Mystery-men.

"We have three that try new experiments, such as themselves think good. These we call Pioneers or Miners.

"We have three that draw the experiments of the former four into titles and tables, to give the better light for the drawing of observations and axioms out of them. These we call Compilers.

"We have three that bend themselves, looking into the experiments of their fellows, and cast about how to draw out of them things of use and practice for man's life and knowledge, as well for works as for plain demonstration of causes, means of natural divinations, and the easy and clear discovery of the virtues and parts of bodies. These we call Dowry-men or Benefactors.

"Then after divers meetings and consults of our whole number, to consider of the former labours and collections, we have three that take care out of them to direct new experiments, of a higher light, more penetrating into Nature than the former. These we call Lamps.

"We have three others that do execute the experiment so directed, and report them. These we call Inoculators.

"Lastly, we have three that raise the former discoveries by experiments into greater observations, axioms, and aphorisms. These we call Intrepreters of Nature.

"We have also, as you must think, novices and apprentices, that the succession of the former employed men do not fail; besides a great number of servants and attendants, men and women. And this we do also: we have consultations, which of the inventions and experiences which we have discovered shall be published, and which not; and take all an oath of secrecy for the concealing of those which we think fit to keep secret: though some of those we do reveal sometime to the state, and some not.

"For our ordinances and rites, we have two very long and fair galleries: in one of these we place patterns and samples of all manner of the more rare and excellent inventions; in the other we place the statues of all principal inventors. There we have the statue of your Columbus, that discovered the West Indies; also the inventor of ships; your Monk that was the inventor of ordnance and of gunpowder; the inventor of music; the inventor of letters; the inventor of printing; the inventor of observations of astronomy; the inventor of works in metal; the inventor of glass; the inventor of silk of the worm; the inventor of wine; the inventor of corn and bread; the inventor of sugars; and all these by more certain tradition than you have. Then we have divers inventors of our own, of excellent works, which since you have not seen, it were too long to make descriptions of them; and besides, in the right understanding of those descriptions you might easily err. For upon every invention of value we erect a statue to the inventor, and give him a liberal and honourable reward. These statues are some of brass, some of marble and touchstone, some of cedar and other special woods gilt and adorned; some of iron, some of silver, some of gold.

"We have certain hymns and services, which we say daily, of laud and thanks to God for His marvellous works. And forms of prayers, imploring His aid and blessing for the illumination of our labours, and the turning of them into good and holy uses.

"Lastly, we have circuits or visits, of divers principal cities of the kingdom; where as it cometh to pass we do publish such new profitable inventions as we think good. And we do also declare natural divinations of diseases, plagues, swarms of hurtful creatures, scarcity, tempest, earthquakes, great inundations, comets, temperature of the year, and divers other things; and we give counsel thereupon, what the people shall do for the prevention and remedy of them."

And when he had said this, he stood up; and I, as I had been taught, knelt down; and he laid his right hand upon my head, and said, "God bless thee, my son, and God bless this relation which I have made. I give thee leave to publish it, for the good of other nations; for we here are in God's bosom, a land unknown." And so he left me; having assigned a value of about two thousand ducats for a bounty to me and my fellows. For they give great largesses, where they come, upon all occasions.

THE REST WAS NOT PERFECTED.

A New Look at the Heavens and Another Trip to the Moon

The universe named after the first-century Greek astronomer Ptolemy placed the earth, unmoving as Aristotle and Plato insisted, at its center, and the other planets, the sun, and even the stars revolving around it. The Ptolemaic scheme made the earth, and humanity, seem supremely important. Because of this, because it fit into the Biblical concept of special creation, and because the mathematical elaboration of epicycles and eccentrics made the system accurate enough for predicting the movement of the planets, the Ptolemaic universe was adopted by the Catholic Church and stubbornly defended for more than a thousand years.

But the system was delicately balanced on a complicated structure of assumptions. The Polish astronomer Copernicus (1473–1543) gave the first shove. Wouldn't it be simpler, he suggested, to suppose that the earth and the planets revolved around the sun? His theories circulated in manuscript for many years before he allowed a book to be published, just before his death. *De Revolutionibus Orbium Coelestium* (1543) was banned by the Catholic Church until 1835. In a sense, the scientific revolution started with Copernicus. Humanity and the earth were removed from the center of things, diminished, their uniqueness removed; in compensation, science gave humanity new control over its fate and over its earthly environment.

Copernicus never looked through a telescope. Galileo (1564–1642) built a telescope, looked through it, and reported what he saw, and was forced by the Inquisition to recant his heresy that the earth moved around the sun. Galileo's work was continued by Johannes Kepler (1571–1630) in Germany.

Educated for the ministry, Kepler was recognized early in his career as a brilliant mathematician, and he soon turned to the teaching of science and the study of astronomy. He adopted the views of Copernicus, worked under the elderly Danish astronomer Tycho Brahe (1546–1601), and inherited Brahe's astronomical observations of the apparent motions of the planets, which he finally explained with his famous three laws of planetary motion.

Most Renaissance scientists needed the protection and support of nobility, and Kepler served as court astronomer for two Holy Roman emperors.

Nevertheless, he often was in financial and other difficulties. Like those of many of his contemporaries, his ideas combined a strange mix of medieval mysticism and modern science. As court astronomer, for instance, he often cast horoscopes for the emperor and others, and he believed in the music of the spheres, but his discovery that the orbits of the planets were ellipses with the sun as one focus put an end to Greek astronomy and cast doubt on the theory behind astrology.

Kepler's contribution to the development of science fiction, *Somnium, or Lunar Astronomy*, seems like a strange mixture of superstition and science, but the references to demons and witchcraft are largely metaphorical. Kepler also may have thought that travel to the moon with the aid of a demon was only slightly less likely than by any other means, and perhaps safer theologically than some physical mechanism that might be taken seriously.

Once Kepler's hero reaches the moon, however, he finds the kind of lunar conditions that Kepler thought actually existed there. Kepler admitted his indebtedness to Lucian, but the stories share little more than the moon. Kepler and Lucian both send characters to the moon for reasons other than telling a good story, but once the characters arrive, Lucian turns to satire and Kepler to the kind of reality he thought a real space traveler would find.

The narrative excitement still is minimal, but the purpose is approaching that of science fiction.

Somnium, which means "a dream," was written about 1610, circulated privately, and may have been responsible for his mother's arrest for witchcraft in 1620 (although she had a reputation for actually dabbling in the occult). She died shortly after Kepler procured her release; the demon-propulsion may not have been so safe after all. The story was not published until 1634, four years after Kepler's death.

Somnium, or Lunar Astronomy

BY JOHANNES KEPLER
TRANSLATED BY EDWARD ROSEN

In the year 1608 there was a heated quarrel between the Emperor Rudolph[1] and his brother, the Archduke Matthias.[2] Their actions universally recalled precedents found in Bohemian history. Stimulated by the widespread public interest, I turned my attention to reading about Bohemia, and came upon the story of the heroine Libussa,[3] renowned for her skill in magic. It happened one night that after watching the stars and the moon, I went to bed and fell into a very deep sleep. In my sleep I seemed to be reading a book brought from the fair. Its contents were as follows.

My name is Duracotus. My country is Iceland, which the ancients called Thule. My mother was Fiolxhilde. Her recent death freed me to write, as I had long wished to do. While she lived, she carefully kept me from writing. For, she said, the arts are loathed by many vicious people who malign what their dull minds fail to understand, and make laws harmful to mankind. Condemned by these laws, not a few persons have perished in the chasms of Hekla. My mother never told me my father's name. But she said he was a fisherman who died at the ripe old age of 150 (when I was three) in about the seventieth year of his marriage.

In the earliest years of my boyhood my mother, leading me by the hand and sometimes hoisting me up on her shoulders, often used to take me up to the lower slopes of Mt. Hekla. These excursions were made especially around St. John's Day, when the sun is visible all twenty-four hours, and there is no night. Gathering some herbs with many rites, she cooked them at home. She made little bags out of goatskin, which she filled and carried to a nearby port to sell to the ship captains. This is how she earned her living.

---

1 Rudolph II (1552–1612), Holy Roman Emperor.

2 Matthias, archduke of Austria (1557–1619).

3 Just as the rule of the Emperor Rudolph was challenged by his younger brother Matthias, so Libussa, a female ruler of the Bohemians, faced an uprising by males.

Once, out of curiosity, I cut a bag open. Suspecting nothing, my mother was about to sell it, when out fell the herbs and linen cloth embroidered with various symbols. Because I had deprived her of this little income, she angrily made me, instead of the bag, the property of the skipper in order to keep the money. On the next day he unexpectedly sailed out of the harbor, and with a favorable wind steered approximately toward Bergen in Norway. After a few days a north wind sprang up and drove the ship between Norway and England. He headed for Denmark and passed through the strait, since he had to deliver a letter from a bishop in Iceland to the Dane, Tycho Brahe, who lived on the island of Hven. The tossing of the boat and the unaccustomed warmth of the air made me violently sick, for I was a youth of fourteen. When the boat reached shore, he put me and the letter in the hands of an island fisherman. Expressing the hope that he would return, he sailed away.

When I delivered the letter, Brahe was quite delighted and began to ask me many questions. These I did not understand, since I was unacquainted with the language except for a few words. He therefore instructed his students, whom he supported in great numbers, to talk to me frequently. So it came about, through Brahe's generosity and a few weeks' practice, that I spoke Danish tolerably well. I was no less ready to talk than they were to ask. For I marveled at many unfamiliar things, and they wondered about the many novelties I related about my country.

Finally the skipper returned to take me back. When he failed, I was very happy.

I was delighted beyond measure by the astronomical activities, for Brahe and his students watched the moon and the stars all night with marvelous instruments. This practice reminded me of my mother, because she, too, used to commune with the moon constantly.

Through this opportunity, then, I, who had come from an entirely destitute background in a half-savage country, acquired knowledge of the most divine science, and this knowledge paved my way to greater things.

For, after spending several years on this island, I was finally overcome by a desire to see my country again. I considered that it would not be hard for me, with the knowledge I had acquired, to rise to some position of importance among my backward people. Hence, having paid my respects to my patron, who gave me his permission to depart, I went to Copenhagen. I found traveling companions, who gladly took me under their protection because of my familiarity with the language and the region. Five years after I had left, I returned to my native land.

What delighted me first on my return was to find my mother still active and engaged in the very same pursuits as before. The fact that I was alive and important put an end to her prolonged grief over the son she had lost through her impetuosity. At that time autumn was approaching, to be followed by those long nights of ours, since during the month in which Christ was born the sun barely rises at noon and sets again at once. On account of this interruption in her work my mother clung to me and did not leave my side, no matter where I went with my letter of recommendation. Sometimes she asked about the countries which I had visited, and sometimes about the heavens. She was deliriously happy that I had become acquainted with that science. Comparing what she had learned with my remarks, she exclaimed that now she was ready to die, since she was leaving behind a son who would inherit her knowledge, the only thing she possessed.

Since I am by nature most eager to acquire new knowledge, I, in turn, questioned her about her arts and her teachers of those arts among a people so remote from all the others. Then one day, choosing the time for her narrative, she went over the whole story from the beginning, about as follows:

Advantages have been conferred, Duracotus my son, not only on all those other regions to which you went but also on our country, too. To be sure, we are burdened with cold and darkness and other discomforts, which I feel only now, after I have learned from you about the salubriousness of the other lands. But we have plenty of clever persons. At our service are very wise spirits, who detest the bright light of the other lands and their noisy people. They long for our shadows, and they talk to us intimately. Among them there are nine chief spirits. Of these one is especially well known to me. The very gentlest and most innocuous of all, he is evoked by one and twenty characters. By his help I am not infrequently whisked in an instant to other shores, whichever I mention to him; or if I am frightened away from some of them on account of their distance, by inquiring about them I gain as much as if I were there in person. Most of the things which you saw with your own eyes or learned by hearsay or absorbed from books, he related to me just as you did. I should like you to become my companion on a visit, particularly, to that region of which he has spoken to me so often. Quite remarkable are the things which he tells about it. The name she uttered was "Levania."

Without any delay I agreed that she should summon her teacher. I sat down, ready to hear the entire plan for the trip and description of the region. It was already spring. The moon, becoming a crescent, began to shine as soon as the sun set below the horizon, and was in conjunction with the planet Saturn in the sign of the Bull. My mother went away from me to the nearest crossroads. Raising a shout, she pronounced just a few words in which she couched her request. Having completed the ceremonies, she returned. With the outstretched palm of her right hand she commanded silence, and sat down beside me. Hardly had we covered our heads with our clothing (in accordance with our covenant) when the rasping of an indistinct and unclear voice became audible. It began at once as follows, albeit in the Icelandic tongue.

THE DAEMON FROM LEVANIA

Fifty thousand German miles up in the ether lies the island of Levania.[4] The road to it from here or from it to this earth is seldom open. When it is open, it is easy for our kind, but for transporting men it is assuredly most difficult and fraught with the greatest danger to life. We admit to this company nobody who is lethargic, fat, or tender. On the contrary, we choose those who spend their time in the constant practice of horsemanship or often sail to the Indies, inured to subsisting on hardtack, garlic, dried fish, and unappetizing victuals. We especially like dried-up old women, experienced from an early age in riding he-goats at night or forked sticks or threadbare cloaks, and in traversing immense expanses of the earth. No men from Germany are acceptable; we do not spurn the firm bodies of Spaniards.

Great as the distance is, the entire trip is consummated in four hours at the most. For we are always very busy, and agree not to start until the moon begins to eclipse on its eastern side. Should it regain its full light while we are still in transit, our departure becomes futile. Because the opportunity is so fleeting, we take few human beings along, and only those who are most devoted to us. Some man of this kind, then, we seize as a group and all of us, pushing from underneath, lift him up into the heavens. In every instance the take-off hits him as a severe shock, for he is hurled just as though he had been shot aloft by gunpowder to sail over mountains and seas. For this reason at the outset he must be lulled to sleep immediately with narcotics and opiates. His limbs must be arranged in such a way that his torso will not be torn away from his buttocks nor his head from his body, but the shock will be distributed among his individual limbs. Then a new difficulty follows: extreme cold and impeded breathing. The cold is relieved by a power which we are born with; the breathing, by applying damp sponges to the nostrils. After the first stage of the trip is finished, the passage becomes easier. At that time we expose their bodies to the open air

---

4 The moon.

and remove our hands. Their bodies roll themselves up, like spiders, into balls which we carry along almost entirely by our will alone, so that finally the bodily mass proceeds towards its destination of its own accord. But this onward drive is of very little use to us, because it is too late. Hence it is by our will, as I said, that we move the body swiftly along, and we forge ahead of it from now on lest it suffer any harm by colliding very hard with the moon. When the humans wake up, they usually complain about an indescribable weariness of all their limbs, from which they later recover well enough to walk.

Many additional difficulties arise which it would be tedious to enumerate. On the other hand, we suffer no harm at all. For as a group we inhabit the earth's shadows, whatever their length. When they reach Levania, there we are as though disembarking from a ship and going ashore. Up there we quickly withdraw into caves and dark places, lest after a short while the sun overpower us in the open, and drive us out of the living quarters we had chosen, and force us to follow the retreating shadow. Up there we are granted leisure to exercise our minds in accordance with our inclinations. We consult with the daemons of that area and enter into a league. As soon as a spot begins to be free from sun, we close ranks and move out into the shadow. If it touches the earth with its apex, as generally happens, we rush toward the earth with our allied forces. This we are permitted to do only when mankind sees the sun in eclipse. Hence it happens that solar eclipses are feared so much.

I have said enough about the trip to Levania. Next I shall talk about the nature of the region itself, starting like the geographers with its view of the heavens.

The fixed stars look the same to all Levania as to us. But its view of the movements and sizes of the planets is very different from what we observe here, so that its entire system of astronomy is quite diverse.

Just as our geographers divide up the sphere of the earth into five zones on the basis of celestial phenomena, so Levania consists of two hemispheres. One of these, the Subvolva,[5] always enjoys its Volva,[6] which among them takes the place of our moon. The other one, the Privolva,[7] is deprived forever of the sight of Volva. The circle which separates the hemispheres passes through the celestial poles, like our solstitial colure, and is called the divisor.

---

5 The hemisphere of the moon that always faces the earth.
6 The earth.
7 The hemisphere of the moon that always faces away from the earth.

In the first place I shall explain what is common to both hemispheres. All Levania experiences the succession of day and night as we do, but they lack the variation that goes on all year among us. For throughout the whole of Levania the days are almost exactly equal to the nights, except that each day is uniformly shorter than its night for the Privolvans, and for the Subvolvans longer. What varies in a period of eight years will be mentioned later on. To produce equal nights at each of the poles, the sun is hidden half the time and shines half the time as it travels around the mountains in a circle. For Levania seems to its inhabitants to remain just as motionless among the moving stars as does our earth to us humans. A night and a day, taken together, equal one of our months, since at sunrise in the morning almost an entire additional sign of the zodiac appears on any day as compared with the previous day. For us in one year there are 365 revolutions of the sun, and 366 of the sphere of the fixed stars, or more accurately, in four years, 1,461 revolutions of the sun but 1,465 of the sphere of the fixed stars. Similarly, for them the sun revolves 12 times in one year and the sphere of the fixed stars 13 times, or more precisely in eight years the sun revolves 99 times and the sphere of the fixed stars 107 times. But they are more familiar with the nineteen-year cycle, for in that interval the sun rises 235 times, but the fixed stars 254 times.

The sun rises for the middle of central Subvolvans when the moon appears to us in its last quarter, but the middle Privolvans when we have the first quarter. What I say about the middle must be understood as applying to complete semicircles drawn through the poles and the middle at right angles to the divisor. These may be called the Midvolvan semicircles.

Halfway between the poles there is a circle corresponding to our terrestrial equator, by which name it too may be denoted. It twice intersects both the divisor and the Midvolva in opposite points. At all places on the equator the sun at noon passes almost exactly overhead daily, and exactly overhead on two opposite days of the year. For all the others, who live on either side of the equator toward the poles, the sun deviates from the zenith at noon.

On Levania they have also some alternation of summer and winter. But the contrast is not to be compared with ours, nor does it always occur, as with us, in the same places at the same time of year. For within a period of ten years their summer shifts from one part of the sidereal year to the opposite part in any given place. The reason is that in a cycle of nineteen sidereal years, or 235 Levanian days, summer occurs twenty times near the poles and winter just as often, but forty times at the equator. Every year they have six summer days, the others winter, like our months. This alternation is scarcely felt near the equator, because in those places the sun deviates no more than 5° back and forth to either side. It is felt much more near the poles, where the sun is present or absent in alternating periods of six months, as is the case among us on earth for those who live near either of the poles. Hence the sphere of Levania, too, is divided into five zones, corresponding somewhat to our terrestrial zones. But their tropical zone, like their arctic zones, contains scarcely 10°. All the rest belongs to zones similar to our temperate zones. The tropical zone passes through the middle of the hemispheres, with half of its longitude in the Subvolva and the other half in the Privolva.

The intersections of the equatorial and zodiacal circles create four cardinal points, like our equinoxes and solstices. These intersections mark the start of the zodiacal circle. But from this start the motion of the fixed stars in the order of the signs is very swift, since they traverse the entire zodiac in twenty tropical years (a tropical year being defined as one summer and one winter). For us this traversing takes almost 26,000 years. So much for the first motion.

The theory of the second motions is for them no less different from what appears to us, and is much more complicated for them than for us. The reason is that all six planets (Saturn, Jupiter, Mars, sun, Venus, Mercury) exhibit, besides the many inequalities which they have in common with us, three others for them. Two of these irregularities are in longitude; one is daily, the other has a period of eight and a half years. The third is in latitude, with a period of nineteen years. For the mid-Privolvans have the sun at their noon, other things being equal, bigger than when it rises, and the Subvolvans smaller. Both agree in believing that the sun diverges by some minutes from the ecliptic back and forth now among these fixed stars, now among those. These oscillations return to the original position, as I said, in a period of nineteen years. Yet this deviation takes a little more time for the Privolvans, a little less for the Subvolvans. And although the sun and the fixed stars are assumed to advance uniformly in the first motion around Levania, nevertheless, the sun barely progresses in relation to the fixed stars at noon for the Privolvans, whereas for the Subvolvans it is very fast at noon. The reverse is true at midnight. Hence the sun seems to make, as it were, certain jumps in relation to the fixed stars, separate jumps every day.

The same statements hold true for Venus, Mercury, and Mars; in the cases of Jupiter and Saturn, these phenomena are almost imperceptible.

Furthermore the diurnal motion is not uniform even at the same hour every day. On the contrary, it is slower at times not only for the sun but also for the fixed stars, while at the opposite season of the year at the like hour of the day it is faster. Moreover, the retardation shifts throughout the days of the year, so that sometimes it occurs on a summer day, sometimes on a winter day, which in another year had experienced the acceleration, one cycle being completed in a period of a little less than nine years. Hence the day sometimes becomes longer (through a natural retardation, not as with us on the earth through the unequal division of natural day), and sometimes the night, in turn, becomes longer.

But if the retardation occurs for the Privolvans during their night, its excess over their day is increased; on the other hand, if the retardation falls in their daytime, then their night and day approach more closely to equality, which is reached once in nine years. The converse is true for the Subvolvans.

So much for the phenomena which in a certain way happen in common to the hemispheres.

THE HEMISPHERE OF THE PRIVOLVANS

Now as for what concerns the individual hemispheres separately, there is an enormous contrast between them. By its presence and absence Volva gives rise to quite different spectacles. Not only that, but the common phenomena themselves produce very divergent effects on the two sides. As a result, the Privolvans' hemisphere may perhaps more properly be called non-temperate, and the Subvolvans', temperate. For among the Privolvans night lasts fifteen or sixteen of our natural days. It is made frightful by as deep an uninterrupted darkness as we have on a moonless night, since it never receives any light even from Volva's rays. Consequently everything turns stiff with ice and frost, abetted by very sharp and very strong winds. Day follows, as long as fourteen of our days or a little less. During this time the sun is quite large and moves slowly with respect to the fixed stars. There are no winds. The result is immense heat. And thus, in the interval of our month or the Levanian day, one and the same place is exposed both to heat fifteen times hotter than our African, and to cold more unbearable than the Quiviran.

It should be especially noted that the planet Mars sometimes appears almost twice as big to the Privolvans as to us; to the mid-Privolvans this happens at midnight, and to the other Privolvans at some particular moment of the night for each.

THE HEMISPHERE OF THE SUBVOLVANS

In making the transition to this topic, I begin with the frontiersmen who inhabit the divisor circle. What is peculiar to them is that the elongations of

Venus and Mercury from the sun seem much bigger to them than to us. Moreover, at certain times Venus looks twice as big to them as to us, especially to those of them who live near the north pole.

But the most beautiful of all the sights on Levania is the view of its Volva. This they enjoy to make up for our moon, of which they and likewise the Privolvans are completely deprived. From the perennial presence of this Volva this region is termed the Subvolvan, just as from the absence of Volva the other region is called the Privolvan, because they are deprived of the sight of Volva.

To us who inhabit the earth, our moon, when it is full and rising and climbing above distant houses, seems equal to the rim of a keg; when it mounts to mid-heaven, it hardly matches the width of the human face. But to the Subvolvans, their Volva in mid-heaven (a position which it occupies for those who live in the center or navel of this hemisphere) looks a little less than four times longer in diameter than our moon does to us. Hence, if the disks are compared, their Volva is fifteen times larger than our moon. However, to those for whom Volva always clings to the horizon, it presents the appearance of a mountain on fire far away.

Consequently, just as we differentiate between regions according to the greater and smaller altitudes of the pole, even through we do not see the pole itself with our eyes, so this same function is performed for them by Volva, which, although it is always visible, differs in altitude from place to place.

For, as I said, Volva stands directly over the heads of some of them; in other places it is seen low down near the horizon; and for the rest its altitude varies from the zenith to the horizon, while remaining forever constant in any given area.

Yet they, too, have their own poles. These are located, not at those fixed stars where our celestial poles are, but around other stars which for us mark the poles of the ecliptic. These poles of the moon-dwellers in a period of nineteen years traverse small circles around the poles of the ecliptic in the constellation of the Dragon and, at the other extremity, in the Swordfish (Dorado), Sparrow (Flying Fish), and the Greater Nebula. Since these poles of the moon-dwellers are about a quadrant's distance from their Volva, their regions can be delimited both according to the poles and according to Volva. Hence it is clear how much more convenient their situation is than ours. For they indicate the longitude of places with reference to their motionless Volva, and the latitude with reference both to Volva and to the poles, whereas for longitudes we have nothing but that most lowly and barely perceptible declination of the magnet.

Their Volva remains fixed in place, then, as though it were attached to the heavens with a nail. Above it the other heavenly bodies, including the sun, move from east to west. There is never a night in which some of the fixed stars in the zodiac do not pass behind this Volva and emerge again on the other side. But the same fixed stars do not do so every night. All those which are within a distance of 6° or 7° from the ecliptic take turns. The cycle is complete in nineteen years, after which the first stars return.

Their Volva waxes and wanes no less than our moon does. In both cases the cause is the same: the presence of the sun or its departure. The length of time involved is also the same, if you look to nature. But they measure it in one way, and we in another. They consider a day and a night the interval in which their Volva passes through all its waxings and wanings. This is the interval which we call a month. On account of its size and brilliance Volva is practically never, not even at new Volva, hidden from the Subvolvans. This is true in particular for those who live near the poles and are deprived of the sun during that time. For them Volva turns its horns upward at noon in the inter-Volvan period. For in general, for those who live between Volva and the poles on the mid-Volvan circle, new Volva is the sign of noon; the first quarter, of evening; full Volva, of midnight; the last quarter, of returning sunlight. For those who have Volva as well as the poles located on the horizon and who live at the intersection of the equator with the divisor, morning or evening occurs at new Volva and full Volva, noon or midnight at the quarters. Let these remarks provide the basis for conclusions regarding those who live in between.

In the daytime, too, they distinguish the hours in this way according to the various phases of their Volva; for example, the closer the approach of the sun and Volva to each other, the nearer is noon for the mid-Volvans, and evening or sunset for those at the equator. But at night, which regularly lasts as long as fourteen of our days and nights, they are much better equipped to measure time than we are. For besides that series of Volva's phases, of which we said that full Volva is the sign of midnight at the mid-Volvan circle, Volva itself also distinguishes the hours for them. For even though it does not seem to have any motion in space, nevertheless, unlike our moon, it rotates in its place and displays in turn a wonderful variety of spots, as these spots move constantly from east to west. One such revolution, in which the same spots return, is regarded by the Subvolvans as one hour of time; it is equal, however, to a little more than one of our days added to one of our nights. This is the only uniform measure of time. For, as was pointed out above, the sun and stars move non-uniformly about the moon-dwellers every day. This non-uniformity is revealed very clearly by this rotation of Volva if it is compared with the distances of the fixed stars from the moon.

So far as its upper, northern part is concerned, Volva in general seems to have two halves. One of them is darker and covered with almost continuous spots. The other is a little lighter, being interpenetrated by a bright belt which lies to the north and serves to distinguish the two halves. In the darker half the shape of the spot is hard to describe. Yet on the eastern side it looks like the front of the human head cut off at the shoulders and leaning forward to kiss a young girl in a long dress, who stretches her hand back to attract a leaping cat. The bigger and broader part of the spot, however, extends westward without any apparent configuration. In the other half of Volva the brightness is more widely diffused than the spot. You might call it the outline of a bell hanging from a rope and swinging westward. What lies above and below cannot be likened to anything.

Besides distinguishing the hours of the day for them in this manner, Volva also furnishes no obscure indication of the seasons of the year to anyone who is observant, or who is unaware of the arrangement of the fixed stars. Even when the sun is in the sign of the Crab, Volva clearly displays the north pole of its rotation. For there is a certain small dark spot which is stuck in the middle of the bright area above the figure of the girl. From the highest and uppermost part of Volva this spot moves toward the east, and then as it drops down over the disk, toward the west; from this side it again turns eastward toward the top of Volva, and thus it is perpetually visible at that time. But when the sun is in the sign of the Goat, this spot is nowhere to be seen since the entire circle with its pole disappears behind the body of Volva. In these two seasons of the year the spots travel westward in a straight line. But in the intervening seasons, when the sun is in the sign of the Ram or the Balance, the spots either drop down or climb up crosswise in a somewhat crooked line. These facts show us that, while the center of the body of Volva remains stationary, the poles of this rotation revolve on an arctic circle once a year around the pole of the moon-dwellers.

More careful observers notice also that Volva does not always retain the same size. For at those hours of the day when the heavenly bodies travel fast, the diameter of Volva is much bigger, so that then it altogether exceeds four times the diameter of our moon.

What shall I say now about the eclipses of the sun and of Volva? Eclipses occur on Levania too, and they occur at the same moments as solar and lunar eclipses here on the globe of the earth, although obviously for the opposite reasons. For when a total eclipse of the sun is visible to us, for them Volva is eclipsed. In turn, when our moon is eclipsed for us, the sun is eclipsed for them. Nevertheless, the correspondence is not complete. For they often see partial eclipses of the sun when no part of the moon is blacked out for us. On the other hand, they not infrequently miss eclipses of Volva when we have partial eclipses of the sun. Volva is eclipsed for them when it is full, just as is the moon for us when it is full; but the sun is eclipsed at new Volva, as it is for us at new moon. Since their days and nights are so long, they experience very frequent darkenings of both bodies. For whereas among us a large percentage of the eclipses passes on to our antipodes, their antipodes, because they are Privolans, see absolutely none of these phenomena, which are all witnessed by the Subvolvans alone.

They never see a total eclipse of Volva. However, for them the body of Volva is traversed by a certain small spot which is reddish around the rim and black in the middle. Entering from the eastern side of Volva, it leaves by the western edge, following the same course as the natural spots of Volva, while surpassing them in speed. It lasts one-sixth of a Levanian hour or four of our hours.

A solar eclipse is caused for them by their Volva, just as it is for us by our moon. This phenomenon is inevitable since Volva has a diameter four times bigger than the sun's. As the sun crosses from the east through the south beyond the motionless Volva to the west, it very often passes behind Volva, which thus occults the sun's body partially or totally. Even though an occultation of the sun's entire body is frequent, it is nevertheless quite remarkable because it lasts several of our hours, while the light of both the sun and Volva is extinguished at the same time. This is a grand spectacle for the Subvolvans. For under other circumstances their nights are not much darker than their days on account of the brilliance and size of Volva, which is always present, whereas in a solar eclipse both luminaries, the sun and Volva, are quenched for them.

Yet among them solar eclipses have the following peculiar feature. Hardly has the sun disappeared behind the body of Volva than, as happens quite frequently, bright light arises on the opposite side. It is as though the sun expanded and embraced the entire body of Volva, whereas at other times the sun appears just as many degrees smaller than Volva. Therefore complete darkness does not always occur, unless the centers of the bodies are almost exactly aligned and the condition of the intervening transparent medium is suitable. Nor, on the other hand, is Volva extinguished so suddenly that it cannot be seen at all, even though the sun is entirely hidden behind it; the only exception takes place at the middle moment of a total eclipse. But at the beginning of a total eclipse in certain localities on the divisor Volva still shines, like an ember which continues to glow after a flame has been put out. When Volva, too, ceases to shine, the middle of the total eclipse has arrived (for if the eclipse is not total, Volva does not cease to shine). When Volva resumes its shining (at the opposite localities on the divisor circle) the sun also approaches visibility. Thus to a certain extent both luminaries are extinguished at the same time in the middle of a total eclipse.

So much for the phenomena in both hemispheres of Levania, the Subvolvan and the Privolvan. From these phenomena, even without my saying anything, it is not difficult to infer how much the Subvolvans differ from the Privolvans in all other respects.

For although the Subvolvan night lasts as long as fourteen of our days and nights, nevertheless by its presence Volva lights up the land and protects it from the cold. Indeed, so huge a mass, so intense a brilliance cannot fail to impart warmth.

On the other hand, even though a day among the Subvolvans has the sun irksomely present for fifteen or sixteen of our days and nights, nevertheless it is a smaller sun, whose strength is not so dangerous. The luminaries, being joined, pull all the water to that hemisphere, where the land is submerged so that only a tiny quantity of it protrudes. By contrast the Privolvan hemisphere is dry and cold because all the water has been drawn off. However, when night begins for the Subvolvans and day for the Privolvans, the hemispheres divide the luminaries between them, and therefore the water is divided too; the fields of the Subvolvans are drained, whereas the moisture provides the Privolvans with some slight relief from the heat.

The whole of Levania does not exceed fourteen hundred German miles in circumference, that is, only a quarter of our earth. Nevertheless, it has very high mountains as well as very deep and wide valleys; to this extent it is much less of a perfect sphere than our earth is. Yet it is all porous and, so to say, perforated with caves and grottoes everywhere, especially in the Privolvan region; these recesses are the inhabitants' principal protection from heat and cold.

Whatever is born on the land or moves about on the land attains a monstrous size. Growth is very rapid. Everything has a short life, since it develops such an immensely massive body. The Privolvans have no fixed abode, no established domicile. In the course of one of their days they roam in crowds over their whole sphere, each according to his own nature: some use their legs, which far surpass some of our camels; some resort to wings; and some follow the receding water in boats; or if a delay of several more days is necessary, then they crawl into caves. Most of them are divers; all of them, since they live naturally, draw their breath very slowly; hence under water they stay down on the bottom, helping nature with art. For in those very deep layers of the water, they say, the cold persists while the waves on top are heated up by the sun; whatever clings to the surface is boiled out by the sun at noon, and becomes food for the advancing hordes of wandering inhabitants. For in general the Subvolvan hemisphere is comparable to our cantons, towns, and gardens; the Privolvan, to our open country, forests, and deserts. Those for whom breathing is more essential introduce the hot water into the caves through a narrow channel in order that it may flow a long time to reach the interior and gradually cool off. There they shut themselves up for the greater part of the day, using the water for drink; when evening comes, they go out looking for food. In plants, the rind; in animals, the skin, or whatever replaces it, takes up the major portion of their bodily mass; it is spongy and porous. If anything is exposed during the day, it becomes hard on top and scorched; when evening comes, its husk drops off. Things born in the ground—they are sparse on the ridges of the mountains—generally begin and end their lives on the same day, with new generations springing up daily.

In general, the serpentine nature is predominant. For in a wonderful manner they expose themselves to the sun at noon as if for pleasure; yet they do so nowhere but behind the mouths of the caves to make sure that they may retreat safely and swiftly.

To certain of them the breath they exhaust and the life they lose on account of the heat of the day return at night; the pattern is the opposite of that governing flies among us. Scattered everywhere on the ground are objects having the shape of pine cones. Their shells are roasted during the day. In the evening when, so to say, they disclose their secrets, they beget living creatures.

Relief from the heat in the Subvolvan hemisphere is provided chiefly by the constant cloud cover and rain, which sometimes prevail over half the region or more.

When I had reached this point in my dream, a wind arose with the rattle of rain, disturbing my sleep and at the same time wiping out the end of the book acquired at Frankfurt. Therefore, leaving behind the Daemon narrator and her auditors, Duracotus the son with his mother, Fiolxhilde, as they were with their heads covered up, I returned to myself and found my head really covered with the pillow and my body with the blankets.

Commuting to the Moon

The moon always had loomed large in men's imaginations. Today, when men have reached and explored at least a limited portion of the moon, the earth's disproportionately large satellite has lost much of its mystery and some of its romantic appeal, but throughout most of man's history the moon affected men's lives in the same way it affected the tides. Civilizations worshiped the moon, considered the lunar month as sacred as the solar year, believed in the affect of the moon on men's minds and fortunes and bodies, and saw it hanging in the sky almost near enough to touch.

The new astronomy turned humanity's eyes toward the night sky, looking at the stars and the planets and the moon through the new telescope invented in 1608 by Hans Lippershey, a Dutch spectacle-maker. The moon, in particular, seemed so close and so obviously like the earth that the notion of getting there by some means, any means, seemed not only feasible but inevitable.

Francis Godwin (1562–1633), an English bishop, wrote *The Man in the Moone* (1638) about a trip to the moon by a tiny rogue named Domingo Gonsales. Set ashore on the island of St. Helena, he trains a flock of swan-like birds called gansas to pull an "engine" through the air. As he is fleeing from savages, the gansas migrate with him to the moon. Godwin describes conditions on the moon in realistic terms, although the inhabitants are fanciful and the society is utopian. Ultimately Gonsales returns safely with his gansas to China.

Another English bishop, John Wilkins (1614–1672), one of the founders and first secretary of the Royal Society, published *Mercury; or the Secret and Swift Messenger* (1641), a nonfictional exploration of the possibilities of new inventions such as "a flying chariot," "a trunk or hollow pipe" for preserving the voice for hours or days, a means for communicating at a distance by gunshots or other loud noises, or through walls by using "magneticall vertues." He also published in 1638 (third edition, including a Book II, in 1640) a nonfictionalized consideration of conditions on the moon, speculation on whether the moon is inhabited, and his belief that man will journey there, *A Discourse Concerning a New World.*

More ingenious and more amusing than any of the moon journeys up to the time of Poe was *Voyage to the Moon* (1657), by Cyrano de Bergerac (1619–1655). An adventurer, swordsman, and wit, who was later immortalized in the romantic play by Edmond Rostand, Cyrano also became well known as a writer. Although none of his works were published during his short life, some of them were circulated in manuscript. Cyrano also wrote another imaginary extraterrestrial journey, the unfinished *Voyage to the Sun* (1662). It describes Cyrano's escape from prison in a box fitted with lenses that focus the sun's rays and create a whirlwind. In it he is drawn to the sun, finds civilized birds, and discusses utopias with Campanella.

Both narratives satirized the institutions of Cyrano's day, mocked at a literal belief in the Old Testament, had a dismal view of man, and described certain scientific and philosophical ideas that were dangerous to publish or to popularize.

The tradition of the extraterrestrial trip, particularly to the moon, continued in literature until the first spaceship reached the moon and man set his foot on it in 1969. Notable examples are Gabriel Daniel's *A Voyage to the World of Cartesius* (1691), Ralph Morris' *John Daniel* (1751), Aratus' *A Voyage to the Moon* (1793), George Fowler's *A Flight to the Moon* (1813), George Tucker's *A Voyage to the Moon* (1827), Edgar Allan Poe's *Hans Pfaall* (1840), Jules Verne's *From the Earth to the Moon* (1865), H. G. Wells's *The First Men in the Moon* (1901), and Robert A. Heinlein's *The Man Who Sold the Moon* (1950).

By the 1890s the Russian scientist Konstantin Tsiolkovsky (1857–1935) was writing seriously about space flight and referring to the necessity for liquid-fuel rockets. By 1914 Robert Goddard (1882–1945) was taking out patents on rocket apparatus; he sent up experimental rockets from the twenties until his death.

The age of space travel began.

From A Voyage to the Moon

BY CYRANO DE BERGERAC

I had been with some Friends at Clamard, a House near Paris, and magnif-icently Entertain'd there by Monsieur de Cuigy, the Lord of it; when upon our return home, about Nine of the Clock at Night, the Air serene, and the Moon in the Full, the Contemplation of that bright Luminary furnished us with such variety of Thoughts as made the way seem shorter than, indeed, it was. Our Eyes being fixed upon that stately Planet, every one spoke what he thought of it: One would needs have it be a Garret Window of Heaven; another presently affirmed, That it was the Pan whereupon *Diana* smoothed *Apollo's* Bands; while another was of Opinion, That it might very well be the Sun himself, who puffing his Locks up under his Cap at Night, peeped through a hole to observe what was doing in the World during his absence.

"And for my part, Gentlemen," said I, "that I may put in for a share, and guess with the rest; not to amuse my self with those curious Notions where-with you tickle and spur on slow-paced Times; I believe, that the Moon is a World like ours, to which this of ours serves likewise for a Moon."

This was received with the general Laughter of the Company. "And per-haps," said I, "(Gentlemen) just so they laugh now in the Moon, at some who maintain, That this Globe, where we are, is a World." But I'd as good have said nothing, as have alledged to them, That a great many Learned Men had been of the same Opinion; for that only made them laugh the faster.

However, this thought, which because of its boldness suited my Humor, being confirmed by Contradiction, sunk so deep into my mind, that during the rest of the way I was big with Definitions of the Moon which I could not be delivered of: Insomuch that by striving to verifie this Comical Fancy by Reasons of appearing weight, I had almost perswaded my self already of the truth on't; when a Miracle, Accident, Providence, Fortune, or what, perhaps, some may call Vision, others Fiction, Whimsey, or (if you will) Folly, furnished me with an occasion that engaged me into this Discourse. Being come home, I went up into my Closet, where I found a Book open upon the Table, which I had not put there. It was a piece of *Cardanus;* and though I had no design to read in it, yet I fell at first sight, as by force, exactly upon a Passage of that Philosopher where he tells us, That Studying one evening by Candle-light, he perceived Two tall old Men enter in through the door that was shut, who after many questions that he put to them, made him answer, That they were Inhabitants of the Moon, and thereupon immediately disappeared.

I was so surprised, not only to see a Book get thither of it self; but also because of the nicking of the Time so patly, and of the Page at which it lay upon, that I looked upon that Concatenation of Accidents as a Revelation, discovering to Mortals that the Moon is a World. "How!" said I to my self, having just now talked of a thing, can a Book, which perhaps is the only Book in the World that treats of that matter so particularly, fly down from the Shelf upon my Table; become capable of Reason, in opening so exactly at the place of so strange an adventure; force my Eyes in a manner to look upon it, and then to suggest to my fancy the Reflexions, and to my Will the Designs which I hatch.

"Without doubt," continued I, "the Two old Men, who appeared to that famous Philosopher, are the very same who have taken down my Book and opened it at that Page, to save themselves the labour of making to me the Harangue which they made to *Cardan*. But," added I, "I cannot be resolved of this Doubt, unless I mount up thither."

"And why not?" said I instantly to myself. *"Prometheus* heretofore went up to Heaven, and stole fire from thence. Have not I as much Boldness as he? And why should not I then, expect as favourable a Success?"

After these sudden starts of Imagination, which may be termed, perhaps, the Ravings of a violent Feaver, I began to conceive some hopes of succeeding in so fair a Voyage. Insomuch that to take my measures aright, I shut myself up in a solitary Country-house; where having flattered my fancy with some means, proportioned to my design, at length I set out for Heaven in this manner.

I planted myself in the middle of a great many Glasses full of Dew, tied fast about me; upon which the Sun so violently darted his Rays, that the Heat, which attracted them, as it does the thickest Clouds, carried me up so high, that at length I found my self above the middle Region of the Air. But seeing that Attraction hurried me up with as much rapidity that instead of drawing near the Moon, as I intended, she seem'd to me to be more distant than at my first setting out; I broke several of my Vials, until I found my weight exceed the force of the Attraction, and that I began to descend again towards the Earth. I was not mistaken in my opinion, for some time after I fell to the ground again; and to reckon from the hour that I set out at it must then have been about midnight. Nevertheless I found the Sun to be in the Meridian, and that it was Noon. I leave it to you to judge, in what Amazement I was; The truth is, I was so strangely surprised, that not knowing what to think of that Miracle, I had the insolence to imagine that in favour of my Boldness God had once more nailed the Sun to the Firmament, to light so generous an Enterprise. That which encreased my Astonishment was, That I knew not the Country where I was; it seemed to me, that having mounted straight up, I should have fallen down again in the same place I parted from.

However, in the Equipage I was in, I directed my course towards a kind of Cottage, where I perceived some smoke; and I was not above a Pistol-shot from it, when I saw my self environed by a great number of People, stark naked: They seemed to be exceedingly surprised at the sight of me; for I was the first, (as I think) that they had ever seen clad in Bottles. Nay, and to baffle all the Interpretations that they could put upon that Equipage, they perceived that I hardly touched the ground as I walked; for, indeed, they understood not that upon the least agitation I gave my Body the Heat of the beams of the Noon-Sun raised me up with my Dew; and that if I had had Vials enough about me, it would possibly have carried me up into the Air in their view. I had a mind to have spoken to them; but as if Fear had changed them into Birds, immediately I lost sight of them in an adjoyning Forest. However, I catched hold of one, whose Legs had, without doubt, betrayed his Heart. I asked him, but with a great deal of pain, (for I was quite choked) how far they reckoned from thence to *Paris?* How long Men had gone naked in *France?* and why they fled from me in so great Consternation? The Man I spoke to was an old tawny Fellow, who presently fell at my Feet, and with lifted-up Hands joyned behind his Head, opened his Mouth and shut his Eyes: He mumbled a long while between his Teeth, but I could not distinguish an articulate Word; so that I took his Language for the muffling noise of a Dumb-man.

Some time after, I saw a Company of Souldiers marching, with Drums beating; and I perceived Two detached from the rest, to come and take speech of me. When they were come within hearing, I asked them, Where I was? "You are in *France*," answered they: "But what Devil hath put you into that Dress? And how comes it that we know you not? Is the Fleet then arrived? Are you going to carry the News of it to the Governor? And why have you divided your Brandy into so many Bottles?" To all this I made answer, That the Devil had not put me into that Dress: That they knew me not; because they could not know all Men: That I knew nothing of the *Seine's* carrying Ships to *Paris:* That I had no news of the *Marshal de l'Hospital;* and that I was not loaded with Brandy. "Ho, ho," said they to me, taking me by the Arm, "you are a merry Fellow indeed; come, the Governor will make a shift to know you, no doubt on't."

They led me to their Company, where I learnt that I was in reality in *France,* but that it was in *New-France:* So that some time after, I was presented before the Governor, who asked me my Country, my Name and Quality; and after that I had satisfied him in all Points, and told him the pleasant Success of my Voyage, whether he believed it, or only pretended to do so, he had the goodness to order me a Chamber in his Apartment. I was very happy, in meeting with a Man capable of lofty Opinions, and who was not at all surprised when I told him that the Earth must needs have turned during my Elevation; seeing that having begun to mount about Two Leagues from *Paris,* I was fallen, as it were, by a perpendicular Line in *Canada.*

Next Day, and the Days following, we had some Discourses to the same purpose: But some time after, since the hurry of Affairs suspended our Philosophy, I fell afresh upon the design of mounting up to the Moon.

So soon as she was up, I walked about musing in the Woods, how I might manage and succeed in my Enterprise; and at length on *St. John's-Eve,* when they were at Council in the Fort, whether they should assist the Wild Natives of the Country against the *Iroqueans;* I went all alone to the top of a little Hill at the back of our Habitation, where I put in Practice what you shall hear. I had made a Machine which I fancied might carry me up as high as I pleased, so that nothing seeming to be wanting to it, I placed my self within, and from the Top of a Rock threw my self in the Air: But because I had not taken my measures aright, I fell with a sosh in the Valley below.

Bruised as I was, however, I returned to my Chamber without losing courage, and with Beef-Marrow I anointed my Body, for I was all over mortified from Head to Foot: Then having taken a dram of Cordial Waters to strengthen my Heart, I went back to look for my Machine; but I could not find it, for some Souldiers, that had been sent into the Forest to cut wood for a Bonefire, meeting with it by chance, had carried it with them to the Fort: Where after a great deal of guessing what it might be, when they had discovered the invention of the Spring, some said, that a good many Fire-Works should be fastened to it, because their Force carrying them up on high, and the Machine playing its large Wings, no Body but would take it for a Fiery Dragon. In the mean time I was long in search of it, but found it at length in the Market-place of *Kebeck* (Quebec), just as they were setting Fire to it. I was so transported with Grief, to find the Work of my Hands in so great Peril, that I ran to the Souldier that was giving Fire to it, caught hold of his Arm, pluckt the Match out of his Hand, and in great rage threw my self into my Machine, that I might undo the Fire-Works that they had stuck about it; but I came too late, for hardly were both my Feet within, when whip, away went I up in a Cloud.

The Horror and Consternation I was in did not so confound the faculties of my Soul, but I have since remembered all that happened to me at that instant. For so soon as the Flame had devoured one tier of Squibs, which were ranked by six and six, by means of a Train that reached every half-dozen, another tier went off, and then another so that the Salt-Peter taking Fire, put off the danger by encreasing it. However, all the combustible matter being spent, there was a period put to the Fire-work; and whilst I thought of nothing less than to knock my Head against the top of some Mountain, I felt, without the least stirring, my elevation continuing; and adieu Machine, for I saw it fall down again towards the Earth.

That extraordinary Adventure puffed up my Heart with so uncommon a Gladness; that, ravished to see my self delivered from certain danger, I had the impudence to philosophize upon it. Whilst then with Eyes and Thought I cast about to find what might be the cause of it, I perceived my flesh blown up, and still greasy with the Marrow, that I had daubed my self over with for the Bruises of my fall: I knew that the Moon being then in the Wain, and that it being usual for her in that Quarter to suck up the Marrow of Animals, she drank up that wherewith I was anointed, with so much the more force that her Globe was nearer to me, and that no interposition of Clouds weakened her Attraction.

When I had, according to the computation I made since, advanced a good deal more than three quarters of the space that divided the Earth from the Moon; all of a sudden I fell with my Heels up and Head down, though I had made no Trip; and indeed, I had not been sensible of it, had not I felt my Head loaded under the weight of my Body: The truth is, I knew very well that I was not falling again towards our World; for though I found my self to be betwixt two Moons, and easily observed, that the nearer I drew to the one, the farther I removed from the other; yet I was certain, that ours was the bigger Globe of the two: Because after one or two days Journey, the remote Refractions of the Sun, confounding the diversity of Bodies and Climates, it appeared to me only as a large Plate of Gold: that made me imagine, that I descended towards the Moon; and I was confirmed in that Opinion, when I began to call to mind, that I did not fall till I was past three quarters of the way. For, said I to myself, that Mass being less than ours, the Sphere of its Activity must be of less Extent also; and by consequence, it was later before I felt the force of its Center.

* * *

In fine, after I had been a very long while in falling, as I judged, for the violence of my Precipitation hindered me from observing it more exactly: The last thing I can remember is, that I found my self under a Tree, entangled with three or four pretty large Branches which I had broken off by my fall; and my face besmeared with an Apple, that had dashed against it.

By good luck that place was, as you shall know by and by the Earthly Paradise and the tree I fell on precisely The Tree of Life. So that you may very well conclude, that had it not been for that Chance, if I had had a thousand lives, they had been all lost. I have many times since reflected upon the vulgar Opinion, That if one precipitate himself from a very high place, his breath is out before he reach the ground; and from my adventure I conclude it to be false, or else that the efficacious Juyce of that Fruit, which squirted into my mouth, must needs have recalled my soul, that was not far from my Carcass, which was still hot and in a disposition of exerting the Functions of Life. The truth is, so soon as I was upon the ground my pain was gone, before I could think what it was; and the Hunger, which I had felt during my Voyage, was fully satisfied with the sense that I had lost it. . . .

The Age of Reason and the
Voice of Dissent

The scientific revolution that had been foreshadowed by Roger Bacon, made possible by the printing press, and set off by Copernicus reached its culmination in the seventeenth century. New discoveries and inventions were appearing almost every year, among them Harvey's discovery of the circulation of the blood, Gascoigne's invention of the micrometer, Torricelli's invention of the barometer, Boyle's findings about the pressure and volume of gases, and Huygens' wave theory of light.

Everything seemed to come to focus in the person of Sir Isaac Newton (1642–1727). Considered by many the greatest mind ever to be born to the human race, Newton made astonishing discoveries in optics, invented a new mathematics called calculus (independently invented by a German philosopher and mathematician, Gottfried Wilhelm, Baron von Leibnitz), built the first reflecting telescope, developed his theory of gravity and his three laws of motion, and served the last twenty-four years of his life as president of the Royal Society.

Of his own work he wrote, "I do not know what I may appear to the world; but to myself I seem to have been only a boy playing on the seashore, and diverting myself in now and then finding a smoother pebble than ordinary, whilst the great ocean of truth lay all undiscovered before me." Wordsworth, looking at his bust, called it:

The marble index of a mind forever
Voyaging through strange seas of thought, alone.

Newton's major work, *Principia Mathematica* (1687), became the foundation for a new world view. It provided an elegant explanation for a universe operating by simple and understandable mechanisms, and it suggested that the rest of the problems troubling scientists could be worked out as easily by careful observation and intellectual rigor. It would not be as simple as that, but it led to a period of scientific optimism that later would be called the Age of Reason. Ironically, Newton also believed in transmutation and mysticism.

Not everyone was an optimist about science. In Dublin, Jonathan Swift (1667–1745), a reluctant Anglican cleric who became dean of St. Patrick's Cathedral, found his true vocation as a satirist, first attacking religion and learning in A *Tale of a Tub* and *The Battle of the Books* (1704), and eventually politics, science, and humanity itself in his masterpiece, *Gulliver's Travels* (1726).

Although Swift wrote *Gulliver's Travels* for satirical purposes, the stories have survived (largely as children's literature) for their narrative values and for the detail and inventiveness of Swift's imagination, as well as the precision of his prose, long after the particular objects of his satire have been forgotten. As voyages to unknown lands, all four parts have science-fiction relevance. Even more, each has something unusual to offer by way of comparison with human existence—comparisons Swift makes effective by differences in scale, social system, or civilized species.

The most famous voyages are the first two: to Lilliput, where Gulliver is a giant who finds pettiness among the little people who at first seem brave and capable; and to Brobdingnag, where he is a Lilliputian among giants, offended at first by their grossness but overwhelmed in the end by their benevolence and enlightenment. In the final episode, which has been called the work of a misanthropist approaching madness, Gulliver finds the Houyhnhmns so admirable that he cannot help seeing himself and all other men as contemptible Yahoos. The final voyage actually was published third but placed last in the collected voyages as a more appropriate conclusion.

The third voyage (initially published after the voyage to the land of the Houyhnhmns), to Laputa, is generally considered inferior to the other three, but it has the greatest science-fiction interest, chiefly because it shows the greatest impact of science and technology upon humanity, first through the flying city, which creates significant social change, and second through a society organized around scientific research, even though that research is satirized not only as ridiculous but also as less than worthless, because it distracts citizens from human concerns.

Swift distrusted science and did not care for scientists, particularly those who tried to find practical uses for their discoveries; he called them projectors. Perhaps his major objection was that science did not encompass the total human person and thus falsified the human experience. His so-called misanthropy was based on his opposition to the contemporary notion that humanity was basically good. He saw man not as a rational animal but as an animal capable only of reason, which was deeply and permanently flawed by its refusal to live up to its capabilities.

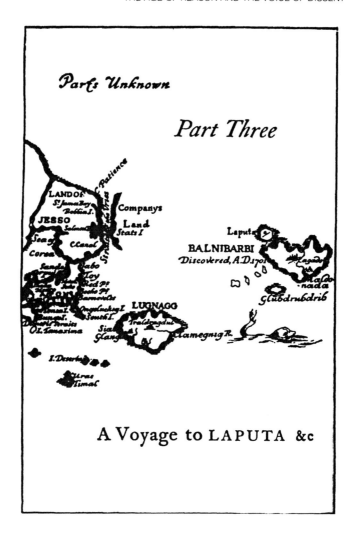

Swift owed a debt to Lucian and perhaps to Cyrano as well. In turn he inspired Wells and through Wells, and his own writing, much of later science fiction.

In the voyage to Laputa Swift particularly satirized the Royal Society founded in response to Francis Bacon's vision, the organization of scientists that played so large a part in the development of science in England, and the world, up to that time.

From "A Voyage to Laputa"

BY JONATHAN SWIFT

Chapter I *The Author sets out on his third voyage, is taken by pirates. The malice of a Dutchman. His arrival at an island. He is received into Laputa.*

I had not been at home above ten days, when Captain William Robinson, a Cornish man, Commander of the *Hopewell,* a stout ship of three hundred tons, came to my house. I had formerly been surgeon of another ship where he was master, and a fourth part owner, in a voyage to the Levant; he had always treated me more like a brother than an inferior officer, and hearing of my arrival made me a visit, as I apprehended only out of friendship, for nothing passed more than what is usual after long absences. But repeating his visits often, expressing his joy to find me in good health, asking whether I were not settled for life, adding that he intended a voyage to the East Indies in two months, at last he plainly invited me, though with some apologies, to be surgeon of the ship; that I should have another surgeon under me besides our two mates; that my salary should be double to the usual pay; and that having experienced my knowledge in sea-affairs to be at least equal to his, he would enter into any engagement to follow my advice, as much as if I had share in the command.

He said so many other obliging things, and I knew him to be so honest a man, that I could not reject his proposal; the thirst I had of seeing the world, notwithstanding my past misfortunes, continuing as violent as ever. The only difficulty that remained was to persuade my wife, whose consent, however, I at last obtained by the prospect of advantage she proposed to her children.

We set out the 5th of August 1706, and arrived at Fort St. George the 11th of April, 1707. We stayed there three weeks to refresh our crew, many of whom were sick. From thence we went to Tonquin, where the Captain resolved to continue some time, because many of the goods he intended to buy were not ready, nor could he expect to be dispatched in some months. Therefore in hopes to defray some of the charges he must be at, he bought a sloop, loaded it with several sorts of goods, wherewith the Tonquinese usually trade to the neighbouring islands, and putting fourteen men on board, whereof three were of the country, he appointed me master of the sloop, and gave me power to traffic for two months, while he transacted his affairs at Tonquin.

We had not sailed above three days, when a great storm arising, we were driven five days to the north-north-east, and then to the east; after which we had fair weather, but still with a pretty strong gale from the west. Upon the tenth day we were chased by two pirates, who soon overtook us; for my sloop was so deep loaden, that she sailed very slow; neither were we in a condition to defend ourselves.

We were boarded about the same time by both the pirates, who entered furiously at the head of their men, but finding us all prostrate upon our faces (for so I gave order) they pinioned us with strong ropes, and setting a guard upon us, went to search the sloop.

I observed among them a Dutchman, who seemed to be of some author-ity, though he was not commander of either ship. He knew us by our coun-tenances to be Englishmen, and jabbering to us in his own language, swore we should be tied back to back, and thrown into the sea. I spoke Dutch tolerably well; I told him who we were, and begged him in consideration of our being Christians and Protestants, of neighbouring countries, in strict al-liance, that he would move the Captains to take some pity on us. This in-flamed his rage; he repeated his threatenings, and turning to his compan-ions, spoke with great vehemence, in the Japanese language, as I suppose, often using the word *Christianos*.

The largest of the two pirate ships was commanded by a Japanese Cap-tain, who spoke a little Dutch, but very imperfectly. He came up to me, and after several questions, which I answered in great humility, he said we should not die. I made the Captain a very low bow, and then turning to the Dutchman, said, I was sorry to find more mercy in a heathen, than a brother Christian. But I had soon reason to repent those foolish words; for that ma-licious reprobate, having often endeavoured in vain to persuade both the Captains that I might be thrown into the sea (which they would not yield to after the promise made me, that I should not die), however prevailed so far as to have a punishment inflicted on me, worse in all human appearance than death itself. My men were sent by an equal division into both the pi-rate ships, and my sloop new manned. As to myself, it was determined that I should be set adrift in a small canoe, with paddles and a sail, and four days' provisions, which last the Japanese Captain was so kind to double out of his own stores, and would permit no man to search me. I got down into the canoe, while the Dutchman standing upon the deck, loaded me with all the curses and injurious terms his language could afford.

About an hour before we saw the pirates, I had taken an observation and found we were in the latitude of 46 N. and of longitude 183. When I was at some distance from the pirates, I discovered by my pocket-glass several islands to the south-east. I set up my sail, the wind being fair, with a design to reach the nearest of those islands, which I made a shift to do in about three hours. It was all rocky; however I got many birds' eggs, and striking fire, I kindled some heath and dry sea-weed, by which I roasted my eggs. I ate no other supper, being resolved to spare my provisions as much as I could. I passed the night under the shelter of a rock, strowing some heath under me, and slept pretty well.

The next day I sailed to another island, and thence to a third and fourth, sometimes using my sail, and sometimes my paddles. But not to trouble the reader with a particular account of my distresses, let it suffice that on the fifth day I arrived at the last island in my sight, which lay south-south-east to the former.

This island was at a greater distance than I expected, and I did not reach it in less than five hours. I encompassed it almost round before I could find a convenient place to land in, which was a small creek about three times the wideness of my canoe. I found the island to be all rocky, only a little intermingled with tufts of grass and sweet smelling herbs. I took out my small provisions, and after having refreshed myself, I secured the remainder in a cave, whereof there were great numbers. I gathered plenty of eggs upon the rocks, and got a quantity of dry sea-weed and parched grass, which I designed to kindle the next day, and roast my eggs as well as I could. (For I had about me my flint, steel, match, and burning-glass.) I lay all night in the cave where I had lodged my provisions. My bed was the same dry grass and sea-weed which I intended for fuel. I slept very little, for the disquiets of my mind prevailed over my weariness, and kept me awake. I considered how impossible it was to preserve my life in so desolate a place, and how miserable my end must be. Yet I found myself so listless and desponding that I had not the heart to rise, and before I could get spirits enough to creep out of my cave the day was far advanced. I walked a while among the rocks; the sky was perfectly clear, and the sun so hot that I was forced to turn my face from it: when all of a sudden it became obscured, as I thought, in a manner very different from what happens by the interposition of a cloud. I turned back and perceived a vast opaque body between me and the sun, moving forwards towards the island: it seemed to be about two miles high, and hid the sun six or seven minutes, but I did not observe the air to be much colder, or the sky more darkened, than if I had stood under the shade of a mountain. As it approached nearer over the place where I was, it appeared to be a firm substance, the bottom flat, smooth, and shining very bright from the reflection of the sea below. I stood upon a height about two hundred yards from the shore, and saw this vast body descending almost to a parallel with me, at less than an English mile distance. I took out my pocket-perspective, and could plainly discover numbers of people moving up and down the sides of it, which appeared to be sloping, but what those people were doing, I was not able to distinguish.

The natural love of life gave me some inward motions of joy, and I was ready to entertain a hope that this adventure might some way or other help to deliver me from the desolate place and condition I was in. But at the same time the reader can hardly conceive my astonishment, to behold an island in the air, inhabited by men, who were able (as it should seem) to raise or sink, or put it into a progressive motion, as they pleased. But not being at that time in a disposition to philosophise upon this phenomenon, I rather chose to observe what course the island would take, because it seemed for a while to stand still. Yet soon after it advanced nearer, and I could see the sides of it, encompassed with several gradations of galleries, and stairs at certain intervals, to descend from one to the other. In the lowest gallery I beheld some people fishing with long angling rods, and others looking on, I waved my cap (for my hat was long since worn out) and my handkerchief towards the island; and upon its nearer approach, I called and shouted with the utmost strength of my voice; and then looking circumspectly, I beheld a crowd gather to that side which was most in my view, I found by their pointing towards me and to each other, that they plainly discovered me, although they made no return to my shouting. But I could see four or five men running in great haste up the stairs to the top of the island, who then disappeared. I happened rightly to conjecture, that these were sent for orders to some person in authority upon this occasion.

The number of people increased, and in less than half an hour the island was moved and raised in such a manner, that the lowest gallery appeared in a parallel of less than an hundred yards distance from the height where I stood. I then put myself into the most supplicating postures, and spoke in the humblest accent, but received no answer. Those who stood nearest over against me seemed to be persons of distinction, as I supposed by their habit. They conferred earnestly with each other, looking often upon me. At length one of them called out in a clear, polite, smooth dialect, not unlike in sound to the Italian; and therefore I returned an answer in that language, hoping at least that the cadence might be more agreeable to his ears. Although neither of us understood the other, yet any meaning was easily known, for the people saw the distress I was in.

They made signs for me to come down from the rock, and go towards the shore, which I accordingly did; and the flying island being raised to a convenient height, the verge directly over me, a chain was let down from the lowest gallery, with a seat fastened to the bottom, to which I fixed myself, and was drawn up by pulleys.

Chapter II *The humours and dispositions of the Laputians described. An account of their learning. Of the King and his Court. The Author's reception there. The inhabitants subject to fear and disquietudes. An account of the women.*

At my alighting I was surrounded by a crowd of people, but those who stood nearest seemed to be of better quality. They beheld me with all the marks and circumstances of wonder; neither indeed was I much in their debt, having never till then seen a race of mortals so singular in their shapes, habits, and countenances. Their heads were all reclined either to the right or the left; one of their eyes turned inward, and the other directly up to the zenith. Their outward garments were adorned with the figures of suns, moons, and stars, interwoven with those of fiddles, flutes, harps, trumpets, guitars, harpsichords, and many other instruments of music, unknown to us in Europe. I observed here and there many in the habit of servants, with a blown bladder fastened like a flail to the end of a short stick, which they carried in their hands. In each bladder was a small quantity of dried pease, or little pebbles (as I was afterwards informed). With these bladders they now and then flapped the mouths and ears of those who stood near them, of which practice I could not then conceive the meaning; it seems the minds of these people are so taken up with intense speculations, that they neither can speak, nor attend to the discourses of others, without being roused by some external faction upon the organs of speech and hearing; for which reason those persons who are able to afford it always keep a flapper (the original is *climenole)* in their family, as one of their domestics, nor ever walk abroad or make visits without him. And the business of this officer is, when two or more persons are in company, gently to strike with his bladder the mouth of him who is to speak, and the right ear of him or them to whom the speaker addresseth himself. This flapper is likewise employed diligently to attend his master in his walks, and upon occasion to give him a soft flap on his eyes, because he is always so wrapped up in cogitation, that he is in manifest danger of falling down every precipice, and bouncing his head against every post, and in the streets, of jostling others, or being jostled himself into the kennel.

It was necessary to give the reader this information, without which he would be at the same loss with me, to understand the proceedings of these people, as they conducted me up the stairs, to the top of the island, and from thence to the royal palace. While we were ascending, they forgot several times what they were about, and left me to myself, till their memories were again roused by their flappers; for they appeared altogether unmoved by the sight of my foreign habit and countenance, and by the shouts of the vulgar, whose thoughts and minds were more disengaged.

At last we entered the palace, and proceeded into the chamber of presence, where I saw the King seated on his throne, attended on each side by persons of prime quality. Before the throne was a large table filled with globes and spheres, and mathematical instruments of all kinds. His Majesty took not the least notice of us, although our entrance was not without sufficient noise, by the concourse of all persons belonging to the court. But he was then deep in a problem, and we attended at least an hour, before he could solve it. There stood by him on each side a young page, with flaps in their hands, and when they saw he was at leisure, one of them gently struck his mouth, and the other his right ear; at which he started like one awaked on the sudden, and looking towards me and the company I was in, recollected the occasion of our coming, whereof he had been informed before. He spoke some words, whereupon immediately a young man with a flap came up to my side, and flapped me gently on the right ear; but I made signs, as well as I could, that I had no occasion for such an instrument; which, as I afterwards found, gave his Majesty and the whole court a very mean opinion of my understanding. The King, as far as I could conjecture, asked me several questions, and I addressed myself to him in all the languages I had. When it was found that I could neither understand nor be understood, I was conducted by the King's order to an apartment in his palace (this prince being distinguished above all his predecessors for his hospitality to strangers), where two servants were appointed to attend me. My dinner was brought, and four persons of quality, whom I remembered to have seen very near the King's person, did me the honour to dine with me. We had two courses of three dishes each. In the first course there was a shoulder of mutton, cut into an equilateral triangle, a piece of beef into a rhomboides, and a pudding into a cycloid. The second course was two ducks, trussed up into the form of fiddles; sausages and puddings resembling flutes and hautboys, and a breast of veal in the shape of a harp. The servants cut our bread into cones, cylinders, parallelograms, and several other mathematical figures.

While we were at dinner, I made bold to ask the names of several things in their language; and those noble persons, by the assistance of their flappers, delighted to give me answers, hoping to raise my admiration of their great abilities, if I could be brought to converse with them. I was soon able to call for bread and drink, or whatever else I wanted.

After dinner my company withdrew, and a person was sent to me by the King's order, attended by a flapper. He brought with him pen, ink, and paper, and three or four books, giving me to understand by signs, that he was sent to teach me the language. We sat together four hours, in which time I wrote down a great number of words in columns, with the translations over against them. I likewise made a shift to learn several short sentences. For my tutor would order one of my servants to fetch something, to turn about, to make a bow, to sit, or stand, or walk, and the like. Then I took down the sentence in writing. He showed me also in one of his books the figures of the sun, moon, and stars, and zodiac, the tropics, and polar circles, together with the denominations of many figures of planes and solids. He gave me the names and descriptions of all the musical instruments, and the general terms of art in playing on each of them. After he had left me, I placed all my words with their interpretations in alphabetical order. And thus in a few days, by the help of a very faithful memory, I got some insight into their language.

The word, which I interpret the *Flying* or *Floating Island,* is in the original *Laputa,* whereof I could never learn the true etymology. *Lap* in the old obsolete language signifieth *high,* and *untuh,* a *governor,* from which they say by corruption was derived *Laputa,* from *Lapuntuh.* But I do not approve of this derivation, which seems to be a little strained. I ventured to offer to the learned among them a conjecture of my own, that *Laputa* was *quasi lap outed; lap* signifying properly the dancing of the sunbeams in the sea, and *outed,* a wing, which however I shall not obtrude, but submit to the judicious reader.

Those to whom the King had entrusted me, observing how ill I was clad, ordered a tailor to come next morning, and take my measure for a suit of clothes. This operator did his office after a different manner from those of his trade in Europe. He first took my altitude by a quadrant, and then with a rule and compasses described the dimensions and outlines of my whole body, all which he entered upon paper, and in six days brought my clothes very ill made, and quite out of shape, by happening to mistake a figure in the calculation. But my comfort was, that I observed such accidents very frequent, and little regarded.

During my confinement for want of clothes, and by an indisposition that held me some days longer, I much enlarged my dictionary; and when I went next to court, was able to understand many things the King spoke, and to return him some kind of answers. His Majesty had given orders that the island should move north-east and by east, to the vertical point over Lagado, the metropolis of the whole kingdom below upon the firm earth. It was about ninety leagues distant, and our voyage lasted four days and an half. I was not in the least sensible of the progressive motion made in the air by the island. On the second morning about eleven o'clock the King himself in person, attended by his nobility, courtiers, and officers, having prepared all their musical instruments, played on them for three hours without intermission, so that I was quite stunned with the noise; neither could I possibly guess the meaning, till my tutor informed me. He said that the people of their island had their ears adapted to hear the music of the spheres, which always played at certain periods, and the court was now prepared to bear their part in whatever instrument they most excelled.

In our journey towards Lagado, the capital city, his Majesty ordered that the island should stop over certain towns and villages, from whence he might receive the petitions of his subjects. And to this purpose several packthreads were let down with small weights at the bottom. On these packthreads the people strung their petitions, which mounted up directly like the scraps of paper fastened by school-boys at the end of the string that holds their kite. Sometimes we received wine and victuals from below, which were drawn up by pulleys.

The knowledge I had in mathematics gave me great assistance in acquiring their phraseology, which depended much upon that science and music; and in the latter I was not unskilled. Their ideas are perpetually conversant in lines and figures. If they would, for example, praise the beauty of a woman, or any other animal, they describe it by rhombs, circles, parallelograms, ellipses, and other geometrical terms, or by words of art drawn from music, needless here to repeat. I observed in the King's kitchen all sorts of mathematical and musical instruments, after the figures of which they cut up the joints that were served to his Majesty's table.

Their houses are very ill built, the walls bevil, without one right angle in any apartment, and this defect ariseth from the contempt they bear for practical geometry, which they despise as vulgar and mechanic, those instructions they give being too refined for the intellectuals of their workmen, which occasions perpetual mistakes. And although they are dexterous enough upon a piece of paper in the management of the rule, the pencil, and the divider, yet in the common actions and behaviour of life, I have not seen a more clumsy, awkward, and unhandy people, nor so slow and perplexed in their conceptions upon all other subjects, except those of mathematics and music. They are very bad reasoners, and vehemently given to opposition, unless when they happen to be of the right opinion, which is seldom in their case. Imagination, fancy, and invention, they are wholly strangers to, nor have any words in their language by which those ideas can be expressed; the whole compass of their thoughts and mind being shut up within the two forementioned sciences.

Most of them, and especially those who deal in the astronomical part, have great faith in judicial astrology, although they are ashamed to own it publicly. But what I chiefly admired, and thought altogether unaccountable, was the strong disposition I observed in them towards news and politics, perpetually enquiring into public affairs, giving their judgments in matters of state, and passionately disputing every inch of a party opinion. I have indeed observed the same disposition among most of the mathematicians I have known in Europe, although I could never discover the least analogy between the two sciences; unless those people suppose, that because the smallest circle hath as many degrees as the largest, therefore the regulation and management of the world require no more abilities than the handling and turning of a globe. But I rather take this quality to spring from a very common infirmity of human nature, inclining us to be more curious and conceited in matters where we have least concern, and for which we are least adapted either by study or nature.

These people are under continual disquietudes, never enjoying a minute's peace of mind; and their disturbances proceed from causes which very little affect the rest of mortals. Their apprehensions arise from several changes they dread in the celestial bodies. For instance, that the earth, by the continual approaches of the sun towards it, must in course of time be absorbed or swallowed up. That the face of the sun will by degrees be encrusted with its own effluvia, and give no more light to the world. That the earth very narrowly escaped a brush from the tail of the last comet, which would have infallibly reduced it to ashes; and that the next, which they have calculated for one and thirty years hence, will probably destroy us. For if in its perihelion it should approach within a certain degree of the sun (as by their calculations they have reason to dread) it will conceive a degree of heat ten thousand times more intense than that of red-hot glowing iron; and in its absence from the sun, carry a blazing tail ten hundred thousand and fourteen miles long; through which if the earth should pass at the distance of one hundred thousand miles from the nucleus or main body of the comet, it must in its passage be set on fire, and reduced to ashes. That the sun daily spending its rays without any nutriment to supply them, will at last be wholly consumed and annihilated;

which must be attended with the destruction of this earth, and of all the planets that receive their light from it.

They are so perpetually alarmed with the apprehensions of these and the like impending dangers, that they can neither sleep quietly in their beds, nor have any relish for the common pleasures or amusements of life. When they meet an acquaintance in the morning, the first question is about the sun's health, how he looked at his setting and rising, and what hopes they have to avoid the stroke of the approaching comet. This conversation they are apt to run into with the same temper that boys discover, in delighting to hear terrible stories of sprites and hobgoblins, which they greedily listen to, and dare not go to bed for fear.

The women of the island have abundance of vivacity: they contemn their husbands, and are exceedingly fond of strangers, whereof there is always a considerable number from the continent below, attending a court, either upon affairs of the several towns and corporations, or their own particular occasions, but are much despised, because they want the same endowments. Among these the ladies choose their gallants: but the vexation is, that they act with too much ease and security, for the husband is always so rapt in speculation, that the mistress and lover may proceed to the greatest familiarities before his face, if he be but provided with paper and implements, and without his flapper at his side.

The wives and daughters lament their confinement to the island, although I think it the most delicious spot of ground in the world; and although they live here in the greatest plenty and magnificence, and are allowed to do whatever they please, they long to see the world, and take the diversions of the metropolis, which they are not allowed to do without a particular licence from the King; and this is not easy to be obtained, because the people of quality have found by frequent experience how hard it is to persuade their women to return from below. I was told that a great court lady, who had several children, is married to the prime minister, the richest subject in the kingdom, a very graceful person, extremely fond of her, and lives in the finest palace of the island, went down to Lagado, on the presence of health, there hid herself for several months, till the King sent a warrant to search for her, and she was found in an obscure eating-house all in rags, having pawned her clothes to maintain an old deformed footman, who beat her every day, and in whose company she was taken much against her will. And although her husband received her with all possible kindness, and without the least reproach, she soon after contrived to steal down again with all her jewels, to the same gallant, and hath not been heard of since.

This may perhaps pass with the reader rather for an European or English story, than for one of a country so remote. But he may please to consider, that the caprices of womankind are not limited by any climate or nation, and that they are much more uniform than can be easily imagined.

In about a month's time I had made a tolerable proficiency in their language, and was able to answer most of the King's questions, when I had the honour to attend him. His Majesty discovered not the least curiosity to enquire into the laws, government, history, religion, or manners of the countries where I had been, but confined his questions to the state of mathematics, and received the account I gave him with great contempt and indifference, though often roused by his flapper on each side.

Chapter III *A phenomenon solved by modern philosophy and astronomy. The Laputian's great improvements in the latter. The King's method of suppressing insurrections.*

I desired leave of this prince to see the curiosities of the island, which he was graciously pleased to grant, and ordered my tutor to attend me. I chiefly wanted to know what cause in art or in nature it owed its several motions, whereof I will now give a philosophical account to the reader.

The Flying or Floating Island is exactly circular, its diameter 7837 yards, or about four miles and a half, and consequently contains ten thousand acres. It is three hundred yards thick. The bottom or under surface, which appears to those who view it from below, is one even regular plate of adamant, shooting up to the height of about two hundred yards. Above it lie the several minerals in their usual order, and over all is a coat of rich mould, ten or twelve foot deep. The declivity of the upper surface, from the circumference to the centre, is the natural cause why all the dews and rains which fall upon the island, are conveyed in small rivulets toward the middle, where they are emptied into four large basins, each of about half a mile in circuit, and two hundred yards distant from the centre. From these basins the water is continually exhaled by the sun in the daytime, which effectually prevents their over-flowing. Besides, as it is in the power of the monarch to raise the island above the region of clouds and vapours, he can prevent the falling of dews and rains whenever he pleases. For the highest clouds cannot rise above two miles, as naturalists agree, at least they were never known to do so in that country.

At the centre of the island there is a chasm about fifty yards in diameter, from whence the astronomers descend into a large dome, which is therefore called *Flandona Gagnole,* or the Astronomer's Cave, situated at the depth of a hundred yards beneath the upper surface of the adamant. In this cave are twenty lamps continually burning, which from the reflection of the adamant cast a strong light into every part. The place is stored with great variety of sextants, quadrants, telescopes, astrolabes, and other astronomical instruments. But the greatest curiosity, upon which the fate of the island depends, is a loadstone of a prodigious size, in shape resembling a weaver's shuttle. It is in length six yards, and in the thickest part at least three yards over. This magnet is sustained by a very strong axle of adamant passing through its middle, upon which it plays, and is poised so exactly that the weakest hand can turn it. It is trooped round with an hollow cylinder of adamant, four foot deep, as many thick, and twelve yards in diameter, placed horizontally, and supported by eight adamantine feet, each six yards high. In the middle of the concave side there is a groove twelve inches deep, in which the extremities of the axle are lodged, and turned round as there is occasion.

The stone cannot be moved from its place by any force, because the hoop and its feet are one continued piece with that body of adamant which constitutes the bottom of the island.

By means of this loadstone, the island is made to rise and fall, and move from one place to another. For with respect to that part of the earth over which the monarch presides, the stone is endued at one of its sides with an attractive power, and at the other with a repulsive. Upon placing the magnet erect with its attracting end towards the earth, the island descends; but when the repelling extremity points downwards, the island mounts directly upwards. When the position of the stone is oblique, the motion of the island is so too. For in this magnet the forces always act in lines parallel to its direction.

By this oblique motion the island is conveyed to different parts of the monarch's dominions. To explain the matter of its progress, let $A B$ represent a line drawn cross the dominions of Balnibarbi, let the line $c d$ represent the loadstone, of which let d be the repelling end, and c the attracting end, the island being over C; let the stone be placed in the position $c d$, with its repelling end downwards; then the island will be driven upwards obliquely towards D. When it is arrived at D, let the stone be turned upon its axle, till its attracting end points toward E, and then the island will be carried obliquely towards E; where if the stone be again turned upon its axle till it stands in the position E F, with its repelling point downwards, the island will rise obliquely towards F, where by directing the attracting end towards G, the island may be carried to G, and from G to E, by turning the stone, so as to make its repelling extremity point directly downwards. And thus by changing the situation of the stone as often as there is occasion, the island is made to rise and fall by turns in an oblique direction, and by those alternate risings and failings (the obliquity being not considerable) is conveyed from one part of the dominions to the other.

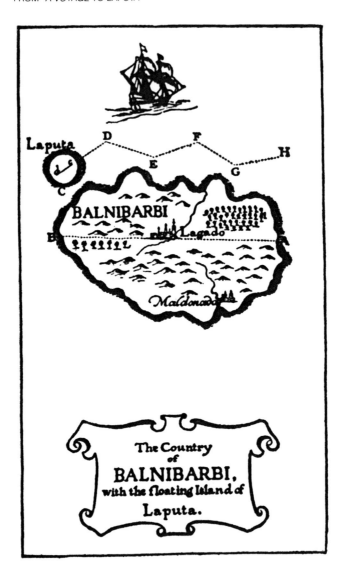

But it must be observed that this island cannot move beyond the extent of the dominions below nor can it rise above the height of four miles. For which the astronomers (who have written large systems concerning the stone) assign the following reason: that the magnetic virtue does not extend beyond the distance of four miles, and that the mineral which acts upon the stone in the bowels of the earth, and in the sea about six leagues distant from the shore, is not diffused through the whole globe, but terminated with the limits of the King's dominions; and it was easy from the great advantage of such a superior situation, for a prince to bring under his obedience whatever country lay within the attraction of that magnet.

When the stone is put parallel to the plane of the horizon, the island standeth still; for in that case the extremities of it being at equal distance from the earth, act with equal force, the one in drawing downwards, the other in pushing upwards, and consequently no motion to ensue.

This loadstone is under the care of certain astronomers, who from time to time give it such positions as the monarch directs. They spend the greatest part of their lives in observing the celestial bodies, which they do by the assistance of glasses far excelling ours in goodness. For although their largest telescopes do not exceed three feet, they magnify much more than those of an hundred yards among us, and at the same time show the stars with greater clearness. This advantage hath enabled them to extend their discoveries much further than our astronomers in Europe; for they have made a catalogue of ten thousand fixed stars, whereas the largest of ours do not contain above one third part of that number. They have likewise discovered two lesser stars, or satellites, which revolve about Mars, whereof the innermost is distant from the centre of the primary planet exactly three of the diameters, and the outermost five; the former revolves in the space of ten hours, and the latter in twenty one and an half; so that the squares of their periodical times are very near in the same proportion with the cubes of their distance from the centre of Mars, which evidently shows them to be governed by the same law of gravitation, that influences the other heavenly bodies.

They have observed ninety-three different comets, and settled their periods with great exactness. If this be true (and they affirm it with great confidence), it is much to be wished that their observations were made public, whereby the theory of comets, which at present is very lame and defective, might be brought to the same perfection with other parts of astronomy.

The King would be the most absolute prince in the universe, if he could but prevail on a ministry to join with him; but these having their estates below on the continent, and considering that the office of a favourite hath a very uncertain tenure, would never consent to the enslaving their country.

If any town should engage in rebellion or mutiny, fall into violent factions, or refuse to pay the usual tribute, the King hath two methods of reducing them to obedience. The first and the mildest course is by keeping the island hovering over such a town, and the lands about it, whereby he can deprive them of the benefit of the sun and the rain, and consequently afflict the inhabitants with dearth and diseases. And if the crime deserve it, they are at the same time pelted from above with great stones, against which they have no defence but by creeping into cellars or caves, while the roofs of their houses are beaten to pieces. But if they still continue obstinate, or offer to raise insurrections, he proceeds to the last remedy, by letting the island drop directly upon their heads, which makes a universal destruction both of houses and men. However, this is an extremity to which the prince is seldom driven, neither indeed is he willing to put it in execution, nor dare his ministers advise him to an action, which as it would render them odious to the people, so it would be a great damage to their own estates, which lie all below, for the island is the King's demesne.

But there is still indeed a more weighty reason, why the kings of this country have been always averse from executing so terrible an action, unless upon the utmost necessity. For if the town intended to be destroyed should have in it any tall rocks, as it generally falls out in the larger cities, a situation probably chosen at first with a view to prevent such a catastrophe; or if it abound in high spires, or pillars of stone, a sudden fall might endanger the bottom or under surface of the island, which, although it consists, as I have said, of one entire adamant two hundred yards thick, might happen to crack by too great a shock, or burst by approaching too near the fires from the houses below, as the backs both of iron and stone will often do in our chimneys. Of all this the people are well apprised and understand how far to carry their obstinacy, where their liberty or property is concerned. And the King, when he is highest provoked, and most determined to press a city to rubbish, orders the island to descend with great gentleness, out of a pretence of tenderness to his people, but indeed for fear of breaking the adamantine bottom; in which case it is the opinion of all their philosophers that the loadstone could no longer hold it up, and the whole mass would fall to the ground.

About three years before my arrival among them, while the King was in his progress over his dominions, there happened an extraordinary accident which had like to have put a period to the fate of that monarchy, at least as it is now instituted. Lindalino, the second city in the kingdom, was the first his Majesty visited in his progress. Three days after his departure the inhabitants, who had often complained of great oppressions, shut the town gates, seized on the governor, and with incredible speed and labour erected four large towers, one at every corner of the city (which is an exact square), equal in height to a strong pointed rock that stands directly in the centre of the city. Upon the top of each tower, as well as upon the rock, they fixed a great loadstone, and in case their design should fail, they had provided a vast quantity of the most combustible fuel, hoping to burst therewith the adamantine bottom of the island, if the loadstone project should miscarry.

It was eight months before the King had perfect notice that the Lindalinians were in rebellion. He then commanded that the island should be wafted over the city. The people were unanimous, and had laid in store of provisions, and a great river runs through the middle of the town. The King hovered over them several days to deprive them of the sun and the rain. He ordered many pack-threads to be let down, yet not a person offered to send up a petition, but instead thereof very bold demands, the redress of all their grievances, great immunities, the choice of their own governor, and other the like exorbitances. Upon which his Majesty commanded all the inhabitants of the island to cast great stones from the lower gallery into the town; but the citizens had provided against this mischief by conveying their persons and effects into the four towers, and other strong buildings, and vaults underground.

The King being now determined to reduce this proud people, ordered that the island should descend gently within forty yards of the top of the towers and rock. This was accordingly done; but the officers employed in that work found the descent much speedier than usual, and by turning the loadstone could not without great difficulty keep it in a firm position, but found the island inclining to fall. They sent the King immediate intelligence of this astonishing event, and begged his Majesty's permission to raise the island higher; the King consented, a general council was called, and the officers of the loadstone ordered to attend. One of the oldest and expertest among them obtained leave to try an experiment. He took a strong line of an hundred yards, and the island being raised over the town above the attracting power they had felt, he fastened a piece of adamant to the end of his line, which had in it a mixture of iron mineral, of the same nature with that whereof the bottom or lower surface of the island is composed, and from the lower gallery let it down slowly towards the top of the towers. The adamant was not descended four yards, before the officer felt it drawn so strongly downwards that he could hardly pull it back. He then threw down several small pieces of adamant, and observed that they were all violently attracted by the top of the tower. The same experiment was made on the other three towers, and on the rock with the same effect.

This incident broke entirely the King's measures, and (to dwell no longer on other circumstances) he was forced to give the town their own conditions.

I was assured by a great minister that if the island had descended so near the town as not to be able to raise itself, the citizens were determined to fix it for ever, to kill the King and all his servants, and entirely change the government.

By a fundamental law of this realm, neither the king, nor either of his two elder sons, are permitted to leave the island; nor the queen, till she is past child-bearing.

Chapter IV *The Author leaves Laputa; is conveyed to Balnibarbi, arrives at the metropolis. A description of the metropolis, and the country adjoining. The Author hospitably received by a great lord. His conversation with that lord.*

Although I cannot say that I was ill treated in this island, yet I must confess I thought myself too much neglected, not without some degree of contempt. For neither prince nor people appeared to be curious in any part of knowledge, except mathematics and music, wherein I was far their inferior, and upon that account very little regarded.

On the other side, after having seen all the curiosities of the island, I was very desirous to leave it, being heartily weary of those people. They were indeed excellent in two sciences for which I have great esteem, and wherein I am not unversed; but at the same time so abstracted and involved in speculation, that I never met with such disagreeable companions. I conversed only with women, tradesmen, flappers, and court-pages, during two months of my abode there, by which at last I rendered myself extremely contemptible; yet these were the only people from whom I could ever receive a reasonable answer.

I had obtained by hard study a good degree of knowledge in their language; I was weary of being confined to an island where I received so little countenance, and resolved to leave it with the first opportunity.

There was a great lord at court, nearly related to the King, and for that reason alone used with respect. He was universally reckoned the most ignorant and stupid person among them. He had performed many eminent services for the crown, had great natural and acquired parts, adorned with integrity and honour, but so ill an ear for music, that his detractors reported he had been often known to beat time in the wrong place; neither could his tutors without extreme difficulty teach him to demonstrate the most easy proposition in the mathematics. He was pleased to show me many marks of favour, often did me the honour of a visit, desired to be informed in the affairs of Europe, the laws and customs, the manners and learning of the several countries where I had travelled. He listened to me with great attention, and made very wise observations on all I spoke. He had two flappers attending him for state, but never made use of them except at court, and in visits of ceremony, and would always command them to withdraw when we were alone together.

I entreated this illustrious person to intercede in my behalf with his Majesty for leave to depart, which he accordingly did, as he was pleased to tell me, with regret: for indeed he had made me several offers very advantageous, which however I refused with expression of the highest acknowledgment.

On the 16th day of February I took leave of his Majesty and the court. The King made me a present to the value of about two hundred pounds English, and my protector his kinsman as much more, together with a letter of recommendation to a friend of his in Lagado, the metropolis. The island being then hovering over a mountain about two miles from it, I was let down from the lowest gallery, in the same manner as I had been taken up.

The continent, as far as it is subject to the monarch of the Flying Island, passes under the general name of *Balnibarbi,* and the metropolis, as I said before, is called *Lagado.* I felt some little satisfaction in finding myself on firm ground. I walked to the city without any concern, being clad like one of the natives, and sufficiently instructed to converse with them. I soon found out the person's house to whom I was recommended, presented my letter from his friend the grandee in the island, and was received with much kindness. This great lord, whose name was Munodi, ordered me an apartment in his own house, where I continued during my stay, and was entertained in a most hospitable manner.

The next morning after my arrival, he took me in his chariot to see the town, which is about half the bigness of London, but the houses very strangely built, and most of them out of repair. The people in the streets walked fast, looked wild, their eyes fixed, and were generally in rags. We passed through one of the town gates, and went about three miles into the country, where I saw many labourers working with several sorts of tools in the ground, but was not able to conjecture what they were about; neither did I observe any expectation either of corn or grass, although the soil appeared to be excellent. I could not forbear admiring at these odd appearances both in town and country, and I made bold to desire my conductor, that he would be pleased to explain to me what could be meant by so many busy heads, hands, and faces, both in the streets and the fields, because I did not discover any good effects they produced; but on the contrary, I never knew a soil so unhappily cultivated, houses so ill contrived and so ruinous, or a people whose countenances and habit expressed so much misery and want.

This Lord Munodi was a person of the first rank, and had been some years Governor of Lagado, but by a cabal of ministers was discharged for insufficiency. However, the King treated him with tenderness, as a well-meaning man, but a low contemptible understanding.

When I gave that free censure of the country and its inhabitants, he made no further answer than by telling me that I had not been long enough among them to form a judgement, and that the different nations of the world had different customs, and other common topics to the same purpose. But when we returned to his palace, he asked me how I liked the building, what absurdities

I observed, and what quarrel I had with the dress or looks of his domestics. This he might safely do, because every thing about him was magnificent, regular, and polite. I answered that his Excellency's prudence, quality, and fortune, had exempted him from those defects which folly and beggary had produced in others. He said if I would go with him to his country-house, about twenty miles distant, where his estate lay, there would be more leisure for this kind of conversation. I told his Excellency that I was entirely at his disposal, and accordingly we set out next morning.

During our journey he made me observe the several methods used by farmers in managing their lands, which to me were wholly unaccountable; for except in some very few places I could not discover one ear of corn or blade of glass. But in three hours travelling the scene was wholly altered; we came into a most beautiful country; farmers' houses at small distances, neatly built; the fields enclosed, containing vineyards, corn-grounds, and meadows. Neither do I remember to have seen a more delightful prospect. His Excellency observed my countenance to clear up; he told me with a sigh that there his estate began, and would continue the same till we should come to his house. That his countrymen ridiculed and despised him for managing his affairs no better, and for setting so ill an example to the kingdom, which however was followed by very few, such as were old, and wilful, and weak like himself.

We came at length to the house, which was indeed a noble structure, built according to the best rules of ancient architecture. The fountains, gardens, walks, avenues, and groves were all disposed with exact judgement and taste. I gave due praises to every thing I saw, whereof his Excellency took not the least notice till after supper, when, there being no third companion, he told me with a very melancholy air that he doubted he must throw down his houses in town and country, to rebuild them after the present mode, destroy all his plantations, and cast others into such a form as modern usage required, and give the same directions to all his tenants, unless he would submit to incur the censure of pride, singularity, affectation, ignorance, caprice, and perhaps increase his Majesty's displeasure.

That the admiration I appeared to be under would cease or diminish when he had informed me of some particulars, which probably I never heard of at court, the people there being too much taken up in their own speculations, to have regard to what passed here below.

The sum of his discourse was to this effect. That about forty years ago certain persons went up to Laputa, either upon business or diversion, and after five months continuance came back with a very little smattering in mathematics, but full of volatile spirits acquired in that airy region. That these persons upon their return began to dislike the management of every thing below, and fell into schemes of putting all art, sciences, languages, and mechanics upon a new foot. To this end they procured a royal patent for erecting an Academy of Projectors in Lagado; and the humour prevailed so strongly among the people, that there is not a town of any consequence in the kingdom without such an academy. In these colleges the professors contrive new rules and methods of agriculture and building, and new instruments and tools for all trades and manufacturers, whereby, as they undertake, one man shall do the work of ten; a palace may be built in a week, of materials so durable as to last for ever without repairing. All the fruits of the earth shall come to maturity at whatever season we think fit to choose, and increase an hundred fold more than they do at present, with innumerable other happy proposals. The only inconvenience is, that none of these projects are yet brought to perfection, and in the mean time, the whole country lies miserably waste, the houses in ruins, and the people without food or clothes. By all which, instead of being discouraged, they are fifty times more violently bent upon prosecuting their schemes, driven equally on by hope and despair; that as for himself, being not of an enterprising spirit, he was content to go on in the old forms, to live in the houses his ancestors had built, and act as they did in every part of life without innovation. That some few other persons of quality and gentry had done the same, but were looked on with an eye of contempt and ill-will as enemies to art, ignorant, and ill commonwealth's-men, preferring their own ease and sloth before the general improvement of their country.

His Lordship added that he would not by any further particulars prevent the pleasure I should certainly take in viewing the grand Academy, whither he was resolved I should go. He only desired me to observe a ruined building upon the side of a mountain about three miles distant, of which he gave me this account. That he had a very convenient mill within half a mile of his house, turned by a current from a large river, and sufficient for his own family as well as a great number of his tenants. That about seven years ago a club of those projectors came to him with proposals to destroy this mill, and build another on the side of that mountain, on the long ridge whereof a long canal must be cut for a repository of water, to be conveyed up by pipes and engines to supply the mill; because the wind and air upon a height agitated the water, and thereby made it fitter for motion; and because the water descending down a declivity would turn the mill with half the current of a river whose course is more upon a level. He said, that being then not very well with the court, and pressed by many of his friends, he complied with the proposal; and after employing an hundred men for two years, the work miscarried, the projectors went off, laying the blame entirely upon him, railing at him ever since, and putting others upon the same experiment, with equal assurance of success, as well as equal disappointment.

In a few days we came back to town, and his Excellency, considering the bad character he had in the Academy, would not go with me himself, but recommended me to a friend of his to bear me company thither. My lord was pleased to represent me as a great admirer of projects, and a person of much curiosity and easy belief; which indeed was not without truth, for I had myself been a sort of projector in my younger days.

> Chapter V *The Author permitted to see the Grand Academy of Lagado. The Academy largely described. The Arts wherein the professors employ themselves.*

This Academy is not an entire single building, but a continuation of several houses on both sides of a street, which growing waste was purchased and applied to that use.

I was received very kindly by the Warden, and went for many days to the Academy. Every room hath in it one or more projectors, and I believe I could not be in fewer than five hundred rooms.

The first man I saw was of a meagre aspect, with sooty hands and face, his hair and beard long, ragged and singed in several places. His clothes, shirt, and skin were all of the same colour. He had been eight years upon a project for extracting sun-beams out of cucumbers, which were to be put into vials hermetically sealed, and let out to warm the air in raw inclement summers. He told me he did not doubt in eight years more he should be able to supply the Governor's gardens with sunshine at a reasonable rate; but he complained that his stock was low, and entreated me to give him something as an encouragement to ingenuity, especially since this had been a very dear season for cucumbers. I made him a small present, for my lord had furnished me with money on purpose, because he knew their practice of begging from all who go to see them.

I went into another chamber, but was ready to hasten back, being almost overcome with a horrible stink. My conductor pressed me forward, conjuring me in a whisper to give no offence, which would be highly resented, and therefore I durst not so much as stop my nose. The projector of this cell was the most ancient student of the Academy; his face and beard were of a pale yellow; his hands and clothes daubed over with filth. When I was presented to him, he gave me a close embrace (a compliment I could well have excused). His employment from his first coming into the Academy, was an operation to reduce human excrement to its original food, by separating the several parts, removing the tincture which it receives from the gall, making the odour exhale, and scumming off the saliva. He had a weekly allowance from the society, of a vessel filled with human ordure, about the bigness of a Bristol barrel.

I saw another at work to calcine ice into gunpowder, who likewise showed me a treatise he had written concerning the malleability of fire, which he intended to publish.

There was a most ingenious architect who had contrived a new method for building houses, by beginning at the roof, and working downwards to the foundation, which he justified to me by the like practice of those two prudent insects, the bee and the spider.

There was a man born blind, who had several apprentices in his own condition: their employment was to mix colours for painters, which their master taught them to distinguish by feeling and smelling. It was indeed my misfortune to find them at that time not very perfect in their lessons, and the professor himself happened to be generally mistaken: this artist is much encouraged and esteemed by the whole fraternity.

In another apartment I was highly pleased with a projector, who had found a device of ploughing the ground with hogs, to save the charges of ploughs, cattle, and labour. The method is this: in an acre of ground you bury, at six inches distance and eight deep, a quantity of acorns, dates, chestnuts, and other mast or vegetables whereof these animals are fondest; then you drive six hundred or more of them into the field, where in a few days they will root up the whole ground in search of their food, and make it fit for sowing, at the same time manuring it with their dung. It is true, upon experiment they found the charge and trouble very great, and they had little or no crop. However, it is not doubted that this invention may be capable of great improvement.

I went into another room, where the walls and ceiling were all hung round with cobwebs, except a narrow passage for the artist to go in and out. At my entrance he called aloud to me not to disturb his webs. He lamented the fatal mistake the world had been so long in of using silk-worms, while we had such plenty of domestic insects, who infinitely excelled the former, because they understood how to weave as well as spin. And he proposed farther that by employing spiders the charge of dyeing silks should be wholly saved, whereof I was fully convinced when he showed me a vast number of flies most beautifully colored, wherewith he fed his spiders, assuring us that the webs would take a tincture from them; and as he had them of all hues, he hoped to fit everybody's fancy, as soon as he could find proper food for the flies, of certain gums, oils, and other glutinous matter to give a strength and consistence to the threads.

There was an astronomer who had undertaken to place a sun-dial upon the great weathercock on the town-house, by adjusting the annual and diurnal motions of the earth and sun, so as to answer and coincide with all accidental turnings by the wind.

I was complaining of a small fit of the colic, upon which my conductor led me into a room, where a great physician resided, who was famous for curing that disease by contrary operations from the same instrument. He had a large pair of bellows with a long slender muzzle of ivory. This he conveyed eight inches up the anus, and drawing in the wind, he affirmed he could make the guts as lank as a dried bladder. But when the disease was more stubborn and violent, he let in the muzzle while the bellows were full of wind, which he discharged into the body of the patient, then withdrew the instrument to replenish it, clapping his thumb strongly against the orifice of the fundament; and this being repeated three or four times, the adventitious wind would rush out, bringing the noxious along with it (like water put into a pump), and the patient recover. I saw him try both experiments upon a dog, but could not discern any effect from the former. After the latter, the animal was ready to burst, and made so violent a discharge, as was very offensive to me and my companions. The dog died on the spot, and we left the doctor endeavouring to recover him by the same operation.

I visited many other apartments, but shall not trouble my reader with all the curiosities I observed, being studious of brevity.

I had hitherto seen only one side of the Academy, the other being appropriated to the advancers of speculative learning, of whom I shall say something when I have mentioned one illustrious person more, who is called among them *the universal artist*. He told us he had been thirty years employing his thoughts for the improvement of human life. He had two large rooms full of wonderful curiosities, and fifty men at work. Some were condensing air into a dry tangible substance by extracting the nitre, and letting the aqueous or fluid particles percolate; others softening marble for pillows and pin-cushions; others petrifying the hoofs of a living horse to preserve them from foundering. The artist himself was at that time busy upon two great designs; the first, to sow land with chaff, wherein he affirmed the true seminal virtue to be contained, as he demonstrated by several experiments which I was not skilful enough to comprehend. The other was, by a certain composition of gums, minerals, and vegetables outwardly applied, to prevent the growth of wool upon two young lambs; and he hoped in a reasonable time to propagate the breed of naked sheep all over the kingdom.

We crossed a walk to the other part of the Academy, where, as I have already said, the projectors in speculative learning resided.

The first professor I saw was in a very large room, with forty pupils about him. After salutation, observing me to look earnestly upon a frame, which took up the greatest part of both the length and breadth of the room, he said perhaps I might wonder to see him employed in a project for improving speculative knowledge by practical and mechanical operations. But the world would soon be sensible of its usefulness, and he flattered himself that a more noble exalted thought never sprang in any other man's head. Every one knew how laborious the usual method is of attaining to arts and sciences; whereas by his contrivance the most ignorant person at a reasonable charge, and with a little bodily labour, may write books in philosophy, poetry, politics, law, mathematics, and theology, without the least assistance from genius or study. He then led me to the frame, about the sides whereof all his pupils stood in ranks. It was twenty foot square, placed in the middle of the room. The superficies was composed of several bits of wood, about the bigness of a die, but some larger than others. They were all linked together by slender wires. These bits of wood were covered on every square with paper pasted on them, and on these papers were written all the words of their language, in their several moods, tenses, and declensions, but without any order. The professor then desired me to observe, for he was going to set his engine at work. The pupils at his command took each of them hold of an iron handle, whereof there were forty fixed round the edges of the frame, and giving them a sudden turn, the whole disposition of the words was entirely changed. He then commanded six and thirty of the lads to read the several lines softly as they appeared upon the frame; and where they found three or four words together that might make part of a sentence, they dictated to the four remaining boys who were scribes. This work was repeated three or four times, and at every turn the engine was so contrived that the words shifted into new places, as the square bits of wood moved upside down.

Six hours a day the young students were employed in this labour, and the professor showed me several volumes in large folio already collected, of broken sentences, which he intended to piece together, and out of those rich materials to give the world a complete body of all arts and sciences; which however might be still improved, and much expedited, if the public would raise a fund for making and employing five hundred such frames in Lagado, and oblige the managers to contribute in common their several collections.

He assured me, that this invention had employed all his thoughts from his youth, that he had emptied the whole vocabulary into his frame, and made the strictest computation of the general proportion there is in books between the numbers of particles, nouns, and verbs, and other parts of speech.

I made my humblest acknowledgement to this illustrious person for his great communicativeness, and promised if ever I had the good fortune to return to my native country, that I would do him justice, as the sole inventor of this wonderful machine; the form and contrivance of which I desired leave to delineate upon paper. I told him, although it were the custom of our learned in Europe to steal inventions from each other, who had thereby at last this advantage, that it became a controversy which was the right owner, yet I would take such caution, that he should have the honour entire without a rival.

We next went to the school of languages, where three professors sat in consultation upon improving that of their own country.

The first project was to shorten discourse by cutting polysyllables into one, and leaving out verbs and participles, because in reality all things imaginable are but nouns.

The other project was a scheme for entirely abolishing all words what-soever; and this was urged as a great advantage in point of health as well as brevity. For it is plain that every word we speak is in some degree a diminu-tion of our lungs by corrosion, and consequently contributes to the short-ening of our lives. An expedient was therefore offered, that since words are only names for *things,* it would be more convenient for all men to carry about them such things as were necessary to express the particular business they are to discourse on. And this invention would certainly have taken place, to the great ease as well as health of the subject, if the women, in conjunction with the vulgar and illiterate, had not threatened to raise a re-bellion, unless they might be allowed the liberty to speak with their tongues, after the manner of their ancestors; such constant irreconcilable enemies to science are the common people. However, many of the most learned and wise adhere to the new scheme of expressing themselves by things, which hath only this inconvenience attending it, that if a man's busi-ness be very great, and of various kinds, he must be obliged in proportion to carry a greater bundle of things upon his back, unless he can afford one or two strong servants to attend him. I have often beheld two of those sages almost sinking under the weight of their packs, like pedlars among us; who, when they met in the streets, would lay down their loads, open their sacks, and hold conversation for an hour together; then put up their implements, help each other to resume their burthens, and take their leave.

But for short conversations a man may carry implements in his pockets and under his arms, enough to supply him, and in his house he cannot be at a loss. Therefore the room where company meet who practice this art, is full of all things ready at hand, requisite to furnish matter for this kind of artificial converse.

Another great advantage proposed by this invention was that it would serve as an universal language to be understood in all civilised nations, whose goods and utensils are generally of the same kind, or nearly resem-bling, so that their uses might easily be comprehended. And thus ambassa-dors would be qualified to treat with foreign princes or ministers of state, to whose tongues they were utter strangers.

I was at the mathematical school, where the master taught his pupils af-ter a method scarce imaginable to us in Europe. The proposition and demonstration were fairly written on a thin wafer, with ink composed of a cephalic tincture. This the student was to swallow upon a fasting stomach, and for three days following eat nothing but bread and water. As the wafer digested, the tincture mounted to his brain, bearing the proposition along with it. But the success hath not hitherto been answerable, partly by some error in the *quantum* or composition, and partly by the perverseness of lads, to whom this bolus is so nauseous, that they generally steal aside, and discharge it upwards before it can operate; neither have they been yet persuaded to use so long an abstinence as the prescription requires.

Chapter VI *A further account of the Academy. The Author proposes some improvements, which are honourably received.*

In the school of political projectors I was but ill entertained, the professors appearing in my judgement wholly out of their senses, which is a scene that never fails to make me melancholy. These unhappy people were proposing schemes for persuading monarchs to choose favourites upon the score of their wisdom, capacity, and virtue; of teaching ministers to consult the public good; of rewarding merit, great abilities, eminent services; of instructing princes to know their true interest by placing it on the same foundation with that of their people; of choosing for employments persons qualified to exercise them; with many other wild impossible chimæras, that never entered before into the heart of man to conceive, and confirmed in me the old observation, that there is nothing so extravagant and irrational which some philosophers have not maintained for truth.

But however I shall so far do justice to this part of the Academy, as to acknowledge that all of them were not so visionary. There was a most ingenious doctor who seemed to be perfectly versed in the whole nature and system of government. This illustrious person had very usefully employed his studies in finding out effectual remedies for all diseases and corruptions, to which the several kinds of public administration are subject by the vices or infirmities of those who govern, as well as by the licentiousness of those who are to obey. For instance, whereas all writers and reasoners have agreed, that there is a strict universal resemblance between the natural and the political body; can there by any thing more evident, than that the health of both must be preserved, and the diseases cured by the same prescriptions? It is allowed that senates and great councils are often troubled with redundant, ebullient, and other peccant humours, with many diseases of the head, and more of the heart; with strong convulsions, with grievous contractions of the nerves and sinews in both hands, but especially the right; with spleen, flatus, vertigoes, and deliriums; with scrofulous tumours full of foetid virulent matter; with sour frothy ructations, with canine appetites and crudeness of digestion, besides many others needless to mention. This doctor therefore proposed, that upon the meeting of a senate, certain physicians should attend at the three first days of their sitting, and at the close of each day's debate, feel the pulses of every senator; after which, having maturely considered, and consulted upon the nature of the several maladies, and the methods of cure, they should on the fourth day return to the senate house, attended by their apothecaries stored with proper medicines; and before the members sat, administer to each of them lenitives, aperitives, abstersives, corrosives, restringents, palliatives, laxatives, cephalalgics, icterics, apophlegmatics, acoustics, as their several cases required; and according as these medicines should operate, repeat, alter, or omit them at the next meeting.

This project could not be of any great expense to the public, and would, in my poor opinion, be of much use for the dispatch of business in those countries where senates have any share in the legislative power; beget unanimity, shorten debates, open a few mouths which were now closed, and close many more which are now open; curb the petulancy of the young, and correct the positiveness of the old; rouse the stupid, and damp the pert.

Again, because it is a general complaint, that the favourites of princes are troubled with short and weak memories, the same doctor proposed, that whoever attended a first minister, after having told his business with the utmost brevity and in the plainest words, should at his departure give the said minister a tweak by the nose, or a kick in the belly, or tread on his corns, or lug him thrice by both ears, or run a pin into his breech, or pinch his arm black and blue to prevent forgetfulness; and at every levee day repeat the same operation, till the business were done or absolutely refused.

He likewise directed, that every senator in the great council of a nation, after he had delivered his opinion, and argued in the defence of it, should be obliged to give his vote directly contrary; because if that were done, the result would infallibly terminate in the good of the public.

When parties in a state are violent, he offered a wonderful contrivance to reconcile them. The method is this. You take a hundred leaders of each party, you dispose them into couples of such whose heads are nearest of a size; then let two nice operators saw off the occiput of each couple at the same time, in such a manner that the brain may be equally divided. Let the occiputs thus cut off be interchanged, applying each to the head of his opposite party-man. It seems indeed to be a work that requireth some exactness, but the professor assured us that if it were dexterously performed the cure would be infallible. For he argued thus: that the two half brains being left to debate the matter between themselves within the space of one skull, would soon come to a good understanding, and produce that moderation, as well as regularity of thinking so much be wished for in the heads of those who imagine they come into the world only to watch and govern its motion: and as to the difference of brains in quantity or quality among those who are directors in faction, the doctor assured us from his own knowledge that it was a perfect trifle.

I heard a very warm debate between two professors, about the most commodious and effectual ways and means of raising money without grieving the subject. The first affirmed the justest method would be to lay a certain tax upon vices and folly, and the sum fixed upon every man to be rated after the fairest manner by a jury of his neighbours. The second was of an opinion directly contrary, to tax those qualities of body and mind for which men chiefly value themselves, the rate to be more or less according to the degrees of excelling, the decision whereof should be left entirely to their own breast. The highest tax was upon men who are the greatest favourites of the other sex, and the assessments according to the number and natures of the favours they have received; for which they are allowed to be their own vouchers. Wit, valour, and politeness were likewise proposed to be largely taxed, and collected in the same manner, by every person's giving his own word for the quantum of what he possessed. But as to honour, justice, wisdom, and learning, they should not be taxed at all, because they are qualifications of so singular a kind, that no man will either allow them in his neighbour, or value them in himself.

The women were proposed to be taxed according to their beauty and skill in dressing, wherein they had the same privilege with the men, to be determined by their own judgment. But constancy, chastity, good sense, and good nature were not rated, because they would not bear the charge of collecting.

To keep senators in the interest of the crown, it was proposed that the members should raffle for employments, every man first taking an oath, and giving security that he would vote for the court, whether he won or no; after which the losers had in their turn the liberty of raffling upon the next vacancy. Thus hope and expectation would be kept alive, none would complain of broken promises, but impute their disappointments wholly to fortune whose shoulders are broader and stronger than those of a ministry.

Another professor showed me a large paper of instructions for discovering plots and conspiracies against the government. He advised great statesmen to examine into the diet of all suspected persons; their times of eating; upon which side they lay in bed; with which hand they wiped their posteriors; to take a strict view of their excrements, and, from the colour, the odour, the taste, the consistence, the crudeness or maturity of digestion, form a judgment of their thoughts and designs. Because men are never so serious, thoughtful, and intent, as when they are at stool, which he found by frequent experiment; for in such conjunctures, when he used merely as a trial to consider which was the best way of murdering the king, his ordure would have a tincture of green, but quite different when he thought only of raising an insurrection or burning the metropolis.

The whole discourse was written with great acuteness, containing many observations both curious and useful for politicians, but as I conceived not altogether complete. This I ventured to tell the author, and offered if he pleased to supply him with some additions. He received my proposition with more compliance than is usual among writers, especially those of the projecting species, professing he would be glad to receive farther information.

I told him that in the kingdom of Tribnia, by the natives called Langden, where I had sojourned some time in my travels, the bulk of the people consist in a manner wholly of discoverers, witnesses, informers, accusers, prosecutors, evidences, swearers, together with their several subservient and subaltern instruments, all under the colours and conduct of ministers of state and their deputies. The plots in that kingdom are usually the workmanship of those persons who desire to raise their own characters of profound politicians, to restore new vigour to a crazy administration, to stifle or divert general discontents, to fill their pockets with forfeiture, and raise or sink the opinion of public credit, as either shall best answer their private advantage. It is first agreed and settled among them, what suspected persons shall be accused of a plot; then, effectual care is taken to secure all their letters and papers, and put the criminals in chains. These papers are delivered to a set of artists, very dexterous in finding out the mysterious meanings of words, syllables, and letters. For instance, they can discover a close-stool to signify a privy council; a flock of geese, a senate; a lame dog, an invader; a codshead, a— —; the plague, a standing army; a buzzard, a prime minister; the gout, a high priest; a gibbet, a secretary of state; a chamber-pot, a committee of grandees; a sieve, a court lady; a broom, a revolution; a mouse-trap, an employment; a bottomless pit, the treasury; a sink, the court; a cap and bells, a favourite; a broken reed, a court of justice; an empty tun, a general; a running sore, the administration.

When this method fails, they have two others more effectual, which the learned among them call acrostics and anagrams. First they can decipher all initial letters into political meanings. Thus, *N.* shall signify a plot; *B.* a regiment of horse; *L.* a fleet at sea; or secondly by transposing the letters of the alphabet in any suspected paper, they can discover the deepest designs of a discontented party. So for example if I should say in a letter to a friend, *Our brother* Tom *has just got the piles,* a skilful decipherer would discover that the same letters which compose that sentence may be analysed into the following words: *Resist, a plot is brought home; The tour.* And this is the anagrammatic method.

The professor made me great acknowledgments for communicating these observations, and promised to make honourable mention of me in his treatise.

I saw nothing in this country that could invite me to a longer continuance, and began to think of returning home to England.

Imaginary Voyages in the
Other Direction

In the eighteenth century inventors began to rival scientists in their impact on the way Western man looked at his world and on his relationship with his environment.

The progress of scientific discovery went on without pause: Du Fay worked out the theory of electrical charges and Franklin gave them names; Linnaeus published his taxonomical masterpiece, *Systema Naturae;* Buffon announced his theory of the formation of the planets by collision of a large heavenly object with the sun and Kant his theory of gaseous condensation; Lavoisier discovered the true nature of combustion; Gauss developed non-Euclidian geometry; and Hutton founded modern geology.

Meanwhile, inventors produced two invaluable aids to navigation, the sextant and the chronometer, and the threshing machine, the weaving machine, the spinning jenny, the circular saw, the steel pen, the steamboat, the manned balloon and the parachute, the iron plow, and power loom, the cotton gin, lithography, and mass production through interchangeable parts. And the most important invention of all, the steam engine.

Inventions were the response of ingenious minds to needs of one sort or another: the need for greater efficiency, the need for greater profit, or the need to do something that man was unable to do up to that time. The use of coal, for instance, came when England was deforested by men seeking firewood, but water seeped into coal mines and made many unusable. Savery and Newcomen invented machines that used steam to pump out the mines, and then James Watt improved their work so radically that he has been credited with inventing the steam engine. By 1769 Watt had produced his first working engine, and soon new applications were being discovered: the steam boat, foundries and textile mills, the steam locomotive, and an apparently endless series of uses for chemical power rather than human labor.

In combination with other inventions, the result was the Industrial Revolution. Cottage industries were unable to compete. Workers, including many farmers, flocked to the new factories. Towns absorbed them. The blessings and the evils of industrialization descended upon humanity. An

economic boon with social problems as a side effect, the Industrial Revolution provided an environment that encouraged expansion, new inventions, and further economic development. Man was set upon a path of
change that could be reversed only at great human sacrifice of lives and the
quality of life.

In addition, the Industrial Revolution created a middle class, a newly literate middle class, and the middle class, in turn, created the modern novel.
A steadily growing reading public demanded information rather than
well-turned phrases and good taste. The *Tatler* and the *Spectator* were followed by a series of popular journals, and the new journalism that appealed
to the new readers attracted new kinds of writers who could make a kind of
subsistence living out of writing. The period came to be called Grub Street.

Daniel Defoe (1660–1731) came out of the period. He turned to fiction
at the age of almost sixty and wrote highly detailed fictitious autobiogra-
phies of adventurers or rogues—men and women of his own class trying to
achieve success, which they defined as accumulation of property. His major work, *Robinson Crusoe* (1719), was the only one of his books to be
widely read outside the middle class.

The episodic narratives of Defoe and the satirical narratives of Swift led
toward what has been called the first English novel, *Pamela* (1740) by
Samuel Richardson (1689–1761). *Pamela,* in turn, would lead to the greater
triumphs of Henry Fielding (1707–1754), Tobias Smollett (1721–1771),
and Laurence Sterne (1713–1768).

Meanwhile the great Danish writer Ludvig Holberg (1684–1754), who
wrote histories, plays (he was called "the Molière of the North"), and essays, wrote a notable imaginary voyage. Unlike the earlier examples, however, Holberg turned inward. His voyage was not a trip to the moon but to
the center of the earth. But like the others, it had an ulterior purpose. *The
Journey of Niels Klim to the World Underground* (1741) was intended, Holberg wrote, "to correct popular errors and to distinguish the semblance of
virtue and vice from the reality." The book was written in Latin but soon
translated into German, Danish, and English.

The story relates how Niels Klim, an impoverished university graduate,
seeks to make a reputation for himself by exploring a mysterious cave in
Norway, falls through the earth, orbits a central planet, fights off a griffin
and is pulled by it to the planet where he discovers intelligent, mobile trees
who consider him so flighty and shallow that he is good for nothing but
carrying messages, tries to get a law passed overthrowing the equality of
the sexes, and is condemned to be flown to the firmament (the inside of the
earth), where he encounters all kinds of civilizations of monkeys, tigers,

bears, gamecocks, bass fiddles, ice creatures, and finally humans. For the humans he trains cavalry, manufactures muskets, builds ships, and leads them into battle, where he is victorious. He succeeds the emperor and subdues most of the kingdoms of the firmament before power corrupts him, his people rebel against his cruelty, and trying to hide, he falls back through a hole in a cave and finds himself in Norway again.

As in *Gulliver's Travels, Journey to the World Underground* has plenty of story to hold the reader's attention. This is one of the two new characteristics the imaginary voyage has developed; the other is credibility achieved through documentation by realistic prefaces, letters, and other kinds of evidence, through concrete detail, and through believable heroes. All of these would be important in the transition of the imaginary voyage to science fiction.

From The Journey to the World Underground

BY LUDVIG HOLBERG

CHAPTER I

THE AUTHOR'S DESCENT TO THE SUBTERRANEAN WORLD

In the year 1664, after I had passed my several examinations in the University of Copenhagen, and had deservedly obtained the character, which is there called laudable, by the votes of my judges, as well philosophers as divines, I prepared for my return into my native country, and accordingly put myself aboard a ship bound for Bergen in Norway, dignified indeed with various marks of honour from the gentlemen of the several faculties, but in my fortunes quite impoverished. This was an evil that attended myself as well as several of the Norwegian students, who returned from the study of the arts and sciences into their own country stripped of all they were worth. As we had a pretty brisk gale, after a voyage of six days we arrived at Bergen harbour. Being thus restored to my country, something wiser indeed, though by no means richer, I was supported for a time at the expense of my near relations, and led a precarious sort of life, yet not altogether indolent and inactive. For in order to clear up by experience some points of natural philosophy, the study I had devoted myself to, I rambled over every corner of the province with an insatiable curiosity to explore the nature of the Earth, and to search into the very bowels of our mountains. No rock so steep but I climbed it, no cavern so hideous and deep but I made a descent into it, to try if haply I could discover anything curious and worth the inquiry of a philosopher. For there are a multitude of things in our country of Norway hardly ever seen or heard of, which if France, Italy, Germany, or any other country so fruitful of the marvelous could boast of, nothing could be more talked of, nothing more sifted and examined.

Among those things which to me appeared most worthy of observation there was a large and deep cave upon the top of that mountain which the natives call Floïen. And because the mouth of the cave used to send forth a gentle murmuring sound, and that too by intervals, as if by its frequent sighs its jaws were now shut, and now opened; hence the literati of Bergen, and particularly the celebrated Master Abeline, and Master Edvard, one of our first geniuses in astronomy and natural philosophy, imagined this affair highly worthy of a philosophical inquiry; and since they themselves were too old for such an enterprise, they excited the younger inhabitants to a closer examination of the nature of the cavern; especially as at stated intervals, after the manner of human respiration, the sound being sometime withheld, issued out with a certain proportional force.

What with these discourses, and what with my own natural inclination, I formed a design of entering into this cavern, and communicated my intention to some of my friends. But they by no means approved of it, plainly declaring that it was a wild and frantic undertaking. But all they could say, so far was it from extinguishing, that it did not even damp the ardour of my mind; and their advice, instead of weakening, administered fuel to my curiosity. For that eagerness with which I pursued the study of nature inspired me to face every danger, and the straitness of my private circumstances gave a spur to my natural inclination. For my own substance was quite wasted, and it seemed to me the greatest hardship to live in a state of dependence in a country where all hopes of preferment were cut off, where I beheld myself condemned to poverty, and every avenue to honour and advantage entirely stopped, unless I would make my way by some flagrant act of dishonour or immorality.

Thus resolved, and having got together what was requisite for such an exploit, upon a Thursday morning, when the heavens were all serene and cloudless, I left the city soon after twilight, to the end that having finished my observations, I might return again that same day; because, being ignorant of futurity, it was not possible I should foresee that I, like another Phaeton, should be flung upon another world, not to revisit my native soil till after a ten years' peregrination.

This expedition was undertaken in the year of our Lord 1665, Hans Munthe and Lars Sorensen being consuls of Bergen, and Christian Bertelsen and Lars Sand being senators. I went out attended by four fellows I had hired, who brought with them such ropes and iron crooks as would be necessary to descend by. We went directly to Sandvik, the most commodious way to climb the mountain. Having with difficulty reached the top, we came to the place where was the fatal cave, and being tired with so troublesome a journey, we all sat down to breakfast.

'Twas then my mind, foreboding as it were the approaching evil, first began to be dismayed. Therefore, turning to my companions, "Will anyone," says I, "undertake this task?" But no reply being made, my ardour, that had languished, kindled anew. I ordered them to fasten the rope about me, and thus equipped, I commended my soul to Almighty God. Being now just ready to be let down, I gave my companions to understand what I would have done, viz., that they should continue letting down the rope till they heard me cry out, upon which signal they should stop, and if I persisted to cry out, that then they should immediately draw me up again. In my right hand I held my harpoon, or iron hook, an instrument that might be of use to me to remove whatever might obstruct my passage, and also to keep my body suspended equally between the sides of the cavern. But scarce had I descended so low as about ten or twelve cubits, when the rope broke. This accident was discovered to me by the sudden outcries of the men I had hired. But their noise soon died away; for with an amazing velocity I was hurried down into the abyss, like a second Pluto, allowing my harpoon to be a sceptre.

For about the fourth part of an hour (as near as I could guess, considering the great consternation I must be in) I was in total darkness, and in the very bosom of night; when at length a thin small light, like twilight, broke in upon me, and I beheld at last a bright serene firmament. I ignorantly thought, therefore, that either by the repercussion or opposite action of the subterranean air, or that by the force of some contrary wind, I had been thrown back, and that the cave had vomited me up again. But neither the sun which I then surveyed, nor the heavens, nor heavenly bodies were at all known to me, since they were considerably less than those of ours. I concluded therefore that either all that whole mass of new heavens existed solely in imagination, excited by the vertigo my head had undergone, or else that I was arrived at the mansions of the Blessed. But this last opinion I soon rejected with scorn, since I viewed myself armed with a harpoon, and dragging a mighty length of rope after me, knowing full well that a man just going to Paradise has no occasion for a rope or a harpoon, and that the celestial inhabitants could not possibly be pleased with a dress which looked as if I intended, after the example of the Titans, to take Heaven by violence, and to expel them from their divine abodes. At last, after the maturest consideration, I fell to imagining that I was sunk into the subterranean world, and that the conjectures of those men are right who hold the Earth to be hollow, and that within the shell or outward crust there is another lesser globe, and another firmament adorned with lesser sun, stars, and planets. And the event discovered that this conjecture was right.

That violence with which I was hurried headlong had now continued for some time, when at length I perceived that it languished gradually in proportion to my approach towards a certain planet, which was the first thing I met with. That same planet increased so sensibly in bulk or magnitude that at last, without much difficulty, I could plainly distinguish mountains, valleys, and seas through that thicker atmosphere with which it was surrounded.

Then I perceived that I did not only swim in a celestial matter or ether, but that my motion which had hitherto been perpendicular was now altered into a circular one. At this my hair stood on end, for I was full of apprehension lest I should be transformed into a planet, or into a satellite of the neighbouring planet, and so be whirled about in an everlasting rotation. But when I reflected that by this metamorphosis my dignity would suffer no great diminution, and that a heavenly body, or at least an attendant upon a heavenly body, would surely move with equal solemnity to a famished philosopher, I took courage again, especially when I found from the benefit of that pure celestial ether that I was no longer pressed by hunger or thirst. Yet upon recollecting that I had in my pocket some of that sort of bread which the people of Bergen call *bolken,* and which is of an oval or oblong figure. I resolved to take it out and make an experiment whether in this situation I had any appetite. But at the first bite perceiving it was quite nauseous, I threw it away as a thing to all intents and purposes useless. The bread thus cast away was not only suspended in air, but (what was very marvelous to behold) it described a little circular motion round my own body. And from thence I learned the true laws of motion, by which it comes to pass that all bodies placed in equilibrium naturally affect a circular motion. Upon this, instead of deploring my wretchedness, as I had done, for being thus the sport of Fortune, I began to plume a little, finding that I was not only a simple planet, but such a planet as would have a perpetual attendant conforming itself to my motions, insomuch that I should have the honour to be reckoned in the number of the greater heavenly bodies or stars of the first magnitude. And to confess my weakness, so elated was I that if I had then met any of our consuls or senators of Bergen, I should have received them with a supercilious air, should have regarded them as atoms, and accounted them unworthy to be saluted or honoured with a touch of my harpoon.

For almost three days I remained in this condition. For as without any intermission I was whirled about the planet that was next me, I could distinguish day from night; and observing the subterranean sun to rise, and set, and retire gradually out of my sight, I could easily perceive when it was night, though it was not altogether such as it is with us. For at sunset the whole face of the firmament appeared of a bright purple, not unlike the countenance of our moon sometimes. This I took to be occasioned by the inner surface of our Earth, which borrowed that light from the subterranean sun, which sun was placed in the center. This hypothesis I framed to myself, being not altogether a stranger to the study of astronomy.

But while I was thus amused with the thoughts of being in the neighbourhood of the gods, and was congratulating myself as a new constellation, together with my satellite that surrounded me, and hoped in a short time to be inserted in the catalogue of stars by the astronomers of the neighbouring planet, behold! an enormous winged monster hovered near me, sometimes on this side, now on that side, and by and by over my head. At first view I took it for one of the twelve heavenly signs in this new world, and accordingly hoped that, if the conjecture was right, it would be that of Virgo, since out of the whole number of the twelve signs, that alone could yield me, in my unhappy solitude, some delight and comfort. But when the figure approached nearer to me, it appeared to be a grim, huge griffin. So great was my terror that, unmindful of my starry dignity to which I was newly advanced, in that disorder of my soul I drew out my university testimonial, which I happened to have in my pocket, to signify to this terrible adversary that I had passed my academical examination, that I was a graduate student, and could plead the privilege of my university against anyone that should attack me.

But my disorder beginning to cool, when I came to myself, I could not but condemn my folly. For it was yet a matter of doubt to what purpose this griffin should approach me, whether as an enemy or a friend; or, what is more likely, whether, led by the sole novelty of the thing, he had only a mind to feast his curiosity. For the sight of a human creature whirling about in air, bearing in his right hand a harpoon, and drawing after him a great length of rope like a tail, was really a phenomenon which might excite even a brute creature to behold the spectacle. For the unusual figure I then exhibited gave to the inhabitants of the globe round which I revolved an occasion of divers conjectures and conversations concerning me, as I afterwards learned; for the philosophers and mathematicians would have me to be a comet, being positive that my rope was the tail; and some there were who, from the appearance of so rare a meteor, prognosticated some impending misfortune, a plague, a famine, or some other such extraordinary catastrophe; some also went further, and delineated my figure, such as it appeared to them at that distance, in very accurate drawings; so that I was described, defined, painted, and engraved before ever I touched their globe. All this I afterward heard with no small pleasure, and even laughter, when I was conveyed to that planet, and had learned their language.

It must be noted that sometimes there appear new stars, which the Subterraneans call *sciscisi,* or blazing stars, which they describe as something looking horrid with fiery hair, and after the manner of our comets, bushy on the top, so as that it projects in form of a long beard; and these, as in our world, so in that, are reckoned ominous.

But to resume my history. The griffin advanced so near at last as to incommode me by the flapping of his wings, and even did not scruple to attack my leg with his teeth, so that now it openly appeared with what disposition he pursued me. Upon this I began to attack this troublesome animal with arms and grasping my harpoon with both my hands, I soon curbed the insolence of my foe, obliging him to look about for a way to escape; and at last, since he persisted to annoy me, I darted my harpoon with such a force into the back of the animal between his wings, that I could not pull it out again. The wounded griffin, setting up a horrible cry, fell headlong upon the planet. As for myself, quite weary of this starry station, this new dignity, which I saw exposed to infinite hazards and evils, I held to the harpoon and fell with him. And now this circular motion I had described altered once more into a perpendicular one. And being for some time agitated and tossed with great violence by the opposite motions of a thicker air, at length by an easy, gentle descent, I alighted upon the aforesaid planet, together with the griffin, who soon after died of his wound.

It was night when I was conveyed to that planet. This I could gather from the sole absence of the sun, and not from the darkness; for there still remained so much light that I could distinctly read my university testimonial by it. That light by night arises from the inward surface of our Earth, whose surface reflects a light like that of the moon among us. And hence, with respect to light alone, there is little difference between the nights and days, only that the sun is absent, and his absence makes the nights a little colder.

Visitors from Space

The eighteenth century brought Enlightenment to the world—the rationalist, liberal, humanitarian, and scientific approach to life, knowledge, and government that gave that era the name of The Age of Reason. It was a new direction in humanity's evaluation of the universe and its position in it that had its origins in the Renaissance recovery of classical manuscripts and philosophies. Thomas Aquinas, in the thirteenth century, adopted Aristotelian logic to defend Catholic dogma; so-called "humanists" emerged in Italy and France in the fourteenth and fifteenth centuries to argue that God was best worshiped by celebrating His crowning creation, humanity. In the sixteenth century François Rabelais, in *Gargantua and Pantagruel* (1532–1562), ridiculed many religious doctrines while Martin Luther was offering a revolutionary alternative to Catholicism and Michel de Montagne in his *Essays* created the foundations for cultural relativism with his repeated question, "What do I know?" In the seventeenth century Galileo displaced Earth as the center of the universe.

In the seventeenth century, as well, René Descartes made a valiant effort to defend faith with logic, but Enlightenment philosophers added something radical to the mix: common sense supported by observation. Though known as the Age of Reason, the eighteenth century also could have been called the Age of Revolution, since it featured two of the three great revolutions in human history, the American and the French (the Russian is the third). One of the major figures whose speech and writings led up to the French Revolution was François Marie Arouet de Voltaire (1694–1778).

The eighteenth century was a period of change in many ways, energized by the wealth brought back from Asia and the Americas to a rising middle class. The ideals of individualism, freedom, and change began to replace the older values of community, authority, and tradition upheld by the Church, the King, and the aristocrats. Voltaire was one of the aristocrats, dining at their tables, taking an aristocratic mistress, counseling monarchs, and charming everyone with his wit.

But wit has its enemies, and Voltaire was unjustly imprisoned twice in his youthful years and then exiled to England where he added an admiration for English liberalism to his hatred of judicial arbitrariness. When he returned to France he wrote tragedies for the stage, including *Brutus* (1730) and *Zaïre* (1732), and *Letters Concerning the English Nation* (1733). After the death of his mistress in 1749, Voltaire went to live at the court of Prussia but left in 1753 after quarreling with Frederick II and settled on an estate near Geneva in Switzerland. He wrote *The Age of Louis XIV* (1751) and *Essay on Manners* (1756), but most important the *Philosophical Dictionary* (1764), setting down his political and religious concerns, and his satirical masterpiece *Candide* (1759).

Candide's only relationship to science fiction is its naïve hero's eventful journey to explore the truth of his tutor's (Dr. Pangloss's) belief that "all is for the best in this best of all possible worlds." Seven years earlier Voltaire published *Micromegas* (1752), which tells of a journey not from here to there but there to here by a giant creature from Sirius who comes to earth accompanied by a companion, a six-thousand-foot dwarf from Saturn. Only with great difficulty do they detect life on Earth, but they finally converse with human beings and find their ideas as petty as their height. The Age of Enlightenment prepared the way for the age of science fiction.

From Micromegas

BY FRANÇOIS MARIE AROUET DE VOLTAIRE

CHAPTER 1. A VOYAGE TO THE
PLANET SATURN BY A NATIVE OF SIRIUS

In one of the planets that revolve round the star known by the name of Sirius was a certain young gentleman of promising parts, whom I had the honor to be acquainted with in his last voyage to this our little ant-hill. His name was Micromegas, an appellation suited to all great men, and his stature amounted to eight leagues in height, that is, twenty-four thousand geometrical paces of five feet each.

Some of your mathematicians, a set of people always useful to the public, will perhaps instantly seize the pen and calculate that Mr. Micromegas, inhabitant of the country of Sirius, being from head to foot four and twenty thousand paces in length, making one hundred and twenty thousand royal feet, that we, denizens of this earth, being at a medium little more than five feet high, and our globe nine thousand leagues in circumference; these things being premised, they will then conclude that the periphery of the globe which produced him must be exactly one and twenty millions six hundred thousand times greater than that of this, our tiny ball. Nothing in nature is more simple and common. The dominions of some sovereigns of Germany or Italy, which may be compassed in half an hour, when compared with the Ottoman, Russian, or Chinese empires, are no other than faint instances of the prodigious difference that nature has made in the scale of beings. The stature of his excellency being of these extraordinary dimensions, all our artists will agree that the measure around his body might amount to fifty thousand royal feet, a very agreeable and just proportion.

His nose being equal in length to one-third of his face, and his jolly countenance engrossing one-seventh part of his height, it must be owned that the nose of this Sirian was six thousand three hundred and thirty-three royal feet, to a hair, which was to be demonstrated. With regard to his understanding, it is one of the best cultivated I have known. He is perfectly well acquainted with abundance of things, some of which are of his own invention; for, when his age did not exceed two hundred and fifty years, he studied according to the custom of the country, at the most celebrated university of the whole planet, and by the force of his genius discovered upwards of fifty propositions of Euclid, having the advantage by more than eighteen of Blaise Pascal, who (as we are told by his own sister), demonstrated two and thirty for his amusement and then left off, choosing rather to be an indifferent philosopher than a great mathematician.

About the four hundred and fiftieth year of his age, or latter end of his childhood, he dissected a great number of small insects not more than one hundred feet in diameter, which are not perceivable by ordinary microscopes, on which he composed a very curious treatise, which involved him in some trouble. The mufti of the nation, though very old and very ignorant, made shift to discover in his book certain lemmas that were suspicious, unseemly, rash, heretic, and unsound, and prosecuted him with great animosity; for the subject of the author's inquiry was whether, in the world of Sirius, there was any difference between the substantial forms of a flea and a snail.

Micromegas defended his philosophy with such spirit as made all the female sex his proselytes; and the process lasted two hundred and twenty years; at the end of which time, in consequence of the mufti's interest, the book was condemned by judges who had never read it, and the author expelled from court for the term of eight hundred years.

Not much affected at his banishment from a court that teemed with nothing but turmoils and trifles, he made a very humorous song upon the mufti, who gave himself no trouble about the matter, and set out on his travels from planet to planet in order (as the saying is) to improve his mind and finish his education. Those who never travel but in a post-chaise or berlin, will doubtless be astonished at the equipages used above, for we that strut upon this little mole-hill are at a loss to conceive anything that surpasses our own customs. But our traveller was a wonderful adept in the laws of gravitation, together with the whole force of attraction and repulsion, and made such seasonable use of his knowledge that sometimes by the help of a sunbeam, and sometimes by the convenience of a comet, he and his retinue glided from sphere to sphere, as the bird hops from one bough to another. He in a very little time posted through the milky way, and I am obliged to own he saw not a twinkle of those stars supposed to adorn that fair empyrean which the illustrious Dr. Derham brags to have observed through his telescope. Not that I pretend to say the doctor was mistaken. God forbid! But Micromegas was upon the spot, an exceeding good observer, and I have no mind to contradict any man. Be that as it may, after many windings and turnings, he arrived at the planet Saturn, and, accustomed as he was to the

sight of novelties, he could not for his life repress a supercilious and conceited smile, which often escapes the wisest philosopher, when he perceived the smallness of that globe and the diminutive size of its inhabitants;
for really Saturn is but about nine hundred times larger than this our earth,
and the people of that country mere dwarfs, about a thousand fathoms high.
In short, he at first derided those poor pygmies, just as an Indian fiddler
laughs at the music of Lully, at his first arrival in Paris; but as this Sirian
was a person of good sense, he soon perceived that a thinking being may
not be altogether ridiculous, even though he is not quite six thousand feet
high; and therefore he became familiar with them, after they had ceased to
wonder at his extraordinary appearance. In particular, he contracted an intimate friendship with the secretary of the Academy of Saturn, a man of
good understanding, who, though in truth he had invented nothing of his
own, gave a very good account of the inventions of others, and enjoyed in
peace the reputation of a little poet and great calculator. And here, for the
edification of the reader, I will repeat a very singular conversation that one
day passed between Mr. Secretary and Micromegas.

CHAPTER 2. THE CONVERSATION BETWEEN
MICROMEGAS AND THE INHABITANT OF SATURN

His excellency having laid himself down, and the secretary approached his
nose:

"It must be confessed," said Micromegas, "that nature is full of variety."

"Yes," replied the Saturnian, "nature is like a parterre, whose flowers—"

"Pshaw!" cried the other, "a truce with your parterres."

"It is," resumed the secretary, "like an assembly of fair and brown
women, whose dresses—"

"What a plague have I to do with your brunettes?" said our traveller.

"Then it is like a gallery of pictures, the strokes of which—"

"Not at all," answered Micromegas, "I tell you, once for all, nature is like
nature, and comparisons are odious."

"Well, to please you," said the secretary—

"I won't be pleased," replied the Sirian, "I want to be instructed; begin,
therefore, without further preamble, and tell me how many senses the people of this world enjoy."

"We have seventy and two," said the academician, "but we are daily
complaining of the small number, as our imagination transcends our wants,
for, with the seventy-two senses, our five moons and ring, we find our-

selves very much restricted; and notwithstanding our curiosity, and the no small number of those passions that result from these few senses, we have still time enough to be tired of idleness."

"I sincerely believe what you say," cried Micromegas, "for, though we Sirians have near a thousand different senses, there still remains a certain vague desire, an unaccountable inquietude incessantly admonishing us of our own unimportance, and giving us to understand that there are other beings who are much our superiors in point of perfection. I have travelled a little, and seen mortals both above and below myself in the scale of being, but I have met with none who had not more desire than necessity, and more want than gratification. Perhaps I shall one day arrive in some country where naught is wanting, but hitherto I have had no certain information of such a happy land."

The Saturnian and his guest exhausted themselves in conjectures upon this subject, and after abundance of argumentation equally ingenious and uncertain, were fain to return to matter of fact.

"To what age do you commonly live?" said the Sirian.

"Lackaday! a mere trifle," replied the little gentleman.

"It is the very same case with us," resumed the other, "the shortness of life is our daily complaint, so that this must be a universal law in nature."

"Alas!" cried the Saturnian, "few, very few on this globe outlive five hundred great revolutions of the sun (these, according to our way of reckoning, amount to about fifteen thousand years). So, you see, we in a manner begin to die the very moment we are born; our existence is no more than a point, our duration an instant, and our globe an atom. Scarce do we begin to learn a little, when death intervenes before we can profit by experience. For my own part, I am deterred from laying schemes when I consider myself as a single drop in the midst of an immense ocean. I am particularly ashamed, in your presence, of the ridiculous figure I make among my fellow-creatures."

To this declaration Micromegas replied:

"If you were not a philosopher, I should be afraid of mortifying your pride by telling you that the term of our lives is seven hundred times longer than the length of your existence; but you are very sensible that when the texture of the body is resolved, in order to reanimate nature in another form, which is the consequence of what we call death—when that moment of change arrives, there is not the least difference betwixt having lived a whole eternity or a single day. I have been in some countries where the people live a thousand times longer than with us, and yet they murmured at the shortness of their time. But one will find everywhere some few persons of good sense, who know how to make the best of their portion and thank the author of nature for his bounty. There is a profusion of variety scattered through the universe, and yet there is an admirable vein of uniformity that runs through the whole; for example, all thinking beings are different among themselves, though at bottom they resemble one another in the powers and passions of the soul. Matter, though interminable, hath different properties in every sphere. How many principal attributes do you reckon in the matter of this world?"

"If you mean those properties," said the Saturnian, "without which we believe this our globe could not subsist, we reckon in all three hundred, such as extent, impenetrability, motion, gravitation, divisibility, et cætera."

"That small number," replied the traveller, "probably answers the views of the Creator on this your narrow sphere. I adore His Wisdom in all His works. I see infinite variety, but everywhere proportion. Your globe is small, so are the inhabitants. You have few sensations, because your matter is endued with few properties. These are the works of unerring providence. Of what color does your sun appear when accurately examined?"

"Of a yellowish white," answered the Saturnian, "and in separating one of his rays we find it contains seven colors."

"Our sun," said the Sirian, "is of a reddish hue, and we have no less than thirty-nine original colors. Among all the suns I have seen there is no sort of resemblance, and in this sphere of yours there is not one face like another."

After divers questions of this nature he asked how many substances, essentially different, they counted in the world of Saturn, and understood that they numbered but thirty, such as God, space, matter, beings endowed with sense and extension, beings that have extension, sense, and reflection; thinking beings who have no extension; those that are penetrable; those that are impenetrable, and also all others. But this Saturnian philosopher was prodigiously astonished when the Sirian told him they had no less than three hundred, and that he himself had discovered three thousand more in the course of his travels. In short, after having communicated to each other what they knew, and even what they did not know, and argued during a complete revolution of the sun, they resolved to set out together on a small philosophical tour.

CHAPTER 3. THE VOYAGE OF
THESE INHABITANTS OF OTHER WORLDS

Our two philosophers were just ready to embark for the atmosphere of Saturn, with a large provision of mathematical instruments, when the Saturnian's mistress, having got an inkling of their design, came all in tears to make her protest. She was a handsome brunette, though not above six hundred and three score fathoms high; but her agreeable attractions made amends for the smallness of her nature.

"Ah! Cruel man," cried she, "after a courtship of fifteen hundred years, when at length I surrendered and became your wife, and scarce have passed two hundred more in thy embraces, to leave me thus, before the honeymoon is over, and go a-rambling with a giant of another world! Go, go, thou art a mere virtuoso, devoid of tenderness and love! If thou were a true Saturnian, thou wouldst be faithful and invariable. Ah! whither art thou going? what is thy design? Our five moons are not so inconstant, nor our ring so changeable as thee! But take this along with thee, henceforth I ne'er shall love another man."

The little gentleman embraced and wept over her, notwithstanding his philosophy; and the lady, after having swooned with great decency, went to console herself with more agreeable company.

Meanwhile our two virtuosi set out, and in one jump leaped upon the ring, which they found pretty flat, according to the ingenious guess of an illustrious inhabitant of this our little earth. From thence they easily slipped from moon to moon; and a comet chancing to pass, they sprang upon it with all their servants and apparatus. Thus carried about one hundred and fifty millions of leagues, they met with the satellites of Jupiter, and arrived upon the body of the planet itself, where they continued a whole year; during which they learned some very curious secrets, which would actually be sent to the press, were it not for fear of the gentlemen inquisitors, who have found among them some corollaries very hard of digestion. Nevertheless, I have read the manuscript in the library of the illustrious archbishop of—, who, with that generosity and goodness which should ever be commended, has granted me permission to peruse his books; wherefore I promised he shall have a long article in the next edition of Moréri, and I shall not forget the young gentlemen, his sons, who give us such pleasing hopes of seeing perpetuated the race of their illustrious father. But to return to our travellers. When they took leave of Jupiter, they traversed a space of about one hundred millions of leagues, and coasting along the planet Mars, which is well known to be five times smaller than our little earth, they descried two moons subservient to that orb which have escaped the observation of all our astronomers. I know Father Castel will write, and that pleasantly enough, against the existence of these two moons; but I entirely refer myself to those who reason by analogy. Those worthy philosophers are very sensible that Mars, which is at such a distance from the sun, must be in a very uncomfortable situation, without the benefit of a couple of moons. Be that as it may, our gentlemen found the planet so small that they were afraid they should not find room to take a little repose, so that they pursued their journey like two travellers who despise the paltry accommodation of a village and push forward to the next market town. But the Sirian and his companion soon repented of their delicacy, for they journeyed a long time without finding a resting-place, till at length they discerned a small speck, which was the Earth. Coming from Jupiter, they could not but be moved with compassion at the sight of this miserable spot, upon which, however, they resolved to land, lest they should be a second time disappointed. They accordingly moved toward the tail of the comet, where, finding an aurora borealis ready to set sail, they embarked, and arrived on the northern coast of the Baltic on the fifth day of July, new style, in the year 1737.

CHAPTER 4. WHAT BEFELL
THEM UPON THIS OUR GLOBE

Having taken some repose, and being desirous of reconnoitering the narrow field in which they were, they traversed it at once from north to south. Every step of the Sirian and his attendants measured about thirty thousand royal feet, whereas the dwarf of Saturn, whose stature did not exceed a thousand fathoms, followed at a distance quite out of breath; because, for every single stride of his companion, he was obliged to make twelve good steps at least. The reader may figure to himself (if we are allowed to make such comparisons) a very little rough spaniel dodging after a captain of the Prussian grenadiers.

As those strangers walked at a good pace, they compassed the globe in six and thirty hours; the sun, it is true, or rather the earth, describes the same space in the course of one day; but it must be observed that it is much easier to turn upon an axis than to walk afoot. Behold them then returned to the spot from whence they had set out, after having discovered that almost imperceptible sea, which is called the Mediterranean, and the other narrow pond that surrounds this mole-hill, under the denomination of the great ocean, in wading through which the dwarf had never wet his mid-leg, while the other scarce moistened his heel. In going and coming through both hemispheres, they did all that lay in their power to discover whether or not the globe was inhabited. They stooped, they lay down, they groped in every corner; but their eyes and hands were not at all proportioned to the small beings that crawl upon this earth, and, therefore, they could not find the smallest reason to suspect that we and our fellow-citizens of this globe had the honor to exist.

The dwarf, who sometimes judged too hastily, concluded at once that there were no living creatures upon earth, and his chief reason was that he had seen nobody. But Micromegas, in a polite manner, made him sensible of the unjust conclusion:

"For," said he, "with your diminutive eyes you cannot see certain stars of the fiftieth magnitude, which I easily perceive; and do you take it for granted that no such stars exist?"

"But I have groped with great care," replied the dwarf.

"Then your sense of feeling must be bad," said the other.

"But this globe," said the dwarf, "is ill contrived, and so irregular in its form as to be quite ridiculous. The whole together looks like a chaos. Do but observe these little rivulets; not one of them runs in a straight line; and these ponds which are neither round, square, nor oval, nor indeed of any regular figure; together with these little sharp pebbles (meaning the mountains) that roughen the whole surface of the globe, and have torn all the skin from my feet. Besides, pray take notice of the shape of the whole, how it flattens at the poles, and turns round the sun in an awkward oblique manner, so that the polar circles cannot possibly be cultivated. Truly, what makes me believe there is no inhabitant on this sphere is a full persuasion that no sensible being would live in such a disagreeable place."

"What then?" said Micromegas; "perhaps the beings that inhabit it come not under that denomination; but, to all appearance, it was not made for nothing. Everything here seems to you irregular, because you fetch all your comparisons from Jupiter or Saturn. Perhaps this is the very reason of the seeming confusion which you condemn; have I not told you that in the course of my travels I have always met with variety?"

The Saturnian replied to all these arguments, and perhaps the dispute would have known no end, if Micromegas, in the heat of the contest, had not luckily broken the string of his diamond necklace, so that the jewels fell to the ground; they consisted of pretty small unequal stones, the largest of which weighed four hundred pounds, and the smallest fifty. The dwarf, in helping to pick them up, perceived, as they approached his eye, that every single diamond was cut in such a manner as to answer the purpose of an excellent microscope. He therefore took up a small one, about one hundred and sixty feet in diameter, and applied it to his eye, while Micromegas chose another of two thousand five hundred feet. Though they were of excellent powers, the observers could perceive nothing by their assistance, so they were altered and adjusted. At length, the inhabitant of Saturn discerned something almost imperceptible moving between two waves in the Baltic. This was no other than a whale, which, in a dextrous manner, he caught with his little finger, and, placing it on the nail of his thumb, showed it to the Sirian, who laughed heartily at the excessive smallness peculiar to the inhabitants of this our globe. The Saturnian, by this time convinced that our world was inhabited, began to imagine we had no other animals than whales; and being a mighty debater, he forthwith set about investigating the origin and motion of this small atom, curious to know whether or not it was furnished with ideas, judgment, and free will. Micromegas was very much perplexed upon this subject. He examined the animal with the most patient attention, and the result of his inquiry was that he could see no reason to believe a soul was lodged in such a body. The two travellers were actually inclined to think there was no such thing as mind in this our habitation, when, by the help of their microscope, they perceived something as large as a whale floating upon the surface of the sea. It is well known that at this period a flock of philosophers were upon their return from the polar circle, where they had been making observations, for which nobody has hitherto been the wiser. The gazettes record that their vessel ran ashore on the coast of Bothnia and that they with great difficulty saved their lives; but in this world one can never dive to the bottom of things. For my own part, I will ingeniously recount the transaction just as it happened, without any addition of my own; and this is no small effort in a modern historian.

CHAPTER 5. THE TRAVELLERS CAPTURE A VESSEL

Micromegas stretched out his hand gently toward the place where the object appeared, and advanced two fingers, which he instantly pulled back, for fear of being disappointed; then opening softly and shutting them all at once, he very dextrously seized the ship that contained those gentlemen, and placed it on his nail, avoiding too much pressure, which might have crushed the whole in pieces.

"This," said Saturnian dwarf, "is a creature very different from the former."

Upon which the Sirian, placing the supposed animal in the hollow of his hand, the passengers and crew, who believed themselves thrown by a hurricane upon some rock, began to put themselves in motion. The sailors having hoisted out some casks of wine, jumped after them into the hand of Micromegas; the mathematicians having secured their quadrants, sectors, and Lapland servants, went overboard at a different place, and made such a bustle in their descent that the Sirian at length felt his fingers tickled by something that seemed to move. An iron bar chanced to penetrate about a foot deep into his forefinger; and from this prick he concluded that something had issued from the little animal he held in his hand; but at first he suspected nothing more, for the microscope, that scarce rendered a whale and a ship visible, had no effect upon an object so imperceptible as man.

I do not intend to shock the vanity of any person whatever; but here I am obliged to request people of importance to consider that, supposing the stature of a man to be about five feet, we mortals make just such a figure upon the earth as an animal the sixty thousandth part of a foot in height would exhibit upon a bowl ten feet in circumference. When you reflect upon a being who could hold this whole earth in the palm of his hand, and is provided with organs proportioned to those we possess, you will easily conceive that there must be a great variety of created substances — and pray, what must such beings think of those battles by which a conqueror gains a small village, to lose it again in the sequel?

I do not at all doubt but if some captain of grenadiers should chance to read this work, he would add two large feet at least to the caps of his company; but I assure him his labor will be in vain, for, do what he will, he and his soldiers will never be other than infinitely diminutive and inconsiderable.

What wonderful address must have been inherent in our Sirian philosopher that enabled him to perceive these atoms of which we have been speaking. When Leuwenhoek and Hartsoeker observed the first rudiments of which we are formed, they did not make such an astonishing discovery. What pleasure, therefore, was the portion of Micromegas in observing the motion of those little machines, in examining all their pranks, and following them in all their operations! With what joy did he put his microscope into his companion's hand; and with what transport did they both at once exclaim:

"I see them distinctly — don't you see them carrying burdens, lying down and rising up again?"

So saying, their hands shook with eagerness to see and apprehension to lose such uncommon objects. The Saturnian, making a sudden transition from the most cautious distrust to the most excessive credulity, imagined he saw them engaged in their devotions, and cried aloud in astonishment.

Nevertheless, he was deceived by appearances; a case too common, whether we do or do not make use of microscopes.

CHAPTER 6. WHAT HAPPENED IN
THEIR INTERCOURSE WITH MEN

Micromegas being a much better observer than the dwarf, perceived distinctly that those atoms spoke; and made the remark to his companion, who was so much ashamed of being mistaken in his first suggestion that he would not believe such a puny species could possibly communicate their ideas, for, though he had the gift of tongues, as well as his companion, he could not hear those particles speak, and, therefore, supposed they had no language.

"Besides, how should such imperceptible beings have the organs of speech? and what in the name of Jove can they say to one another? In order to speak, they must have something like thought, and if they think, they must surely have something equivalent to a soul. Now, to attribute anything like a soul to such an insect species appears a mere absurdity."

"But just now," replied the Sirian, "you believed they were engaged in devotional exercises; and do you think this could be done without thinking, without using some sort of language, or at least some way of making themselves understood? Or do you suppose it is more difficult to advance an argument than to engage in physical exercise? For my own part, I look upon all faculties as alike mysterious."

"I will no longer venture to believe or deny," answered the dwarf, "in short, I have no opinion at all. Let us endeavor to examine these insects, and we will reason upon them afterward."

"With all my heart," said Micromegas, who, taking out a pair of scissors which he kept for paring his nails, cut off a paring from his thumb nail, of which he immediately formed a large kind of speaking trumpet, like a vast tunnel, and clapped the pipe to his ear; as the circumference of this machine included the ship and all the crew, the most feeble voice was conveyed along the circular fibres of the nail; so that, thanks to his industry, the philosopher could distinctly hear the buzzing of our insects that were below. In a few hours he distinguished articulate sounds, and at last plainly understood the French language. The dwarf heard the same, though with more difficulty.

The astonishment of our travellers increased every instant. They heard a nest of mites talk in a very sensible strain: and that *lusus naturæ* seemed to them inexplicable. You need not doubt but the Sirian and his dwarf glowed with impatience to enter into conversation with such atoms. Micromegas being afraid that his voice, like thunder, would deafen and confound the mites, without being understood by them, saw the necessity of diminishing the sound; each, therefore, put into his mouth a sort of small toothpick, the slender end of which reached to the vessel. The Sirian setting the dwarf upon his knees, and the ship and crew upon his nail, held down his head and spoke softly. In fine, having taken these and a great many more precautions, he addressed himself to them in these words:

"O ye invisible insects, whom the hand of the Creator hath designed to produce in the abyss of infinite littleness! I give praise to His goodness, in that He hath been pleased to disclose unto me those secrets that seemed to be impenetrable."

If ever these was such a thing as astonishment, it seized upon the people who heard this address, and who could not conceive from whence it proceeded. The chaplain of the ship repeated exorcisms, the sailors swore, and the philosophers formed a system; but, notwithstanding all their systems, they could not divine who the person was that spoke to them. Then the dwarf of Saturn, whose voice was softer than that of Micromegas, gave them briefly to understand what species of beings they had to do with. He related the particulars of their voyage from Saturn, made them acquainted with the rank and quality of Monsieur Micromegas, and, after having pitied their smallness, asked if they had always been in that miserable state so near akin to annihilation; and what their business was upon that globe which seemed to be the property of whales. He also desired to know if they were happy in their situation? if they were inspired with souls? and put a hundred questions of the like nature.

A certain mathematician on board, braver than the rest and shocked to hear his soul called in question, planted his quadrant, and having taken two observations of this interlocutor, said: "You believe then, Mr. what's your name, that because you measure from head to foot a thousand fathoms—"

"A thousand fathoms!" cried the dwarf, "good heavens! How should he know the height of my nature. A thousand fathoms! My very dimensions to a hair. What, measured by a mite! This atom, forsooth, is a geometrician, and knows exactly how tall I am; while I, who can scarce perceive him through a microscope, am utterly ignorant of his extent!"

"Yes, I have taken your measure," answered the philosopher, "and I will now do the same by your tall companion."

The proposal was embraced; his excellency reclined upon his side, for, had he stood upright, his head would have reached too far above the clouds. Our mathematicians planted a tall tree near him, and then, by a series of triangles joined together, they discovered that the object of their observation was a strapping youth, exactly one hundred and twenty thousand royal feet in length. In consequence of this calculation, Micromegas uttered this words:

"I am now more than ever convinced that we ought to judge of nothing by its external magnitude. O God! Who hast bestowed understanding upon such contemptible substances, Thou canst with equal ease produce that which is infinitely small, as that which is incredibly great; and if it be possible that among Thy works there are beings still more diminutive that these, they may, nevertheless, be undued with understanding superior to the intelligence of those stupendous animals I have seen in heaven, a single foot of whom is larger than this whole globe on which I have alighted."

One of the philosophers assured him that there were intelligent beings much smaller than men, and recounted not only Virgil's whole fable of the bees, but also described all that Swammerdam hath discovered and Reaumur dissected. In a word, he informed him that there are animals which bear the same proportion to bees that bees bear to man, the same as the Sirian himself compared to those vast beings whom he had mentioned, and as those huge animals are to other substances, before whom they would appear like so many particles of dust. Here the conversation became very interesting, and Micromegas proceeded in these words:

"O ye intelligent atoms, in whom the Supreme Being hath been pleased to manifest his omniscience and power, without all doubt your joys on this earth must be pure and exquisite; for, being unencumbered with matter, and, to all appearance, little else than soul, you must spend your lives in the delights of pleasure and reflection, which are the true enjoyments of a perfect spirit. True happiness I have nowhere found; but certainly here it dwells."

At this harangue all the philosophers shook their heads, and one among them, more candid than his brethren, frankly owned that, excepting a very small number of inhabitants who were very little esteemed by their fellows, all the rest were a parcel of knaves, fools, and miserable wretches.

"We have matter enough," said he, "to do abundance of mischief, if mischief comes from matter; and too much understanding, if evil flows from understanding. You must know, for example, that at this very moment, while I am speaking, there are one hundred thousand animals of our own species, covered with hats, slaying an equal number of their fellow-creatures who wear turbans; at least they are either slaying or being slain; and this hath usually been the case all over the earth from time immemorial."

The Sirian, shuddering at this information, begged to know the cause of those horrible quarrels among such a puny race, and was given to understand that the subject of the dispute was a pitiful mole-hill (called Palestine), no larger than his heel. Not that any one of those millions who cut one another's throats pretends to have the least claim to the smallest particle of that clod. The question is, whether it shall belong to a certain person who is known by the name of Sultan, or to another whom (for what reason I know not) they dignify with the appellation of Pope. Neither the one nor the other has seen or ever will see the pitiful corner in question; and probably none of these wretches, who so madly destroy each other, ever beheld the ruler on whose account they are so mercilessly sacrificed!

"Ah, miscreants!" cried the indignant Sirian, "such excess of desperate rage is beyond conception. I have a good mind to take two or three steps, and trample the whole nest of such ridiculous assassins under my feet."

"Don't give yourself the trouble," replied the philosopher; "they are industrious enough in procuring their own destruction. At the end of ten years the hundredth part of those wretches will not survive; for you must know that, though they should not draw a sword in the cause they have espoused, famine, fatigue, and intemperance would sweep almost all of them from the face of the earth. Besides, the punishment should not be inflicted upon them, but upon those sedentary and slothful barbarians, who, from their palaces, give orders for murdering a million of men and then solemnly thank God for their success."

Our traveller was moved with compassion for the entire human race, in which he discovered such astonishing contrasts. "Since you are of the small number of the wise," said he, "and in all likelihood do not engage yourselves in the trade of murder for hire, be so good as to tell me your occupation."

"We anatomize flies," replied the philosopher, "we measure lines, we make calculations, we agree upon two or three points which we understand, and dispute upon two or three thousand that are beyond our comprehension."

"How far," said the Sirian, "do you reckon the distance between the great star of the constellation Gemini and that called Canicula?"

To this question all of them answered with one voice: "Thirty-two degrees and a half."

"And what is the distance from thence to the moon?"

"Sixty semi-diameters of the earth."

He then thought to puzzle them by asking the weight of the air; but they answered distinctly that common air is about nine hundred times specifically lighter than an equal column of the lightest water, and nineteen hundred times lighter than current gold. The little dwarf of Saturn, astonished at their answers, was now tempted to believe those people sorcerers who, but a quarter of an hour before, he would not allow were inspired with souls.

"Well," said Micromegas, "since you know so well what is without you, doubtless you are still more perfectly acquainted with that which is within. Tell me what is the soul, and how do your ideas orginate?"

Here the philosophers spoke altogether as before; but each was of a different opinion. The eldest quoted Aristotle, another pronounced the name of Descartes, a third mentioned Malebranche, a fourth Leibnitz, and a fifth Locke. An old peripatetical lifting up his voice, exclaimed with an air of confidence: "The soul is perfection and reason, having power to be such as it is, as Aristotle expressly declares, page 633, of the Louvre edition:

"Ἐυτελεχεῖά τις ἐστί καὶ λόγος τοῦ δύναμιυ ἔχοντος τσιοῦδι εἰ ταῖ."

"I am not very well versed in Greek," said the giant.

"Nor I, either," replied the philosophical mite.

"Why, then, do you quote that same Aristotle in Greek," resumed the Sirian.

"Because," answered the other, "it is but reasonable we should quote what we do not comprehend in a language we do not understand."

Here the Cartesian interposing: "The soul," said he, "is a pure spirit or intelligence, which hath received before birth all the metaphysical ideas; but after that event it is obliged to go to school and learn anew the knowledge which it hath lost."

"So it is necessary," replied the animal of eight leagues, "that thy soul should be learned before birth, in order to be so ignorant when thou hast got a beard upon thy chin. But what dost thou understand by spirit?"

"I have no idea of it," said the philosopher; "indeed, it is supposed to be immaterial."

"At least, thou knowest what matter is?" resumed the Sirian.

"Perfectly well," answered the other. "For example: that stone is gray, is of a certain figure, has three dimensions, specific weight, and divisibility."

"I want to know," said the giant, "what that object is, which, according to thy observation, hath a gray color, weight, and divisibility. Thou seest a few qualities, but dost thou know the nature of the thing itself?"

"Not I, truly," answered the Cartesian.

Upon which the Sirian admitted that he also was ignorant in regard to this subject. Then addressing himself to another sage, who stood upon his thumb, he asked: "What is the soul? and what are its functions?"

"Nothing at all," replied this disciple of Malebranche; "God hath made everything for my convenience. In Him I see everything, by Him I act; He is the universal agent, and I never meddle in His work."

"That is being a nonentity indeed," said the Sirian sage; and then, turning to a follower of Leibnitz, he exclaimed: "Hark ye, friend, what is thy opinion of the soul?"

"In my opinion," answered this metaphysician, "the soul is the hand that points at the hour, while my body does the office of the clock; or, if you please, the soul is the clock, and the body is the pointer; or again, my soul is the mirror of the universe, and my body the frame. All this is clear and uncontrovertible."

A little partisan of Locke, who chanced to be present, being asked his opinion on the same subject, said: "I do not know by what power I think; but well I know that I should never have thought without the assistance of my senses. That there are immaterial and intelligent substances I do not at all doubt; but that it is impossible for God to communicate the faculty of thinking to matter, I doubt very much. I revere the Eternal Power, to which it would ill become me to prescribe bounds. I affirm nothing, and am contented to believe that many more things are possible than are usually thought so."

The Sirian smiled at this declaration, and did not look upon the author as the least sagacious of the company; and as for the dwarf of Saturn, he would have embraced this adherent of Locke, had it not been for the extreme disproportion in their respective sizes. But unluckily there was another animalcule in a square cap, who, taking the word from all his philosophical brethren, affirmed that he knew the whole secret, which was contained in the abridgment of St. Thomas. He surveyed the two celestial strangers from top to toe, and maintained to their faces that their persons, their fashions, their suns, and their stars were created solely for the use of man. At this wild assertion our two travellers were seized with a fit of that uncontrollable laughter, which (according to Homer) is the portion of the immortal gods; their bellies quivered, their shoulders rose and fell, and, during these convulsions, the vessel fell from the Sirian's nail into the Saturnian's pocket, where these worthy people searched for it a long time with great diligence. At length, having found the ship and set everything to rights again, the Sirian resumed the discourse with those diminutive mites, and promised to compose for them a choice book of philosophy which would demonstrate the very essence of things. Accordingly, before his departure, he made them a present of the book, which was brought to the Academy of Sciences at Paris, but when the old secretary came to open it he saw nothing but blank paper, upon which—

"Ay, ay," said he, "this is just what I suspected."

Science and Literature:
When Worlds Collide

Although the Flemish anatomist Andreas Vesalius (1514–1564) had revolutionized the study of human anatomy with his *De humani corporis fabrica* in 1543 and William Harvey (1578–1657) published his discoveries on the circulation of the blood in 1628, the major concern of scientists seemed to be focused on astronomy, physics, and chemistry. In the late eighteenth century the excitement spread to biology and psychology: Mesmer's theory of animal magnetism (called mesmerism and later associated with hypnotism, it would inspire a generation of early science-fiction writers), Luigi Galvani's experiments with muscles and static electricity, Erasmus Darwin's attempts to codify natural history in verse and his previsions of evolution that later would be spelled out by his grandson, Lamarck's evolutionary theories, Malthus's ideas about population and food supply published in his famous *Essay on the Principle of Population,* and William Smith's work on stratigraphic dating and fossils.

The Bible's authority on creation and the age of earth was being overthrown, and it seemed only a matter of time until scientists could create life itself.

Meanwhile a new form of popular literature had sprung out of the eighteenth-century revival of interest in the Gothic; it exhibited itself in a new popularity of Gothic architecture, in pseudo-Gothic poems and epics, and in an aesthetic pleasure in fancy and extravagance in literature and art. In the midst of the Enlightenment (and perhaps as a reaction to it), Horace Walpole (1717–1797) created a new kind of novel in his tiny, pseudo-Gothic castle, Strawberry Hill. In *The Castle of Otranto* (1764), the first Gothic novel, nightmare replaced probability; it contained all the elements that would distinguish the genre: a young woman facing danger in a medieval castle with trap doors, mysterious rooms, ancient secrets, ghostly apparitions, clanking armor, and a growing menace creating an atmosphere of terror. *Otranto* was followed by William Beckford's *Vathek* (1786), Mrs. Ann Radcliffe's *The Mysteries of Udolpho* (1794), and Matthew "Monk" Lewis's *The Monk* (1796). The Gothic novel has retained its popularity down to contemporary times. Gloomy mansions and psychological explanations have replaced the castles and supernatural elements, but the same atmosphere of brooding terror is achieved in works such as Henry James's *The Turn of the Screw* (1898) and Daphne du Maurier's *Rebecca* (1938). For a time the Gothic novel was a standard category on the newsstands, easily recognizable by the face of a terrified young woman on the cover while behind her looms a dark, ominous mansion.

These elements—the new developments in biological science and the invention of the Gothic novel—combined with discoveries in electricity, particularly the creation of an electric current by Alessandro Volta, came together in the imagination of a twenty-year-old woman to produce what was if not the first science-fiction novel (as some scholars contend) at least the first novel that showed what a science-fiction novel might be. That novel was Mary Shelley's *Frankenstein* (1818).

The Gothic and the scientific actually played a part in the creation of the novel. Mary Shelley (1797–1851) was the daughter of William Godwin (1756–1836), a liberal philosopher and novelist (he wrote a Gothic novel himself), and Mary Wollstonecraft (1759–1797), a writer and early feminist. They married late in life, and Mary Wollstonecraft survived the birth of her daughter by only ten days. In 1814 Mary Godwin eloped to Switzerland with her father's friend, Percy Bysshe Shelley, already a promising poet, and was married to him in 1816, after the birth of two children, both of whom died in infancy, and the suicide of his first wife.

Frankenstein's birth pangs are recorded in Mary Shelley's preface to the edition of 1831. Lord Byron, his friend Dr. Polidori, and the Shelleys were reading aloud some German ghost stories one evening; Byron decided that everyone should write a tale founded on some supernatural occurrence. Mary was the only one who persevered (Shelley urged her on) to produce a book, but only after a long search for a subject. Then, one evening, Byron and Shelley were discussing Erasmus Darwin's experiments, "among others the nature of the principle of life, and whether there was any probability of its ever being discovered and communicated. . . . Perhaps a corpse would be reanimated; galvanism had given token of such things: perhaps the component parts of a creature might be manufactured, brought together, and endued with vital warmth."

That night, Mary recalled, she dreamed about "the pale student of unhallowed arts kneeling beside the thing he had put together. I saw the hideous phantasm of a man stretched out, and then, on the working of some powerful engine, show signs of life, and stir with an uneasy, half vital motion."

The novel is written in the form of letters from Captain Robert Walton to his sister in England, a manuscript of the scientist Victor Frankenstein's story prepared by Walton, and Walton's letters again. Mary Shelley's readers were accustomed to the epistolary style from the novels of Samuel Richardson, but modern readers may find it strange. Readers who are familiar only with the film version, or the exploitations that followed the definitive 1931 film starring Boris Karloff, will be surprised to discover that the monster is literate and born good, only to be soured by the universal horror with which he is greeted by everyone, including his creator.

In his history of science fiction, *Billion Year Spree* (and its revision, *Trillion Year Spree*), Brian Aldiss stated his belief that science fiction begins with *Frankenstein*. Certainly Mary Shelley intended to write convincingly about the possibilities of the new science. The preface to the edition of 1818 (though written by Shelley) cites Darwin and some German physiological writers as offering an opinion that reanimation is "not of impossible occurrence," and "however impossible as a physical fact, affords a point of view to the imagination for the delineating of human passions more comprehensive and commanding than any which the ordinary relations of existing events can yield." A current science-fiction writer could provide no better justification for his work.

But there are non-science-fiction aspects to the novel as well. Aldiss believes that science fiction "is characteristically cast in the Gothic or post-Gothic mold." Other critics believe science fiction to be cast in a more rational, skeptical mold in which the Gothic element is a foreign intrusion. The Gothic element in *Frankenstein*, the medieval elements of impiety and guilt, battle the scientific concerns . . . and win. The belief that "there are things man was not meant to know," though common enough in the Gothic novel and in early science fiction, and still prevalent in the science-fiction film (John Baxter, in *Science Fiction and the Cinema*, says it has a different origin than printed science fiction), is not the philosophy that runs through science fiction's hard core.

Mary Shelley also wrote a novel of the future in which a worldwide plague wipes out all humanity except one man. *The Last Man* (1826) takes place in the twenty-first century and might be considered the first novel of the future, but like the anonymous *Reign of King George VI: 1900–1925* (1763), it exhibits no awareness that the future will be any different from the present.

From Frankenstein
(or, The Modern Prometheus)

BY MARY SHELLEY

CHAPTER 5

It was on a dreary night of November that I beheld the accomplishment of my toils. With an anxiety that almost amounted to agony, I collected the instruments of life around me, that I might infuse a spark of being into the lifeless thing that lay at my feet. It was already one in the morning; the rain pattered dismally against the panes, and my candle was nearly burnt out, when, by the glimmer of the half-extinguished light, I saw the dull yellow eye of the creature open; it breathed hard, and a convulsive motion agitated its limbs.

How can I describe my emotions at this catastrophe, or how delineate the wretch whom with such infinite pains and care I had endeavoured to form? His limbs were in proportion, and I had selected his features as beautiful. Beautiful!—Great God! His yellow skin scarcely covered the work of muscles and arteries beneath; his hair was of a lustrous black, and flowing; his teeth of a pearly whiteness; but these luxuriances only formed a more horrid contrast with his watery eyes, that seemed almost of the same colour as the dun white sockets in which they were set, his shrivelled complexion and straight black lips.

The different accidents of life are not so changeable as the feelings of human nature. I had worked hard for nearly two years, for the sole purpose of infusing life into an inanimate body. For this I had deprived myself of rest and health. I had desired it with an ardour that far exceeded moderation; but now that I had finished, the beauty of the dream vanished, and breathless horror and disgust filled my heart. Unable to endure the aspect of the being I had created, I rushed out of the room, and continued a long time traversing my bedchamber, unable to compose my mind to sleep. At length lassitude succeeded to the tumult I had before endured; and I threw myself on the bed in my clothes, endeavouring to seek a few moments of forgetfulness. But it was in vain: I slept, indeed, but I was disturbed by the wildest dreams. I thought I saw Elizabeth, in the bloom of health, walking in the streets of Ingolstadt. Delighted and surprised, I embraced her; but as I imprinted the first kiss on her lips, they became livid with the hue of death; her features appeared to change, and I thought that I held the corpse of my dead mother in my arms; a shroud enveloped her form, and I saw the graveworms crawling in the folds of the flannel. I started from my sleep with horror; a cold dew covered my forehead, my teeth chattered, and every limb became convulsed: when, by the dim and yellow light of the moon, as it forced its way through the window shutters, I beheld the wretch—the miserable monster whom I had created. He held up the curtain of the bed; and his eyes, if eyes they may be called, were fixed on me. His jaws opened, and he muttered some inarticulate sounds, while a grin wrinkled his cheeks. He might have spoken, but I did not hear; one hand was stretched out, seemingly to detain me, but I escaped, and rushed down stairs. I took refuge in the courtyard belonging to the house which I inhabited; where I remained during the rest of the night, walking up and down in the greatest agitation, listening attentively, catching and fearing each sound as if it were to announce the approach of the demoniacal corpse to which I had so miserably given life.

Oh! no mortal could support the horror of that countenance. A mummy again endued with animation could not be so hideous as that wretch. I had gazed on him while unfinished; he was ugly then; but when those muscles and joints were rendered capable of motion, it became a thing such as even Dante could not have conceived.

I passed the night wretchedly. Sometimes my pulse beat so quickly and hardly that I felt the palpitation of every artery; at others, I nearly sank to the ground through languor and extreme weakness. Mingled with this horror, I felt the bitterness of disappointment; dreams that had been my food and pleasant rest for so long a space were now become a hell to me; and the change was so rapid, the overthrow so complete!

Morning, dismal and wet, at length dawned, and discovered to my sleepless and aching eyes the church of Ingolstadt, its white steeple and clock, which indicated the sixth hour. The porter opened the gates of the court, which had that night been my asylum, and I issued into the streets, pacing them with quick steps, as if I sought to avoid the wretch whom I feared every turning of the street would present to my view. I did not dare return to the apartment which I inhabited, but felt impelled to hurry on, although drenched by the rain which poured from a black and comfortless sky.

I continued walking in this manner for some time, endeavouring, by bodily exercise, to ease the load that weighed upon my mind. I traversed the streets, without any clear conception of where I was, or what I was doing. My heart palpitated in the sickness of fear; and I hurried on with irregular steps, not daring to look about me: —

> *"Like one who, on a lonely road,*
>   *Doth walk in fear and dread,*
> *And, having once turned round, walks on,*
>   *And turns no more his head;*
> *Because he knows a frightful fiend*
>   *Doth close behind him tread."*[1]

Continuing thus, I came at length opposite to the inn at which various diligences and carriages usually stopped. Here I paused, I knew not why; but I remained some minutes with my eyes fixed on a coach that was coming towards me from the other end of the street. As it drew nearer, I observed that it was the Swiss diligence: it stopped just where I was standing, and, on the door being opened, I perceived Henry Clerval, who, on seeing me, instantly sprung out. "My dear Frankenstein," exclaimed he, "how glad I am to see you! how fortunate that you should be here at the very moment of my alighting!"

Nothing could equal my delight on seeing Clerval; his presence brought back to my thoughts my father, Elizabeth, and all those scenes of home so dear to my recollection. I grasped his hand, and in a moment forgot my horror and misfortune; I felt suddenly, and for the first time during many months, calm and serene joy. I welcomed my friend, therefore, in the most cordial manner, and we walked towards my college. Clerval continued talking for some time about our mutual friends, and his own good fortune in being permitted to come to Ingolstadt. "You may easily believe," said he, "how great was the difficulty to persuade my father that all necessary knowledge was not comprised in the noble art of bookkeeping; and, indeed, I believe I left him incredulous to the last, for his constant answer to my unwearied entreaties was the same as that of the Dutch schoolmaster in the *Vicar of Wakefield:*— 'I have ten thousand florins a year without Greek, I eat heartily without Greek.' But his affection for me at length overcame his dislike of learning, and he has permitted me to undertake a voyage of discovery to the land of knowledge."

"It gives me the greatest delight to see you; but tell me how you left my father, brothers, and Elizabeth."

"Very well, and very happy, only a little uneasy that they hear from you so seldom. By the by, I mean to lecture you a little upon their account myself.—But, my dear Frankenstein," continued he, stopping short, and gazing full in my face, "I did not before remark how ill you appear; so thin and pale; you look as if you had been watching for several nights."

---

1 Coleridge's *Ancient Mariner.*

"You have guessed right; I have lately been so deeply engaged in one occupation that I have not allowed myself sufficient rest, as you see; but I hope, I sincerely hope, that all these employments are now at an end, and that I am at length free."

I trembled excessively; I could not endure to think of, and far less to allude to, the occurrences of the preceding night. I walked with a quick pace, and we soon arrived at my college. I then reflected, and the thought made me shiver, that the creature whom I had left in my apartment might still be there, alive, and walking about. I dreaded to behold this monster; but I feared still more that Henry should see him. Entreating him, therefore, to remain a few minutes at the bottom of the stairs, I darted up towards my own room. My hand was already on the lock of the door before I recollected myself. I then paused; and a cold shivering came over me. I threw the door forcibly open, as children are accustomed to do when they expect a spectre to stand in waiting for them on the other side; but nothing appeared. I stepped fearfully in: the apartment was empty; and my bedroom was also freed from its hideous guest. I could hardly believe that so great a good fortune could have befallen me; but when I became assured that my enemy had indeed fled, I clapped my hands for joy, and ran down to Clerval.

We ascended into my room, and the servant presently brought breakfast; but I was unable to contain myself. It was not joy only that possessed me; I felt my flesh tingle with excess of sensitiveness, and my pulse beat rapidly. I was unable to remain for a single instant in the same place; I jumped over the chairs, clapped my hands, and laughed aloud. Clerval at first attributed my unusual spirits to joy on his arrival; but when he observed me more attentively he saw a wildness in my eyes for which he could not account; and my loud, unrestrained, heartless laughter, frightened and astonished him.

"My dear Victor," cried he, "what, for God's sake, is the matter? Do not laugh in that manner. How ill you are! What is the cause of all this?"

"Do not ask me," cried I, putting my hands before my eyes, for I thought I saw the dreaded spectre glide into the room, "*he* can tell.—Oh save me! save me!" I imagined that the monster seized me; I struggled furiously, and fell down in a fit.

Poor Clerval! what must have been his feelings? A meeting, which he anticipated with such joy, so strangely turned to bitterness. But I was not the witness of his grief; for I was lifeless, and did not recover my senses for a long, long time.

This was the commencement of a nervous fever, which confined me for several months. During all that time Henry was my only nurse. I afterwards learned that, knowing my father's advanced age, and unfitness for so long a journey, and how wretched my sickness would make Elizabeth, he spared them this grief by concealing the extent of my disorder. He knew that I could not have a more kind and attentive nurse than himself; and, firm in the hope he felt of my recovery, he did not doubt that, instead of doing harm, he performed the kindest action that he could towards them.

But I was in reality very ill; and surely nothing but the unbounded and unremitting attentions of my friend could have restored me to life. The form of the monster on whom I had bestowed existence was for ever before my eyes, and I raved incessantly concerning him. Doubtless my words surprised Henry: he at first believed them to be the wanderings of my disturbed imagination; but the pertinacity with which I continually recurred to the same subject, persuaded him that my disorder indeed owed its origin to some uncommon and terrible event.

By very slow degrees, and with frequent relapses that alarmed and grieved my friend, I recovered. I remember the first time I became capable of observing outward objects with any kind of pleasure, I perceived that the fallen leaves had disappeared, and that the young buds were shooting forth from the trees that shaded my window. It was a divine spring; and the season contributed greatly to my convalescence. I felt also sentiments of joy and affection revive in my bosom; my gloom disappeared, and in a short time I became as cheerful as before I was attacked by the fatal passion.

"Dearest Clerval," exclaimed I, "how kind, how very good you are to me. This whole winter, instead of being spent in study, as you promised yourself, has been consumed in my sick room. How shall I ever repay you? I feel the greatest remorse for the disappointment of which I have been the occasion: but you will forgive me."

"You will repay me entirely, if you do not discompose yourself, but get well as fast as you can; and since you appear in such good spirits, I may speak to you on one subject, may I not?"

I trembled. One subject! what could it be? Could he allude to an object on whom I dared not even think?

"Compose yourself," said Clerval, who observed my change of colour, "I will not mention it, if it agitates you; but your father and cousin would be very happy if they received a letter from you in your own handwriting. They hardly know how ill you have been, and are uneasy at your long silence."

"Is that all, my dear Henry? How could you suppose that my first thoughts would not fly towards those dear, dear friends whom I love, and who are so deserving of my love."

"If this is your present temper, my friend, you will perhaps be glad to see a letter that has been lying here some days for you; it is from your cousin, I believe." . . .

CHAPTER 10

I spent the following day roaming through the valley. I stood beside the sources of the Arveiron, which take their rise in a glacier, that with slow pace is advancing down from the summit of the hills, to barricade the valley. The abrupt sides of vast mountains were before me; the icy wall of the glacier overhung me; a few shattered pines were scattered around; and the solemn silence of this glorious presence-chamber of imperial Nature was broken only by the brawling waves, or the fall of some vast fragment, the thunder sound of the avalanche, or the cracking reverberated along the mountains of the accumulated ice, which, through the silent working of immutable laws, was ever and anon rent and torn, as if it had been but a plaything in their hands. These sublime and magnificent scenes afforded me the greatest consolation that I was capable of receiving. They elevated me from all littleness of feeling; and although they did not remove my grief, they subdued and tranquillised it. In some degree, also, they diverted my mind from the thoughts over which it had brooded for the last month. I retired to rest at night; my slumbers, as it were, waited on and ministered to by the assemblance of grand shapes which I had contemplated during the day. They congregated round me; the unstained snowy mountain-top, the glittering pinnacle, the pine woods, and ragged bare ravine; the eagle, soaring amidst the clouds—-they all gathered round me, and bade me be at peace.

Where had they fled when the next morning I awoke? All of soul-inspiriting fled with sleep, and dark melancholy clouded every thought. The rain was pouring in torrents, and thick mists hid the summits of the mountains, so that I even saw not the faces of those mighty friends. Still I would penetrate their misty veil, and seek them in their cloudy retreats. What were rain and storm to me? My mule was brought to the door, and I resolved to ascend to the summit of Montanvert. I remembered the effect that the view of the tremendous and ever-moving glacier had produced upon my mind when I first saw it. It had then filled me with a sublime ecstasy that gave wings to the soul, and allowed it to soar from the obscure world to light and joy. The sight of the awful and majestic in nature had indeed always the effect of solemnising my mind, and causing me to forget the passing cares of life. I determined to go without a guide, for I was well acquainted with the path, and the presence of another would destroy the solitary grandeur of the scene.

The ascent is precipitous, but the path is cut into continual and short windings, which enable you to surmount the perpendicularity of the mountain. It is a scene terrifically desolate. In a thousand spots the traces of the winter avalanche may be perceived, where trees lie broken and skewed on the ground; some entirely destroyed, others bent, leaning upon the jutting rocks of the mountain, or transversely upon other trees. The path, as you ascend higher, is intersected by ravines of snow, down which stones continually roll from above; one of them is particularly dangerous, as the slightest sound, such as even speaking in a loud voice, produces a concussion of air sufficient to draw destruction upon the head of the speaker. The pines are not tall or luxuriant, but they are sombre, and add an air of severity to the scene. I looked on the valley beneath; vast mists were rising from the rivers which ran through it, and curling in thick wreaths around the opposite mountains, whose summits were hid in the uniform clouds, while rain poured from the dark sky, and added to the melancholy impression I received from the objects around me. Alas! why does man boast of sensibilities superior to those apparent in the brute; it only renders them more necessary beings. If our impulses were confined to hunger, thirst, and desire, we might be nearly free; but now we are moved by every wind that blows, and a chance word or scene that that word may convey to us.

> "We rest; a dream has power to poison sleep.
>   We rise; one wandering thought pollutes the day.
> We feel, conceive, or reason; laugh or weep,
>   Embrace fond woe, or cast our cares away;
> It is the same; for, be it joy or sorrow,
>   The path of its departure still is free.
> Man's yesterday may ne'er be like his morrow;
>   Nought may endure but mutability!"

It was nearly noon when I arrived at the top of the ascent. For some time I sat upon the rock that overlooks the sea of ice. A mist covered both that and the surrounding mountains. Presently a breeze dissipated the cloud, and I descended upon the glacier. The surface is very uneven, rising like the waves of a troubled sea, descending low, and interspersed by rifts that sink deep. The field of ice is almost a league in width, but I spent nearly two hours in crossing it. The opposite mountain is a bare perpendicular rock. From the side where I now stood Montanvert was exactly opposite, at the distance of a league; and above it rose Mont Blanc, in awful majesty. I remained in a recess of the rock, gazing on this wonderful and stupendous scene. The sea, or rather the vast river of ice, wound among its dependent mountains, whose aerial summits hung over its recesses. Their icy and glittering peaks shone in the sunlight over the clouds. My heart, which was before sorrowful, now swelled with something like joy; I exclaimed— "Wandering spirits, if indeed ye wander, and do not rest in your narrow beds, allow me this faint happiness, or take me, as your companion, away from the joys of life."

As I said this, I suddenly beheld the figure of a man, at some distance, advancing towards me with superhuman speed. He bounded over the crevices in the ice, among which I had walked with caution; his stature, also, as he approached, seemed to exceed that of man. I was troubled: a mist came over my eyes, and I felt a faintness seize me; but I was quickly restored by the cold gale of the mountains. I perceived, as the shape came nearer (sight tremendous and abhorred!) that it was the wretch whom I had created. I trembled with rage and horror, resolving to wait his approach and then close with him in mortal combat. He approached; his countenance bespoke bitter anguish, combined with disdain and malignity, while its unearthly ugliness rendered it almost too horrible for human eyes. But I scarcely observed this; rage and hatred had at first deprived me of utterance, and I recovered only to overwhelm him with words expressive of furious detestation and contempt.

"Devil," I exclaimed, "do you dare approach me? and do not you fear the fierce vengeance of my arm wreaked on your miserable head? Begone, vile insect! or rather, stay, that I may trample you to dust! and, oh! that I could, with the extinction of your miserable existence, restore those victims whom you have so diabolically murdered!"

"I expected this reception," said the dœmon. "All men hate the wretched; how, then, must I be hated, who am miserable beyond all living things! Yet you, my creator, detest and spurn me, thy creature, to whom thou art bound by ties only dissoluble by the annihilation of one of us. You purpose to kill me. How dare you sport thus with life? Do your duty towards me, and I will do mine towards you and the rest of mankind. If you will comply with my conditions, I will leave them and you at peace; but if you refuse, I will glut the maw of death, until it be satiated with the blood of your remaining friends."

"Abhorred monster! fiend that thou art! the tortures of hell are too mild a vengeance for thy crimes. Wretched devil! you reproach me with your creation; come on, then, that I may extinguish the spark which I so negligently bestowed."

My rage was without bounds; I sprang on him, impelled by all the feelings which can arm one being against the existence of another.

He easily eluded me, and said—

"Be calm! I entreat you to hear me, before you give vent to your hatred on my devoted head. Have I not suffered enough that you seek to increase my misery? Life, although it may only be an accumulation of anguish, is dear to me, and I will defend it. Remember, thou hast made me more powerful than thyself; my height is superior to thine; my joints more supple. But I will not be tempted to set myself in opposition to thee. I am thy creature, and I will be even mild and docile to my natural lord and king, if thou wilt also perform thy part, the which thou owest me. Oh, Frankenstein, be not equitable to every other, and trample upon me alone, to whom thy justice, and even thy clemency and affection, is most due. Remember, that I am thy creature; I ought to be thy Adam; but I am rather the fallen angel, whom thou drivest from joy for no misdeed. Everywhere I see bliss, from which I alone am irrevocably excluded. I was benevolent and good; misery made me a fiend. Make me happy, and I shall again be virtuous."

"Begone! I will not hear you. There can be no community between you and me; we are enemies. Begone, or let us try our strength in a fight, in which one must fall."

"How can I move thee? Will no entreaties cause thee to turn a favourable eye upon thy creature, who implores thy goodness and compassion? Believe me, Frankenstein: I was benevolent; my soul glowed with love and humanity: but am I not alone, miserably alone? You my creator, abhor me; what hope can I gather from your fellow-creatures, who owe me nothing? they spurn and hate me. The desert mountains and dreary glaciers are my refuge. I have wandered here many days; the caves of ice, which I only do not fear, are a dwelling to me, and the only one which man does not grudge. These black skies I hail, for they are kinder to me than your fellow-beings. If the multitude of mankind knew of my existence, they would do as you do, and arm themselves for my destruction. Shall I not then hate them who abhor me? I will keep no terms with my enemies. I am miserable, and they shall share my wretchedness. Yet it is in your power to recompense me, and deliver them from an evil which it only remains for you to make so great that not only you and your family, but thousands of others, shall be swallowed up in the whirlwinds of its rage. Let your compassion be moved, and do not disdain me. Listen to my tale: when you have heard that, abandon or commiserate me, as you shall judge that I deserve. But hear me. The guilty are allowed, by human laws, bloody as they are, to speak in their own defence before they are condemned. Listen to me, Frankenstein. You accuse me of murder; and yet you would, with a satisfied conscience, destroy your own creature. Oh, praise the eternal justice of man! Yet I ask you not to spare me: listen to me; and then, if you can, and if you will, destroy the work of your hands."

"Why do you call to my remembrances," I rejoined, "circumstances, of which I shudder to reflect, that I have been the miserable origin and author? Cursed be the day, abhorred devil, in which you first saw light! Cursed (although I curse myself) be the hands that formed you! You have made me wretched beyond expression. You have left me no power to consider whether I am just to you or not. Begone! relieve me from the sight of your detested form."

"Thus I relieve thee, my creator," he said, and placed his hated hands before my eyes, which I flung from me with violence; "thus I take from thee a sight which you abhor. Still thou canst listen to me, and grant me thy compassion. By the virtues that I once possessed, I demand this from you. Hear my tale; it is long and strange, and the temperature of this place is not fitting to your fine sensations; come to the hut upon the mountain. The sun is yet high in the heavens; before it descends to hide itself behind yon snowy precipices, and illuminate another world, you will have heard my story, and can decide. On you it rests whether I quit for ever the neighbourhood of man, and lead a harmless life, or become the scourge of your fellow-creatures, and the author of your own speedy ruin."

As he said this, he led the way across the ice: I followed. My heart was full, and I did not answer him; but, as I proceeded, I weighed the various arguments that he had used, and determined at least to listen to his tale. I was partly urged by curiosity, and compassion confirmed my resolution. I had hitherto supposed him to be the murderer of my brother, and I eagerly sought a confirmation or denial of this opinion. For the first time, also, I felt what the duties of a creator towards his creature were, and that I ought to render him happy before I complained of his wickedness. These motives urged me to comply with his demand. We crossed the ice, therefore, and ascended the opposite rock. The air was cold, and the rain again began to descend: we entered the hut, the fiend with an air of exultation, I with a heavy heart and depressed spirits. But I consented to listen; and, seating myself by the fire which my odious companion had lighted, he thus began his tale. . . .

Science as Symbol

The flywheel of scientific discovery and technological invention picked up speed throughout the first half of the nineteenth century with Dalton's atomic theory, Wollaston's discovery of dark lines in the solar spectrum, the synthesis of organic compounds by Wohler, the discovery of electromagnetic induction by Faraday, the announcement of the first law of thermodynamics by von Mayer, Joule, and von Helmholtz and the second law by Clasius, and the discovery of ether as an anesthetic by Long; and the inventions of the practical steamboat, the breech-loading rifle, the bicycle, the stethoscope, the cultivator, the camera, cement, the tractor, the reaper, the revolver, the telegraph, electrotype, nitroglycerin, the safety pin, and the rifle bullet.

But electricity was in the air, beginning with Volta's battery and Ritter's storage battery, Faraday's electric motor, Sturgeon's electromagnet, Ohm's law of electrical conduction, and Pixii's electric generator. Electricity was a miracle, invisible but powerful like magic or the will of God, and the groundwork was being laid for the miracles of application that began with the telegraph but would multiply rapidly in the last few decades of the century.

The wonders that science might achieve seemed endless. Public acceptance was so high that when Richard Adams Locke published a series of articles in the New York *Sun* headlined "Discoveries in the Moon Lately Made at the Cape of Good Hope, by Sir John Herschel" (1835) readers believed that a telescope had been built that would make visible objects on the moon as small as eighteen inches across, and that living creatures and buildings had been sighted. The articles would be reprinted under the title of *The Moon Hoax* (1859).

In 1791 Erasmus Darwin wrote:

Soon shall thy arm, UNCONQUER'D STEAM! afar
Drag the slow barge, or drive the rapid car,
Or on wide-waving wings expanded bear
The flying chariot through the field of air.
Fair crews triumphant, leaning from above,
Shall wave their fluttering kerchiefs as they move;

Or warrior-bands alarm the gaping crowd,
And armies shrink beneath the shadowy cloud.

Better writers, such as Goethe, himself an amateur scientist as Darwin
had been an amateur poet, exclaimed about the way in which, throughout
his life, "one great discovery has followed another." And Tennyson in
"Locksley Hall" (1842) wrote of "nourishing a youth sublime/With the
fairy tales of science, and the long result of time . . ." and went on to foresee a future in which commerce and warfare would be conducted in the air
until the creation of "the Parliament of man, the Federation of the World."

But not everyone was pleased with the accomplishments of science and
the industrialization that was changing the old ways of life. William Blake
complained about "the dark satanic mills" that were despoiling the green
landscape of England and polluting the English skies, and Ralph Waldo
Emerson wrote that "things are in the saddle and ride mankind."

It was not yet time for the literary mind to make dramatic sense out of
scientific innovation. The reaction of a few writers who were attracted by
the new material for fiction began with fascination and ended with reaffir-
mation of traditional values. Nathaniel Hawthorne (1804–1864) is a case in
point. In his notebooks he wrote, just like any science-fiction writer:

> Questions as to unsettled points of History, and Mysteries of Nature, to be
> asked of a mesmerized person.
>   Madame Calderon de la B (in Life in Mexico) speaks of persons who have
> been inoculated with the venom of rattlesnakes, by pricking them in various
> places with the tooth. These persons are thus secured forever against the bite
> of any venomous reptile. They have the power of calling snakes, and feel great
> pleasure in playing with and handling them. Their own bite becomes poison-
> ous to people not inoculated in the same manner. Thus a part of the serpent's
> nature appears to be tranfused into them.

But when Hawthorne turned these materials into fiction, his instinct told
him that meddling with life's mysteries was a presumption that would be
punished. In "The Birthmark" (1843), for instance, an eighteenth-century
"man of science," named Aylmer, marries a beautiful woman with a small
birthmark on her cheek; in an attempt to remove the defect and make her
perfect, Aylmer gives her a medicine that removes the birthmark but takes
her life. At one point in the story, Hawthorne wrote:

> The latter pursuit, however, Aylmer had long laid aside in unwilling recogni-
> tion of the truth—against which all seekers sooner or later stumble—that our

great creative Mother, while she amuses us with apparently working in the broadest sunshine, is yet severely careful to keep her own secrets, and, in spite of her pretended openness, shows us nothing but results. She permits us, indeed, to mar, but seldom to mend, and, like a jealous patentee, on no account to make.

Hawthorne tried to make a living at writing, turning out some well-regarded short stories but considerable hackwork before he secured job sinecures that allowed him to write his famous novels *The Scarlet Letter* and *The House of the Seven Gables,* dealing with the symbolic expression of Puritan guilt. But he was fascinated by the new science and kept returning to the fundamental questions he jotted into his notebooks: the possibilities of mesmerism, for one, which he turned into a novel called *The Blithedale Romance* (1852), and the elixir of life, which inspired "Dr. Heidigger's Experiment" (1837). He also wrote "The Artist of the Beautiful" (1841), about an obsessed watchmaker who devotes his life to the creation of a mechanical butterfly, and "Rappaccini's Daughter" (1844).

Hawthorne seemed sincerely interested in the possibilities of science, but he had no feel for the dramatic potential of science considered realistically, of science as environment rather than science as moral choice. He used science, like Puritan guilt, for its symbolic value.

Rappaccini's Daughter

BY NATHANIEL HAWTHORNE

A young man, named Giovanni Guasconti, came, very long ago, from the more southern region of Italy, to pursue his studies at the University of Padua. Giovanni, who had but a scanty supply of gold ducats in his pocket, took lodgings in a high and gloomy chamber of an old edifice which looked not unworthy to have been the palace of a Paduan noble, and which, in fact, exhibited over its entrance the armorial bearings of a family long since extinct. The young stranger, who was not unstudied in the great poem of his country, recollected that one of the ancestors of this family, and perhaps an occupant of this very mansion, had been pictured by Dante as a partaker of the immortal agonies of his Inferno. These reminiscences and associations, together with the tendency to heartbreak natural to a young man for the first time out of his native sphere, caused Giovanni to sigh heavily as he looked around the desolate and ill-furnished apartment.

"Holy Virgin, signor!" cried old Dame Lisabetta, who, won by the youth's remarkable beauty of person, was kindly endeavoring to give the chamber a habitable air, "what a sigh was that to come out of a young man's heart! Do you find this old mansion gloomy? For the love of Heaven, then, put your head out of the window, and you will see as bright sunshine as you have left in Naples."

Guasconti mechanically did as the old woman advised, but could not quite agree with her that the Paduan sunshine was as cheerful as that of southern Italy. Such as it was, however, it fell upon a garden beneath the window and expended its fostering influences on a variety of plants, which seemed to have been cultivated with exceeding care.

"Does this garden belong to the house?" asked Giovanni.

"Heaven forbid, signor, unless it were fruitful of better pot herbs than any that grow there now," answered old Lisabetta. "No; that garden is cultivated by the own hands of Signor Giacomo Rappaccini, the famous doctor, who, I warrant him, has been heard of as far as Naples. It is said that he distils these plants into medicines that are as potent as a charm. Oftentimes you may see the signor doctor at work, and perchance the signora, his daughter, too, gathering the strange flowers that grow in the garden."

The old woman had now done what she could for the aspect of the chamber; and, commending the young man to the protection of the saints, took her departure.

Giovanni still found no better occupation than to look down into the garden beneath his window. From its appearance, he judged it to be one of those botanic gardens which were of earlier date in Padua than elsewhere in Italy or in the world. Or, not improbably, it might once have been the pleasure-place of an opulent family; for there was the ruin of a marble fountain in the centre, sculptured with rare art, but so woefully shattered that it was impossible to trace the original design from the chaos of remaining fragments. The water, however, continued to gush and sparkle into the sunbeams as cheerfully as ever. A little gurgling sound ascended to the young man's window and made him feel as if the fountain were an immortal spirit, that sung its song unceasingly and without heeding the vicissitudes around it, while one century imbodied it in marble and another scattered the perishable garniture on the soil. All about the pool into which the water subsided grew various plants, that seemed to require a plentiful supply of moisture for the nourishment of gigantic leaves, and, in some instances, flowers gorgeously magnificent. There was one shrub in particular, set in a marble vase in the midst of the pool, that bore a profusion of purple blossoms, each of which had the lustre and richness of a gem; and the whole together made a show so resplendent that it seemed enough to illuminate the garden, even had there been no sunshine. Every portion of the soil was peopled with plants and herbs, which, if less beautiful, still bore tokens of assiduous care, as if all had their individual virtues, known to the scientific mind that fostered them. Some were placed in urns, rich with old carving, and others in common garden pots; some crept serpent-like along the ground or climbed on high, using whatever means of ascent was offered them. One plant had wreathed itself round a statue of Vertumnus, which was thus quite veiled and shrouded in a drapery of hanging foliage, so happily arranged that it might have served a sculptor for a study.

While Giovanni stood at the window he heard a rustling behind a screen of leaves, and became aware that a person was at work in the garden. His figure soon emerged into view, and showed itself to be that of no common laborer, but a tall, emaciated, sallow, and sickly-looking man, dressed in a scholar's garb of black. He was beyond the middle term of life, with gray hair, a thin, gray beard, and a face singularly marked with intellect and cultivation, but which could never, even in his more youthful days, have expressed much warmth of heart.

Nothing could exceed the intentness with which this scientific gardener examined every shrub which grew in his path; it seemed as if he was looking into their inmost nature, making observations in regard to their creative essence, and discovering why one leaf grew in this shape and another in that, and wherefore such and such flowers differed among themselves in hue and perfume. Nevertheless, in spite of this deep intelligence on his part, there was no approach to intimacy between himself and these vegetable existences. On the contrary, he avoided their actual touch or the direct inhaling of their odors with a caution that impressed Giovanni most disagreeably; for the man's demeanor was that of one walking among malignant influences, such as savage beasts, or deadly snakes, or evil spirits; which, should he allow them one moment of license, would wreak upon him some terrible fatality. It was strangely frightful to the young man's imagination to see this air of insecurity in a person cultivating a garden, that most simple and innocent of human toils, and which had been alike the joy and labor of the unfallen parents of the race. Was this garden, then, the Eden of the present world? And this man, with such a perception of harm in what his own hands caused to grow,—was he the Adam?

The distrustful gardener, while plucking away the dead leaves or pruning the too luxuriant growth of the shrubs, defended his hands with a pair of thick gloves. Nor were these his only armor. When, in his walk through the garden, he came to the magnificent plant that hung its purple gems beside the marble fountain, he placed a kind of mask over his mouth and nostrils, as if all this beauty did but conceal a deadlier malice; but, finding his task still too dangerous, he drew back, removed the mask, and called loudly, but in the infirm voice of a person affected with inward disease,—

"Beatrice! Beatrice!"

"Here am I, my father. What would you?" cried a rich and youthful voice from the window of the opposite house—a voice as rich as a tropical sunset, and which made Giovanni, though he knew not why, think of deep hues of purple or crimson and of perfumes heavily delectable. "Are you in the garden?"

"Yes, Beatrice," answered the gardener; "and I need your help."

Soon there emerged from under a sculptured portal the figure of a young girl, arrayed with as much richness of taste as the most splendid of the flowers, beautiful as the day, and with a bloom so deep and vivid that one shade more would have been too much. She looked redundant with life, health, and energy; all of which attributes were bound down and compressed, as it were, and girdled tensely, in their luxuriance, by her virgin zone. Yet Giovanni's fancy must have grown morbid while he looked down into the garden; for the impression which the fair stranger made upon him was as if here were another flower, the human sister of those vegetable ones, as beautiful as they, more beautiful than the richest of them, but still to be touched only with a glove, nor to be approached without a mask. As Beatrice came down the garden path, it was observable that she handled and inhaled the odor of several of the plants which her father had most sedulously avoided.

"Here, Beatrice," said the latter, "see how many needful offices require to be done to our chief treasure. Yet, shattered as I am, my life might pay the penalty of approaching it so closely as circumstances demand. Henceforth, I fear, this plant must be consigned to your sole charge."

"And gladly will I undertake it," cried again the rich tones of the young lady, as she bent towards the magnificent plant and opened her arms as if to embrace it. "Yes, my sister, my splendor, it shall be Beatrice's task to nurse and serve thee; and thou shalt reward her with thy kisses and perfumed breath, which to her is as the breath of life."

Then, with all the tenderness in her manner that was so strikingly expressed in her words, she busied herself with such attentions as the plant seemed to require; and Giovanni, at his lofty window, rubbed his eyes, and almost doubted whether it were a girl tending her favorite flower, or one sister performing the duties of affection to another. The scene soon terminated. Whether Dr. Rappaccini had finished his labors in the garden, or that his watchful eye had caught the stranger's face, he now took his daughter's arm and retired. Night was already closing in; oppressive exhalations seemed to proceed from the plants and steal upward past the open window, and Giovanni, closing the lattice, went to his couch and dreamed of a rich flower and beautiful girl. Flower and maiden were different, and yet the same, and fraught with some strange peril in either shape.

But there is an influence in the light of morning that tends to rectify whatever errors of fancy, or even of judgment, we may have incurred during the sun's decline, or among the shadows of the night, or in the less wholesome glow of moonshine. Giovanni's first movement on starting from sleep, was to throw open the window and gaze down into the garden which his dreams had made so fertile of mysteries. He was surprised, and a little ashamed, to find how real and matter-of-fact an affair it proved to be, in the first rays of the sun which gilded the dewdrops that hung upon leaf and blossom, and, while giving a brighter beauty to each rare flower, brought every thing within the limits of ordinary experience. The young man rejoiced that, in the heart of the barren city, he had the privilege of overlooking this spot of lovely and luxuriant vegetation. It would serve, he said to himself, as a symbolic language to keep him in communion with Nature. Neither the sickly and thought-worn Dr. Giacomo Rappaccini, it is true, nor his brilliant daughter, were now visible; so that Giovanni could not determine how much of the singularity which he attributed to both was due to their own qualities and how much to his wonder-working fancy; but he was inclined to take a most rational view of the whole matter.

In the course of the day he paid his respects to Signor Pietro Baglioni, professor of medicine in the university, a physician of eminent repute, to whom Giovanni had brought a letter of introduction. The professor was an elderly personage, apparently of genial nature and habits that might almost be called jovial. He kept the young man to dinner, and made himself very agreeable by the freedom and liveliness of his conversation, especially when warmed by a flask or two of Tuscan wine. Giovanni, conceiving that men of science, inhabitants of the same city, must needs be on familiar terms with one another, took an opportunity to mention the name of Dr. Rappaccini. But the professor did not respond with so much cordiality as he had anticipated.

"Ill would it become a teacher of the divine art of medicine," said Professor Pietro Baglioni, in answer to a question of Giovanni, "to withhold due and well-considered praise of a physician so eminently skilled as Rappaccini; but, on the other hand, I should answer it but scantily to my conscience were I to permit a worthy youth like yourself, Signor Giovanni, the son of an ancient friend, to imbibe erroneous ideas respecting a man who might hereafter chance to hold your life and death in his hands. The truth is, our worshipful Dr. Rappaccini has as much science as any member of the faculty—with perhaps one single exception—in Padua, or all Italy; but there are certain grave objections to his professional character."

"And what are they?" asked the young man.

"Has my friend Giovanni any disease of body or heart, that he is so inquisitive about physicians?" said the professor, with a smile. "But as for Rappaccini, it is said of him—and I, who know the man well, can answer for its truth—that he cares infinitely more for science than for mankind. His patients are interesting to him only as subjects for some new experiment. He would sacrifice human life, his own among the rest, or whatever else was dearest to him, for the sake of adding so much as a grain of mustard seed to the great heap of his accumulated knowledge."

"Methinks he is an awful man indeed," remarked Guasconti, mentally recalling the cold and purely intellectual aspect of Rappaccini. "And yet, worshipful professor, is it not a noble spirit? Are there many most capable of so spiritual a love of science?"

"God forbid," answered the professor, somewhat testily; "at least, unless they take sounder views of the healing art than those adopted by Rappaccini. It is his theory that all medicinal virtues are comprised within those substances which we term vegetable poisons. These he cultivates with his own hands, and is said even to have produced new varieties of poison, more horribly deleterious than Nature, without the assistance of this learned person, would ever have plagued the world withal. That the signor doctor does less mischief than might be expected with such dangerous substances, is undeniable. Now and then, it must be owned, he has effected, or seemed to effect, a marvellous cure; but, to tell you my private mind, Signor Giovanni, he should receive little credit for such instances of success,—they being probably the work of chance,—but should be held strictly accountable for his failures, which may justly be considered his own work."

The youth might have taken Baglioni's opinions with many grains of allowance had he known that there was a professional warfare of long continuance between him and Dr. Rappaccini, in which the latter was generally thought to have gained the advantage. If the reader be inclined to judge for himself, we refer him to certain black-letter tracts on both sides, preserved in the medical department of the University of Padua.

"I know not, most learned professor," returned Giovanni, after musing on what had been said of Rappaccini's exclusive zeal for science,—"I know not how dearly this physician may love his art; but surely there is one object more dear to him. He has a daughter."

"Aha!" cried the professor, with a laugh. "So now our friend Giovanni's secret is out. You have heard of this daughter, whom all the young men in Padua are wild about, though not half a dozen have ever had the good hap to see her face. I know little of the Signora Beatrice save that Rappaccini is said to have instructed her deeply in his science, and that, young and beautiful as fame reports her, she is already qualified to fill a professor's chair. Perchance her father destines her for mine! Other absurd rumors there be, not worth talking about or listening to. So now, Signor Giovanni, drink off your glass of lachryma."

Guasconti returned to his lodgings somewhat heated with the wine he had quaffed, and which caused his brain to swim with strange fantasies in reference to Dr. Rappaccini and the beautiful Beatrice. On his way, happening to pass by a florist's, he bought a fresh bouquet of flowers.

Ascending to his chamber, he seated himself near the window, but within the shadow thrown by the depth of the wall, so that he could look down into the garden with little risk of being discovered. All beneath his eye was a solitude. The strange plants were basking in the sunshine, and now and then nodding gently to one another, as if in acknowledgment of sympathy and kindred. In the midst, by the shattered fountain, grew the magnificent shrub, with its purple gems clustering all over it; they glowed in the air, and gleamed back again out of the depths of the pool, which thus seemed to overflow with colored radiance from the rich reflection that was steeped in it. At first, as we have said, the garden was a solitude. Soon, however,—as Giovanni had half hoped, half feared, would be the case,—a figure appeared beneath the antique sculptured portal, and came down between the rows of plants, inhaling their various perfumes as if she were one of those beings of old classic fables that lived upon sweet odors. On again beholding Beatrice, the young man was even startled to perceive how much her beauty exceeded his recollection of it; so brilliant, so vivid, was its character, that she glowed amid the sunlight, and, as Giovanni whispered to himself, positively illuminated the more shadowy intervals of the garden path. Her face being now more revealed than on the former occasion, he was struck by its expression of simplicity and sweetness—qualities that had not entered into his idea of her character, and which made him ask anew what manner of mortal she might be. Nor did he fail again to observe, or imagine, an analogy between the beautiful girl and the gorgeous shrub that hung its gemlike flowers over the fountain—a resemblance which Beatrice seemed to have indulged a fantastic humor in heightening, both by the arrangement of her dress and the selection of its hues.

Approaching the shrub, she threw open her arms, as with a passionate ardor, and drew its branches into an intimate embrace—so intimate that her features were hidden in its leafy bosom and her glistening ringlets all intermingled with the flowers.

"Give me thy breath, my sister," exclaimed Beatrice; "for I am faint with common air. And give me this flower of thine, which I separate with gentlest fingers from the stem and place it close beside my heart."

With these words the beautiful daughter of Rappaccini plucked one of the richest blossoms of the shrub, and was about to fasten it in her bosom. But now, unless Giovanni's draughts of wine had bewildered his senses, a singular incident occurred. A small orange-colored reptile, of the lizard or chameleon species, chanced to be creeping along the path, just at the feet of Beatrice. It appeared to Giovanni,—but, at the distance from which he gazed, he could scarcely have seen any thing so minute,—it appeared to him, however, that a drop or two of moisture from the broken stem of the flower descended upon the lizard's head. For an instant the reptile contorted itself violently, and then lay motionless in the sunshine. Beatrice observed this remarkable phenomenon, and crossed herself, sadly, but without surprise; nor did she therefore hesitate to arrange the fatal flower in her bosom. There it blushed, and almost glimmered with the dazzling effect of a precious stone, adding to her dress and aspect the one appropriate charm which nothing else in the world could have supplied. But Giovanni, out of the shadow of his window, bent forward and shrank back, and murmured and trembled.

"Am I awake? Have I my senses?" said he to himself. "What is this being? Beautiful shall I call her, or inexpressibly terrible?"

Beatrice now strayed carelessly through the garden, approaching closer beneath Giovanni's window, so that he was compelled to thrust his head quite out of its concealment in order to gratify the intense and painful curiosity which she excited. At this moment there came a beautiful insect over the garden wall: it had, perhaps, wandered through the city, and found no flowers or verdure among those antique haunts of men until the heavy perfumes of Dr. Rappaccini's shrubs had lured it from afar. Without alighting on the flowers, this winged brightness seemed to be attracted by Beatrice, and lingered in the air and fluttered about her head. Now, here it could not be but that Giovanni Guasconti's eyes deceived him. Be that as it might, he fancied that, while Beatrice was gazing at the insect with childish delight, it grew faint and fell at her feet; its bright wings shivered; it was dead — from no cause that he could discern, unless it were the atmosphere of her breath. Again Beatrice crossed herself and sighed heavily as she bent over the dead insect.

An impulsive movement of Giovanni drew her eyes to the window. There she beheld the beautiful head of the young man — rather a Grecian than an Italian head, with fair, regular features, and a glistening of gold among his ringlets — gazing down upon her like a being that hovered in mid air. Scarcely knowing what he did, Giovanni threw down the bouquet which he had hitherto held in his hand.

"Signora," said he, "there are pure and healthful flowers. Wear them for the sake of Giovanni Guasconti."

"Thanks, signor," replied Beatrice, with her rich voice, that came forth as it were like a gush of music, and with a mirthful expression half childish and half womanlike. "I accept your gift, and would fain recompense it with this precious purple flower; but, if I toss it into the air, it will not reach you. So Signor Guasconti must even content himself with my thanks."

She lifted the bouquet from the ground, and then, as if inwardly ashamed at having stepped aside from her maidenly reserve to respond to a stranger's greeting, passed swiftly homeward through the garden. But, few as the moments were, it seemed to Giovanni, when she was on the point of vanishing beneath the sculptured portal, that his beautiful bouquet was already beginning to wither in her grasp. It was an idle thought; there could be no possibility of distinguishing a faded flower from a fresh one at so great a distance.

For many days after this incident the young man avoided the window that looked into Dr. Rappaccini's garden, as if something ugly and monstrous would have blasted his eyesight had he been betrayed into a glance. He felt conscious of having put himself, to a certain extent, within the influence of an unintelligible power by the communication which he had opened with Beatrice. The wisest course would have been, if his heart were in any real danger, to quit his lodgings and Padua itself at once; the next wiser, to have accustomed himself, as far as possible, to the familiar and daylight view of Beatrice—thus bringing her rigidly and systematically within the limits of ordinary experience. Least of all, while avoiding her sight, ought Giovanni to have remained so near this extraordinary being that the proximity and possibility even of intercourse should give a kind of substance and reality to the wild vagaries which his imagination ran riot continually in producing. Guasconti had not a deep heart—or, at all events, its depths were not sounded now; but he had a quick fancy, and an ardent southern temperament, which rose every instant to a higher fever pitch. Whether or no Beatrice possessed those terrible attributes, that fatal breath, the affinity with those so beautiful and deadly flowers which were indicated by what Giovanni had witnessed, she had at least instilled a fierce and subtle poison into his system. It was not love, although her rich beauty was a madness to him; nor horror, even while he fancied her spirit to be imbued with the same baneful essence that seemed to pervade her physical frame; but a wild offspring of both love and horror that had each parent in it, and burned like one and shivered like the other. Giovanni knew not what to dread; still less did he know what to hope; yet hope and dread kept a continual warfare in his breast, alternately vanquishing one another and starting up afresh to renew the contest. Blessed are all simple emotions, be they dark or bright! It is the lurid intermixture of the two that produces the illuminating blaze of the infernal regions.

Sometimes he endeavoured to assuage the fever of his spirit by a rapid walk through the streets of Padua or beyond its gates: his footsteps kept time with the throbbings of his brain, so that the walk was apt to accelerate itself to a race. One day he found himself arrested; his arm was seized by a portly-personage, who had turned back on recognizing the young man and expended much breath in overtaking him.

"Signor Giovanni! Stay, my young friend!" cried he. "Have you forgotten me? That might well be the case if I were as much altered as yourself."

It was Baglioni, whom Giovanni had avoided ever since their first meeting, from a doubt that the professor's sagacity would look too deeply into his secrets. Endeavoring to recover himself, he stared forth wildly from his inner world into the outer one and spoke like a man in a dream.

"Yes; I am Giovanni Guasconti. You are Professor Pietro Baglioni. Now let me pass!"

"Not yet, not yet, Signor Giovanni Guasconti," said the professor, smiling, but at the same time scrutinizing the youth with an earnest glance. "What! did I grow up side by side with your father? and shall his son pass me like a stranger in these old streets of Padua? Stand still, Signor Giovanni; for we must have a word or two before we part."

"Speedily, then, most worshipful professor, speedily," said Giovanni, with feverish impatience. "Does not your worship see that I am in haste?"

Now, while he was speaking there came a man in black along the street, stooping and moving feebly like a person in inferior health. His face was all overspread with a most sickly and sallow hue, but yet so pervaded with an expression of piercing and active intellect that an observer might easily have overlooked the merely physical attributes and have seen only this wonderful energy. As he passed, this person exchanged a cold and distant salutation with Baglioni, but fixed his eyes upon Giovanni with an intentness that seemed to bring out whatever was within him worthy of notice. Nevertheless, there was a peculiar quietness in the look, as if taking merely a speculative, not a human, interest in the young man.

"It is Dr. Rappaccini!" whispered the professor when the stranger had passed. "Has he ever seen your face before?"

"Not that I know," answered Giovanni, starting at the name.

"He *has* seen you! he must have seen you!" said Baglioni, hastily. "For some purpose or other, this man of science is making a study of you. I know that look of his! It is the same that coldly illuminates his face as he bends over a bird, a mouse, or a butterfly which, in pursuance of some experiment, he has killed by the perfume of a flower; a look as deep as Nature itself, but without Nature's warmth of love. Signor Giovanni, I will stake my life upon it, you are the subject of one of Rappaccini's experiments!"

"Will you make a fool of me?" cried Giovanni, passionately. "*That,* signor professor, were an untoward experiment."

"Patience! patience!" replied the imperturbable professor. "I tell thee, my poor Giovanni, that Rappaccini has a scientific interest in thee. Thou hast fallen into fearful hands! And the Signora Beatrice,—what part does she act in this mystery?"

But Guasconti, finding Baglioni's pertinacity intolerable, here broke away, and was gone before the professor could again seize his arm. He looked after the young man intently and shook his head.

"This must not be," said Baglioni to himself. "The youth is the son of my old friend, and shall not come to any harm from which the arcana of medical science can preserve him. Besides, it is too insufferable an impertinence in Rappaccini thus to snatch the lad out of my own hands, as I may say, and make use of him for his infernal experiments. This daughter of his! It shall be looked to. Perchance, most learned Rappaccini, I may foil you where you little dream of it!"

Meanwhile Giovanni had pursued a circuitous route, and at length found himself at the door of his lodgings. As he crossed the threshold he was met by old Lisabetta, who smirked and smiled, and was evidently desirous to attract his attention; vainly, however, as the ebullition of his feelings had momentarily subsided into a cold and dull vacuity. He turned his eyes full upon the withered face that was puckering itself into a smile, but seemed to behold it not. The old dame, therefore, laid her grasp upon his cloak.

"Signor! signor!" whispered she, still with a smile over the whole breadth of her visage, so that it looked not unlike a grotesque carving in wood, darkened by centuries. "Listen, signor! There is a private entrance into the garden!"

"What do you say?" exclaimed Giovanni, turning quickly about, as if an inanimate thing should start into feverish life. "A private entrance into Dr. Rappaccini's garden?"

"Hush! hush! not so loud!" whispered Lisabetta, putting her hand over his mouth. "Yes; into the worshipful doctor's garden, where you may see all his fine shrubbery. Many a young man in Padua would give gold to be admitted among those flowers."

Giovanni put a piece of gold into her hand.

"Show me the way," said he.

A surmise, probably excited by his conversation with Baglioni, crossed his mind, that this interposition of old Lisabetta might perchance be connected with the intrigue, whatever were its nature, in which the professor seemed to suppose that Dr. Rappaccini was involving him. But such a suspicion, though it disturbed Giovanni, was inadequate to restrain him. The instant that he was aware of the possibility of approaching Beatrice, it seemed an absolute necessity of his existence to do so. It mattered not whether she were angel or demon; he was irrevocably within her sphere, and must obey the law that whirled him onward, in ever-lessening circles, towards a result which he did not attempt to foreshadow; and yet, strange to say, there came across him a sudden doubt whether this intense interest on his part were not delusory; whether it were really of so deep and positive a nature as to justify him in now thrusting himself into an incalculable position; whether it were not merely the fantasy of a young man's brain, only slightly or not at all connected with his heart.

He paused, hesitated, turned half about, but again went on. His withered guide led him along several obscure passages, and finally undid a door, through which, as it was opened, there came the sight and sound of rustling leaves, with the broken sunshine glimmering among them. Giovanni stepped forth, and, forcing himself through the entanglement of a shrub that wreathed its tendrils over the hidden entrance, stood beneath his own window in the open area of Dr. Rappaccini's garden.

How often is it the case that, when impossibilities have come to pass and dreams have condensed their misty substance into tangible realities, we find ourselves calm, and even coldly self-possessed, amid circumstances which it would have been a delirium of joy or agony to anticipate! Fate delights to thwart us thus. Passion will choose his own time to rush upon the scene, and lingers sluggishly behind when an appropriate adjustment of events would seem to summon his appearance. So was it now with Giovanni. Day after day his pulses had throbbed with feverish blood at the improbable idea of an interview with Beatrice, and of standing with her, face to face, in this very garden, basking in the Oriental sunshine of her beauty, and snatching from her full gaze the mystery which he deemed the riddle of his own existence. But now there was a singular and untimely equanimity within his breast. He threw a glance around the garden to discover if Beatrice or her father were present, and, perceiving that he was alone, began a critical observation of the plants.

The aspect of one and all of them dissatisfied him; their gorgeousness seemed fierce, passionate, and even unnatural. There was hardly an individual shrub which a wanderer, straying by himself through a forest, would not have been startled to find growing wild, as if an unearthly face had glared at him out of the thicket. Several also would have shocked a delicate instinct by an appearance of artificiality indicating that there had been such commixture, and, as it were, adultery of various vegetable species, that the production was no longer of God's making, but the monstrous offspring of man's depraved fancy, glowing with only an evil mockery of beauty. They were probably the result of experiment, which in one or two cases had succeeded in mingling plants individually lovely into a compound possessing the questionable and ominous character that distinguished the whole growth of the garden. In fine, Giovanni recognized but two or three plants in the collection, and those of a kind that he well knew to be poisonous. While busy with these contemplations he heard the rustling of a silken garment, and, turning, beheld Beatrice emerging from beneath the sculptured portal.

Giovanni had not considered with himself what should be his deportment; whether he should apologize for his intrusion into the garden, or assume that he was there with the privity at least, if not by the desire, of Dr. Rappaccini or his daughter; but Beatrice's manner placed him at his ease, though leaving him still in doubt by what agency he had gained admittance. She came lightly along the path and met him near the broken fountain. There was surprise in her face, but brightened by a simple and kind expression of pleasure.

"You are a connoisseur in flowers, signor," said Beatrice, with a smile, alluding to the bouquet which he had flung her from the window. "It is no marvel, therefore, if the sight of my father's rare collection has tempted you to take a nearer view. If he were here, he could tell you many strange and interesting facts as to the nature and habits of these shrubs; for he has spent a lifetime in such studies, and this garden is his world."

"And yourself, lady," observed Giovanni, "if fame says true,—you likewise are deeply skilled in the virtues indicated by these rich blossoms and these spicy perfumes. Would you deign to be my instructress, I should prove an apter scholar than if taught by Signor Rappaccini himself."

"Are there such idle rumors?" asked Beatrice, with the music of a pleasant laugh. "Do people say that I am skilled in my father's science of plants? What a jest is there! No; though I have grown up among these flowers, I know no more of them than their hues and perfume; and sometimes methinks I would fain rid myself of even that small knowledge. There are many flowers here, and those not the least brilliant, that shock and offend me when they meet my eye. But pray, signor, do not believe these stories about my science. Believe nothing of me save what you see with your own eyes."

"And must I believe all that I have seen with my own eyes?" asked Giovanni, pointedly, while the recollection of former scenes made him shrink. "No, signora; you demand too little of me. Bid me believe nothing save what comes from your own lips."

It would appear that Beatrice understood him. There came a deep flush to her cheek; but she looked full into Giovanni's eyes, and responded to his gaze of uneasy suspicion with a queenlike haughtiness.

"I do so bid you, signor," she replied. "Forget whatever you may have fancied in regard to me. If true to the outward senses, still it may be false in its essence; but the words of Beatrice Rappaccini's lips are true from the depths of the heart outward. Those you may believe."

A fervor glowed in her whole aspect and beamed upon Giovanni's consciousness like the light of truth itself; but while she spoke there was a fra-

grance in the atmosphere around her, rich and delightful, though evanes-
cent, yet which the young man, from an indefinable reluctance, scarcely
dared to draw into his lungs. It might be the odor of the flowers. Could it
be Beatrice's breath which thus embalmed her words with a strange richness, as if by steeping them in her heart? A faintness passed like a shadow
over Giovanni and flitted away; he seemed to gaze through the beautiful
girl's eyes into her transparent soul, and felt no more doubt or fear.

The tinge of passion that had colored Beatrice's manner vanished; she became gay, and appeared to derive a pure delight from her communion with
the youth not unlike what the maiden of a lonely island might have felt conversing with a voyager from the civilized world. Evidently her experience of
life had been confined within the limits of that garden. She talked now about
matters as simple as the daylight or summer clouds, and now asked questions in reference to the city, or Giovanni's distant home, his friends, his
mother, and his sisters—questions indicating such seclusion, and such lack
of familiarity with modes and forms, that Giovanni responded as if to an in-
fant. Her spirit gushed out before him like a fresh rill that was just catching
its first glimpse of the sunlight and wondering at the reflections of earth and
sky which were flung into its bosom. There came thoughts, too, from a deep
source, and fantasies of a gemlike brilliancy, as if diamonds and rubies
sparkled upward among the bubbles of the fountain. Ever and anon there
gleamed across the young man's mind a sense of wonder that he should be
walking side by side with the being who had so wrought upon his imagination, whom he had idealized in such hues of terror, in whom he had positively witnessed such manifestations of dreadful attributes—that he should
be conversing with Beatrice like a brother, and should find her so human and
so maidenlike. But such reflections were only momentary; the effect of her
character was too real not to make itself familiar at once.

In this free intercourse they had strayed through the garden, and now, after many turns among its avenues, were come to the shattered fountain, beside which grew the magnificent shrub, with its treasury of glowing blossoms. A fragrance was diffused from it which Giovanni recognized as
identical with that which he had attributed to Beatrice's breath, but incom-
parably more powerful. As her eyes fell upon it, Giovanni beheld her press
her hand to her bosom as if her heart were throbbing suddenly and
painfully.

"For the first time in my life," murmured she, addressing the shrub, "I
had forgotten thee."

"I remember, signora," said Giovanni, "that you once promised to reward
me with one of these living gems for the bouquet which I had the happy

boldness to fling to your feet. Permit me now to pluck it as a memorial of this interview."

He made a step towards the shrub with extended hand; but Beatrice darted forward, uttering a shriek that went through his heart like a dagger. She caught his hand and drew it back with the whole force of her slender figure. Giovanni felt her touch thrilling through his fibres. "Touch it not!" exclaimed she, in a voice of agony. "Not for thy life! It is fatal!"

Then, hiding her face, she fled from him and vanished beneath the sculptured portal. As Giovanni followed her with his eyes, he beheld the emaciated figure and pale intelligence of Dr. Rappaccini, who had been watching the scene, he knew not how long, within the shadow of the entrance.

No sooner was Guasconti alone in his chamber than the image of Beatrice came back to his passionate musings, invested with all the witchery that had been gathering around it ever since his first glimpse of her, and now likewise imbued with a tender warmth of girlish womanhood. She was human; her nature was endowed with all gentle and feminine qualities; she was worthiest to be worshipped; she was capable, surely, on her part, of the height and heroism of love. Those tokens which he had hitherto considered as proofs of a frightful peculiarity in her physical and moral system were now either forgotten or by the subtle sophistry of passion transmitted into a golden crown of enchantment, rendering Beatrice the more admirable by so much as she was the more unique. Whatever had looked ugly was now beautiful; or, if incapable of such a change, it stole away and hid itself among those shapeless half ideas which throng the dim region beyond the daylight of our perfect consciousness. Thus did he spend the night, nor felt asleep until the dawn had begun to awake the slumbering flowers in Dr. Rappaccini's garden, whither Giovanni's dreams doubtless led him. Up rose the sun in his due season, and, flinging his beams upon the young man's eyelids, awoke him to a sense of pain. When thoroughly aroused, he became sensible of a burning and tingling agony in his hand—in his right hand—the very hand which Beatrice had grasped in her own when he was on the point of plucking one of the gemlike flowers. On the back of that hand there was now a purple print like that of four small fingers, and the likeness of a slender thumb upon his wrist.

O, how stubbornly does love,—or even that cunning semblance of love which flourishes in the imagination, but strikes no depth of root into the heart,—how stubbornly does it hold its faith until the moment comes when it is doomed to vanish into thin mist! Giovanni wrapped a handkerchief about his hand and wondered what evil thing had stung him, and soon forgot his pain in a revery of Beatrice.

After the first interview, a second was in the inevitable course of what we call fate. A third; a fourth; and a meeting with Beatrice in the garden was no longer an incident in Giovanni's daily life, but the whole space in which he might be said to live; for the anticipation and memory of that ecstatic hour made up the remainder. Nor was it otherwise with the daughter of Rappaccini. She watched for the youth's appearance and flew to his side with confidence as unreserved as if they had been playmates from early infancy—as if they were such playmates still. If, by any unwonted chance, he failed to come at the appointed moment, she stood beneath the window and sent up the rich sweetness of her tones to float around him in his chamber and echo and reverberate throughout his heart: "Giovanni! Giovanni! Why tarriest thou? Come down!" And down he hastened into that Eden of poisonous flowers.

But, with all this intimate familiarity, there was still a reserve in Beatrice's demeanor, so rigidly and invariably sustained that the idea of infringing it scarcely occurred to his imagination. By all appreciable signs, they loved; they had looked love with eyes that conveyed the holy secret from the depths of one soul into the depths of the other, as if it were too sacred to be whispered by the way; they had even spoken love in those gushes of passion when their spirits darted forth in articulated breath like tongues of long hidden flame; and yet there had been no seal of lips, no clasp of hands, nor any slightest caress such as love claims and hallows. He had never touched one of the gleaming ringlets of her hair; her garment—so marked was the physical barrier between them—had never been waved against him by a breeze. On the few occasions when Giovanni had seemed tempted to overstep the limit, Beatrice grew so sad, so stern, and withal wore such a look of desolate separation, shuddering at itself, that not a spoken word was requisite to repel him. At such time he was startled at the horrible suspicions that rose, monsterlike, out of the caverns of his heart and stared him in the face; his love grew thin and faint as the morning mist; his doubts alone had substance. But, when Beatrice's face brightened again after the momentary shadow, she was transformed at once from the mysterious, questionable being whom he had watched with so much awe and horror; she was now the beautiful and unsophisticated girl whom he felt that his spirit knew with a certainty beyond all other knowledge.

A considerable time had now passed since Giovanni's last meeting with Baglioni. One morning, however, he was disagreeably surprised by a visit from the professor, whom he had scarcely thought of for whole weeks, and would willingly have forgotten still longer. Given up as he had long been to a pervading excitement, he could tolerate no companions except upon condition of their perfect sympathy with his present state of feeling. Such sympathy was not to be expected from Professor Baglioni.

The visitor chatted carelessly for a few moments about the gossip of the city and the university, and then took up another topic.

"I have been reading an old classic author lately," said he, "and met with a story that strangely interested me. Possibly you may remember it. It is of an Indian prince, who sent a beautiful woman as a present to Alexander the Great. She was as lovely as the dawn and gorgeous as the sunset; but what especially distinguished her was a certain rich perfume in her breath—richer than a garden of Persian roses. Alexander, as was natural to a youthful conqueror, fell in love at first sight with this magnificent stranger; but a certain sage physician, happening to be present, discovered a terrible secret in regard to her."

"And what was that?" asked Giovanni, turning his eyes downward to avoid those of the professor.

"That this lovely woman," continued Baglioni, with emphasis, "had been nourished with poisons from her birth upward, until her whole nature was so imbued with them that she herself had become the deadliest poison in existence. Poison was her element of life. With that rich perfume of her breath she blasted the very air. Her love would have been poison—her embrace death. Is not this a marvellous tale?"

"A childish fable," answered Giovanni, nervously starting from his chair. "I marvel how your worship finds time to read such nonsense among your graver studies."

"By the by," said the professor, looking uneasily about him, "what singular fragrance is this in your apartment? Is it the perfume of your gloves? It is faint, but delicious; and yet, after all, by no means agreeable. Were I to breathe it long, methinks it would make me ill. It is like the breath of a flower; but I see no flowers in the chamber."

"Nor are there any," replied Giovanni, who had turned pale as the professor spoke; "nor, I think, is there any fragrance except in your worship's imagination. Odors, being a sort of element combined of the sensual and the spiritual, are apt to deceive us in this matter. The recollection of a perfume, the bare idea of it, may easily be mistaken for a present reality."

"Ay; but my sober imagination does not often play such tricks," said Baglioni; "and, were I to fancy any kind of odor, it would be that of some vile apothecary drug, wherewith my fingers are likely enough to be imbued. Our worshipful friend Rappaccini, as I have heard, tinctures his medicaments with odors richer than those of Araby. Doubtless, likewise, the fair and learned Signora Beatrice would minister to her patients with draughts as sweet as a maiden's breath; but woe to him that sips them!"

Giovanni's face evinced many contending emotions. The tone in which the professor alluded to the pure and lovely daughter of Rappaccini was a torture to his soul; and yet the intimation of a view of her character, opposite to his own, gave instantaneous distinctness to a thousand dim suspicions, which now grinned at him like so many demons. But he strove hard to quell them and to respond to Baglioni with a true lover's perfect faith.

"Signor professor," said he, "you were my father's friend; perchance, too, it is your purpose to act a friendly part towards his son. I would fain feel nothing towards you save respect and deference; but I pray you to observe, signor, that there is one subject on which we must not speak. You know not the Signora Beatrice. You cannot, therefore, estimate the wrong—the blasphemy, I may even say—that is offered to her character by a light or injurious word."

"Giovanni! my poor Giovanni!" answered the professor, with a calm expression of pity, "I know this wretched girl far better than yourself. You shall hear the truth in respect to the poisoner Rappaccini and his poisonous daughter; yes, poisonous as she is beautiful. Listen; for, even should you do violence to my gray hairs, it shall not silence me. That old fable of the Indian woman has become a truth by the deep and deadly science of Rappaccini and in the person of the lovely Beatrice."

Giovanni groaned and hid his face.

"Her father," continued Baglioni, "was not restrained by natural affection from offering up his child in this horrible manner as the victim of his insane zeal for science; for, let us do him justice, he is as true a man of science as ever distilled his own heart in an alembic. What, then, will be your fate? Beyond a doubt you are selected as the material of some new experiment. Perhaps the result is to be death; perhaps a fate more awful still. Rappaccini with what he calls the interest of science before his eyes, will hesitate at nothing."

"It is a dream," muttered Giovanni to himself; "surely it is a dream."

"But," resumed the professor, "be of good cheer, son of my friend. It is not yet too late for the rescue. Possibly we may even succeed in bringing back this miserable child within the limits of ordinary nature, from which her father's madness has estranged her. Behold this little silver vase! It was wrought by the hands of the renowned Benvenuto Cellini, and is well worthy to be a love gift to the fairest dame in Italy. But its contents are invaluable. One little sip of this antidote would have rendered the most virulent poisons of the Borgias innocuous. Doubt not that it will be as efficacious against those of Rappaccini. Bestow the vase, and the precious liquid within it, on your Beatrice, and hopefully await the result."

Baglioni laid a small, exquisitely wrought silver vial on the table and withdrew, leaving what he had said to produce its effect upon the young man's mind.

"We will thwart Rappaccini yet," thought he, chuckling to himself, as he descended the stairs; "but, let us confess the truth of him, he is a wonderful man—a wonderful man indeed; a vile empiric, however, in his practice, and therefore not to be tolerated by those who respect the good old rules of the medical profession."

Throughout Giovanni's whole acquaintance with Beatrice, he had occasionally, as we have said, been haunted by dark surmises as to her character; yet so thoroughly had she made herself felt by him as a simple, natural, most affectionate, and guileless creature, that the image now held up by Professor Baglioni looked as strange and incredible as if it were not in accordance with his own original conception. True, there were ugly recollections connected with his first glimpses of the beautiful girl; he could not quite forget the bouquet that withered in her grasp, and the insect that perished amid the sunny air, by no ostensible agency save the fragrance of her breath. These incidents, however, dissolving in the pure light of her character, had no longer the efficacy of facts, but were acknowledged as mistaken fantasies, by whatever testimony of the senses they might appear to be substantiated. There is something truer and more real than what we can see with the eyes and touch with the finger. On such better evidence had Giovanni founded his confidence in Beatrice, though rather by the necessary force of her high attributes than by any deep and generous faith on his part. But now his spirit was incapable of sustaining itself at the height to which the early enthusiasm of passion had exalted it; he fell down, grovelling among earthly doubts, and defiled therewith the pure whiteness of Beatrice's image. Not that he gave her up; he did but distrust. He resolved to institute some decisive test that should satisfy him, once for all, whether there were those dreadful peculiarities in her physical nature which could not be supposed to exist without some corresponding monstrosity of soul. His eyes, gazing down afar, might have deceived him as to the lizard, the insect, and the flowers; but if he could witness, at the distance of a few paces, the sudden blight of one fresh and healthful flower in Beatrice's hand, there would be room for no further question. With this idea he hastened to the florist's and purchased a bouquet that was still gemmed with the morning dewdrops.

It was now the customary hour of his daily interview with Beatrice. Before descending into the garden, Giovanni failed not to look at his figure in the mirror—a vanity to be expected in a beautiful young man, yet, as displaying itself at that troubled and feverish moment, the token of a certain shallowness of feeling and insincerity of character. He did gaze, however, and said to himself that his features had never before possessed so rich a grace, nor his eyes such vivacity, nor his cheeks so warm a hue of super-abundant life.

"At least," thought he, "her poison has not yet insinuated itself into my system. I am no flower to perish in her grasp."

With that thought he turned his eyes on the bouquet, which he had never once laid aside from his hand. A thrill of indefinable horror shot through his frame on perceiving that those dewy flowers were already beginning to droop; they wore the aspect of things that had been fresh and lovely yesterday. Giovanni grew white as marble, and stood motionless before the mirror, staring at his own reflection there as at the likeness of something frightful. He remembered Baglioni's remark about the fragrance that seemed to pervade the chamber. It must have been the poison in his breath! Then he shuddered—shuddered at himself. Recovering from his stupor, he began to watch with curious eye a spider that was busily at work hanging its web from the antique cornice of the apartment, crossing and recrossing the artful system of interwoven lines—as vigorous and active a spider as ever dangled from an old ceiling. Giovanni bent towards the insect, and emitted a deep, long breath. The spider suddenly ceased its toil; the web vibrated with a tremor originating in the body of the small artisan. Again Giovanni sent forth a breath, deeper, longer, and imbued with a venomous feeling out of his heart: he knew not whether he were wicked, or only desperate. The spider made a convulsive gripe with his limbs and hung dead across the window.

"Accursed! accursed!" muttered Giovanni, addressing himself. "Hast thou grown so poisonous that this deadly insect perishes by thy breath?"

At that moment a rich, sweet voice came floating up from the garden.

"Giovanni! Giovanni! It is past the hour! Why tarriest thou? Come down!"

"Yes," muttered Giovanni again. "She is the only being whom my breath may not slay! Would that it might!"

He rushed down, and in an instant was standing before the bright and loving eyes of Beatrice. A moment ago his wrath and despair had been so fierce that he could have desired nothing so much as to wither her by a glance; but with her actual presence there came influences which had too real an existence to be at once shaken off; recollections of the delicate and benign power of her feminine nature, which had so often enveloped him in a religious calm; recollections of many a holy and passionate outgush of her heart, when the pure fountain had been unsealed from its depths and made visible in its transparency to his mental eye; recollections which, had Giovanni known how to estimate them, would have assured him that all this ugly mystery was but an earthly illusion, and that, whatever mist of evil might seem to have gathered over her, the real Beatrice was a heavenly angel. Incapable as he was of such high faith, still her presence had not utterly lost its magic. Giovanni's rage was quelled into an aspect of sullen insensibility. Beatrice, with a quick spiritual sense, immediately felt that there was a gulf of blackness between them which neither he nor she could pass. They walked on together, sad and silent, and came thus to the marble fountain and to its pool of water on the ground, in the midst of which grew the shrub that bore gemlike blossoms. Giovanni was affrighted at the eager enjoyment—the appetite, as it were—with which he found himself inhaling the fragrance of the flowers.

"Beatrice," asked he, abruptly, "whence came this shrub?"

"My father created it," answered she, with simplicity.

"Created it! created it!" repeated Giovanni. "What mean you, Beatrice?"

"He is a man fearfully acquainted with the secrets of Nature" replied Beatrice; "and, at the hour when I first drew breath, this plant sprang from the soil, the offspring of his science, of his intellect, while I was but his earthly child. Approach it not!" continued she, observing with terror that Giovanni was drawing nearer to the shrub. "It has qualities that you little dream of. But I, dearest Giovanni,—I grew up and blossomed with the plant and was nourished with its breath. It was my sister, and I loved it with a human affection; for, alas!—hast thou not suspected it?—there was an awful doom."

Here Giovanni frowned so darkly upon her that Beatrice paused and trembled. But her faith in his tenderness reassured her, and made her blush that she had doubted for an instant.

"There was an awful doom," she continued, "the effect of my father's fatal love for science, which estranged me from all society of my kind. Until Heaven sent thee, dearest Giovanni, O, how lonely was thy poor Beatrice!"

"Was it a hard doom?" asked Giovanni, fixing his eyes upon her.

"Only of late have I known how hard it was," answered she, tenderly. "O, yes; but my heart was torpid, and therefore quiet."

Giovanni's rage broke forth from his sullen gloom like a lightning flash out of a dark cloud.

"Accursed one!" cried he, with venomous scorn and anger. "And, finding thy solitude wearisome, thou hast severed me likewise from all the warmth of life and enticed me into thy region of unspeakable horror!"

"Giovanni!" exclaimed Beatrice, turning her large bright eyes upon his face. The force of his words had not found its way into her mind; she was merely thunderstruck.

"Yes, poisonous thing!" repeated Giovanni, beside himself with passion. "Thou hast done it! Thou hast blasted me! Thou hast filled my veins with poison! Thou hast made me as hateful, as ugly, as loathsome and deadly a creature as thyself—a world's wonder of hideous monstrosity! Now, if our breath be happily as fatal to ourselves as to all others, let us join our lips in one kiss of unutterable hatred, and so die!"

"What has befallen me?" murmured Beatrice, with a low moan out of her heart. "Holy Virgin, pity me, a poor heartbroken child!"

"Thou,—dost thou pray?" cried Giovanni, still with the same fiendish scorn. "Thy very prayers, as they come from thy lips, taint the atmosphere with death. Yes, yes; let us pray! Let us to church and dip our fingers in the holy water at the portal! They that come after us will perish as by a pestilence! Let us sign crosses in the air! It will be scattering curses abroad in the likeness of holy symbols!"

"Giovanni," said Beatrice, calmly, for her grief was beyond passion, "why dost thou join thyself with me thus in those terrible words? I, it is true, am the horrible thing thou namest me. But thou,—what hast thou to do, save with one other shudder at my hideous misery to go forth out of the garden and mingle with thy race, and forget that there ever crawled on earth such a monster as poor Beatrice?"

"Dost thou pretend ignorance?" asked Giovanni, scowling upon her. "Behold! this power have I gained from the pure daughter of Rappaccini."

There was a swarm of summer insects flitting through the air in search of the food promised by the flower odors of the fatal garden. They circled round Giovanni's head, and were evidently attracted towards him by the same influence which had drawn them for an instant within the sphere of several of the shrubs. He sent forth a breath among them, and smiled bitterly at Beatrice as at least a score of the insects fell dead upon the ground.

"I see it! I see it!" shrieked Beatrice. "It is my father's fatal science! No, no, Giovanni; it was not I. Never! never! I dreamed only to love thee and be with thee a little time, and so to let thee pass away, leaving but thine image in mine heart; for, Giovanni, believe it, though my body be nourished with poison, my spirit is God's creature, and craves love as its daily food. But my father,—he has united us in this fearful sympathy. Yes; spurn me, tread upon me, kill me! O, what is death after such words as thine? But it was not I. Not for a world of bliss would I have done it."

Giovanni's passion had exhausted itself in its outburst from his lips. There now came across him a sense, mournful, and not without tenderness, of the intimate and peculiar relationship between Beatrice and himself. They stood, as it were, in an utter solitude, which would be made none the less solitary by the densest throng of human life. Ought not, then, the desert of humanity around them to press this insulated pair closer together? If they should be cruel to one another, who was there to be kind to them? Besides, thought Giovanni, might there not still be a hope of his returning within the limits of ordinary nature, and leading Beatrice, the redeemed Beatrice, by the hand? O, weak, and selfish, and unworthy spirit, that could dream of an earthly union and earthly happiness as possible, after such deep love had been so bitterly wronged as was Beatrice's love by Giovanni's blighting words! No, no; there could be no such hope. She must pass heavily, with that broken heart, across the borders of Time — she must bathe her hurts in some fount of paradise, and forget her grief in the light of immortality, and *there* be well.

But Giovanni did not know it.

"Dear Beatrice," said he, approaching her, while she shrank away as always at his approach, but now with a different impulse, "dearest Beatrice, our fate is not yet so desperate. Behold! there is a medicine, potent, as a wise physician has assured me, and almost divine in its efficacy. It is composed of ingredients the most opposite to those by which thy awful father has brought this calamity upon thee and me. It is distilled of blessed herbs. Shall we not quaff it together, and thus be purified from evil?"

"Give it me!" said Beatrice, extending her hand to receive the little silver vial which Giovanni took from his bosom. She added, with a peculiar emphasis, "I will drink; but do thou await the result."

She put Baglioni's antidote to her lips; and, at the same moment, the figure of Rappaccini emerged from the portal and came slowly towards the marble fountain. As he drew near, the pale man of science seemed to gaze with a triumphant expression at the beautiful youth and maiden, as might an artist who should spend his life in achieving a picture or a group of statuary and finally be satisfied with his success. He paused; his bent form grew erect with conscious power; he spread out his hands over them in the attitude of a father imploring a blessing upon his children; but those were the same hands that had thrown poison into the stream of their lives. Giovanni trembled. Beatrice shuddered nervously, and pressed her hand upon her heart.

"My daughter," said Rappaccini, "thou art no longer lonely in the world. Pluck one of those precious gems from thy sister shrub and bid thy bridegroom wear it in his bosom. It will not harm him now. My science and the sympathy between thee and him have so wrought within his system that he now stands apart from common men, as thou dost, daughter of my pride and triumph, from ordinary women. Pass on, then, through the world, most dear to one another and dreadful to all besides!"

"My father," said Beatrice, feebly,—and still as she spoke she kept her hand upon her heart,—"wherefore didst thou inflict this miserable doom upon thy child?"

"Miserable!" exclaimed Rappaccini. "What mean you, foolish girl? Dost thou deem it misery to be endowed with marvellous gifts against which no power nor strength could avail an enemy—misery, to be able to quell the mightiest with a breath—misery, to be as terrible as thou art beautiful? Wouldst thou, then, have preferred the condition of a weak woman, exposed to all evil and capable of none?"

"I would fain have been loved, not feared," murmured Beatrice, sinking down upon the ground. "But now it matters not. I am going, father, where the evil which thou hast striven to mingle with my being will pass away like a dream—like the fragrance of these poisonous flowers, which will no longer taint my breath among the flowers of Eden. Farewell, Giovanni! Thy words of hatred are like lead within my heart; but they, too, will fall away as I ascend. O, was there not, from the first, more poison in thy nature than in mine?"

To Beatrice,—so radically had her earthly part been wrought upon by Rappaccini's skill,—as poison had been life, so the powerful antidote was death; and thus the poor victim of man's ingenuity and of thwarted nature, and of the fatality that attends all such efforts of perverted wisdom, perished there, at the feet of her father and Giovanni. Just at that moment Professor Pietro Baglioni looked forth from the window, and called loudly, in a tone of triumph mixed with horror, to the thunder-stricken man of science,—

"Rappaccini! Rappaccini! and is *this* the upshot of your experiment?"

Anticipations of the Future

Edgar Allan Poe (1809–1849) was a major figure in American (and European) literature, and a major figure, as well, in the developing literature of science fiction. Neurotic, tragic, alcoholic, he was also a genius who excelled in poetry, fiction, essays, and criticism. Some critics say that Poe founded science fiction.

Sam Moskowitz, who gives the credit for the founding of science fiction to Mary Shelley, wrote in *Explorers of the Infinite* (1963): "The full range of Poe's influence upon science fiction is incalculable, but his greatest contribution to the advancement of the genre was the precept that every departure from norm must be explained *scientifically.*"

Poe was one of the three writers Hugo Gernsback pointed to when he tried to describe what he was going to publish in the first science-fiction magazine, his *Amazing Stories* (1926).

Poe tried to live by his pen, and much of what he wrote was hasty or commercial. Critics of our technological age who recommend a return to simpler, more congenial times might reflect upon the experience of authors throughout the greater part of man's history: in most periods authors have been imprisoned because of their writing or had to be cautious of what they wrote or published for fear of prison, or were unable to support themselves by their art because few could read and fewer yet had the money to spend for literature.

Seldom, until the middle of the nineteenth century, was it possible for a person to find financial success in writing who did not have an independent income or the support of a patron.

Poe, the orphaned son of actors, became the ward of a Richmond merchant, John Allan. Their relationship was troubled by Poe's dissipation and gambling debts at college, and Allan's lack of sympathy for Poe's ambitions. They quarreled, Poe left home, and the rest of his career was a story of struggle, jobs lost or abandoned, a tragic marriage, and at last, literary success. He served some time in the army, tried to get through West Point and lasted less than a year, published three youthful volumes of poetry, and tried to live by hack writing.

His first short stories were published in 1832, his first pseudoscientific story, "MS. Found in a Bottle," in 1833, winning a prize offered by the *Baltimore Saturday Visitor.*

He found various editorial positions with the small-circulation literary journals of his day, performed brilliantly as an editor, but lost each job through drinking and personal problems. In 1836 he married a fourteen-year-old tubercular cousin, Virginia Clemm; she died in 1847.

Finally he achieved recognition with the publication of "The Gold Bug" in 1843, another prize-winning story, and "The Raven" and a major volume of poetry in 1845. Collections of his stories were published beginning in 1840. His critical articles and reviews, including a major statement in his review of Hawthorne's *Twice-Told Tales,* were beginning to shape a new theory of poetry and of short-story writing that would be a significant contribution to the history of literature.

In 1849 he proposed to a widowed childhood sweetheart and was accepted, but two months later, while on a Philadelphia business trip, he disappeared for six days and was found unconscious on the streets of Baltimore, where he died in delirium.

His contribution to literature was an emphasis on the creative act to the exclusion of other purposes. Hawthorne was often didactic. Poe's stories had no moral statements; he sought a single effect and shaped everything to it. The poem, he said, should aim at beauty and produce an elevating excitement; the short story, at truth.

Poe created the detective story, gave poetry a new direction, and helped shape the short story. His contribution to science fiction was almost as important.

He wrote several kinds of stories: detective stories such as "The Gold Bug" and those featuring the first fictional detective, Auguste Dupin; terror stories, mostly about death, such as "The Fall of the House of Usher," "The Tell-Tale Heart," "The Premature Burial," "The Pit and the Pendulum," and "The Black Cat"; allegories such as "The Masque of the Red Death"; and fantasies related more or less to science fiction.

Some of his fantasies had only a trace of the speculation that suggests science fiction. "MS. Found in a Bottle," for instance, is a sea voyage that turns into a fantasy of the Flying Dutchman variety; only at the end is the protagonist caught in a giant whirlpool at the South Pole that may take him into the unknown. The only unusual element in "A Descent into the Maelstrom" is the size and power of the whirlpool. Poe's novel, *The Narrative of Arthur Gordon Pym*, is an adventure story that includes a stowaway on board ship, a mutiny, a violent storm, cannibalism, an attack by savages, escape by giant canoe; only at the end, as in "MS. Found in a Bottle," do the two survivors floating toward the South Pole encounter the fantastic.

Other stories were inspired by the new science, and Poe, unlike Hawthorne, was capable of looking at the scientist and the results of science without prejudice. Mesmerism was the inspiration for several stories, including "A Tale of the Ragged Mountains," "The Facts in the Case of M. Valdemar," and "Mesmeric Revelation." "The Unparalleled Adventure of One Hans Pfaall" is a long story about a Dutch bankrupt who gets to the moon by means of a balloon, taking along equipment to protect himself against the rarefaction of the air; when Richard Adams Locke's "Moon Hoax" appeared, Poe accused him of stealing material Poe had prepared as a sequel. Ironically, Poe later published a story (that was to become known as "The Balloon-Hoax") in the New York *Sun,* describing the crossing of the Atlantic by balloon.

Some of Poe's stories, however, exhibited a unique understanding of the nature of change, perhaps the single most important characteristic of later science fiction. "The Thousand-and-Second Tale of Scheherazade" described the science and technology of Poe's time as Sindbad might have experienced it—more marvelous, and to the king more fantastic, than any of the other tales.

"Mellonta Tauta" (1849) may be the first true story of the future. Dated one thousand years from the time Poe wrote it in 1848 (and on April 1), the story incorporates an important recognition that the future will be so different that it will have forgotten its past (Poe's present) almost completely, and what it remembers will be confused and often wrong. The novel effect on the reader is the intellectual counterpoint between our knowledge and Mellonta Tauta's understanding, and our recognition of why these differ.

Mellonta Tauta

BY EDGAR ALLAN POE

ON BOARD BALLOON "SKYLARK,"

April 1, 2848.

Now, my dear friend—now, for your sins, you are to suffer the infliction of a long gossiping letter. I tell you distinctly that I am going to punish you for all your impertinences by being as tedious, as discursive, as incoherent and as unsatisfactory as possible. Besides, here I am, cooped up in a dirty balloon, with some one or two hundred of the *canaille,* all bound on a *pleasure* excursion (what a funny idea some people have of pleasure!), and I have no prospect of touching *terra firma* for a month at least. Nobody to talk to. Nothing to do. When one has nothing to do, then is the time to correspond with one's friends. You perceive, then, why it is that I write you this letter—it is on account of my *ennui* and your sins.

Get ready your spectacles and make up your mind to be annoyed. I mean to write at you every day during this odious voyage.

Heigho! when will any *Invention* visit the human pericranium? Are we forever to be doomed to the thousand inconveniences of the balloon? Will *nobody* contrive a more expeditious mode of progress? This jog-trot movement, to my thinking, is little less than positive torture. Upon my word we have not made more than a hundred miles the hour since leaving home! The very birds beat us—at least some of them. I assure you that I do not exaggerate at all. Our motion, no doubt, seems slower than it actually is—this on account of our having no objects about us by which to estimate our velocity, and on account of our going *with* the wind. To be sure, whenever we meet a balloon we have a chance of perceiving our rate, and then, I admit, things do not appear so very bad. Accustomed as I am to this mode of traveling, I cannot get over a kind of giddiness whenever a balloon passes us in a current directly overhead. It always seems to me like an immense bird of prey about to pounce upon us and carry us off in its claws. One went over us this morning about sunrise, and so nearly overhead that its drag-rope actually brushed the network suspending our car, and caused us very serious apprehension.

Our captain said that if the material of the bag had been the trumpery varnished "silk" of five hundred or a thousand years ago, we should inevitably
have been damaged. This silk, as he explained it to me, was a fabric composed of the entrails of a species of earthworm. The worm was carefully fed
on mulberries—a kind of fruit resembling a water-melon—and, when sufficiently fat, was crushed in a mill. The paste thus arising was called *papyrus*
in its primary state, and went through a variety of processes until finally became "silk." Singular to relate, it was once much admired as an article of *female dress!* Balloons were also very generally constructed from it. A better
kind of material, it appears, was subsequently found in the down surrounding the seed-vessels of a plant vulgarly called *euphorbium,* and at that time
botanically termed milkweed. This latter kind of silk was designated as
silk-buckingham, on account of its superior durability, and was usually prepared for use by being varnished with a solution of gum caoutchouc—a substance which in some respects must have resembled the *gutta percha* now in
common use. This caoutchouc was occasionally called India rubber or rubber of whist, and was no doubt one of the numerous *fungi.* Never tell me
again that I am not at heart an antiquarian

   Talking of drag-ropes—our own, it seems, has this moment knocked a
man overboard from one of the small magnetic propellers that swarm in the
ocean below us—a boat of about six thousand tons, and, from all accounts,
shamefully crowded. These diminutive barques should be prohibited from
carrying more than a definite number of passengers. The man, of course,
was not permitted to get on board again, and was soon out of sight, he and
his life-preserver. I rejoice, my dear friend, that we live in an age so en-
lightened that no such a thing as an individual is supposed to exist. It is the
mass for which the true Humanity cares. By the by, talking of Humanity, do
you know that our immortal Wiggins is not so original in his views of the
Social Condition and so forth, as his contemporaries are inclined to suppose? Pundit assures me that the same ideas were put, nearly in the same
way, about a thousand years ago, by an Irish philosopher called Furrier, on
account of his keeping a retail shop for cat-peltries and other furs. Pundit
knows, you know; there can be no mistake about it. How very wonderfully
do we see verified, every day, the profound observation of the Hindoo Aries
Tottle (as quoted by Pundit)—"Thus must we say that, not once or twice or
a few times, but with almost infinite repetitions, the same opinions come
round in a circle among men."

   April 2.—Spoke to-day the magnetic cutter in charge of the middle section of floating telegraph wires. I learn that when this species of telegraph
was first put into operation by Horse, it was considered quite impossible to

convey the wires over sea; but now we are at a loss to comprehend where the difficulty lay! So wags the world. *Tempora mutantur*—excuse me for quoting the Etruscan. What *would* we do without the Atalantic telegraph? (Pundit says Atlantic was the ancient adjective.) We lay to a few minutes to ask the cutter some questions, and learned, among other glorious news, that civil war is raging in Africa, while the plague is doing its good work beautifully both in Yurope and Ayesher. Is it not truly remarkable that, before the magnificent light shed upon philosophy by Humanity, the world was accustomed to regard War and Pestilence calamities? Do you know that prayers were actually offered up in the ancient temples to the end that these *evils* (!) might not be visited upon mankind? Is it not really difficult to comprehend upon what principle of interest our forefathers acted? Were they so blind as not to perceive that the destruction of a myriad of individuals is only so much positive advantage to the mass!

April 3.—It is really a very fine amusement to ascend the rope-ladder leading to the summit of the balloon-bag and thence survey the surrounding world. From the car below, you know, the prospect is not so comprehensive—you can see little vertically. But seated here (where I write this) in the luxuriously-cushioned open piazza of the summit, one can see everything that is going on in all directions. Just now, there is quite a crowd of balloons in sight, and they present a very animated appearance, while the air is resonant with the hum of so many millions of human voices. I have heard it asserted that when Yellow or (as Pundit *will* have it) Violet, who is supposed to have been the first aeronaut, maintained the practicability of traversing the atmosphere in all directions, by merely ascending or descending until a favorable current was attained, he was scarcely hearkened to at all by his contemporaries, who looked upon him as merely an ingenious sort of madman, because the philosophers (?) of the day declared the thing impossible. Really now it does seem to me *quite* unaccountable how anything so obviously feasible could have escaped the sagacity of the ancient *savans.* But in all ages the great obstacles to advancement in Art have been opposed by the so-called men of science. To be sure, *our* men of science are not quite so bigoted as those of old:—oh, I have something *so* queer to tell you on this topic. Do you know that it is not more than a thousand years ago since the metaphysicians consented to relieve the people of the singular fancy that there existed but *two possible roads for the attainment of Truth!* Believe it if you can! It appears that long, long ago, in the night of Time, there lived a Turkish philosopher (or Hindoo possibly) called Aries Tottle. This person introduced, or at all events propagated what was termed the deductive or *à priori* mode of investigation. He started with

what he maintained to be *axioms* or "self-evident truths," and thence proceeded "logically" to results. His greatest disciples were one Neuclid and
one Cant. Well, Aries Tottle flourished supreme until the advent of one
Hog, surnamed the "Ettrick Shepherd," who preached an entirely different
system, which he called the *à posteriori* or inductive. His plan referred altogether to Sensation. He proceeded by observing, analyzing and classifying
facts—*instantiae naturae,* as they were affectedly called—into general
laws. Aries Tottle's mode, in a word, was based on *noumena;* Hog's on *phenomena.* Well, so great was the admiration excited by this latter system that,
at its first introduction, Aries Tottle fell into disrepute; but finally he recovered ground, and was permitted to divide the realm of Truth with his
more modern rival. The *savans* now maintained that the Aristotelian and
Baconian roads were the sole possible avenues to knowledge. "Baconian,"
you must know, was an adjective invented as equivalent to Hog-ian and
more euphonious and dignified.

Now, my dear friend, I do assure you, most positively, that I represent this
matter fairly, on the soundest authority; and you can easily understand how
a notion so absurd on its very face must have operated to retard the progress
of all true knowledge—which makes its advances almost invariably by in-
tuitive bounds. The ancient idea confined investigation to *crawling;* and for
hundreds of years so great was the infatuation about Hog especially, that a
virtual end was put to all thinking properly so called. No man dared utter a
truth to which he felt himself indebted to his *Soul* alone. It mattered not
whether the truth was even *demonstrably* a truth, for the bullet-headed *savans* of the time regarded only *the road* by which he had attained it. They
would not even *look* at the end. "Let us see the means," they cried, "the
means!" If, upon investigation of the means, it was found to come neither
under the category Aries (that is to say Ram) nor under the category Hog,
why then the savans went no farther, but pronounced the "theorist" a fool,
and would have nothing to do with him or his truth.

Now, it cannot be maintained, even, that by the crawling system the
greatest amount of truth would be attained in any long series of ages, for
the repression of *imagination* was an evil not to be compensated for by any
superior *certainty* in the ancient modes of investigation. The error of these
Jurmains, these Vrinch, these Inglitch and these Amriccans, (the latter, by
the way, were our own immediate progenitors) was an error quite analo-
gous with that of the wiseacre who fancies that he must necessarily see an
object the better the more closely he holds it to his eyes. These people
blinded themselves by details. When they proceeded Hoggishly, their
"facts" were by no means always facts—a matter of little consequence had

it not been for assuming that they *were* facts and must be facts because they appeared to be such. When they proceeded on the path of the Ram, their course was scarcely as straight as a ram's horn, for they *never had* an axiom which was an axiom at all. They must have been very blind not to see this, even in their own day; for even in their own day many of the long "established" axioms had been rejected. For example—*"Ex nihilo nihil fit"*; "a body cannot act where it is not"; "there cannot exist antipodes"; "darkness cannot come out of light"—all these, and a dozen other similar propositions, formerly admitted without hesitation as axioms, were, even at the period of which I speak, seen to be untenable. How absurd in these people, then, to persist in putting faith in "axioms" as immutable bases of Truth! But even out of the mouths of their soundest reasoners it is easy to demonstrate the futility, the impalpability of their axioms in general. Who was the soundest of their logicians? Let me see! I will go and ask Pundit and be back in a minute . . . Ah, here we have it! Here is a book written nearly a thousand years ago and lately translated from the Inglitch—which, by the way, appears to have been the rudiment of the Amriccan. Pundit says it is decidedly the cleverest ancient work on its topic, Logic. The author (who was much thought of in his day) was one Miller, or Mill; and we find it recorded of him, as a point of some importance, that he had a mill-horse called Bentham. But let us glance at the treatise!

Ah!—"Ability or inability to conceive," says Mr. Mill very properly, "is in no case to be received as a criterion of axiomatic truth." What *modern* in his senses would ever think of disputing this truism? The only wonder with us must be, how it happened that Mr. Mill conceived it necessary even to hint at any thing so obvious. So far good—but let us turn over another page. What have we here?—"Contradictories cannot both be true that is, cannot co-exist in nature." Here Mr. Mill means, for example, that a tree must be either a tree or not a tree—that it cannot be at the same time a tree and not a tree. Very well; but I ask him *why*. His reply is this—and never pretends to be any thing else than this—"Because it is impossible to conceive that contradictories can both be true." But this is no answer at all, by his own showing; for has he not just admitted as a truism that "ability—or inability to conceive is *in no* case to be received as a criterion of axiomatic truth."

Now I do not complain of these ancients so much because their logic is, by their own showing, utterly baseless, worthless and fantastic altogether, as because of their pompous and imbecile proscription of all *other* roads of Truth, of all *other* means for its attainment than the two preposterous paths—the one of creeping and the one of crawling—to which they have dared to confine the Soul that loves nothing so well as to *soar.*

By the by, my dear friend, do you not think it would have puzzled these ancient dogmaticians to have determined by *which* of their two roads it was that the most important and most sublime of *all* their truths was, in effect, attained? I mean the truth of Gravitation. Newton owed it to Kepler. Kepler admitted that his three laws were *guessed at*—these three laws of all laws which led the great Inglitch mathematician to his principle, the basis of all physical principle—to go behind which we must enter the Kingdom of Metaphysics. Kepler guessed—that is to say, *imagined.* He was essentially a "theorist"—that word now of so much sanctity, formerly an epithet of contempt. Would it not have puzzled these old moles, too, to have explained by which of the two "roads" a cryptographist unriddles a cryptograph of more than usual secrecy, or by which of these two roads Champollion directed mankind to those enduring and almost innumerable truths which resulted from his deciphering the Hieroglyphics?

One word more on this topic and I will be done boring you. Is it not *passing* strange that, with their eternal prating about *roads* to Truth, these bigoted people missed what we now so clearly perceive to be the great highway—that of Consistency? Does it not seem singular how they should have failed to deduce from the works of God the vital fact that a perfect consistency *must be* an absolute truth! How plain has been our progress since the late announcement of this proposition! Investigation has been taken out of the hands of the ground-moles and given, as a task, to the true and only true thinkers, the men of ardent imagination. These latter *theorize.* Can you not fancy the shout of scorn with which my words would be received by our progenitors were it possible for them to be now looking over my shoulder? These men, I say, *theorize;* and their theories are simply corrected, reduced, systematized—cleared, little by little, of their dross of inconsistency—until, finally, a perfect consistency stands apparent which even the most stolid admit, because it is a consistency, to be an absolute and an unquestionable *truth.*

April 4.—The new gas is doing wonders, in conjunction with the new improvement with gutta percha. How very safe, commodious, manageable, and in every respect convenient are our modern balloons! Here is an immense one approaching us at the rate of at least a hundred and fifty miles an hour. It seems to be crowded with people—perhaps there are three or four hundred passengers—and yet it soars to an elevation of nearly a mile, looking down upon poor us with sovereign contempt. Still a hundred or even two hundred miles an hour is slow traveling, after all. Do you remember our flight on the railroad across the Kanadaw continent?—fully three hundred miles the hour—*that* was traveling. Nothing to be seen, though—nothing to be done but flirt, feast and dance in the magnificent saloons. Do you remember what an odd sensation was experienced when, by chance, we caught a glimpse of external objects while the cars were in full flight? Everything seemed unique—in one mass. For my part, I cannot say but that I preferred the traveling by the slow train of a hundred miles the hour. Here we were permitted to have glass windows—even to have them open—and something like a distinct view of the country was attainable . . . . Pundit says that *the route* for the great Kanadaw railroad must have been in some measure marked out about nine hundred years ago! In fact, he goes so far as to assert that actual traces of a road are still discernible—traces referable to a period quite as remote as that mentioned. The track, it appears, was *double* only; ours, you know, has twelve paths; and three or four new ones are in preparation. The ancient rails were very slight, and placed so close together as to be, according to modern notions, quite frivolous, if not dangerous in the extreme. The present width of track—fifty feet—is considered, indeed, scarcely secure enough. For my part, I make no doubt that a track of some sort *must* have existed in very remote times, as Pundit asserts; for nothing can be clearer, to my mind, than that, at some period—not less than seven centuries ago, certainly—the Northern and Southern Kanadaw continents were *united;* the Kanawdians, then, would have been driven, by necessity, to a great railroad across the continent.

April 5.—I am almost devoured by *ennui.* Pundit is the only conversible person on board; and he, poor soul! can speak of nothing but antiquities. He has been occupied all the day in the attempt to convince me that the ancient Amriccans *governed themselves!*—did ever anybody hear of such an absurdity?—that they existed in a sort of every-man-for-himself confederacy, after the fashion of the "prairie dogs" that we read of in fable. He says that they started with the queerest idea conceivable, viz: that all men are born free and equal—this in the very teeth of the laws of *gradation* so visibly impressed upon all things both in the moral and physical universe. Every man "voted," as they called it—that is to say, meddled with public affairs—until, at length, it was discovered that what is everybody's business is nobody's, and that the "Republic" (so the absurd thing was called) was without a government at all. It is related, however, that the first circumstance which disturbed, very particularly, the self-complacency of the philosophers who constructed this "Republic," was the startling discovery that universal suffrage gave opportunity for fradulent schemes, by means of which any desired number of votes might at any time be polled, without the possibility of prevention or even detection, by any party which should be merely villainous enough not to be ashamed of the fraud. A little reflection upon this discovery sufficed to render evident the consequences, which were that rascality must predominate—in a word, that a republican government *could* never be anything but a rascally one. While the philosophers, however, were busied in blushing at their stupidity in not have foreseen these inevitable evils, and intent upon the invention of new theories, the matter was put to an abrupt issue by a fellow of the name of *Mob,* who took everything into his own hands and set up a despotism, in comparison with which those of the fabulous Zeros and Hellofagabaluses were respectable and delectable. This Mob (a foreigner, by the by), is said to have been the most odious of all men that ever encumbered the earth. He was a giant in stature—insolent, rapacious, filthy; had the gall of a bullock with the heart of an hyena and the brains of a peacock. He died, at length, by dint of his own energies, which exhausted him. Nevertheless, he had his uses, as everything has, however vile, and taught mankind a lesson which to this day it is in no danger of forgetting—never to run directly contrary to the natural analogies. As for Republicanism, no analogy could be found for it upon the face of the earth—unless we except the case of the "prairie dogs," an exception which seems to demonstrate, if anything, that democracy is a very admirable form of government—for dogs.

April 6.—Last night had a fine view of the Alpha Lyræ, whose disk, through our captain's spy-glass, subtends an angle of half a degree, looking very much as our sun does to the naked eye on a misty day. Alpha Lyræ, although so very much larger than our sun, by the by, resembles him closely as regards its spots, its atmosphere, and in many other particulars. It is only within the last century, Pundit tells me, that the binary relation existing between these two orbs began even to be suspected. The evident motion of our system in the heavens was (strange to say!) referred to an orbit about a prodigious star in the centre of the galaxy. About this star, or at all events about a centre of gravity common to all the globes of the Milky Way and supposed to be near Alcyome in the Pleiades, every one of these globes was declared to be revolving, our own performing the circuit in a period of 117,000,000 of years! *We,* with our present lights, our vast telescopic improvements and so forth, of course find it difficult to comprehend *the ground* of an idea such as this. Its first propagator was one Mudler. He was led, we must presume, to this wild hypothesis by mere analogy in the first instance; but, this being the case, he should have at least adhered to analogy in its development. A great central orb was, in fact, suggested; so far Mudler was consistent. This central orb, however, dynamically, should have been greater than all its surrounding orbs taken together. The question might then have been asked—"Why do we not see it?"—*we,* especially, who occupy the mid region of the cluster—the very locality *near* which, at least, must be situated this inconceivable central sun. The astronomer, perhaps, at this point, took refuge in the suggestion of non-luminosity; and here analogy was suddenly let fall. But even admitting the central orb non-luminous, how did he manage to explain its failure to be rendered visible by the incalculable host of glorious suns glaring in all directions about it? No doubt what he finally maintained was merely a centre of gravity common to all the revolving orbs — but here again analogy must have been let fall. Our system revolves, it is true, about a common centre of gravity, but it does this in connection with and in consequence of a material sun whose mass more than counterbalances the rest of the system. The mathematical circle is a curve composed of an infinity of straight lines; but the idea of the circle — this idea of it which, in regard to all earthly geometry, we consider as merely the mathematical, in contradistinction from the practical, idea — is, in sober fact, the *practical* conception which alone we have any right to entertain in respect to those Titanic circles with which we have to deal, at least in fancy, when we suppose our system, with its fellows, revolving about a point in the centre of the galaxy. Let the most vigorous of human imaginations but attempt to take a single step towards the comprehension of a circuit so unutterable! It would scarcely be paradoxical to say that a flash of lightning itself, traveling *forever* upon the circumference of this inconceivable circle, would still *forever* be traveling in a straight line. That the path of our sun along such a circumference — that the direction of our system in such an orbit — would, to any human perception, deviate in the slightest degree from a straight line even in a million of years, is a proposition not to be entertained; and yet these ancient astronomers were absolutely cajoled, it appears, into believing that a decisive curvature had become apparent during the brief period of their astronomical history — during the mere point — during the utter nothingness of two or three thousand years! How incomprehensible, that considerations such as this did not at once indicate to them the true state of affairs — that of the binary revolution of our sun and Alpha Lyræ around a common centre of gravity!

April 7.—Continued last night our astronomical amusements. Had a fine view of the five Nepturian asteroids, and watched with much interest the putting up of a huge impost on a couple of lintels in the new temple at Daphnis in the moon. It was amusing to think that creatures so diminutive as the lunarians, and bearing so little resemblance to humanity, yet evinced a mechanical ingenuity so much superior to our own. One finds it difficult, too, to conceive the vast masses which these people handle so easily, to be as light as our reason tells us they actually are.

April 8.—Eureka! Pundit is in his glory. A balloon from Kanadaw spoke us to-day and threw on board several late papers: they contain some exceedingly curious information relative to Kanawdian or rather to Amriccan antiquities. You know, I presume, that laborers have for some months been employed in preparing the ground for a new fountain at Paradise, the emperor's principal pleasure garden. Paradise, it appears, has been, *literally* speaking, an island time out of mind—that is to say, its northern boundary was always (as far back as any records extend) a rivulet, or rather a very narrow arm of the sea. This arm was gradually widened until it attained its present breadth—a mile. The whole length of the island is nine miles; the breadth varies materially. The entire area (so Pundit says) was, about eight hundred years ago, densely packed with houses, some of them twenty stories high; land (for some most unaccountable reason) being considered as especially precious just in this vicinity. The disastrous earthquake, however, of the year 2050, so totally uprooted and overwhelmed the town (for it was almost too large to be called a village) that the most indefatigable of our antiquarians have never yet been able to obtain from the site any sufficient data (in the shape of coins, medals or inscriptions) wherewith to build up even the ghost of a theory concerning the manners, customs, &c. &c. &c., of the aboriginal inhabitants. Nearly all that we have hitherto known of them is, that they were a portion of the Knickerbocker tribe of savages infesting the continent at its first discovery by Recorder Riker, a knight of the Golden Fleece. They were by no means uncivilized, however, but cultivated various arts and even sciences after a fashion of their own. It is related of them that they were acute in many respects, but were oddly afflicted with a monomania for building what, in the ancient Amriccan, was denominated "churches"—a kind of pagoda instituted for the worship of two idols that went by the names of Wealth and Fashion. In the end, it is said, the island became, nine-tenths of it, church. The women, too, it appears, were oddly deformed by a natural protuberance of the region just below the small of the back—although, most unaccountably, this deformity was looked upon altogether in the light of a beauty. One or two pictures of these singular women have, in fact, been miraculously preserved. They look very odd, *very*—like something between a turkey-cock and a dromedary.

Well, these few details are nearly all that have descended to us respecting the ancient Knickerbockers. It seems, however, that while digging in the centre of the emperor's garden, (which, you know, covers the whole island,) some of the workmen unearthed a cubical and evidently chiseled block of granite, weighing several hundred pounds. It was in good preservation, having received, apparently, little injury from the convulsion which entombed it. On one of its surfaces was a marble slab with (only think of it!) *an inscription—a legible inscription.* Pundit is in ecstasies. Upon detaching the slab, a cavity appeared, containing a leaden box filled with various coins, a long scroll of names, several documents which appear to resemble newspapers, with other matters of intense interest to the antiquarian! There can be no doubt that all these are genuine Amriccan relics belonging to the tribe called Knickerbocker. The papers thrown on board our balloon are filled with fac-similes of the coins, MSS., typography, &c &c. I copy for your amusement the Knickerbocker inscription on the marble slab:—

THIS CORNER STONE OF A MONUMENT TO THE
MEMORY OF
GEORGE WASHINGTON,
WAS LAID WITH APPROPRIATE CEREMONIES ON THE
19TH DAY OF OCTOBER, 1847,
THE ANNIVERSARY OF THE SURRENDER OF
LORD CORNWALLIS
TO GENERAL WASHINGTON AT YORKTOWN,
A.D. 1781,
UNDER THE AUSPICES OF THE
WASHINGTON MONUMENT ASSOCIATION OF THE
CITY OF NEW YORK

This, as I give it, is a verbatim translation done by Pundit himself, so there *can* be no mistake about it. From the few words thus preserved, we glean several important items of knowledge, not the least interesting of which is the fact that a thousand years ago *actual* monuments had fallen into disuse—as was all very proper—the people contenting themselves, as we do now, with a mere indication of the design to erect a monument at some future time; a corner-stone being cautiously laid by itself "solitary and alone" (excuse me for quoting the great Amriccan poet Benton!) as a guarantee of the magnanimous *intention.* We ascertain, too, very distinctly, from this admirable inscription, the how, as well as the where and the what, of the great surrender in question. As to the *where,* it was Yorktown (wherever that was), and as to the *what,* it was General Cornwallis (no doubt some wealthy dealer in corn). *He* was surrendered. The inscription commemorates the surrender of—what?—why, "of Lord Cornwallis." The only question is what could the savages wish him surrendered for. But when we remember that these savages were undoubtedly cannibals, we are led to the conclusion that they intended him for sausage. As to the *how* of the surrender, no language can be more explicit. Lord Cornwallis was surrendered (for sausage) "under the auspices of the

Washington Monument Association"—no doubt a charitable institution for the depositing of corner-stones.—But, Heaven bless me! what is the matter? Ah! I see—the balloon has collapsed, and we shall have a tumble into the sea. I have, therefore, only time enough to add that, from a hasty inspection of fac-similes of newspapers, &c., I find that *the* great men in those days among the Amriccans were one John, a smith, and one Zacchary, a tailor.

Good bye, until I see you again. Whether you ever get this letter or not is a point of little importance, as I write altogether for my own amusement. I shall cork the MS. up in a bottle however, and throw it into the sea.

Yours everlastingly,
PUNDITA.

Expanding the Vision

Hawthorne and Poe had discovered an appropriate subject for fiction in the new science, and a suitably dramatic figure to serve as protagonist in the scientist. Science fiction was being shaped, and writers of all kinds occasionally would publish stories that later would be recognized as belonging to the science-fiction tradition or even at the time were clearly influenced by the possibilities of science and technology.

Honoré de Balzac (1799–1850), the great French realistic novelist, wrote a couple of stories, somewhat Gothic in tone, about an elixir of life and an effort to transmute base elements into gold. Edward Everett Hale (1822–1909) wrote a novel about a brick moon that accidentally gets launched into space while the workmen are living in it. Mark Twain (1835–1910) wrote his famous time-travel novel, *A Connecticut Yankee in King Arthur's Court* (1889) and a foreshadowing of television in "From the 'London Times' of 1904" (1898); there were science-fiction elements also in his *Extracts from Captain Stromfield's Visit to Heaven* and *Letters from the Earth.* Even Herman Melville had a story about an automaton. And a group of utopian writers in the last three decades of the nineteenth century wrote for or against science and technology. Prof. H. Bruce Franklin, in his pioneer study *Future Perfect* (1966, revised 1978) commented: "There was no major nineteenth-century American writer of fiction, and indeed few in the second rank, who did not write some science fiction or at least one utopian romance."

One of the most important of the sometime science-fiction writers was a prolific magazine writer of the 1850s, Fitz-James O'Brien (1828–1862). A dashing, romantic figure, O'Brien was born in Ireland, where he ran through an inheritance of eight thousand pounds, tried to elope with the wife of an English officer, and fled to the United States.

He had already published some stories and verse. In New York he began to write seriously and became a literary and social success in a profligate career that lasted only ten years. In the first year of the Civil War, he enlisted in the Union army, received a slight wound in a duel with a Confederate officer, and after inadequate treatment died at the age of thirty-three.

O'Brien was published in many of the literary journals of the time, including *Harper's* and the *Atlantic,* but few literary histories even mention his name. He would be little remembered if it were not for a handful of strikingly original fantasy and science-fiction stories, such as "The Wondersmith," about gypsies who manufacture an army of toy soldiers to kill all the Christian children at Christmas; "From Hand to Mouth," about a man who sits in a hotel room surrounded by disembodied hands and mouths; "What Was It? A Mystery," perhaps the earliest of the invisible-creature stories; "The Lost Room," in which the narrator returns to find his hotel room occupied by strangers he cannot evict; and "How I Overcame My Gravity," about an inventor who makes an antigravity machine by the use of the gyroscope.

His most effective story, and most original notion, was the often-reprinted "The Diamond Lens" (1858). It is the first known story in which another world is perceived through a microscope (although at the time of publication O'Brien was accused of stealing the idea from an unpublished story by a friend, a controversy resolved in O'Brien's favor). It would be followed by hundreds of stories about microscopic creatures, including many in which characters accomplish what O'Brien's microscopist cannot do: they descend into the microscopic world.

O'Brien's story opened up another world, not just for readers but for writers as well. Just as later writers would open galactic vistas, O'Brien let writers into the world of the very small. Perhaps just as important to the development of science fiction was O'Brien's realistic treatment of the fantastic.

One part of science fiction's appeal is the wonderful; another, and perhaps more important part, is the manner in which science fiction relates the wonderful to the everyday world of reality. Up to this time, Mary Shelley had written a romantic story with Gothic elements, Hawthorne had dealt with the symbolic figure of the scientist making moral choices, and Poe had shown the man of extreme and sometimes poetic sensibility facing the unusual; Poe sometimes became matter-of-fact but always jocularly.

O'Brien includes elements of the Gothic in the séance that puts the microscopist in touch with the spirit of Leeuwenhoek, and the murder of an acquaintance to obtain a diamond for the microscope. The microscopist's obsession is as romantic as Frankenstein's, though redeemed from the Gothic by the absence of guilt. But throughout the rest of the story, and even the Gothic parts, O'Brien's tone is colloquial and realistic.

Hugely popular in its own time, "The Diamond Lens" may be the first modern science-fiction story.

The Diamond Lens

BY FITZ-JAMES O'BRIEN

I

THE BENDING OF THE TWIG

From a very early period of my life the entire bent of my inclinations had been towards microscopic investigations. When I was not more than ten years old, a distant relative of our family, hoping to astonish my inexperience, constructed a simple microscope for me, by drilling in a disk of copper a small hole, in which a drop of pure water was sustained by capillary attraction. This very primitive apparatus, magnifying some fifty diameters, presented, it is true, only indistinct and imperfect forms, but still sufficiently wonderful to work up my imagination to a preternatural state of excitement.

Seeing me so interested in this rude instrument, my cousin explained to me all that he knew about the principles of the microscope, related to me a few of the wonders which had been accomplished through its agency, and ended by promising to send me one regularly constructed, immediately on his return to the city. I counted the days, the hours, the minutes, that intervened between that promise and his departure.

Meantime I was not idle. Every transparent substance that bore the remotest resemblance to a lens I eagerly seized upon, and employed in vain attempts to realize that instrument, the theory of whose construction I as yet only vaguely comprehended. All panes of glass containing those oblate spheroidal knots familiarly known as "bull's eyes" were ruthlessly destroyed, in the hope of obtaining lenses of marvellous power. I even went so far as to extract the crystalline humor from the eyes of fishes and animals, and endeavored to press it into the microscopic service. I plead guilty to having stolen the glasses from my Aunt Agatha's spectacles, with a dim idea of grinding them into lenses of wondrous magnifying properties,—in which attempt it is scarcely necessary to say that I totally failed.

At last the promised instrument came. It was of that order known as Field's simple microscope, and had cost perhaps about fifteen dollars. As far as educational purposes went, a better apparatus could not have been selected. Accompanying it was a small treatise on the microscope,—its history, uses, and discoveries. I comprehended then for the first time the "Arabian Nights Entertainments." The dull veil of ordinary existence that hung across the world seemed suddenly to roll away, and to lay bare a land of enchantments. I felt towards my companions as the seer might feel towards the ordinary masses of men. I held conversations with Nature in a tongue which they could not understand. I was in daily communication with living wonders, such as they never imagined in their wildest visions. I penetrated beyond the external portal of things, and roamed through the sanctuaries. Where they beheld only a drop of rain slowly rolling down the window-glass, I saw a universe of beings animated with all the passions common to physical life, and convulsing their minute sphere with struggles as fierce and protracted as those of men. In the common spots of mould, which my mother, good housekeeper that she was, fiercely scooped away from her jam pots, there abode for me, under the name of mildew, enchanted gardens, filled with dells and avenues of the densest foliage and most astonishing verdure, while from the fantastic boughs of these microscopic forests hung strange fruits glittering with green, and silver, and gold.

It was no scientific thirst that at this time filled my mind. It was the pure enjoyment of a poet to whom a world of wonders has been disclosed. I talked of my solitary pleasures to none. Alone with my microscope, I dimmed my sight, day after day and night after night, poring over the marvels which it unfolded to me. I was like one who, having discovered the ancient Eden still existing in all its primitive glory, should resolve to enjoy it in solitude, and never betray to mortal the secret of its locality. The rod of my life was bent at this moment. I destined myself to be a microscopist.

Of course, like every novice, I fancied myself a discoverer. I was ignorant at the time of the thousands of acute intellects engaged in the same pursuit as myself, and with the advantage of instruments a thousand times more powerful than mine. The names of Leeuwenhoek, Williamson, Spencer, Ehrenberg, Schultz, Dujardin, Schact, and Schleiden were then entirely unknown to me, or if known, I was ignorant of their patient and wonderful researches. In every fresh specimen of cryptogamia which I placed beneath my instrument I believed that I discovered wonders of which the world was as yet ignorant. I remember well the thrill of delight and admiration that shot through me the first time that I discovered the common wheel animalcule (Rotifera vulgaris) expanding and contracting its flexible spokes, and seemingly rotating through the water. Alas! as I grew older, and obtained some works treating of my favorite study, I found that I was only on the threshold of a science to the investigation of which some of the greatest men of the age were devoting their lives and intellects.

As I grew up, my parents, who saw but little likelihood of anything practical resulting from the examination of bits of moss and drops of water through a brass tube and a piece of glass, were anxious that I should choose a profession. It was their desire that I should enter the counting-house of my uncle, Ethan Blake, a prosperous merchant, who carried on business in New York. This suggestion I decisively combated. I had no taste for trade; I should only make a failure; in short, I refused to become a merchant.

But it was necessary for me to select some pursuit. My parents were staid New England people, who insisted on the necessity of labor; and therefore, although, thanks to the bequest of my poor Aunt Agatha, I should, on coming of age, inherit a small fortune sufficient to place me above want, it was decided that, instead of waiting for this, I should act the nobler part, and employ the intervening years in rendering myself independent.

After much cogitation I complied with the wishes of my family, and selected a profession. I determined to study medicine at the New York Academy. This disposition of my future suited me. A removal from my relatives would enable me to dispose of my time as I pleased without fear of detection. As long as I paid my Academy fees, I might shirk attending the lectures if I chose; and as I never had the remotest intention of standing an examination, there was no danger of my being "plucked." Besides, a metropolis was the place for me. There I could obtain excellent instruments, the newest publications, intimacy with men of pursuits kindred with my own,—in short, all things necessary to insure a profitable devotion of my life to my beloved science. I had an abundance of money, few desires that were not bounded by my illuminating mirror on one side and my object-glass on the other; what, therefore, was to prevent my becoming an illustrious investigator of the veiled worlds? It was with the most buoyant hopes that I left my New England home and established myself in New York.

II

THE LONGING OF A MAN OF SCIENCE

My first step, of course, was to find suitable apartments. These I obtained, after a couple of days' search, in Fourth Avenue; a very pretty second-floor unfurnished, containing sitting-room, bedroom, and a smaller apartment which I intended to fit up as a laboratory. I furnished my lodgings simply, but rather elegantly, and then devoted all my energies to the adornment of the temple of my worship. I visited Pike, the celebrated optician, and passed in review his splendid collection of microscopes,—Field's Compound, Hingham's, Spencer's, Nachet's Binocular (that founded on the principles of the stereoscope), and at length fixed upon that form known as Spencer's Trunnion Microscope, as combining the greatest number of improvements with an almost perfect freedom from tremor. Along with this I purchased every possible accessory,—draw-tubes, micrometers, a *camera-lucida,* lever-stage, achromatic condensers, white cloud illuminators, prisms, parabolic condensers, polarizing apparatus, forceps, aquatic boxes, fishing-tubes, with a host of other articles, all of which would have been useful in the hands of an experienced microscopist, but, as I afterwards discovered, were not of the slightest present value to me. It takes years of practice to know how to use a complicated microscope. The optician looked suspiciously at me as I made these wholesale purchases. He evidently was uncertain whether to set me down as some scientific celebrity or a madman. I think he inclined to the latter belief. I suppose I was mad. Every great genius is mad upon the subject in which he is greatest. The unsuccessful madman is disgraced and called a lunatic.

Mad or not, I set myself to work with a zeal which few scientific students have ever equalled. I had everything to learn relative to the delicate study upon which I had embarked,—a study involving the most earnest patience, the most rigid analytic powers, the steadiest hand, the most untiring eye, the most refined and subtile manipulation.

For a long time half my apparatus lay inactively on the shelves of my laboratory, which was now most amply furnished with every possible contrivance for facilitating my investigations. The fact was that I did not know how to use some of my scientific accessories,—never having been taught microscopics,—and those whose use I understood theoretically were of little avail, until by practice I could attain the necessary delicacy of handling. Still, such was the fury of my ambition, such the untiring perseverance of my experiments, that, difficult of credit as it may be, in the course of one year I became theoretically and practically an accomplished microscopist.

During this period of my labors, in which I submitted specimens of every substance that came under my observation to the action of my lenses, I became a discoverer,—in a small way, it is true, for I was very young, but still a discoverer. It was I who destroyed Ehrenberg's theory that the *Volvox globator* was an animal, and proved that his "monads" with stomachs and eyes were merely phases of the formation of a vegetable cell, and were, when they reached their mature state, incapable of the act of conjugation, or any true generative act, without which no organism rising to any stage of life higher than vegetable can be said to be complete. It was I who resolved the singular problem of rotation in the cells and hairs of plants into ciliary attraction, in spite of the assertions of Mr. Wenham and others, that my explanation was the result of an optical illusion.

But notwithstanding these discoveries, laboriously and painfully made as they were, I felt horribly dissatisfied. At every step I found myself stopped by the imperfections of my instruments. Like all active microscopists, I gave my imagination full play. Indeed, it is a common complaint against many such, that they supply the defects of their instruments with the creations of their brains. I imagined depths beyond depths in Nature which the limited power of my lenses prohibited me from exploring. I lay awake at night constructing imaginary microscopes of immeasurable power, with which I seemed to pierce through all the envelopes of matter down to its original atom. How I cursed those imperfect mediums which necessity through ignorance compelled me to use! How I longed to discover the secret of some perfect lens, whose magnifying power should be limited only by the resolvability of the object, and which at the same time should be free from spherical and chromatic aberrations, in short from all the obstacles over which the poor microscopist finds himself constantly stumbling! I felt convinced that the simple microscope, composed of a single lens of such vast yet perfect power was possible of construction. To attempt to bring the compound microscope up to such a pitch would have been commencing at the wrong end; this latter being simply a partially successful endeavor to remedy those very defects of the simple instrument, which, if conquered, would leave nothing to be desired.

It was in this mood of mind that I became a constructive microscopist. After another year passed in this new pursuit, experimenting on every imaginable substance,—glass, gems, flints, crystals, artificial crystals formed of the alloy of various vitreous materials,—in short, having constructed as many varieties of lenses as Argus had eyes, I found myself precisely where I started, with nothing gained save an extensive knowledge of glass-making. I was almost dead with despair. My parents were surprised at my apparent want of progress in my medical studies, (I had not attended one lecture since my arrival in the city) and the expenses of mad pursuit had been so great as to embarrass me very seriously.

I was in this frame of mind one day, experimenting in my laboratory on a small diamond,—that stone, from its great refracting power, having always occupied my attention more than any other,—when a young Frenchman, who lived on the floor above me, and who was in the habit of occasionally visiting me, entered the room.

I think that Jules Simon was a Jew. He had many traits of the Hebrew character: a love of jewelry, of dress, and of good living. There was something mysterious about him. He always had something to sell, and yet went into excellent society. When I say sell, I should perhaps have said peddle; for his operations were generally confined to the disposal of single articles,—-a picture, for instance, or a rare carving in ivory, or a pair of dueling-pistols, or the dress of a Mexican *caballero*. When I was first furnishing my rooms, he paid me a visit, which ended in my purchasing an antique silver lamp, which he assured me was a Cellini,—it was handsome enough even for that,—-and some other knickknacks for my sitting-room. Why Simon should pursue this petty trade I never could imagine. He apparently had plenty of money, and had the *entrée* of the best houses in the city,— taking care, however, I suppose, to drive no bargains within the enchanted circle of the Upper Ten. I came at length to the conclusion that this peddling was but a mask to cover some greater object, and even went so far as to believe my young acquaintance to be implicated in the slave-trade. That, however, was none of my affair.

On the present occasion, Simon entered my room in a state of considerable excitement.

"*Ah! mon ami!*" he cried, before I could even offer him the ordinary salutation, "it has occurred to me to be the witness of the most astonishing things in the world. I promenade myself to the house of Madame——How does the little animal—*le renard*—name himself in the Latin?"

"Vulpes," I answered.

"Ah! yes,—Vulpes. I promenade myself to the house of Madame Vulpes."

"The spirit medium?"

"Yes, the great medium. Great Heavens! what a woman! I write on a slip of paper many of questions concerning affairs the most secret,—affairs that conceal themselves in the abysses of my heart the most profound; and behold! by example! what occurs? This devil of a woman makes me replies the most truthful to all of them. She talks to me of things that I do not love to talk of to myself. What am I to think? I am fixed to the earth!"

"Am I to understand you, M. Simon, that this Mrs. Vulpes replied to questions secretly written by you, which questions related to events known only to yourself?"

"Ah! more than that, more than that," he answered, with an air of some alarm. "She related to me things—But," he added, after a pause, and suddenly changing his manner, "why occupy ourselves with these follies? It was all the biology, without doubt. It goes without saying that it has not my

credence.—But why are we here, *mon ami*? It has occurred to me to discover the most beautiful thing as you can imagine,—a vase with green
lizards on it, composed by the great Bernard Palissy. It is in my apartment;
let us mount. I go to show it to you."

I followed Simon mechanically; but my thoughts were far from Palissy
and his enamelled ware, although I, like him, was seeking in the dark after
a great discovery. This casual mention of the spiritualist, Madame Vulpes,
set me on a new track. What if this spiritualism should be really a great
fact? What if, through communication with subtiler organisms than my
own, I could reach at a single bound the goal, which perhaps a life of ago-
nizing mental toil would never enable me to attain?

While purchasing the Palissy vase from my friend Simon, I was mentally
arranging a visit to Madame Vulpes.

III

THE SPIRIT OF LEEUWENHOEK

Two evenings after this, thanks to an arrangement by letter and the promise of an ample fee, I found Madame Vulpes awaiting me at her residence
alone. She was a coarse-featured woman, with a keen and rather cruel
dark eye, and an exceedingly sensual expression about her mouth and
under jaw. She received me in perfect silence, in an apartment on the
ground floor, very sparely furnished. In the centre of the room, close to
where Mrs. Vulpes sat, there was a common round mahogany table. If I
had come for the purpose of sweeping her chimney, the woman could not
have looked more indifferent to my appearance. There was no attempt to
inspire the visitor with any awe. Everything bore a simple and practical
aspect. This intercourse with the spiritual world was evidently as familiar an occupation with Mrs. Vulpes as eating her dinner or riding in an
omnibus.

"You come for a communication, Mr. Linley?" said the medium, in a dry,
business-like tone of voice.

"By appointment,—yes."

"What sort of communication do you want?—a written one?"

"Yes,—I wish for a written one."

"From any particular spirit?"

"Yes."

"Have you ever known this spirit on this earth?"

"Never. He died long before I was born. I wish merely to obtain from him some information which he ought to be able to give better than any other."

"Will you seat yourself at the table, Mr. Linley," said the medium, "and place your hands upon it?"

I obeyed,—Mrs. Vulpes being seated opposite me, with her hands also on the table. We remained thus for about a minute and a half, when a violent succession of raps came on the table, on the back of my chair, on the floor immediately under my feet, and even on the windowpanes. Mrs. Vulpes smiled composedly.

"They are very strong to-night," she remarked. "You are fortunate." She then continued, "Will the spirits communicate with this gentleman?"

Vigorous affirmative.

"Will the particular spirit he desires to speak with communicate?"

A very confused rapping followed this question.

"I know what they mean," said Mrs. Vulpes, addressing herself to me; "they wish you to write down the name of the particular spirit that you desire to converse with. Is that so?" she added, speaking to her invisible guests.

That it was so was evident from the numerous affirmatory responses. While this was going on, I tore a slip from my pocket-book, and scribbled a name, under the table.

"Will this spirit communicate in writing with this gentleman?" asked the medium once more.

After a moment's pause, her hand seemed to be seized with a violent tremor, shaking so forcibly that the table vibrated. She said that a spirit had seized her hand and would write. I handed her some sheets of paper that were on the table, and a pencil. The latter she held loosely in her hand, which presently began to move over the paper with a singular and seemingly involuntary motion. After a few moments had elapsed, she handed me the paper, on which I found written, in a large, uncultivated hand, the words, "He is not here, but has been sent for." A pause of a minute or so now ensued, during which Mrs. Vulpes remained perfectly silent, but the raps continued at regular intervals. When the short period I mention had elapsed, the hand of the medium was again seized with its convulsive tremor, and she wrote, under this strange influence, a few words on the paper, which she handed to me. They were as follows:—

"I am here. Question me.
                    "LEEUWENHOEK."

I was astounded. The name was identical with that I had written beneath the table, and carefully kept concealed. Neither was it at all probable that an uncultivated woman like Mrs. Vulpes should know even the name of the great father of microscopics. It may have been biology; but this theory was soon doomed to be destroyed. I wrote on my slip—still concealing it from Mrs. Vulpes—a series of questions, which, to avoid tediousness, I shall place with the responses, in the order in which they occurred.

I.—Can the microscope be brought to perfection?

SPIRIT.—Yes.

I.—Am I destined to accomplish this great task?

SPIRIT.—You are.

I.—I wish to know how to proceed to attain this end. For the love which you bear to science, help me!

SPIRIT.—A diamond of one hundred and forty carats, submitted to electromagnetic currents for a long period, will experience a rearrangement of its atoms *inter se*, and from that stone you will form the universal lens.

I.—Will great discoveries result from the use of such a lens?

SPIRIT.—So great that all that has gone before is as nothing.

I.—But the refractive power of the diamond is so immense, that the image will be formed within the lens. How is that difficulty to be surmounted?

SPIRIT.—Pierce the lens through its axis, and the difficulty is obviated. The image will be formed in the pierced space, which will itself serve as a tube to look through. Now I am called. Good night.

I cannot at all describe the effect that these extraordinary communications had upon me. I felt completely bewildered. No biological theory could account for the *discovery* of the lens. The medium might, by means of biological *rapport* with my mind, have gone so far as to read my questions, and reply to them coherently. But biology could not enable her to discover that magnetic currents would so alter the crystals of the diamond as to remedy its previous defects, and admit of its being polished into a perfect lens. Some such theory may have passed through my head, it is true; but if so, I had forgotten it. In my excited condition of mind there was no course left but to become a convert, and it was in a state of the most painful nervous exaltation that I left the medium's house that evening. She accompanied me to the door, hoping that I was satisfied. The raps followed us as we went through the hall, sounding on the balusters, the flooring, and even the lintels of the door. I hastily expressed my satisfaction, and escaped hurriedly into the cool night air. I walked home with but one thought possessing me,—how to obtain a diamond of the immense size required. My entire means multiplied a hundred times over would have been inadequate to its purchase. Besides, such stones are rare, and become historical. I could find such only in the regalia of Eastern or European monarchs

IV

THE EYE OF MORNING

There was a light in Simon's room as I entered my house. A vague impulse urged me to visit him. As I opened the door of his sitting-room unannounced, he was bending, with his back toward me, over a carcel lamp, apparently engaged in minutely examining some object which he held in his hands. As I entered, he started suddenly, thrust his hand into his breast pocket, and turned to me with a face crimson with confusion.

"What!" I cried, "poring over the miniature of some fair lady? Well, don't blush so much; I won't ask to see it."

Simon laughed awkwardly enough, but made none of the negative protestations usual on such occasions. He asked me to take a seat.

"Simon," said I, "I have just come from Madame Vulpes."

This time Simon turned as white as a sheet, and seemed stupefied, as if a sudden electric shock had smitten him. He babbled some incoherent words, and went hastily to a small closet where he usually kept his liquors. Although astonished at his emotion, I was too preoccupied with my own idea to pay much attention to anything else.

"You say truly when you call Madame Vulpes a devil of a woman," I continued. "Simon, she told me wonderful things to-night, or rather was the means of telling me wonderful things. Ah! if I could only get a diamond that weighed one hundred and forty carats!"

Scarcely had the sigh with which I uttered this desire died upon my lips, when Simon, with the aspect of a wild beast, glared at me savagely, and, rushing to the mantelpiece, where some foreign weapons hung on the wall, caught up a Malay creese, and brandished it furiously before him.

"No!" he cried in French, into which he always broke when excited. "No! you shall not have it! You are perfidious! You have consulted with that demon, and desire my treasure! But I will die first! Me! I am brave! You cannot make me fear!"

All this, uttered in a loud voice trembling with excitement, astounded me. I saw at a glance that I had accidentally trodden upon the edges of Simon's secret, whatever it was. It was necessary to reassure him.

"My dear Simon," I said, "I am entirely at a loss to know what you mean. I went to Madame Vulpes to consult with her on a scientific problem, to the solution of which I discovered that a diamond of the size I just mentioned was necessary. You were never alluded to during the evening, nor, so far as I was concerned, even thought of. What can be the meaning of this outburst? If you happen to have a set of valuable diamonds in your possession, you need fear nothing from me. The diamond which I require you could not possess; or, if you did possess it, you would not be living here."

Something in my tone must have completely reassured him; for his expression immediately changed to a sort of constrained merriment, combined, however, with a certain suspicious attention to my movements. He laughed, and said that I must bear with him; that he was at certain moments subject to a species of vertigo, which betrayed itself in incoherent speeches, and that the attacks passed off as rapidly as they came. He put his weapon aside while making this explanation, and endeavored, with some success, to assume a more cheerful air.

All this did not impose on me in the least. I was too much accustomed to analytical labors to be baffled by so flimsy a veil. I determined to probe the mystery to the bottom.

"Simon," I said, gayly, "let us forget all this over a bottle of Burgundy. I have a case of Lausseure's *Clos Vougeot* down-stairs, fragrant with the odors and ruddy with the sunlight of the Côte d'Or. Let us have up a couple of bottles. What say you?"

"With all my heart," answered Simon, smilingly.

I produced the wine and we seated ourselves to drink. It was of a famous vintage, that of 1848, a year when war and wine throve together,—and its pure but powerful juice seemed to impart renewed vitality to the system. By the time we had half finished the second bottle, Simon's head, which I knew was a weak one, had begun to yield, while I remained calm as ever, only that every draught seemed to send a flush of vigor through my limbs. Simon's utterance became more and more indistinct. He took to singing French *chansons* of a not very moral tendency. I rose suddenly from the table just at the conclusion of one of those incoherent verses, and, fixing my eyes on him with a quiet smile, said: "Simon, I have deceived you. I learned your secret this evening. You may as well be frank with me. Mrs. Vulpes, or rather one of her spirits, told me all."

He started with horror. His intoxication seemed for the moment to fade away, and he made a movement towards the weapon that he had a short time before laid down. I stopped him with my hand.

"Monster!" he cried, passionately, "I am ruined! What shall I do? You shall never have it! I swear by my mother!"

"I don't want it," I said; "rest secure, but be frank with me. Tell me all about it."

The drunkenness began to return. He protested with maudlin earnestness that I was entirely mistaken,—that I was intoxicated; then asked me to swear eternal secrecy, and promised to disclose the mystery to me. I pledged myself, of course, to all. With an uneasy look in his eyes, and hands unsteady with drink and nervousness, he drew a small case from his breast and opened it. Heavens! How the mild lamplight was shivered into a thousand prismatic arrows, as it fell upon a vast rose-diamond that glittered in the case! I was no judge of diamonds, but I saw at a glance that this was a gem of rare size and purity. I looked at Simon with wonder, and—must I confess it—with envy. How could he have obtained this treasure: In reply to my questions, I could just gather from his drunken statements (of which, I fancy, half the incoherence was affected) that he had been superintending a gang of slaves engaged in diamond-washing in Brazil; that he had seen one of them secrete a diamond, but, instead of informing his employers, had quietly watched the negro until he saw him bury his treasure; that he had dug it up and fled with it, but that as yet he was afraid to attempt to dispose of it publicly, so valuable a gem being almost certain to attract too much attention to its owner's antecedents,—and he had not been able to discover any of those obscure channels by which such matters are conveyed away safely. He added, that, in accordance with the oriental practice, he had named his diamond by the fanciful title of "The Eye of Morning."

While Simon was relating this to me, I regarded the great diamond attentively. Never had I beheld anything so beautiful. All the glories of light, ever imagined or described, seemed to pulsate in its crystalline chambers. Its weight, as I learned from Simon, was exactly one hundred and forty carats. Here was an amazing coincidence. The hand of Destiny seemed in it. On the very evening when the spirit of Leeuwenhoek communicates to me the great secret of the microscope, the priceless means which he directs me to employ start up within my easy reach! I determined, with the most perfect deliberation, to possess myself of Simon's diamond.

I sat opposite to him while he nodded over his glass, and calmly revolved the whole affair. I did not for an instant contemplate so foolish an act as a common theft, which would of course be discovered, or at least necessitate flight and concealment, all of which must interfere with my scientific plans. There was but one step to be taken,—to kill Simon. After all, what was the life of a little peddling Jew, in comparison with the interests of science? Human beings are taken every day from the condemned prisons to be experimented on by surgeons. This man, Simon, was by his own confession a criminal, a robber, and I believed on my soul a murderer. He deserved death quite as much as any felon condemned by the laws; why should I not, like government, contrive that his punishment should contribute to the progress of human knowledge?

The means for accomplishing everything I desired lay within my reach. There stood upon the mantelpiece a bottle half full of French laudanum. Simon was so occupied with his diamond, which I had just restored to him, that it was an affair of no difficulty to drug his glass. In a quarter of an hour he was in a profound sleep.

I now opened his waistcoat, took the diamond from the inner pocket in which he had placed it, and removed him to the bed, on which I laid him so that his feet hung down over the edge. I had possessed myself of the Malay creese, which I held in my right hand, while with the other I discovered as accurately as I could by pulsation the exact locality of the heart. It was essential that all the aspects of his death should lead to the surmise of self-murder. I calculated the exact angle at which it was probable that the weapon, if levelled by Simon's own hand, would enter his breast; then with one powerful blow I thrust it up to the hilt in the very spot which I desired to penetrate. A convulsive thrill ran through Simon's limbs. I heard a smothered sound issue from his throat, precisely like the bursting of a large air-bubble, sent up by a diver, when it reaches the surface of the water; he turned half round on his side, and, as if to assist my plans more effectually, his right hand, moved by some mere spasmodic impulse, clasped the handle of the creese, which it remained holding with extraordinary muscular tenacity. Beyond this there was no apparent struggle. The laudanum, I presume, paralyzed the usual nervous action. He must have died instantaneously.

There was yet something to be done. To make it certain that all suspicion of the act should be diverted from any inhabitant of the house to Simon himself, it was necessary that the door should be found in the morning *locked on the inside.* How to do this, and afterwards escape myself? Not by the window; that was a physical impossibility. Besides, I was determined that the windows *also* should be found bolted. The solution was simple enough. I descended softly to my own room for a peculiar instrument which I had used for holding small slippery substances, such as minute spheres of glass, etc. This instrument was nothing more than a long slender hand-vice, with a very powerful grip, and a considerable leverage, which last was accidentally owing to the shape of the handle. Nothing was simpler than, when the key was in the lock, to seize the end of its stem in this vice, through the keyhole, from the outside, and so lock the door. Previously, however, to doing this, I burned a number of papers on Simon's hearth. Suicides almost always burn papers before they destroy themselves. I also emptied some more laudanum into Simon's glass,—having first removed from it all traces of wine,—cleaned the other wine-glass, and brought the bottles away with me. If traces of two persons drinking had been found in the room, the question naturally would have arisen, Who was the second? Besides, the wine-bottles might have been identified as belonging to me. The laudanum I poured out to account for its presence in his stomach, in case of a *post-mortem* examination. The theory naturally would be, that he first intended to poison himself, but, after swallowing a little of the drug, was either disgusted with its taste, or changed his mind from other motives, and chose the dagger. These arrangements made, I walked out, leaving the gas burning, locked the door with my vice, and went to bed.

Simon's death was not discovered until nearly three in the afternoon. The servant, astonished at seeing the gas burning,—the light streaming on the dark landing from under the door,—peeped through the keyhole and saw Simon on the bed. She gave the alarm. The door was burst open, and the neighborhood was in a fever of excitement.

Every one in the house was arrested, myself included. There was an inquest; but no clew to his death beyond that of suicide could be obtained. Curiously enough, he had made several speeches to his friends the preceding week, that seemed to point to self-destruction. One gentleman swore that Simon had said in his presence that "he was tired of life." His landlord affirmed that Simon, when paying him his last month's rent, remarked that "he would not pay him rent much longer." All the other evidence corresponded,—the door locked inside, the position of the corpse, the burnt papers. As I anticipated, no one knew of the possession of the diamond by Simon, so that no motive was suggested for his murder. The jury, after a prolonged examination, brought in the usual verdict, and the neighborhood once more settled down into its accustomed quiet.

V

ANIMULA

The three months succeeding Simon's catastrophe I devoted night and day to my diamond lens. I had constructed a vast galvanic battery, composed of nearly two thousand pairs of plates,—a higher power I dared not use, lest the diamond should be calcined. By means of this enormous engine I was enabled to send a powerful current of electricity continually through my great diamond, which it seemed to me gained in lustre every day. At the expiration of a month I commenced the grinding and polishing of the lens, a work of intense toil and exquisite delicacy. The great density of the stone, and the care required to be taken with the curvatures of the surfaces of the lens, rendered the labor the severest and most harassing that I had yet undergone.

At last the eventful moment came; the lens was completed. I stood trembling on the threshold of new worlds. I had the realization of Alexander's famous wish before me. The lens lay on the table, ready to be placed upon its platform. My hand fairly shook as I enveloped a drop of water with a thin coating of oil of turpentine, preparatory to its examination,— a process necessary in order to prevent the rapid evaporation of the water. I now placed the drop on a thin slip of glass under the lens, and throwing upon it, by the combined aid of a prism and a mirror, a powerful stream of light, I approached my eye to the minute hole drilled through the axis of the lens. For an instant I saw nothing save what seemed to be an illuminated chaos, a vast luminous abyss. A pure white light, cloudless and serene, and seemingly limitless as space itself, was my first impression. Gently, and with the greatest care, I depressed the lens a few hair's-breadths. The wondrous illumination still continued, but as the lens approached the object a scene of indescribable beauty was unfolded to my view.

I seemed to gaze upon a vast space, the limits of which extended far beyond my vision. An atmosphere of magical luminousness permeated the entire field of view. I was amazed to see no trace of animalculous life. Not a living thing, apparently, inhabited that dazzling expanse. I comprehended instantly that, by the wondrous power of my lens, I had penetrated beyond the grosser particles of aqueous matter, beyond the realms of infusoria and protozoa, down to the original gaseous globule, into whose luminous interior I was gazing, as into an almost boundless dome filled with a supernatural radiance.

It was, however, no brilliant void into which I looked. On every side I beheld beautiful inorganic forms, of unknown texture, and colored with the most enchanting hues. These forms presented the appearance of what might be called, for want of a more specific definition, foliated clouds of the highest rarity; that is, they undulated and broke into vegetable formations, and were tinged with splendors compared with which the gilding of our autumn woodlands is as dross compared with gold. Far away into the illimitable distance stretched long avenues of these gaseous forests, dimly transparent, and painted with prismatic hues of unimaginable brilliancy. The pendent branches waved along the fluid glades until every vista seemed to break through half-lucent ranks of many-colored drooping silken pennons. What seemed to be either fruits or flowers, pied with a thousand hues, lustrous and ever varying, bubbled from the crowns of this fairy foliage. No hills, no lakes, no rivers, no forms animate or inanimate, were to be seen, save those vast auroral copses that floated serenely in the luminous stillness, with leaves and fruits and flowers gleaming with unknown fires, unrealizable by mere imagination.

How strange, I thought, that this sphere should be thus condemned to solitude! I had hoped, at least, to discover some new form of animal life, perhaps of a lower class than any with which we are at present acquainted,—but still, some living organism. I found my newly discovered world, if I may so speak, a beautiful chromatic desert.

While I was speculating on the singular arrangements of the internal economy of Nature, with which she so frequently splinters into atoms our most compact theories, I thought I beheld a form moving slowly through the glades of one of the prismatic forests. I looked more attentively, and found that I was not mistaken. Words cannot depict the anxiety with which I awaited the nearer approach of this mysterious object. Was it merely some inanimate substance, held in suspense in the attenuated atmosphere of the globule? or was it an animal endowed with vitality and motion? It approached, flitting behind the gauzy, colored veils of cloud-foliage, for seconds dimly revealed, then vanishing. At last the violet pennons that trailed nearest to me vibrated; they were gently pushed aside, and the Form floated out into the broad light.

It was a female human shape. When I say "human," I mean it possessed the outlines of humanity,—but there the analogy ends. Its adorable beauty lifted it illimitable heights beyond the loveliest daughter of Adam.

I cannot, I dare not, attempt to inventory the charms of this divine revelation of perfect beauty. Those eyes of mystic violet, dewy and serene, evade my words. Her long, lustrous hair following her glorious head in a golden wake, like the track sown in heaven by a falling star, seems to quench my most burning phrases with its splendors. If all the bees of Hybla nestled upon my lips, they would still sing but hoarsely the wondrous harmonies of outline that enclosed her form.

She swept out from between the rainbow curtains of the cloud-trees into the broad sea of light that lay beyond. Her motions were those of some graceful Naiad, cleaving, by a mere effort of her will, the clear, unruffled waters that fill the chambers of the sea. She floated forth with the serene grace of a frail bubble ascending through the still atmosphere of a June day. The perfect roundness of her limbs formed suave and enchanting curves. It was like listening to the most spiritual symphony of Beethoven the divine, to watch the harmonious flow of lines. This, indeed, was a pleasure cheaply purchased at any price. What cared I, if I had waded to the portal of this wonder through another's blood? I would have given my own to enjoy one such moment of intoxication and delight.

Breathless with gazing on this lovely wonder, and forgetful for an instant of everything save her presence, I withdrew my eye from the microscope eagerly,—alas! As my gaze fell on the thin slide that lay beneath my instrument, the bright light from mirror and from prism sparkled on a colorless drop of water! There, in that tiny bead of dew, this beautiful being was forever imprisoned. The planet Neptune was not more distant from me than she. I hastened once more to apply my eye to the microscope.

Animula (let me now call her by that dear name which I subsequently bestowed on her) had changed her position. She had again approached the wondrous forest, and was gazing earnestly upwards. Presently one of the trees—as I must call them—unfolded a long ciliary process, with which it seized one of the gleaming fruits that glittered on its summit, and, sweeping slowly down, held it within reach of Animula. The sylph took it in her delicate hand and began to eat. My attention was so entirely absorbed by her, that I could not apply myself to the task of determining whether this singular plant was or was not instinct with volition.

I watched her, as she made her repast, with the most profound attention. The suppleness of her motions sent a thrill of delight through my frame; my heart beat madly as she turned her beautiful eyes in the direction of the spot in which I stood. What would I not have given to have had the power to precipitate myself into that luminous ocean, and float with her through those groves of purple and gold! While I was thus breathlessly following her every movement, she suddenly started, seemed to listen for a moment, and then cleaving the brilliant ether in which she was floating, like a flash of light, pierced through the opaline forest, and disappeared.

Instantly a series of the most singular sensations attacked me. It seemed as if I had suddenly gone blind. The luminous sphere was still before me, but my daylight had vanished. What caused this sudden disappearance? Had she a lover or a husband? Yes, that was the solution! Some signal from a happy fellow-being had vibrated through the avenues of the forest, and she had obeyed the summons.

The agony of my sensations, as I arrived at this conclusion, startled me. I tried to reject the conviction that my reason forced upon me. I battled against the fatal conclusion,—but in vain. It was so. I had no escape from it. I loved an animalcule!

It is true that, thanks to the marvellous power of my microscope, she appeared of human proportions. Instead of presenting the revolting aspect of the coarser creatures, that live and struggle and die, in the more easily resolvable portions of the water-drop, she was fair and delicate and of surpassing beauty. But of what account was all that? Every time that my eye was withdrawn from the instrument, it fell on a miserable drop of water, within which, I must be content to know, dwelt all that could make my life lovely.

Could she but see me once! Could I for one moment pierce the mystical walls that so inexorably rose to separate us, and whisper all that filled my soul, I might consent to be satisfied for the rest of my life with the knowledge of her remote sympathy. It would be something to have established even the faintest personal link to bind us together,—to know that at times, when roaming through those enchanted glades, she might think of the wonderful stranger, who had broken the monotony of her life with his presence, and left a gentle memory in her heart!

But it could not be. No invention of which human intellect was capable could break down the barriers that Nature had erected. I might feast my soul upon her wondrous beauty, yet she must always remain ignorant of the adoring eyes that day and night gazed upon her, and, even when closed, beheld her in dreams. With a bitter cry of anguish I fled from the room, and, flinging myself on my bed, sobbed myself to sleep like a child.

VI

THE SPILLING OF THE CUP

I arose the next morning almost at daybreak, and rushed to my microscope. I trembled as I sought the luminous world in miniature that contained my all. Animula was there. I had left the gas-lamp, surrounded by its moderators, burning, when I went to bed the night before. I found the sylph bathing, as it were, with an expression of pleasure animating her features, in the brilliant light which surrounded her. She tossed her lustrous golden hair over her shoulders with innocent coquetry. She lay at full length in the transparent medium, in which she supported herself with ease, and gambolled with the enchanting grace that the nymph Salmacis might have exhibited when she sought to conquer the modest Hermaphroditus. I tried an experiment to satisfy myself if her powers of reflection were developed. I lessened the lamp-light considerably. By the dim light that remained, I could see an expression of pain flit across her face. She looked upward suddenly, and her brows contracted. I flooded the stage of the microscope again with a full stream of light, and her whole expression changed. She sprang forward like some substance deprived of all weight. Her eyes sparkled and her lips moved. Ah! if science had only the means of conducting and reduplicating sounds, as it does the rays of light, what carols of happiness would then have entranced my ears! what jubilant hymns to Adonaïs would have thrilled the illumined air!

I now comprehended how it was that the Count de Gabalis peopled his mystic world with sylphs,—beautiful beings whose breath of life was lambent fire, and who sported forever in regions of purest ether and purest light. The Rosicrucian had anticipated the wonder that I had practically realized.

How long this worship of my strange divinity went on thus I scarcely know. I lost all note of time. All day from early dawn, and far into the night, I was to be found peering through that wonderful lens. I saw no one, went nowhere, and scarce allowed myself sufficient time for my meals. My whole life was absorbed in contemplation as rapt as that of any of the Romish saints. Every hour that I gazed upon the divine form strengthened my passion, a passion that was always overshadowed by the maddening conviction, that, although I could gaze on her at will, she never, never could behold me!

At length, I grew so pale and emaciated, from want of rest, and continual brooding over my insane love and its cruel conditions, that I determined to make some effort to wean myself from it. "Come," I said, "this is at best but a fantasy. Your imagination has bestowed on Animula charms which in reality she does not possess. Seclusion from female society has produced this morbid condition of mind. Compare her with the beautiful women of your own world, and this false enchantment will vanish."

I looked over the newspapers by chance. There I beheld the advertisement of a celebrated *danseuse* who appeared nightly at Niblo's. The Signorina Caradolce had the reputation of being the most beautiful as well as the most graceful woman in the world. I instantly dressed and went to the theatre.

The curtain drew up. The usual semicircle of fairies in white muslin were standing on the right toe around the enamelled flower-bank, of green canvas, on which the belated prince was sleeping. Suddenly a flute is heard. The fairies start. The trees open, the fairies all stand on the left toe, and the queen enters. It was the Signorina. She bounded forward amid thunders of applause, and, lighting on one foot, remained poised in air. Heavens! was this the great enchantress that had drawn monarchs at her chariot-wheels? Those heavy muscular limbs, those thick ankles, those cavernous eyes, that stereotyped smile, those crudely painted cheeks! Where were the vermeil blooms, the liquid expressive eyes, the harmonious limbs of Animula?

The Signorina danced. What gross, discordant movements! The play of her limbs was all false and artificial. Her bounds were painful athletic efforts; her poses were angular and distressed the eye. I could bear it no longer; with an exclamation of disgust that drew every eye upon me, I rose from my seat in the very middle of the Signorina's *pas-de-fascination*, and abruptly quitted the house.

I hastened home to feast my eyes once more on the lovely form of my sylph I felt that henceforth to combat this passion would be impossible. I applied my eye to the lens. Animula was there,—but what could have happened? Some terrible change seemed to have taken place during my absence. Some secret grief seemed to cloud the lovely features of her I gazed upon. Her face had grown thin and haggard; her limbs trailed heavily; the wondrous lustre of her golden hair had faded. She was ill!—ill, and I could not assist her! I believe at that moment I would have gladly forfeited all claims to my human birthright, if I could only have been dwarfed to the size of an animalcule, and permitted to console her from whom fate had forever divided me.

I racked my brain for the solution of this mystery. What was it that afflicted the sylph? She seemed to suffer intense pain. Her features contracted, and she even writhed, as if with some internal agony. The wondrous forests appeared also to have lost half their beauty. Their hues were dim and in some places faded away altogether. I watched Animula for hours with a breaking heart, and she seemed absolutely to wither away under my very eye. Suddenly I remembered that I had not looked at the water-drop for several days. In fact, I hated to see it; for it reminded me of the natural barrier between Animula and myself. I hurriedly looked down on the stage of the microscope. The slide was still there,—but, great heavens! the water-drop had vanished! The awful truth burst upon me; it had evaporated, until it had become so minute as to be invisible to the naked eye; I had been gazing on its last atom, the one that contained Animula,—and she was dying!

I rushed again to the front of the lens, and looked through. Alas! the last agony had seized her. The rainbow-hued forests had all melted away, and Animula lay struggling feebly in what seemed to be a spot of dim light. Ah! the sight was horrible: the limbs once so round and lovely shrivelling up into nothings; the eyes—those eyes that shone like heaven—being quenched into black dust; the lustrous golden hair now lank and discolored. The last throe came. I beheld that final struggle of the blackening form—and I fainted.

When I awoke out of a trance of many hours, I found myself lying amid the wreck of my instrument, myself as shattered in mind and body as it. I crawled feebly to my bed, from which I did not rise for months.

They say now that I am mad; but they are mistaken. I am poor, for I have neither the heart nor the will to work; all my money is spent, and I live on charity. Young men's associations that love a joke invite me to lecture on Optics before them, for which they pay me, and laugh at me while I lecture. "Linley, the mad microscopist," is the name I go by. I suppose that I talk incoherently while I lecture. Who could talk sense when his brain is haunted by such ghastly memories, while ever and anon among the shapes of death I behold the radiant form of my lost Animula!

The Indispensable Frenchman

If the writers who have contributed to the development of science fiction up to the second half of the nineteenth century had decided to write something else instead, conceivably science fiction would have developed much the same. That cannot be said about Jules Verne (1828–1905). Paradoxical as it may sound, Verne was greatly influenced by writers who preceded him; the technology that fueled his novels was not visionary, yet what he wrote about and the way he wrote about it was indispensable to the evolution and popular acceptance of the new literature of science and technology.

Verne was born into an age when engineers were reshaping the world, most dramatically in transportation. They were making the world a smaller place, and a more convenient place for man. Previous generations had taken what nature made available. They had built their cities on seacoasts or on rivers because water transportation was cheap. Now engineers began dredging canals where rivers did not run (the Bridgewater Canal in England was completed in 1761, the Erie Canal in the United States in 1825, the Suez Canal in 1869), and where canals were not feasible, they built railways (beginning in 1825 in England, in 1830 in the United States). Steamboats turned the crossing of the Atlantic into a two-week jaunt. The transatlantic submarine cable was completed in 1866 and brought Europe and the United States into instantaneous communication.

Distant parts of the world were being explored: dark Africa, strange islands, the frozen wastes of the Arctic and the Antarctic; explorers were the heroes of the age. New sources of energy and materials were being developed. The age of chemistry was beginning with the creation of chemical fertilizer and plastics. Electricity was being applied to a variety of marvelous mechanisms—phonographs, electric lights, street railways—and it soon would replace steam as the new scientific miracle.

Verne, the son of a lawyer, himself educated as a lawyer, was a man of his times, fascinated by geography and invention, but instead of turning to a career in science or engineering, he wrote about the romance of science and technology. His early ambition was to write for the stage, and his father supported him for some years while he wrote plays and librettos, none of which brought him fame or wealth. Finally Verne married a young widow with two daughters, persuaded his father to buy him a seat on the Paris Stock Exchange, and apparently settled down to a middle-class career. But he continued to write, working early in the morning until the exchange opened at ten.

He was an admirer of James Fenimore Cooper, of Sir Walter Scott, of *Robinson Crusoe* and *Swiss Family Robinson,* but particularly of Poe, who enjoyed a greater reputation in Europe than in the United States. The engineering excitement of the times and Poe's example ("The Balloon-Hoax") combined with Verne's friendship with a balloonist to produce a book about ballooning. At the suggestion of the man who would become his lifelong publisher, Jules Hetzel, Verne reworked the book into a novel. It was published in 1863 as *Five Weeks in a Balloon* and launched Verne on a career of writing two books a year for the rest of his long life.

His first book was an adventure story—a *voyage extraordinaire,* as Verne called his scientific romances, most of which were journeys of one sort or another—but it was only remotely science fiction; ballooning was eighty years old in 1863, and Verne's balloon was only an improved model, just as his submarine in *Twenty Thousand Leagues Under the Sea* was only an improved model of submarines already in existence. Verne's next book was science fiction without a doubt: *A Journey to the Center of the Earth* (1864); it was inspired by Holberg's book and by new discoveries in geology. Then came *From the Earth to the Moon* (1865) and its sequel (although he made his impatient readers wait five years to find out what happened to the travelers in his projectile), *Round the Moon* (1870).

Verne spent most of his life writing about one unusual journey after another, many of them science fiction as well. The best known of these were *Twenty Thousand Leagues Under the Sea* (1870) and its sequel, *The Mysterious Island* (1875), *Hector Servadac, or Off on a Comet* (1877), *Robur the Conqueror* (1886), and *The Master of the World* (1905). He also wrote other kinds of fiction, including *Around the World in Eighty Days* (1873), which made his fortune, *Matthias Sandorf,* and *Michael Strogoff,* but aside from the first of these it is for his science fiction that he is remembered today.

Verne wrote simple stories about uncomplicated people. His ideas were not particularly original; most of them he got from authors he admired. His plots consisted of abductions, searches, mysteries, and ambitious undertakings; the events of the stories were often marked by accident and coincidence (which he considered to be evidence of divine intervention in human affairs). He was commended by Pope Leo XIII for the purity of his writing.

Verne was tremendously popular in his own time, and he created a mass audience for suspenseful stories in which travel was a principal motif, but the mechanism of travel belonged to the technology of the future. He was the second of the two writers Gernsback pointed at in 1926 when he told his readers what he was going to publish in *Amazing Stories*.

Because he devoted most of his career to writing science fiction (and made a fortune at it), Verne can be called the first science-fiction writer.

From Twenty Thousand Leagues Under the Sea

BY JULES VERNE

CHAPTER X

THE MAN OF THE SEAS

It was the commander of the vessel who thus spoke.

At these words, Ned Land rose suddenly. The steward, nearly strangled, tottered out on a sign from his master; but such was the power of the commander on board, that not a gesture betrayed the resentment which this man must have felt toward the Canadian. Conseil interested in spite of himself, I stupefied, awaited in silence the result of this scene.

The commander, leaning against a corner of the table with his arms folded, scanned us with profound attention. Did he hesitate to speak? Did he regret the words which he had just spoken in French? One might almost think so.

After some moments of silence, which not one of us dreamed of breaking, "Gentlemen," said he, in a calm and penetrating voice, "I speak French, English, German, and Latin equally well. I could, therefore, have answered you at our first interview, but I wished to know you first, then to reflect. The story told by each one, entirely agreeing in the main points, convinced me of your identity. I know now that chance has brought before me M. Pierre Aronnax, Professor of Natural History at the Museum of Paris, intrusted with a scientific mission abroad; Conseil, his servant; and Ned Land, of Canadian origin, harpooner on board the frigate *Abraham Lincoln* of the navy of the United States of America."

I bowed assent. It was not a question that the commander put to me. Therefore there was no answer to be made. This man expressed himself with perfect ease, without any accent. His sentences were well turned, his words clear, and his fluency of speech remarkable. Yet I did not recognize in him a fellow-countryman.

"You have doubtless thought, sir, that I have delayed long in paying you this second visit. The reason is that, your identity recognized, I wished to weigh maturely what part to act toward you. I have hesitated much. Most annoying circumstances have brought you into the presence of a man who has broken all the ties of humanity. You have come to trouble my existence."

"Unintentionally!" said I.

"Unintentionally?" replied the stranger, raising his voice a little; "was it unintentionally that the *Abraham Lincoln* pursued me all over the seas? Was it unintentionally that you took passage in this frigate? Was it unintentionally that your cannon-balls rebounded off the plating of my vessel? Was it unintentionally that Mr. Ned Land struck me with his harpoon?"

I detected a restrained irritation in these words. But to these recriminations I had a very natural answer to make, and I made it.

"Sir," said I, "no doubt you are ignorant of the discussions which have taken place concerning you in America and Europe. You do not know that divers accidents, caused by collisions with your submarine machine, have excited public feeling in the two continents. I omit the hypotheses without number by which it was sought to explain the inexplicable phenomenon of which you alone possess the secret. But you must understand that, in pursuing you over the high seas of the Pacific, the *Abraham Lincoln* believed itself to be chasing some powerful sea-monster, of which it was necessary to rid the ocean at any price."

A half-smile curled-the lips of the commander; then, in a calmer tone, "M. Aronnax," he replied, "dare you affirm that your frigate would not as soon have pursued and cannonaded a submarine boat as a monster?"

This question embarrassed me, for certainly Captain Farragut might not have hesitated. He might have thought it his duty to destroy a contrivance of this kind, as he would a gigantic narwhal.

"You understand then, sir," continued the stranger, "that I have the right to treat you as enemies?"

I answered nothing, purposely. For what good would it be to discuss such a proposition, when force could destroy the best arguments?

"I have hesitated for some time," continued the commander; "nothing obliged me to show hospitality. If I chose to separate myself from you, I should have no interest in seeing you again; I could place you upon the deck of this vessel which has served you as a refuge, I could sink beneath the waters, and forget that you had ever existed. Would not that be my right?"

"It might be the right of a savage," I answered, "but not that of a civilized man."

"Professor," replied the commander quickly, "I am not what you call a civilized man! I have done with society entirely, for reasons which I alone have the right of appreciating. I do not therefore obey its laws, and I desire you never to allude to them before me again!"

This was said plainly. A flash of anger and disdain kindled in the eyes of the Unknown, and I had a glimpse of a terrible past in the life of this man. Not only had he put himself beyond the pale of human laws, but he had made himself independent of them, free in the strictest acceptation of the word, quite beyond their reach! Who then would dare to pursue him at the bottom of the sea, when, on its surface, he defied all attempts made against him? What vessel could resist the shock of his submarine monitor? What cuirass, however thick, could withstand the blows of his spur? No man could demand from him an account of his actions; God, if he believed in one—his conscience, if he had one—were the sole judges to whom he was answerable.

These reflections crossed my mind rapidly, while the strange personage was silent, absorbed, and as if wrapped up in himself. I regarded him with fear mingled with interest, as, doubtless, Oedipus regarded the Sphinx.

After a silence, the commander resumed the conversation.

"I have hesitated," said he, "but I have thought that my interest might be reconciled, with that pity to which every human being has a right. You will remain on board my vessel, since fate has cast you there. You will be free; and in exchange for this liberty, I shall only impose one single condition. Your word of honor to submit to it will suffice."

"Speak, sir," I answered. "I suppose this condition is one which a man of honor may accept?"

"Yes, sir; it is this. It is possible that certain events, unforeseen, may oblige me to consign you to your cabins for some hours or some days, as the case may be. As I desire never to use violence, I expect from you, more than all the others, a passive obedience. In thus acting, I take all the responsibility: I acquit you entirely, for I make it an impossibility for you to see what ought not to be seen. Do you accept this condition?"

Then things took place on board which, to say the least, were singular, and which ought not to be seen by people who were not placed beyond the pale of social laws. Among the surprises which the future was preparing for me, this might not be the least.

"We accept," I answered; "only I will ask your permission, sir, to address one question to you—one only."

"Speak, sir."

"You said that we should be free on board."

"Entirely."

"I ask you, then, what you mean by this liberty?"

"Just the liberty to go, to come, to see, to observe even all that passes here—save under rare circumstances—the liberty, in short, which we enjoy ourselves, my companions and I."

It was evident that we did not understand one another.

"Pardon me, sir," I resumed, "but this liberty is only what every prisoner has of pacing his prison. It can not suffice us."

"It must suffice you, however."

"What! we must renounce forever seeing our country, our friends, our relations again?"

"Yes, sir. But to renounce that unendurable worldly yoke which men believe to be liberty is not perhaps so painful as you think."

"Well," exclaimed Ned Land, "never will I give my word of honor not to try to escape."

"I did not ask you for your word of honor, Master Land," answered the commander coldly.

"Sir," I replied, beginning to get angry in spite of myself, "you abuse your situation toward us; it is cruelty to demand this."

"No, sir, it is clemency. You are my prisoners of war. I keep you, when I could, by a word, plunge you into the depths of the ocean. You attacked me. You came to surprise a secret which no man in the world must penetrate— the secret of my whole existence. And you think that I am going to send you back to the world which must know me no more? Never! In retaining you, it is not you whom I guard—it is myself."

These words indicated a resolution taken on the part of the commander, against which no arguments would prevail.

"So, sir," I rejoined, "you give us simply the choice between life and death?"

"Simply."

"My friends," said I, "to a question thus put, there is nothing to answer. But no word of honor binds us to the master of this vessel."

"None, sir," answered the Unknown.

Then, in a gentler tone, he continued: "Now, permit me to finish what I have to say to you. I know you, M. Aronnax. You and your companions will not, perhaps, have so much to complain of in the chance which has bound you to my fate. You will find among the books which are my favorite study the work which you have published on 'the depths of the sea.' I have often read it. You have earned your work as far as terrestrial science permitted you. But you do not know all— you have not seen all. Let me tell you then, professor, that you will not regret the time passed on board my vessel. You are going to visit the land of marvels."

These words of the commander had a great effect upon me. I cannot deny it. My weak point was touched; and I forgot, for a moment, that the contemplation of these sublime subjects was not worth the loss of liberty. Besides, I trusted to the future to decide this grave question. So I contented myself with saying, "By what name ought I to address you?"

"Sir," replied me commander, "I am nothing to you but Captain Nemo; and you and your companions are nothing to me but the passengers of the *Nautilus.*"

Captain Nemo called. A steward appeared. The captain gave him his orders in that strange language which I did not understand. Then, turning toward the Canadian and Conseil, "A repast awaits you in your cabin," said he. "Be so good as to follow this man. And now, M. Aronnax, our breakfast is ready. Permit me to lead the way."

"I am at your service, Captain."

I followed Captain Nemo; and as soon as I had passed through the door, I found myself in a kind of passage lighted by electricity, similar to the waist of a ship. After we had proceeded a dozen yards, a second door opened before me.

I then entered a dining room, decorated and furnished in severe taste. High oaken sideboards, inlaid with ebony, stood at the two extremities of the room, and upon their shelves glittered china, porcelain, and glass of inestimable value.

The plate on the table sparkled in the rays which the luminous ceiling shed around, while the light was tempered and softened by exquisite paintings.

In the center of the room was a table richly laid out. Captain Nemo indicated the place I was to occupy.

The breakfast consisted of a certain number of dishes, the contents of which were furnished by the sea alone; and I was ignorant of the nature and mode of preparation of some of them. I acknowledged that they were good though they had a peculiar flavor, which I easily became accustomed to. These different aliments appeared to me to be rich in phosphorus, and I thought that they must have a marine origin.

Captain Nemo looked at me. I asked him no questions, but he guessed my thoughts, and answered of his own accord the questions which I was burning to address to him.

"The greater part of these dishes are unknown to you," he said to me. "However, you may partake of them without fear. They are wholesome and nourishing. For a long time I have renounced the food of the earth, and I am never ill now. My crew, who are healthy, are fed on the same food."

"So," said I, "all these eatables are the produce of the sea?"

"Yes, professor, the sea supplies all my wants. Sometimes I cast my nets in tow, and I draw them in ready to break. Sometimes I hunt in the midst of this element, which appears to be inaccessible to man, and quarry the game which dwells in my submarine forests. My flocks, like those of Neptune's old shepherds, graze fearlessly in the immense prairies of the ocean. I have a vast property there, which I cultivate myself, and which is always sown by the hand of the Creator of all things."

"I can understand perfectly, sir, that your nets furnish excellent fish for your table; I can understand also that you hunt aquatic game in your submarine forests; but I cannot understand at all how a particle of meat, no matter how small can figure in your bill of fare."

"This, which you believe to be meat, professor, is nothing else than fillet of turtle. Here are also some dolphin's livers, which you take to be ragout of pork. My cook is a clever fellow, who excels in dressing these various products of the ocean. Taste all these dishes. Here is a preserve of holothuria, which a Malay would declare to be unrivaled in the world; here is a cream, of which the milk has been furnished by the cetacea, and the sugar by the great fucus of the North Sea; and lastly, permit me to offer you some preserve of anemones, which is equal to that of the most delicious fruits."

I tasted, more from curiosity than as a connoisseur, while Captain Nemo enchanted me with his extraordinary stories.

"You like the sea, Captain?"

"Yes, I love it! The sea is everything. It covers seven-tenths of the terrestrial globe. Its breath is pure and healthy. It is an immense desert, where man is never lonely, for he feels life stirring on all sides. The sea is only the embodiment of a supernatural and wonderful existence. It is nothing but love and emotion; it is the 'Living Infinite,' as one of your poets said. In fact, professor, Nature manifests herself in it by her three kingdoms, mineral, vegetable, and animal. The sea is the vast reservoir of Nature. The globe began with sea, so to speak; and who knows if it will not end with it? In it is supreme tranquillity. The sea does not belong to despots. Upon its surface men can still exercise unjust laws, fight, tear one another to pieces, and be carried away with terrestrial horrors. But at thirty feet below its level, their reign ceases, their influence is quenched, and their power disappears. Ah! sir, live—live in the bosom of the waters! There only is independence! There I recognize no masters! There I am free!"

Captain Nemo suddenly became silent in the midst of this enthusiasm, by which he was quite carried away. For a few moments he paced up and down, much agitated. Then he became more calm, regained his accustomed coldness of expression, and turning toward me, "Now, professor," said he, "if you wish to go over the *Nautilus*. I am at your service."

Captain Nemo rose. I followed him. A double door, contrived at the back of the dining-room, opened, and I entered a room equal in dimensions to that which I had just quitted.

It was a library. High pieces of furniture, of black violet ebony inlaid with brass, supported upon their wide shelves a great number of books uniformly bound. They followed the shape of the room, terminating at the lower part in huge divans, covered with brown leather, which were curved, to afford the greatest comfort. Light movable desks, made to slide in and out at will, allowed one to rest one's book while reading. In the center stood an immense table, covered with pamphlets, among which were some newspapers, already of old date. The electric light flooded everything; it was shed from four unpolished globes half sunk in the volutes of the ceiling. I looked with real admiration at this room, so ingeniously fitted-up, and I could scarcely believe my eyes

"Captain Nemo," said I to my host, who had just thrown himself on one of the divans, "this is a library which would do honor to more than one of the continental palaces, and I am absolutely astounded when I consider that it can follow you to the bottom of the seas."

"Where could one find greater solitude or silence, professor?" replied Captain Nemo. "Did your study in the Museum afford you such perfect quiet?"

"No, sir; and I must confess that it is a very poor one after yours. You must have six or seven thousand volumes."

"Twelve thousand, M. Aronnax. These are the only ties which bind me to the earth. But I had done with the world on the day when my *Nautilus* plunged for the first time beneath the waters. That day I bought my last volumes, my last pamphlets, my last papers, and from that time I wish to think that men no longer think or write. These books, professor, are at your service besides, and you can make use of them freely."

I thanked Captain Nemo, and went up to the shelves of the library. Works of science, morals, and literature abounded in every language; but I did not see one single work on political economy; that subject appeared to be strictly proscribed. Strange to say, all these books were irregularly arranged, in whatever language they were written; and this medley proved that the captain of the *Nautilus* must have read indiscriminately the books which he took up by chance.

"Sir," said I to the captain, "I thank you for having placed this library at my disposal. It contains treasures of science, and I shall profit by them."

"This room is not only a library," said Captain Nemo, "it is also a smoking-room."

"A smoking-room!" I cried. "Then one may smoke on board?"

"'Certainly."

"Then sir, I am forced to believe that you have kept up a communication with Havana."

"Not any," answered the captain. "Accept this cigar, M. Aronnax; and though it does not come from Havana, you will be pleased with it, if you are a connoisseur."

I took the cigar which was offered me; its shape recalled the London ones, but it seemed to be made of leaves of gold. I lighted it at a little brazier, which was supported upon an elegant bronze stem, and drew the first whiffs with the delight of a lover of smoking who has not smoked for two days.

"It is excellent," said I, "but it is not tobacco."

"No!" answered the captain, "this tobacco comes neither from Havana nor from the East. It is a kind of seaweed, rich in nicotine, with which the sea provides me, but somewhat sparingly."

At that moment Captain Nemo opened a door which stood opposite to that by which I had entered the library, and I passed into an immense drawing-room splendidly lighted.

It was a vast four-sided room, thirty feet long, eighteen wide, and fifteen high. A luminous ceiling, decorated with light arabesques, shed a soft clear light over all the marvels accumulated in this museum. For it was in fact a museum, in which an intelligent and prodigal hand had gathered all the treasures of nature and art, with the artistic confusion which distinguishes a painter's studio. Thirty first-rate pictures, uniformly framed, separated by bright drapery, ornamented the walls, which were hung with tapestry of severe design. I saw works of great value, the greater part of which I had admired in the special collections of Europe, and in the exhibitions of paintings. The several schools of the old masters were represented by a Madonna of Raphael, a Virgin of Leonardo da Vinci, a nymph of Correggio, a woman of Titian, an Adoration of Veronese, an Assumption of Murillo, a portrait of Holbein, a monk of Velasquez, a martyr of Ribeira, a fair of Rubens, two Flemish landscapes of Teniers, three little "genre" pictures of Gérard Dow, Metsu, and Paul Potter, two specimens of Géricault and Prudhon, and some sea-pieces of Backhuysen and Vernet. Among the works of modern painters were pictures with the signatures of Delacroix, Ingres, Decamp, Troyon, Meissonnier, Daubigny, etc.; and some admirable statues in marble and bronze, after the finest antique models, stood upon pedestals in the corners of this magnificent museum. Amazement, as the captain of the *Nautilus* had predicted, had already begun to take possession of me.

"Professor," said this strange man, "you must excuse the unceremonious way in which I receive you, and the disorder of this room."

"Sir," I answered, "without seeking to know who you are, I recognize in you an artist."

"An amateur, nothing more, sir. Formerly I loved to collect these beautiful works created by the hand of men. I sought them greedily and ferreted them out indefatigably, and I have been able to bring together some objects of great value. These are my last souvenirs of that world which is dead to me. In my eyes, your modern artists are already old; they have two or three thousand years of existence; I confound them in my own mind. Masters have no age."

"And these musicians?" said I, pointing out some works of Weber, Rossini, Mozart, Beethoven, Haydn, Meyerbeer, Hérold, Wagner, Auber, Gounod, and a number of others scattered over a large model piano organ which occupied one of the panels of the drawing-room.

"These musicians," replied Captain Nemo, "are the contemporaries of Orpheus; for in the memory of the dead all chronological differences are effaced; and I am dead, professor; as much dead as those of your friends who are sleeping six feet under the earth!"

Captain Nemo was silent, and seemed lost in a profound reverie. I contemplated him with deep interest, analyzing in silence the strange expression of his countenance. Leaning on his elbow against an angle of a costly mosaic table, he no longer saw me—he had forgotten my presence.

I did not disturb this reverie, and continued my observation of the curiosities which enriched this drawing-room.

Under elegant glass cases, fixed by copper rivets, were classed and labeled the most precious productions of the sea which had ever been presented to the eye of a naturalist. My delight as a professor may be conceived.

Apart, in separate compartments, were spread out chaplets of pearls of the greatest beauty, which reflected the electric light in little sparks of fire; pink pearls, torn from the pinna-marina of the Red Sea; green pearls of the haliotyde iris; yellow, blue, and black pearls, the curious productions of the divers mollusks of every ocean, and certain mussels of the watercourses of the North; lastly, several specimens of inestimable value which had been gathered from the rarest pintadines. Some of these pearls were larger than a pigeon's egg, and were worth as much, and more than that which the traveler Tavernier sold to the Shah of Persia for three millions, and surpassed the one in the possession of the Imaum of Muscat, which I had believed to be unrivaled in the world.

Therefore, to estimate the value of this collection was simply impossible. Captain Nemo must have expended millions in the acquirement of these various specimens, and I was thinking what source he could have drawn from, to have been able thus to gratify his fancy for collecting, when I was interrupted by these words:

"You are examining my shells, professor? Unquestionably they must be interesting to a naturalist; but for me they have a far greater charm, for I have collected them all with my own hand, and there is not a sea on the face of the globe which has escaped my researches."

"I can understand, Captain, the delight of wandering about in the midst of such riches. You are one of those who have collected their treasures themselves. No museum in Europe possesses such a collection of the produce of the ocean. But if I exhaust all my admiration upon it, I shall have none left for the vessel which carries it. I do not wish to pry into your secrets; but I must confess that this *Nautilus,* with the motive power which is confined in it, the contrivances which enable it to be worked, the powerful agent which propels it, all excite my curiosity to the highest pitch. I see suspended on the walls of this room instruments of whose use I am ignorant."

"You will find these same instruments in my own room, professor, where I shall have much pleasure in explaining their use to you. But first come and inspect the cabin which is set apart for your own use. You must see how you will be accommodated on board the *Nautilus.*"

I followed Captain Nemo, who, by one of the doors opening from each panel of the drawing-room, regained the waist. He conducted me toward the bow, and there I found, not a cabin, but an elegant room, with a bed, dressing-table, and several other pieces of furniture.

I could only thank my host.

"Your room adjoins mine," said he, opening a door, "and mine opens into the drawing-room that we have just quitted."

I entered the captain's room; it had a severe, almost a monkish, aspect. A small iron bedstead, a table, some articles for the toilet; the whole lighted by a skylight. No comforts, the strictest necessaries only.

Captain Nemo pointed to a seat. "Be so good as to sit down," he said. I seated myself, and he began thus:

CHAPTER XI

ALL BY ELECTRICITY

"Sir," said Captain Nemo, showing me the instruments hanging on the walls of his room, "here are the contrivances required for the navigation of the *Nautilus*. Here, as in the drawing-room, I have them always under my eyes, and they indicate my position and exact direction in the middle of the ocean. Some are known to you, such as the thermometer, which gives the internal temperature of the *Nautilus;* the barometer, which indicates the weight of the air and foretells the changes of the weather; the hygrometer, which marks the dryness of the atmosphere; the storm-glass, the contents of which, by decomposing, announce the approach of tempests; the compass, which guides my course; the sextant, which shows the latitude by the altitude of the sun; chronometers, by which I calculate the longitude; and glasses for day and night, which I use to examine the points of the horizon when the *Nautilus* rises to the surface of the waves."

"These are the usual nautical instruments," I replied, "and I know the use of them. But these others, no doubt, answer to the particular requirements of the *Nautilus*. This dial with the movable needle is a manometer, is it not?"

"It is actually a manometer. But by communication with the water, whose external pressure it indicates, it gives our depth at the same time."

"And these other instruments, the use of which I can not guess?"

"Here, professor, I ought to give you some explanations. Will you be kind enough to listen to me?" He was silent for a few moments, then he said: "There is a powerful agent, obedient, rapid, easy, which conforms to every use, and reigns supreme on board my vessel. Everything is done by means of it. It lights it, warms it, and is the soul of my mechanical apparatus. This agent is electricity."

"Electricity?" I cried in surprise.

"Yes, sir."

"Nevertheless, captain, you possess an extreme rapidity of movement, which does not agree well with the power of electricity. Until now its dynamic force has remained under restraint, and has only been able to produce a small amount of power."

"Professor," said Captain Nemo, "my electricity is not everybody's. You know what sea-water is composed of. In a thousand grams are found ninety-six and a half per cent of water, and about two and two-thirds per cent of chloride of sodium; then, in a smaller quantity, chlorides of magnesium and of potassium, bromide of magnesium, sulphate of magnesia, sulphate and carbonate of lime. You see, then, that chloride of sodium forms a large part of it. So it is this sodium that I extract from sea-water, and of which I compose my ingredients. I owe all to the ocean; it produces electricity, and electricity gives heat, light, motion, and, in a word, life to the *Nautilus*."

"But not the air you breathe?"

"Oh, I could manufacture the air necessary for my consumption, but it is useless, because I go up to the surface of the water when I please. However, if electricity does not furnish me with air to breathe, it works at least the powerful pumps that are stored in spacious reservoirs, and which enable me to prolong at need, and as long as I will, my stay in the depths of the sea. It gives a uniform and unintermittent light, which the sun does not. Now look at this clock; it is electrical, and goes with a regularity that defies the best chronometers. I have divided it into twenty-four hours, like the Italian clocks, because for me there is neither night nor day, sun nor moon, but only that factitious light that I take with me to the bottom of the sea. Look! just now, it is ten o'clock in the morning."

"Exactly."

"Another application of electricity. This dial hanging in front of us, indicates the speed of the *Nautilus*. An electric thread puts it in communication with the screw, and the needle indicates the real speed. Look! now we are spinning along with a uniform speed of fifteen miles an hour."

"It is marvelous! and I see, captain, you were right to make use of this agent that takes the place of wind, water, and steam."

"We have not finished, M. Aronnax," said Captain Nemo, rising; "if you will follow me, we will examine the stern of the *Nautilus*."

Really, I knew already the front part of this submarine boat, of which this is the exact division, starting from the ship's waist: the dining-room, five yards long, separated from the library by a water-tight partition; the library, five yards long; the large drawing-room, ten yards long, separated from the captain's room by a second water-tight partition; the said room, five yards in length; mine, two and half yards; and lastly, a reservoir of air, seven and a half yards, that extended to the bows. Total length thirty-five yards, or one hundred and five feet. The partitions had doors that were shut hermetically by means of india-rubber instruments, and they insured the safety of the *Nautilus* in case of a leak.

I followed Captain Nemo through the waist, and arrived at the center of the boat. There was a sort of well that opened between two partitions. An iron ladder, fastened with an iron hook to the partition, led to the upper end. I asked the captain what the ladder was used for.

"It leads to the small boat," he said.

"What! have you a boat?" I exclaimed in surprise.

"Of course; an excellent vessel, light and insubmersible, that serves either as a fishing or as a pleasure boat."

"But then, when you wish to embark, you are obliged to come to the surface of the water?"

"Not at all. This boat is attached to the upper part of the hull of the *Nautilus,* and occupies a cavity made for it. It is decked, quite water-tight, and held together by solid bolts. This ladder leads to a man-hole made in the hull of the *Nautilus,* that corresponds with a similar hole made in the side of the boat. By this double opening I get into the small vessel. They shut the one belonging to the *Nautilus,* I shut the other by means of screw pressure. I undo the bolts, and the little boat goes up to the surface of the sea with prodigious rapidity. I then open the panel of the bridge, carefully shut till then; I mast it, hoist my sail, take my oars, and I'm off."

"But how do you get back on board?"

"I do not come back, M. Arronnax; the *Nautilus* comes to me."

"By your orders?"

"By my orders. An electric thread connects us. I telegraph to it, and that is enough."

"Really," I said, astonished at these marvels, "nothing can be more simple."

After having passed by the cage of the staircase that led to the platform, I saw a cabin six feet long, in which Conseil and Ned Land, enchanted with their repast, were devouring it with avidity. Then a door opened into a kitchen nine feet long situated between the large storerooms. There electricity, better than gas itself, did all the cooking. The streams under the furnaces gave out to the sponges of platina a heat which was regularly kept up and distributed. They also heated a distilling apparatus, which, by evaporation, furnished excellent drinkable water. Near this kitchen was a bath-room comfortably furnished, with hot and cold water taps.

Next to the kitchen was the berth-room of the vessel, sixteen feet long. But the door was shut, and I could not see the management of it, which might have given me an idea of the number of men employed on board the *Nautilus.*

At the bottom was a fourth partition, that separated this office from the engine-room. A door opened, and I found myself in the compartment where Captain Nemo—certainly an engineer of a very high order—had arranged his locomotive machinery. This engine-room, clearly lighted, did not measure less than sixty-five feet in length. It was divided into two parts; the first contained the materials for producing electricity, and the second the machinery that connected it with the screw. I examined it with great interest, in order to understand the machinery of the *Nautilus.*

"You see," said the captain, "I use Bunsen's contrivances, not Ruhmkorff's. Those would not have been powerful enough. Bunsen's are fewer in number, but strong and large, which experience proves to be the best. The electricity produced passes forward, where it works, by electro-magnets of great size, on a system of levers and cog-wheels that transmit the movement to the axle of the screw. This one, the diameter of which is nineteen feet, and the thread twenty-three feet, performs about a hundred and twenty revolutions in a second."

"And you get then?"

"A speed of fifty miles an hour."

"I have seen the *Nautilus* maneuver before the *Abraham Lincoln,* and I have my own ideas as to its speed. But this is not enough. We must see where we go. We must be able to direct it to the right, to the left, above, below. How do you get to the great depths, where you find an increasing resistance, which is rated by hundreds of atmospheres? How do you return to the surface of the ocean? And how do you maintain yourselves in the requisite medium? Am I asking too much?"

"Not at all, professor," replied the captain with some hesitation; "since you may never leave this submarine boat. Come into the saloon; it is our usual study, and there you will learn all you want to know about the *Nautilus.*"

CHAPTER XII

SOME FIGURES

A moment after we were seated on a divan in the saloon smoking. The captain showed me a sketch that gave the plan, section, and elevation of the *Nautilus.* Then he began his description in these words:

"Here, M. Aronnax, are the several dimensions of the boat you are in. It is an elongated cylinder with conical ends. It is very like a cigar in shape, a shape already adopted in London in several constructions of the same sort. The length of this cylinder, from stern to stern, is exactly 232 feet, and its maximum breadth is twenty-six feet. It is not built quite like your long-voyage steamers, but its lines are sufficiently long, and its curves prolonged enough, to allow the water to slide off easily, and oppose no obstacle to its passage. These two dimensions enable you to obtain by a simple calculation the surface and cubic contents of the *Nautilus.* Its area measures 6,032 feet; and its contents about 1,500 cubic yards; that is to say, when completely immersed it displaces 50,000 feet of water, or weighs 1,500 tons.

"When I made the plans for this submarine vessel, I meant that nine-tenths should be submerged; consequently, it ought only to displace nine-tenths of its bulk, that is to say, only to weigh that number of tons. I ought not, therefore, to have exceeded that weight, constructing it on the aforesaid dimensions.

"The *Nautilus* is composed of two hulls, one inside, the other outside, joined by T-shaped irons, which render it very strong. Indeed, owing to this cellular arrangement it resists like a block, as if it were solid. Its sides cannot yield; it coheres spontaneously, and not by the closeness of its rivets; and the homogeneity of its construction, due to the perfect union of the materials, enables it to defy the roughest seas.

"These two hulls are composed of steel plates, whose density is from .07 to .08 that of water. The first is not less than two inches and a half thick, and weighs 394 tons. The second envelope, the keel, twenty inches high and ten thick, weighs alone sixty-two tons. The engine, the ballast, the several accessories and apparatus appendages, the partitions and bulkheads, weigh 961.62 tons. Do you follow all this?"

"I do."

"Then, when the *Nautilus* is afloat under these circumstances, one-tenth is out of the water. Now, if I have made reservoirs of a size equal to this tenth, or capable of holding 150 tons, and if I fill them with water, the boat, weighing then 1,507 tons, will be completely immersed. That would happen, professor. These reservoirs are in the lower parts of the *Nautilus*. I turn on taps and they fill, and the vessel sinks that had just been level with the surface."

"Well, captain, but now we come to the real difficulty. I can understand your rising to the surface; but diving below the surface, does not your submarine contrivance encounter a pressure, and consequently undergo an upward thrust of one atmosphere for every thirty feet of water, just about fifteen pounds per square inch?"

"Just so, sir."

"Then unless you quite fill the *Nautilus*, I do not see how you can draw it down to those depths which at times you reach."

"Professor, you must not confound statics with dynamics, or you will be exposed to grave errors. There is very little labor spent in attaining the lower regions of the ocean, for all bodies have a tendency to sink. When I wanted to find out the necessary increase of weight required to sink the *Nautilus*, I had only to calculate the reduction of volume that seawater acquires according to the depth."

"That is evident."

"Now, if water is not absolutely incompressible, it is at least capable of very slight compression. Indeed, after the most recent calculations this reduction is only 0.000436 of an atmosphere for each thirty feet of depth. If we want to sink 3,000 feet, I should keep account of the reduction of bulk under a pressure equal to that of a column of water of a thousand feet. The calculation is easily verified. Now I have supplementary reservoirs capable of holding a hundred tons. Therefore I can sink to a considerable depth. When I wish to rise to the level of the sea, I only let off the water, and empty all the reservoirs if I should desire the *Nautilus* to emerge from the tenth part of her total capacity."

I had nothing to object to these reasonings.

"I admit your calculations, captain," I replied; "I should be wrong to dispute them since daily experience confirms them; but I foresee a real difficulty in the way."

"What, sir?"

"When you are about 1,000 feet deep, the walls of the *Nautilus* bear a pressure of 100 atmospheres. If, then, just now you were to empty the supplementary reservoirs, to lighten the vessel, and to go up to the surface, the pumps must overcome the pressure of 100 atmospheres, which is 1,500 lbs. per square-inch. From that a power— —"

"That electricity alone can give," said the captain hastily. "I repeat, sir, that the dynamic power of my engines is almost infinite. The pumps of the *Nautilus* have an enormous power, as you must have observed when their jets of water burst like a torrent upon the *Abraham Lincoln.* Besides, I use subsidiary reservoirs only to attain a mean depth of 750 to 1,000 fathoms, and that with a view of managing my machines. Also, when I have a mind to visit the depths of the ocean five or six miles below the surface. I make use of slower but not less infallible means."

"What are they, captain?"

"That involves my telling you how the *Nautilus* is worked."

"I am impatient to learn."

"To steer this boat to starboard or port, to turn, in a word, following a horizontal plan, I use an ordinary rudder fixed on the back of the stern post, and with one wheel and some tackle to steer by. But I can also make the *Nautilus* rise and sink, and sink and rise, by a vertical movement by means of two inclined planes fastened to its sides, opposite the center of flotation, planes that move in every direction, and that are worked by powerful levers from the interior. If the planes are kept parallel with the boat, it moves horizontally. If slanted, the *Nautilus,* according to this inclination, and under the influence of the screw, either sinks diagonally or rises diagonally as it suits me. And even if I wish to rise more quickly to the surface, I ship the screw, and the pressure of the water causes the *Nautilus to* rise vertically like a balloon filled with hydrogen."

"Bravo, captain! But how can the steersman follow the route in the middle of the waters?"

"The steersman is placed in a glazed box, that is raised above the hull of the *Nautilus,* and which is furnished with lenses."

"Are these lenses capable of resisting such pressure?"

"Perfectly. Glass, which breaks at a blow, is, nevertheless, capable of offering considerable resistance. During some experiments of fishing by electric light in 1864 in the Northern Seas, we saw plates less than a third of an inch thick resist a pressure of sixteen atmospheres. Now, the glass that I use is not less than thirty times thicker."

"Granted. But, after all, in order to see, the light must exceed the darkness, and in the midst of the darkness in the water, how can you see?"

"Behind the steersman's cage is placed a powerful electric reflector, the rays from which light up the sea for half a mile in front."

"Ah! bravo, bravo, captain! Now I can account for this phosphorescence in the supposed narwhal that puzzled us so. I now ask you if the boarding of the *Nautilus* and of the *Scotia,* that has made such a noise, has been the result of a chance rencounter?"

"Quite accidental, sir. I was sailing only one fathom below the surface of the water when the shock came. It had no bad result."

"None, sir. But now, about your rencounter with the *Abraham Lincoln?*"

"Professor, I am sorry for one of the best vessels in the American navy; but they attacked me, and I was bound to defend myself. I contented myself, however, with putting the frigate *hors de combat;* she will not have any difficulty in getting repaired at the next port."

"Ah, commander! your *Nautilus* is certainly a marvelous boat."

"Yes, professor; and I love it as if it were part of myself. If danger threatens one of your vessels on the ocean, the first impression is the feeling of an abyss above and below. On the *Nautilus* men's hearts never fail them. No defects to be afraid of, for the double shell is as firm as iron; no rigging to attend to; no sails for the wind to carry away; no boilers to burst; no fire to fear, for the vessel is made of iron, not of wood; no coal to run short, for electricity is the only mechanical agent; no collision to fear, for it alone swims in deep water; no tempest to brave, for when it dives below the water, it reaches absolute tranquillity. There, sir! that is the perfection of vessels! And if it is true that the engineer has more confidence in the vessel than the builder, and the builder than the captain himself, you understand the trust I repose in my *Nautilus;* for I am at once captain, builder, and engineer."

"But how could you construct this wonderful *Nautilus* in secret?"

"Each separate portion, M. Aronnax, was brought from different parts of the globe. The keel was forged at Creusot, the shaft of the screw at Penn & Co.'s, London, the iron plates of the hull at Laird's of Liverpool, the screw itself at Scott's at Glasgow. The reservoirs were made by Cail & Co. at Paris, the engine by Krupp in Prussia, its beak in Motala's workshop in

Sweden, its mathematical instruments by Hart Brothers, of New York, etc.; and each of these people had my orders under different names."

"But these parts had to be put together and arranged?"

"Professor, I had set up my workshops upon a desert island in the ocean. There my workmen, that is to say, the brave men that I instructed and educated, and myself have put together our *Nautilus*. Then, when the work was finished, fire destroyed all trace of our proceedings on this island, that I could have jumped over if I had liked."

"Then the cost of this vessel is great?"

"M. Aronnax, an iron vessel costs £45 per ton. Now the *Nautilus* weighed 1,500. It came therefore to £67,500 and £80,000 more for fitting it up, and about £200,000 with the works of art and the collections it contains."

"One last question, Captain Nemo."

"Ask it, professor."

"You are rich?"

"Immensely rich, sir; and I could, without missing it, pay the national debt of France."

I stared at the singular person who spoke thus. Was he playing upon my credulity? The future would decide that.

From Around the Moon

BY JULES VERNE

CHAPTER XVII

TYCHO

At six in the evening the projectile passed the south pole at less than forty miles off, a distance equal to that already reached at the north pole. The elliptical curve was being rigidly carried out.

At this moment the travelers once more entered the blessed rays of the sun. They saw once more those stars which move slowly from east to west. The radiant orb was saluted by a triple hurrah. With its light it also sent heat, which soon pierced the metal walls. The glass resumed its accustomed appearance. The layers of ice melted as if by enchantment; and immediately, for economy's sake, the gas was put out, the air apparatus alone consuming its usual quantity.

"Ah!" said Nicholl, "these rays of heat are good. With what impatience must the Selenites wait the reappearance of the orb of day."

"Yes," replied Michel Ardan, "imbibing as it were the brilliant ether, light and heat, all life is contained in them."

At this moment the bottom of the projectile deviated somewhat from the lunar surface, in order to follow the slightly lengthened elliptical orbit. From this point, had the earth been at the full, Barbicane and his companions could have seen it, but immersed in the sun's irradiation she was quite invisible. Another spectacle attracted their attention, that of the southern part of the moon, brought by the glasses to within 450 yards. They did not again leave the scuttles, and noted every detail of this fantastical continent.

Mounts Doerfel and Leibnitz formed two separate groups very near the south pole. The first group extended from the pole to the eighty-fourth parallel, on the eastern part of the orb; the second occupied the eastern border, extending from the 65° of latitude to the pole.

On their capriciously formed ridge appeared dazzling sheets, as mentioned by Pere Secchi. With more certainty than the illustrious Roman astronomer, Barbicane was enabled to recognize their nature.

"They are snow," he exclaimed.

"Snow?" repeated Nicholl.

"Yes, Nicholl, snow; the surface of which is deeply frozen. See how they reflect the luminous rays. Cooled lava would never give out such intense reflection. There must then be water, there must be air on the moon. As little as you please, but the fact can no longer be contested." No, it could not be. And if ever Barbicane should see the Earth again, his notes will bear witness to this great fact in his Selenographic observations.

These mountains of Doerfel and Leibnitz rose in the midst of plains of a medium extent, which were bounded by an indefinite succession of circles and annular ramparts. These two chains are the only ones not within this region of circles. Comparatively but slightly marked, they throw up here and there some sharp points, the highest summit of which attains an altitude of 24,600 feet.

But the projectile was high above all this landscape, and the projections disappeared in the intense brilliancy of the disc. And to the eyes of the travelers there reappeared that original aspect of the lunar landscapes, raw in tone, without gradation of colors, and without degrees of shadow, roughly black and white, from the want of diffusion of light.

But the sight of this desolate world did not fail to captivate them by its very strangeness. They were moving over this region as if they had been borne on the breath of some storm, watching heights defile under their feet, piercing the cavities with their eyes, going down into the rifts, climbing the ramparts, sounding these mysterious holes, and leveling all cracks. But no trace of vegetation, no appearance of cities; nothing but stratification, beds of lava, overflowings polished like immense mirrors, reflecting the sun's rays with overpowering brilliancy. Nothing belonging to the *living* world— everything to a dead world, where avalanches, rolling from the summits of the mountains, would disperse noiselessly at the bottom of the abyss, retaining the motion but wanting the sound. In any case it was the image of death, without its being possible even to say that life had ever existed there.

Michel Ardan, however, thought he recognized a heap of ruins, to which he drew Barbicane's attention. It was about the 80th parallel, in 30° longitude. This heap of stones, rather regularly placed, represented a vast fortress, overlooking a long rift, which in former days had served as a bed to the rivers of prehistorical times. Not far from that, rose to a height of 17,400 feet the annular mountain of Short, equal to the Asiatic Caucasus. Michel Ardan, with his accustomed ardor, maintained "the evidences" of his fortress. Beneath it he discerned the dismantled ramparts of a town; here the still intact arch of a portico, there two or three columns lying under their base; farther on, a succession of arches which must have supported the conduit of an aqueduct; in another part the sunken pillars of a gigantic bridge, run into the thickest parts of the rift. He distinguished all this, but with so much imagination in his glance, and through glasses so fantastical, that we must mistrust his observation. But who could affirm, who would dare to say, that the amiable fellow did not really see that which his two companions would not see?

Moments were too precious to be sacrificed in idle discussion. The Selenite city, whether imaginary or not, had already disappeared afar off. The distance of the projectile from the lunar disc was on the increase, and the details of the soil were being lost in a confused jumble. The reliefs, the circles, the craters and plains alone remained, and still showed their boundary lines distinctly. At this moment, to the left, lay extended one of the finest circles of lunar orography, one of the curiosities of this continent. It was Newton, which Barbicane recognized without trouble, by referring to the *Mappa Selenographica.*

Newton is situated in exactly 77° south latitude, and 16° east longitude. It forms an annular crater, the ramparts of which, rising to a height of 21,300 feet, seemed to be impassible.

Barbicane made his companions observe that the height of this mountain above the surrounding plain was far from equaling the depth of its crater. This enormous hole was beyond all measurement, and formed a gloomy abyss, the bottom of which the sun's rays could never reach. There, according to Humboldt, reigns utter darkness, which the light of the sun and the earth cannot break. Mythologists could well have made it the mouth of hell.

"Newton," said Barbicane, "is the most perfect type of these annular mountains, of which the earth possesses no sample. They prove that the moon's formation, by means of cooling, is due to violent causes; for whilst under the pressure of internal fires the reliefs rise to considerable height, the depths withdraw far below the lunar level."

"I do not dispute the fact," replied Michel Ardan.

Some minutes after passing Newton, the projectile directly overlooked the annular mountain of Moret. It skirted at some distance the summits of Blancanus, and at about half-past seven in the evening reached the circle of Clavius.

This circle, one of the most remarkable of the disc, is situated in 58° south lat., and 15° east long. Its height is estimated at 22,950 feet. The travelers, at a distance of twenty-four miles (reduced to four by their glasses), could admire this vast crater in its entirety.

"Terrestrial volcanoes," said Barbicane, "are but molehills compared with those of the moon. Measuring the old craters formed by the first eruptions of Vesuvius and Etna, we find them little more than three miles in breadth. In France the circle of Cantal measures six miles across; at Ceyland the circle of the island is forty miles, which is considered the largest on the globe. What are these diameters against that of Clavius, which we overlook at this moment?"

"What is its breadth?" asked Nicholl.

"It is 150 miles," replied Barbicane. "This circle is certainly the most important on the moon, but many others measure 150, 100, or 75 miles."

"Ah! my friends," exclaimed Michel, "can you picture to yourselves what this now peaceful orb of night must have been when its craters, filled with thunderings, vomited at the same time smoke and tongues of flame. What a wonderful spectacle then, and now what decay! This moon is nothing more than a thin carcass of fireworks, whose squibs, rockets, serpents and suns, after a superb brilliancy, have left but sadly broken cases."

The projectile was still advancing. Circles, craters, and uprooted mountains succeeded each other incessantly. No more plains; no more seas. A never ending Switzerland and Norway. And lastly, in the center of this region of crevasses, the most splendid mountain on the lunar disc, the dazzling Tycho, in which posterity will ever preserve the name of the illustrious Danish astronomer.

In observing the full moon in a cloudless sky no one has failed to remark this brilliant point of the southern atmosphere. Michel Ardan used every metaphor that his imagination could supply to designate it by. To him this Tycho was a focus of light, a center of irradiation, a crater vomiting rays. It was the tire of a brilliant wheel, an *asteria* enclosing the disc with its silver tentacles, an enormous eye filled with flames, a glory carved for Pluto's head, a star launched by the Creator's hand, and crushed against the face of the moon! Tycho forms such a concentration of light that the inhabitants of the earth can see it without glasses, though at a distance of 240,000 miles! Imagine, then, its intensity to the eye of observers placed at a distance of only fifty miles! Seen through thus pure ether, its brilliancy was so intolerable that Barbicane and his froends were obliged to blacken their glasses with the gas smoke before they could bear the splendor. Then silent, scarcely uttering an interjection of admiration, they gazed, they contemplated. All their feelings, all their impressions, were concentrated in that look, as under any violent emotion all life is concentrated at the heart.

Tycho belongs to the system of radiating mountains, like Aristarchus and Copernicus; but it is of all the most complete and decided, showing unquestionably the frightful volcanic action to which the formation of the moon is due. Tycho is situated in 43° south lat., and 12° east long. Its center is occupied by a crater fifty miles broad. It assumes a slightly elliptical form, and is surrounded by an enclosure of annular ramparts, which on the east and west overlook the outer plain from a height of 15,000 feet. It is a group of Mont Blancs, placed round one common center, and crowned by radiating beams.

What this incomparable mountain really is, with all the projections converging towards it, and the interior excrescences of its crater, photography itself could never represent. Indeed, it is during the full moon that Tycho is seen in all its splendor. Then all shadows disappear, the fore-shortening of perspective disappears, and all proofs become white—a disagreeable fact; for this strange region would have been marvelous if reproduced with photographic exactness. It is but a group of hollows, craters, circles, a network of crests; then, as far as the eye could see, a whole volcanic network cast upon this encrusted soil. One can then understand that the bubbles of this central eruption have kept their first form. Crystallized by cooling, they have stereotyped that aspect which the moon formerly presented when under the Plutonian forces.

The distance which separated the travelers from the annular summits of Tycho was not so great but that they could catch the principal details. Even on the causeway forming the fortifications of Tycho, the mountains hanging on to the interior and exterior sloping flanks rose in stories like gigantic terraces. They appeared to be higher by 300 or 400 feet to the west than to the east. No system of terrestrial encampment could equal these natural fortifications. A town built at the bottom of this circular cavity would have been utterly inaccessible.

Inaccessible and wonderfully extended over this soil covered with picturesque projections! Indeed, nature had not left the bottom of this crater flat and empty. It possessed its own peculiar orography, a mountainous system, making it a world in itself. The travelers could distinguish clearly cones, central hills, remarkable positions of the soil, naturally placed to receive the chefs-d'œuvre of Selenite architecture. There was marked out the place for a temple, here the ground of a forum, on this spot the plan of a palace, in another the plateau for a citadel; the whole overlooked by a central mountain of 1,500 feet. A vast circle, in which ancient Rome could have been held in its entirety ten times over.

"Ah!" exclaimed Michel Ardan, enthusiastic at the sight; "what a grand town might be constructed within that ring of mountains! A quiet cry, a peaceful refuge, beyond all human misery. How calm and isolated those misanthropes, those haters of humanity might live there, and all who have a distaste for social life!"

"All! It would be too small for them," replied Barbicane simply.

CHAPTER XVIII

GRAVE QUESTIONS

But the projectile had passed the enceinte of Tycho, and Barbicane and his two companions watched with scrupulous attention the brilliant rays which the celebrated mountain shed so curiously all over the horizon.

What was this radiant glory? What geological phenomenon had designed these ardent beams? This question occupied Barbicane's mind.

Under his eyes ran in all directions luminous furrows, raised at the edges and concave in the center, some twelve miles, others thirty miles broad. These brilliant trains extended in some places to within 600 miles of Tycho, and seemed to cover, particularly towards the east, the northeast and the north, the half of the southern hemisphere. One of these jets extended as far as the circle of Neander, situated on the 40th meridian. Another by a slight curve furrowed the Sea of Nectar, breaking against the chain of Pyrenees, after a circuit of 800 miles. Others, towards the west, covered the Sea of Clouds and the Sea of Humors with a luminous network. What was the origin of these sparkling rays, which shone on the plains as well as on the reliefs, at whatever height they might be? All started from a common center, the crater of Tycho. They sprang from him. Herschel attributed their brilliancy to currents of lava congealed by the cold; an opinion, however, which has not been generally adopted. Other astronomers have seen in these inexplicable rays, a kind of *moraines,* rows of erratic blocks, which had been thrown up at the period of Tycho's formation.

"And why not?" asked Nicholl of Barbicane, who was relating and rejecting these different opinions.

"Because the regularity of these luminous lines, and the violence necessary to carry volcanic matter to such distances, is inexplicable."

"Eh! by Jove!" replied Michel Ardan, "it seems easy enough to me to explain the origin of these rays."

"Indeed?" said Barbicane.

"Indeed," continued Michel. "It is enough to say that it is a vast star, similar to that produced by a ball or a stone thrown at a square of glass!"

"Well," replied Barbicane, smiling. "And what hand would be powerful enough to throw a ball to give such a shock as that?"

"The hand is not necessary," answered Michel, not at all confounded: "and as to the stone, let us suppose it to be a comet."

"Ah! those much-abused comets!" exclaimed Barbicane. "My brave Michel, your explanation is not bad; but your comet is useless. The shock which produced that rent must have come from the inside of the star. A violent contraction of the lunar crust, while cooling, might suffice to imprint this gigantic star."

"A contraction! something like a lunar stomachache," said Michel Ardan.

"Besides," added Barbicane, "this opinion is that of an English savant, Nasmyth, and it seems to me to sufficiently explain the radiation of these mountains."

"That Nasmyth was no fool!" replied Michel.

Long did the travelers, whom such a sight could never weary, admire the splendors of Tycho. Their projectile, saturated with luminous gleams in the double irradiation of sun and moon, must have appeared like an incandescent globe. They had passed suddenly from excessive cold to intense heat. Nature was thus preparing them to become Selenites. Become Selenites! That idea brought up once more the question of the habitability of the moon. After what they had seen, could the travelers solve it? Would they decide for or against it? Michel Ardan persuaded his two friends to form an opinion, and asked them directly if they thought that men and animals were represented in the lunar world.

"I think that we can answer," said Barbicane; "but according to my idea the question ought not to be put in that form. I ask it to be put differently."

"Put it your own way," replied Michel.

"Here it is," continued Barbicane. "The problem is a double one, and requires a double solution. Is the moon *habitable?* Has the moon ever been *inhabited?*"

"Good!" replied Nicholl. "First let us see whether the moon is habitable."

"To tell the truth, I know nothing about it," answered Michel.

"And I answer in the negative," continued Barbicane. "In her actual state, with her surrounding atmosphere certainly very much reduced, her seas for the most part dried up, her insufficient supply of water, restricted vegetation, sudden alternations of cold and heat, her days and nights of 354 hours; the moon does not seem habitable to me, nor does she seem propitious to animal development, nor sufficient for the wants of existence as we understand it."

"I agree with you," replied Nicholl. "But is not the moon habitable for creatures differently organized from ourselves?"

"That question is more difficult to answer, but I will try; and I ask Nicholl if *motion* appears to him to be a necessary result of *life,* whatever be its organization?"

"Without a doubt!" answered Nicholl.

"Then, my worthy companion, I would answer that we have observed the lunar continent at a distance of 500 yards at most, and that nothing seemed to us to move on the moon's surface. The presence of any kind of life would have been betrayed by its attendant marks, such as divers buildings, and even by ruins. And what have we seen? Everywhere and always the geological works of nature, never the work of man. If, then, there exist representatives of the animal kingdom on the moon, they must have fled to those unfathomable cavities which the eye can not reach; which I can not admit, for they must have left traces of their passage on those plains which the atmosphere must cover, however slightly raised it may be. These traces are nowhere visible. There remains but one hypothesis, that of a living race to which motion, which is life, is foreign."

"One might as well say, living creatures which do not live," replied Michel.

"Just so," said Barbicane, "which for us has no meaning."

"Then we may form our opinion?" said Michel.

"Yes," replied Nicholl.

"Very well," continued Michel Ardan, "the Scientific Commission assembled in the projectile of the Gun Club, after having founded their argument on facts recently observed, decide unanimously upon the question of the habitability of the moon— '*No!* the moon is not habitable.'"

This decision was consigned by President Barbicane to his notebook, where the process of the sitting of the 6th of December may be seen.

"Now," said Nicholl, "let us attack the second question, an indispensable complement of the first. I ask the honorable Commission, if the moon is not habitable, has she ever been inhabited, Citizen Barbicane?"

"My friends," replied Barbicane, "I did not undertake this journey in order to form an opinion on the past habitability of our satellite; but I will add that our personal observations only confirm me in this opinion. I believe, indeed, I affirm, that the moon has been inhabited by a human race organized like our own; that she has produced animals anatomically formed like the terrestrial animals; but I add that these races, human or animal, have had their day, and are now forever extinct!"

"Then," asked Michael, "the moon must be older than the earth?"

"No!" said Barbicane decidedly, "but a world which has *grown old* quicker, and whose formation and deformation have been more rapid. Relatively, the organizing force of matter has been much more violent in the interior of the moon than in the interior of the terrestrial globe. The actual state of this cracked, twisted, and burst disc abundantly proves this. The moon and the earth were nothing but gaseous masses originally. These gases have passed into liquid state under different influences, and the solid masses have been formed later. But most certainly our sphere was still gaseous or liquid, when the moon was solidified by cooling, and had become habitable."

"I believe it," said Nicholl.

"Then," continued Barbicane, "an atmosphere surrounded it, the waters contained within this gaseous envelope could not evaporate. Under the influence of air, water, light, solar heat, and central heat, vegetation took possession of the continents prepared to receive it, and certainly life showed itself about this period for nature does not expend herself in vain; and a world so wonderfully formed for habitation must necessarily be inhabited."

"But," said Nicholl, "many phenomena inherent in our satellite might cramp the expansion of the animal and vegetable kingdom. For example, its days and nights of 354 hours?"

"At the terrestrial poles they last six months," said Michel.

"An argument of little value, since the poles are not inhabited."

"Let us observe, my friends," continued Barbicane, "that if in the actual state of the moon its long nights and long days created differences of temperature insupportable to organization, it was not so at the historical period of time. The atmosphere enveloped the disc with a fluid mantle; vapor deposited itself in the shape of clouds; this natural screen tempered the ardor of the solar rays, and retained the nocturnal radiation. Light, like heat, can diffuse itself in the air; hence an equality between the influences which no longer exist, now that that atmosphere has almost entirely disappeared. And now I am going to astonish you."

"Astonish us?" said Michel Ardan.

"I firmly believe that at the period when the moon was inhabited, the nights and days were shorter and did not last 354 hours!"

"And why?" asked Nicholl quickly.

"Because most probably then the rotary motion of the moon upon her axis was not equal to her revolution, an equality which presents each part of her disc during fifteen days to the action of the solar rays."

"Granted," replied Nicholl, "but why should not these two motions have been equal, as they are really so?"

"Because that equality has only been determined by terrestrial attraction. And who can say that this attraction was powerful enough to alter the motion of the moon at that period when the earth was still fluid?"

"Just so," replied Nicholl; "and who can say that the moon has always been a satellite of the earth?"

"And who can say," exclaimed Michel Ardan, "that the moon did not exist before the earth?"

Their imagination carried them away into an indefinite field of hypothesis. Barbicane sought to restrain them.

"These speculations are too high," said he; "problems utterly insoluble. Do not let us enter upon them. Let us only admit the insufficiency of the primordial attraction; and then by the inequality of the two motions of rotation and revolution, the days and nights could have succeeded each other on the moon as they succeed each other on the earth. Besides, even without these conditions, life was possible."

"And so," asked Michel Ardan, "humanity has disappeared from the moon?"

"Yes," replied Barbicane, "after having doubtless remained persistently for millions of centuries; by degrees the atmosphere becoming rarefied, the disc became uninhabitable, as the terrestrial globe will one day become by cooling."

"By cooling?"

"Certainly," replied Barbicane; "as the internal fires became extinguished, and the incandescent matter concentrated itself, the lunar crust cooled. By degrees the consequences of these phenomena showed themselves in the disappearance of organized beings, and by the disappearance of vegetation. Soon the atmosphere was rarefied, probably withdrawn by terrestrial attraction; then aerial departure of respirable air, and disappearance of water by means of evaporation. At this period the moon becoming uninhabitable, was no longer inhabited. It was a dead world, such as we see it to-day."

"And you say that the same fate is in store for the earth?"

"Most probably."

"But when?"

"When the cooling of its crust shall have made it uninhabitable."

"And have they calculated the time which our unfortunate sphere will take to cool?"

"Certainly."

"And you know these calculations?"

"Perfectly."

"But speak, then my clumsy savant," exclaimed Michel Ardan, "for you make me boil with impatience!"

"Very well, my good Michel," replied Barbicane quietly, "we know what diminution of temperature the earth undergoes in the lapse of a century. And according to certain calculations, this mean temperature will, after a period of 400,000 years, be brought down to zero!"

"Four hundred thousand years!" exclaimed Michel. "Ah! I breathe again. Really I was frightened to hear you; I imagined that we had not more than 50,000 years to live."

Barbicane and Nicholl could not help laughing at their companion's uneasiness. Then Nicholl, who wished to end the discussion, put the second question which had just been considered again.

"Has the moon been inhabited?" he asked.

The answer was unanimously in the affirmative. But during this discussion, fruitful in somewhat hazardous theories, the projectile was rapidly leaving the moon; the lineaments faded away from the travelers' eyes, mountains were confused in the distance; and of all the wonderful, strange, and fantastical form of the earth's satellite, there soon remained nothing but the imperishable remembrance.

Lost Civilizations and Ancient Knowledge

The growing industrialization of England and the straitlaced Victorian society sent Englishmen in search of adventure elsewhere, usually in Africa, just as it sent Americans in pursuit of the frontier. Unknown worlds still waited to be discovered, and adventurous men such as Richard Burton, David Livingstone, Henry M. Stanley, Robert Peary, and Roald Amundsen went to find them. Something strange, mysterious, perhaps surviving from ancient or prehistoric times, might wait just beyond the horizon.

This elusive hope found its way into the romantic literature of the times. In some ways it reversed the direction taken by the literature of the new science and the growing belief in progress that was sweeping Western civilization. In stories of lost worlds and lost civilizations, writers were intimating that perhaps the greater wonders waited in the past; and the journey necessary to reach the few remaining untouched spots of the world forced adventurers to discard civilization and rely on more primitive virtues such as courage, strength, and endurance.

Thomas D. Clareson suggested that part of the reason for the popularity of the lost-race novels was the emotional repressiveness of Victorian society; the novels allowed their readers to indulge their less civilized instincts and to find, at the end of their perilous journey, "a pagan princess of their very own." But the novels also inherited several elements from the traditional travel stories that began with *Gilgamesh* and the *Odyssey* and continued through *Sir John Mandeville.*

The lost-race story had a basic formula, just as, in the twentieth century, formulas would be developed for the western and the formal detective story. First came a long and hazardous journey, sometimes of exploration, sometimes of flight, sometimes in search of a lost treasure, a lost world, or the source of strange objects or strange stories; the discovery of a hidden valley, an inaccessible plateau, an uncharted island; and amid marvelous and ancient architecture, including all sorts of wisdom and knowledge long lost to the world, the adventurers find a civilization that has survived the ages, perhaps one of the lost tribes of Israel, a forgotten outpost of the Egyptian dynasties or of ancient Greece or Rome, or a race that was powerful before recorded history such as Atlantis. In this setting the courageous hero from Western civilization assumes his proper role as leader, defeats his enemies, wins the love of a princess who is passionate and unashamed but pure of spirit, and settles down with her to found a noble line. Occasionally the hero loses his princess through accident or because she throws herself between him and death, and the hero must return to England (or the United States) often with the ancient civilization destroyed behind him.

Other variations were played upon the formula: sometimes the hero had to leave behind him in England the girl he loved and he would have to fight to return to her, sometimes against his own baser instincts; the discovery might be of prehistoric animals rather than an ancient civilization, or of noble savages; in later times, after the surface of the earth was more completely explored, the journey would end in another world (often through astral projection), or the interior of the earth, or an atom, or another dimension, or in the past, in which case the civilization usually was Atlantis and the novel ended with its destruction by earthquake and volcano.

The most famous of the lost-race authors was H. Rider Haggard (1856–1925). The sixth son of a well-to-do lawyer, Haggard became secretary to the governor of Natal at the age of nineteen and found his imagination permanently stimulated by the mysteries of Africa; later he spent other periods of time in South Africa and other parts of the continent. On his return to England he married a Norfolk heiress and studied law, but the success of *King Solomon's Mine* (1885) directed the rest of his life toward romantic writing, as well as agriculture and service to the British empire.

King Solomon's Mine had some of the elements of the lost-race story, but *She* (1887) had them all. Perennially popular, never out of print since its first publication, *She* inspired a thousand imitations, some of them by Haggard himself, who wrote three sequels. He was fond of series books, and wrote fifteen novels about the hero of *King Solomon's Mine,* Allan Quatermain, including one which brought together his two great characters, *She and Allan.*

In *She,* Leo Vincey, his guardian, Horace Holly, and their servant, Job, set out for Africa in search of the truth behind a family legend that the Vinceys were descended from an Egyptian priest of Isis named Kallikrates. They reach the eastern shore of central Africa and after great difficulties make their way through swamps, are captured by savages, and are finally taken to Kôr, an ancient civilization hidden inside an extinct volcano. It is now inhabited by savages ruled by the beautiful and immortal She-who-must-be-obeyed, who sees in Vincey the reincarnation of her lost love, Kallikrates, for whom she had been waiting some two thousand years. She offers Vincey the same immortality she has enjoyed so that they may live and love forever—an interesting parallel to the *Odyssey* and the episode in which Calypso offers Odysseus immortality and ageless youth if he will stay with her.

The major inheritors of the lost-race tradition were Edgar Rice Burroughs (1875–1950), with his Mars, Venus, and Pellucidar stories, his moon stories, his *Land That Time Forgot,* and even some of his *Tarzan* episodes; and A. Merritt (1880–1943), who, starting with *The Moon Pool,* created lush fantasies with their own special appeal. A. Conan Doyle (1859–1930) wrote a variation of the lost-race story with *The Lost World* (1912). Perhaps the last, major lost-race story was James Hilton's *Lost Horizon* (1933); interestingly, it had all the elements, including a hidden civilization, two beautiful "princesses," great wealth, great knowledge, and near immortality.

Today the kind of romantic conviction that made the lost-race stories possible is hard to find. Perhaps it goes into other kinds of works—heroic fantasies, perhaps, or UFO experiences, or books about ancient mysteries in the Erich von Däniken tradition.

From She

BY H. RIDER HAGGARD

CHAPTER XXIV

WALKING THE PLANK

Next day the mutes woke us before the dawn. By the time that we had rubbed the sleep out of our eyes, and refreshed ourselves by washing at a spring which still welled up into the remains of a marble basin in the centre of the north quadrangle of the vast outer court, we found *She* standing near the litter ready to start, while old Billali and the two bearer-mutes were busy collecting the baggage. As usual, Ayesha was veiled like the marble Truth, and it struck me then that she might have taken the idea of covering up her beauty from that statue. I noticed, however, that she seemed very depressed, and had none of that proud and buoyant bearing which would have betrayed her among a thousand women of the same stature, even if they had been veiled like herself. She looked up as we came—for her head was bowed—and greeted us. Leo asked her how she had slept.

"Ill, my Kallikrates," she answered, "ill! This night strange and hideous dreams have come creeping through my brain, and I know not what they may portend. Almost do I feel as though some evil overshadowed me; and yet, how can evil touch me? I wonder," she went on with a sudden outbreak of womanly tenderness, "I wonder, should aught happen to me, so that I slept awhile and left thee waking, if thou wouldst think gently of me? I wonder, my Kallikrates, if thou wouldst tarry till *I* came again, as for so many centuries I have tarried for *thy* coming?"

Then, without waiting for an answer, she went on: "Let us be setting forth, for we have far to go, and before another day is born in yonder blue we should stand in the place of Life."

In five minutes we were once more on our way through the ruined city, which loomed on either side through the grey dawning in a fashion at once grand and oppressive. Just as the first ray of the rising sun shot like a golden arrow athwart this storied desolation we gained the further gateway of the outer wall. Here, having given one more glance at the hoar and pillared majesty through which we had journeyed, and—with the exception of Job, for whom ruins had no charms—breathed a sigh of regret that we lacked time to explore it, we passed through the encircling moat, and on to the plain beyond.

As the sun rose so did Ayesha's spirits, till at length they had regained their normal level, and she laughingly attributed her sadness to the associations of the spot where she had slept.

"These barbarians swear that Kôr is haunted," she said, "and of a truth I believe their saying, for never did I know so ill a night save once. I remember it now. It was on that very spot, when thou didst lie dead at my feet, Kallikrates. Never will I visit it again; it is a place of evil omen."

After a very brief halt for breakfast we pressed on with such good will that by two o'clock in the day we were at the foot of the vast wall of rock forming the lip of the volcano, which at this point towered up precipitously above us for fifteen hundred or two thousand feet. Here we halted, certainly not to my astonishment, for I did not see how it was possible that we should advance any farther.

"Now," said Ayesha, as she descended from her litter "our labours but commence, for here we part with these men, and henceforward must we bear ourselves." Then she added, addressing Billali, "Do thou and these slaves remain here, and abide our return. By to-morrow at the midday we shall be with thee—if not, wait."

Billali bowed humbly, and said that her august bidding should be obeyed if they stopped there till they grew old.

"And this man, O Holly," said *She,* pointing to Job; "it is best that he should tarry also, for his heart be not high and his courage great, perchance some evil might overtake him. Also, the secrets of the place whither we go are not fit for common eyes."

I translated this to Job, who instantly and earnestly entreated me, almost with tears, not to leave him behind. He said he was sure that he could see nothing worse than he had already seen, and that he was terrified to death at the idea of being left alone with those "dumb folk," who, he thought, would probably take the opportunity to "hot-pot" him.

I translated what he said to Ayesha, who shrugged her shoulders, and answered, "Well, let him come, it is naught to me; on his own head be it. He will serve to bear the lamp and this," and she pointed to a narrow board, some sixteen feet in length, which had been bound above the long bearing-pole of her hammock, I had thought to give the curtains a wider spread, but, as it now appeared, for some unknown purpose connected with our extraordinary undertaking.

Accordingly the plank, which, though tough, was very light, was given to Job to carry, and also one of the lamps. I slung the other on to my back, together with a spare jar of oil, while Leo loaded himself with the provisions and some water in a kid's skin. When this was done *She* bade Billali and the six bearer-mutes to retreat behind a grove of flowering magnolias about a hundred yards away, and there to remain under pain of death till we had vanished. They bowed humbly, and went. As he departed, old Billali gave me a friendly shake of the hand, and whispered that he had rather that it were I than he who was going on this wonderful expedition with *"She-who must-be-obeyed"* a view with which I felt inclined to agree. In another minute they were gone; then, having briefly asked us if we were ready, Ayesha turned and gazed at the towering cliff.

"Great heavens, Leo," I said, "surely we are not going to climb that precipice!"

Leo, who was in a state of half-fascinated, half-expectant mystification, shrugged his shoulders, and at that moment Ayesha with a sudden spring began to scale the cliff, whither of course we must follow her. It was almost marvellous to see the ease and grace with which she sprang from rock to rock, and swung herself along the ledges. The ascent, however, was not so difficult as it seemed, although we passed one or two nasty places where it was unpleasant to look back; for here the rock still sloped, and was not absolutely precipitous, as it became above.

In this way, with no great toil—for the only troublesome thing to manage was Job's board—we mounted to the height of some fifty feet beyond our last standing-place, and in so doing drew sixty or seventy paces to the left of our starting-point, for we ascended as crabs walk, sideways. Presently we reached a ledge, narrow enough at first, but which widened as we followed it, and sloped inwards, moreover, like the petal of a flower, so that we sank gradually into a kind of rut or fold of rock that grew deeper and deeper, till at last it resembled a Devonshire lane in stone, and hid us perfectly from the gaze of persons on the slope below, had anybody been there to gaze. This lane, which appeared to be a natural formation, continued for some thirty or forty yards, then suddenly ended in a cave, also natural, running at right angles to it. That it was not hollowed by the labour of man I am sure, because of its irregular, contorted shape and course, which gave it the appearance of having been blasted in the thickness of the mountain by some frightful eruption of gas following the line of the least resistance. All the caverns hollowed by the ancients of Kôr, on the other hand, were cut out with a symmetrical and perfect regularity.

At the mouth of this cave Ayesha halted, and bade us light the two lamps, which I did, giving one to her and keeping the other myself. Then, taking the lead, she advanced down the cavern, picking her way with great care, as indeed it was necessary to do, for the floor was most irregular—strewn with boulders like the bed of a stream, and in some places pitted with deep holes, in which it would have been easy to break a limb.

This cavern we pursued for twenty minutes or more. It was about a quarter of a mile long, so far as I could form a judgment, which, owing to its numerous twists and turns, was not an easy task.

At last, however, we halted at its farther end, and whilst I was still trying to accustom my eyes to the twilight without a great gust of air came tearing down the cave, and extinguished both the lamps.

Ayesha called to us, and we crept up to her, for she was a little in front, to be rewarded with a view that was positively appalling in its gloom and grandeur. Before us was a mighty chasm in the black rock, jagged, torn, and splintered through it in a far past age by some awful convulsion of Nature, as though it had been cleft by stroke upon stroke of the lightning. This chasm, which was bounded by precipices, although at the moment we could not see that on the farther side, may have measured any width across, but from its darkness I do not think it can have been very broad. It was impossible to make out much of its outline, or how far it ran, for the simple reason that the point where we were standing was so far from the upper surface of the cliff, at least fifteen hundred or two thousand feet, that only a very dim light struggled down to us from above. The mouth of the cavern that we had been following gave on to a most curious and tremendous spur of rock, which jutted out through mid air into the gulf before us for a distance of some fifty yards, coming to a sharp point at its termination, and in shape resembling nothing that I can think of so much as the spur upon the leg of a cock. This huge spur was attached only to the parent precipice at its base, which was, of course, enormous, just as the cock's spur is attached to its leg. Otherwise it was utterly unsupported.

"Here must we pass," said Ayesha. "Be careful lest giddiness overcome you, or the wind sweep you into the gulf beneath, for of a truth it has no bottom"; and, without giving us further time to grow frightened, she began to walk along the spur, leaving us to follow her as best we might. I was next to her, then came Job, painfully dragging his plank, while Leo brought up the rear. It was a wonderful sight to see this intrepid woman gliding fearlessly along that dreadful place. For my part, when I had gone but a very few yards, what between the pressure of the air and the awful sense of the consequences that a slip would entail, I found it necessary to drop on to my hands and knees and crawl, and so did the others.

But Ayesha never condescended to this humble expedient. On she went, leaning her body against the gusts of wind, not seeming to lose either her head or her balance.

In a few minutes we had crossed some twenty paces of this awful bridge, which grew narrower at every step, when of a sudden a great gust tore along the gorge. I saw Ayesha lean herself against it, but the strong draught forced itself beneath her dark cloak, wrenching it from her and away it went down the wind flapping like a wounded bird. It was dreadful to see it go, till it was lost in the blackness.

I clung to the saddle of rock, and looked about me, while, like a living thing, the great spur vibrated with a humming sound beneath us. The sight was truly awesome. There we were poised in the gloom between earth and heaven. Beneath us stretched hundreds upon hundreds of feet of emptiness that gradually grew darker, till at last it was absolutely black; and at what depth it ended is more than I can guess. Above were measureless spaces of giddy air, and far, far away a line of blue sky. And down this vast gulf in which we were pinnacled the great draught dashed and roared, driving clouds and misty wreaths of vapour before it, till we were nearly blinded, and utterly confused.

Indeed the position was so tremendous and so absolutely unearthly, that I believe it actually lulled our sense of terror; but to this hour I often see it in my dreams, and at its mere phantasy wake up dripping with cold sweat.

"On! on!" cried the white form before us, for now that her cloak had gone *She* was robed in white, and looked more like a spirit riding down the gale than a woman; "On, or ye will fall and be dashed to pieces. Fix your eyes upon the ground, and cling closely to the rock."

We obeyed her, and crept painfully along the quivering path, against which the wind shrieked and wailed as it shook it, causing it to murmur like some gigantic tuning-fork. On we went, I do not know for how long, only gazing round now and again when it was absolutely necessary, until at last we saw that we had reached the very tip of the spur, a slab of rock, but little larger than an ordinary table, that throbbed and jumped like any over-engined steamer. There we lay, clinging to the stone, and stared round us, while, absolutely heedless of the hideous depth that yawned beneath, Ayesha stood leaning out against the wind, down which her long hair streamed, and pointed before her. Then we saw why the narrow plank had been provided, which Job and I had borne so painfully between us. In front yawned an empty space, on the other side of which was something, as yet we could not see what, for here either—owing to the shadow of the opposite cliff, or from some other cause—the gloom was that of a cloudy night.

"We must wait awhile," called Ayesha; "soon there will be light."

At the moment I could not imagine what she meant. How could more light than there was ever come to this dreadful spot? While I was still wondering, suddenly, like a great sword of flame, a beam from the setting sun pierced the Stygian gloom, and smote upon the point of rock whereon we lay, illuminating Ayesha's lovely form with an unearthly splendour. I only wish I could describe the wild and marvellous beauty of that sword of fire, laid across the darkness and rushing mist-wreaths of the gulf. How it came there I do not to this moment know, but I presume that there was some cleft or hole in the opposing cliff, through which light flowed when the setting orb was in a direct line with it. All I can say is, the effect was the most wonderful that I ever saw. Right through the heart of the darkness that flaming sword was stabbed, and where it lay the light was surpassingly vivid, so vivid that even at a distance we could see the grain of the rock, while outside of it—yes, within a few inches of its keen edge—was naught but clustering shadows.

And now, by this vast sunbeam, for which *She* had been waiting, and timed our arrival to meet, knowing that at this season for thousands of years it had always struck thus at eve, we saw what was before us. Within eleven or twelve yards of the very tip of the tongue-like rock whereon we stood there arose, presumably from the far bottom of the gulf, a sugarloaf-shaped cone, of which the summit was exactly opposite to us. But had there been a summit only it would not have helped us much, for the nearest point of its circumference was some forty feet from where we were. On the lip of this summit, however, which was circular and hollow, rested a tremendous flat boulder, something like a glacier stone—perhaps it was one, for all I know to the contrary—and the end of the boulder approached to within twelve feet of us. This huge mass was nothing more nor less than a gigantic rocking-stone, accurately balanced upon the edge of the cone or miniature crater, like a half-crown set on the rim of a wine-glass; for, in the fierce light that played upon it and us, we could see it oscillating in the gusts of wind.

"Quick!" said Ayesha; "the plank—we must cross while the light endures; presently it will be gone."

"Oh, Lord, sir! surely she don't mean us to walk across this here place on that there thing," groaned Job, as in obedience to my directions he thrust the long board towards me.

"That's it, Job," I holloaed in ghastly merriment, though the idea of walking the plank was no pleasanter to me than to him.

I passed the board to Ayesha, who ran it deftly across the yards of the very tip of the tongue-like rock whereon we stood there arose, presumably from the far bottom of the gulf so that one end of it rested on the rocking-stone, the other remaining upon the extremity of the trembling spur. Then, placing her foot upon it to prevent it from being blown away, she turned to me.

"Since last I was here, O Holly," she called, "the support of the moving stone hath lessened somewhat, so that I am not sure whether it will bear our weight. Therefore I must cross the first, because no hurt will overtake me," and, without further ado, she trod lightly but firmly across the frail bridge, and in another second had gained the heaving stone.

"It is safe," she called. "See, hold thou the plank! I will stand on the farther side of the rock, so that it may not over balance with your greater weights. Now come, O Holly, for presently the light will fail us."

I struggled to my knees, and if ever I felt terrified in my life it was then; indeed, I am not ashamed to say that I hesitated and hung back.

"Surely thou art not afraid," cried this strange creature, in a lull of the gale, from where she stood poised like a bird on the highest point of the rocking-stone. "Make way, then, for Kallikrates."

This decided me; it is better to fall down a precipice and die than be laughed at by such a woman! so I clenched my teeth, and in another instant I was on that narrow, bending plank, with bottomless space beneath and around me. I have always hated a great height, but never before did I appreciate the full horrors of which such a position is capable. Oh, the sickening sensation of that yielding board resting on the two moving supports. I grew dizzy, and thought that I must fall; my spine *crept;* it seemed to me that I was falling, and my delight at finding myself stretched upon the stone, which rose and fell beneath me like a boat in a swell, cannot be expressed in words. All I know is that briefly, but earnestly enough, I thanked Providence for preserving me thus far.

Then came Leo's turn, and, though he looked rather white, he ran across like a rope-dancer. Ayesha stretched out her hand to clasp his own, and I heard her say, "Bravely done, my love—bravely done! The old Greek spirit lives in thee yet!"

And now only poor Job remained on the farther side of the gulf. He crept up to the plank, and yelled out, "I can't do it, sir. I shall fall into that beastly place."

"You must," I remember answering with inappropriate facetiousness—"you must, Job, it's as easy as catching flies." I suppose that I must have said this to satisfy my conscience, because, although the expression conveys a wonderful idea of facility, as a matter of fact I know no more difficult operation in the whole world than catching flies—that is, in warm weather, unless, indeed, it is catching mosquitoes.

"I can't, sir—I can't indeed."

"Let the man come, or let him stay and perish there. See, the light is dying! In a moment it will be gone!" said Ayesha.

I looked. She was right. The sun was passing below the level of the hole or cleft in the precipice through which the ray reached us.

"If you stop there, Job, you will die alone," I called; "the light is going."

"Come, be a man, Job," shouted Leo; "it's quite easy."

Thus adjured, with a most awful yell, the miserable Job precipitated himself face downwards on the plank—he did not dare, small blame to him, to try to walk it—and commenced to draw himself across in little jerks, his poor legs hanging down on either side into the nothingness beneath.

His violent jerks at the frail board caused the great stone, which was only balanced on a few inches of rock, to oscillate in a most dreadful manner, and, to make matters worse, when he was halfway across the flying ray of lurid light suddenly went out, just as though a lamp had been extinguished in a curtained room, leaving the whole howling wilderness of air black with darkness.

"Come on, Job, for God's sake!" I shouted in an agony of fear, while the stone, gathering motion with every swing, rocked so violently that it was difficult to cling on to it. It was a truly awful position.

"Lord have mercy on me!" cried poor Job from the darkness. "Oh, the plank's slipping!" and I heard a violent struggle, and thought that he was gone.

But at that moment his outstretched hand, clasping in agony at the air, met my own, and I tugged—ah! how I did tug, putting out all the strength that it had pleased Providence to give me in such abundance—till to my joy in another minute Job was gasping on the rock beside me. But the plank! I felt it slip, and heard it knock against a projecting knob of rock. Then it was gone.

"Great heavens!" I exclaimed. "How shall we get back?"

"I don't know," answered Leo out of the gloom. "'Sufficient to the day is the evil thereof.' I am thankful enough to be here."

But Ayesha merely called to me to take her hand and follow her.

CHAPTER XXV

THE SPIRIT OF LIFE

I did as I was bidden, and in fear and trembling felt myself guided over the edge of the stone. I thrust my legs out, but could touch nothing.

"I am going to fall!" I gasped.

"Fall then, and trust to me," answered Ayesha.

Now, if the position is considered, it will be easily understood that this was a heavier tax upon my confidence than was justified by my knowledge of Ayesha's character. For all I knew she might be in the very act of consigning me to a horrible doom. But in life we must sometimes lay our faith upon strange altars, and so it was now.

"Let thyself fall!" she cried again, and, having no choice, I did.

I felt myself slide a pace or two down the sloping surface of the rock, and then pass into the air, and the thought flashed through my brain that I was lost. But no! In another instant my feet struck against a rocky floor, and I knew that I was standing on something solid, out of reach of the wind, which I could hear singing overhead. As I stood there thanking Heaven for these small mercies, there was a slip and a scuffle, and down came Leo alongside of me.

"Hulloa, old fellow!" he exclaimed, "are you there? This is interesting, is it not?"

Just then, with a terrific howl, Job arrived right on the top of us, knocking us both down. By the time that we had struggled to our feet again Ayesha was standing among us, bidding us light the lamps, which fortunately remained uninjured, and with them the spare jar of oil.

I found my box of wax matches, and they struck as merrily there, in that awful place, as they could have done in a London drawing-room.

In another minute both lamps were alight, and they revealed a curious scene. We were huddled together in a rocky chamber, some ten feet square, and very scared we looked; that is, with the exception of Ayesha, who stood calmly, her arms folded, waiting for the lamps to burn up. This chamber appeared to be partly natural and partly hollowed out of the top of the crater. The roof of the natural part was formed by the swinging stone, and that over the back of the chamber, which sloped downwards, was hewn from the live rock. For the rest, the place was warm and dry—a perfect haven of rest compared to the giddy pinnacle above, and the quivering spur that shot out to meet it in mid-air.

"So!" said *She,* "safely have we come, though once I feared that the rocking-stone would fall with you, and hurl you into the bottomless deeps beneath, for I do believe that yonder cleft goes down to the very womb of the world, and the rock whereon the boulder rests has crumbled beneath its swinging weight. But now that he," nodding towards Job, who was seated on the floor, feebly wiping his forehead with a red cotton pocket-handkerchief, "whom they rightly call the 'Pig,' for as a pig is he stupid, hath let fall the plank, it will not be easy to return across the gulf, and to that end I must make some plan. Rest you a while, and look upon this place. What think ye that it is?"

"We cannot say," I answered.

"Wouldst thou believe, O Holly, that once a man did choose this airy nest for a daily habitation, and here he dwelt for many years, leaving it but one day in every twelve to seek food and water and oil that the people brought, more than he could carry, and laid as an offering in the mouth of that tunnel through which we passed hither?"

I looked at her in question, and she continued—

"Yet so it was. There was a man—Noot, he named himself—who, though he lived in the latter days, had of the wisdom of the sons of Kôr. A hermit, and a philosopher, greatly skilled in the secrets of Nature, he it was who discovered the Fire that I shall show you, which is Nature's blood and life, and that the man who bathes therein and breathes thereof shall live while Nature lives. But like unto thee, O Holly, this Noot would not turn his knowledge to account. 'Ill,' he said, 'was it for man to live, for man is born to die.' Therefore he told his secret to none, and therefore did he abide here, where the seeker after Life must pass, and was revered of the Amahagger of that day as holy, and a hermit.

"Now, when first I came to this country—knowest thou how I came, Kallikrates? Another time I will tell thee; it is a strange tale—I heard of this philosopher, and waited for him when he sought his food yonder, and returned with him here, though I greatly feared to tread the gulf. Then did I beguile him with my beauty and my wit, and flatter him with my tongue, so that he led me down to the home of the Fire, and told me the secrets of the Fire; but he would not suffer me to step therein, and, fearing lest he should slay me, I refrained, knowing that the man was very old, and soon would die. So I returned, having learned from him all that he knew of the wonderful Spirit of the World, and that was much, for this man was wise and very ancient, and by purity and abstinence, and the contemplations of his innocent mind, had worn thin the evil between that which we see and those great Invisible truths, the whisper of whose wings we hear at times as they sweep through the gross air of the world. Then—it was but a very few days after, I met thee, my Kallikrates, who hadst wandered hither with the beautiful Egyptian Amenartas, and I learned to love for the first and last time, once and for ever, so that it entered into my mind to come hither with thee, and receive the gift of Life for thee and me. Therefore came we, with that Egyptian who would not be left behind, and, behold! we found the old man Noot lying but newly dead. *There* he lay, and his white beard covered him like a garment," and she pointed to a spot near to which I was sitting;

"but surely he has long since crumbled away, and the wind hath borne his ashes hence."

Here I put out my hand and felt in the dust, till presently my fingers touched something. It was a human tooth, very yellow, but sound. I held it up and showed it to Ayesha, who laughed.

"Yes," she said, "it is his without a doubt. Behold what remains of Noot and the wisdom of Noot—one little tooth! Yet that man had all life at his command, but for his conscience's sake he would have none of it. Well, he lay there newly dead, and we descended whither I shall lead you, and then, gathering up all my courage, and courting death that I might perchance win so glorious a crown of life, I stepped into the flames, and behold! Life such as ye can never know until ye feel it also flowed into me, and I came forth undying, and lovely beyond imagining. And I stretched out mine arms to thee, Kallikrates, bidding thee take thine own immortal bride, and behold! blinded by my naked beauty, thou didst turn from me, to hide thine eyes upon the breast of Amenartas. Then a great fury filled me, making me mad, and I seized the javelin that thou didst bear, and stabbed thee, so that, at my feet, in the very place of Life, thou didst groan and go down in to death. I knew not then that I had strength to slay with mine eyes and by the power of my will, therefore in my madness I slew with the javelin.[1]

"And when thou wast dead, ah! I wept, because I was undying and thou wast dead. I wept there in the place of Life so that had I been mortal any more my heart had surely broken. And she, the swart Egyptian—she cursed me by her gods. By Osiris did she curse me and by Isis, by Nephthys and by Anubis, by Sekhet, the cat-headed, and by Set, calling down evil on me, evil and everlasting desolation. Ah! I can see her dark face now lowering o'er me like a storm, but she could not harm me, and I—I know not if I could harm her. I did not try; it was naught to me then; so together we bore thee hence. Afterwards I sent her—the Egyptian—away through the swamps, and it seems that she lived to bear a son and to write the tale that should lead thee, her husband, back to me, her rival and thy murderess.

---

1 It will be observed that Ayesha's account of the death of Kallikrates differs materially from that written on the potsherd by Amenartas. The writing on the sherd says, "Then in her rage did she smite him *by her magic,* and he died." We never ascertained which was the correct version, but it will be remembered that the body of Kallikrates showed a spear-wound in the breast, which seems conclusive, unless, indeed, it was inflicted after death. Another thing that we never ascertained was *how* the two women—*She* and the Egyptian Amenartas—were able to bear the corpse of the man they both loved across the dread gulf and down the shaking spur. What a spectacle the two distracted creatures must have presented in their grief and loveliness as they toiled along that awful place with the dead man between them! Probably, however, its passage was easier then. — L. H. H.

"Such is the tale, my love, and now the hour is at hand that shall set a crown upon it. Like all things on the earth, it is compounded of evil and of good—more of evil than of good, perchance; and writ in a scroll of blood. It is the truth; I have hidden nothing from thee, Kallikrates. And now, one thing before the moment of thy trial. We go down into the presence of Death, for Life and Death are very near together, and—who knoweth—that might happen which shall separate us for another space of waiting? I am but a woman, and no prophetess, and I cannot read the future. But this I know—for I learned it from the lips of the wise man Noot—that my life is but prolonged and made more bright. It cannot endure for aye. Therefore, ere we go, tell me, O Kallikrates, that of a truth thou dost forgive me, and dost love me from thy heart. See, Kallikrates: much evil have I done— perchance it was evil but two nights since to strike that girl who loved thee cold in death, but she disobeyed me and angered me, prophesying misfortune to me, and I smote. Be careful when power comes to thee also, lest thou too shouldst smite in thine anger or thy jealousy, for unconquerable strength is a sore weapon in the hands of erring man. Yes, I have sinned—out of the bitterness born of a great love have I sinned—yet do I know the good from the evil, nor is my heart altogether hardened. Thy love, Kallikrates, shall be the gate of my redemption, even as aforetime my passion was the path down which I ran to ill. For deep love unsatisfied is the hell of noble hearts and a portion for the accursed, but love that is mirrored back more perfect from the soul of our desired doth fashion wings to lift us above ourselves, and make us what we might be. Therefore, Kallikrates, take me by the hand, and lift my veil with no more fear than though I were some peasant girl, and not the wisest and most beauteous woman in this wide world, and look me in the eyes, and tell me that thou dost forgive me with all thine heart, and that with all thine heart thou dost worship me."

She paused, and the infinite tenderness in her voice seemed to hover round us like some memory of the dead. I know that it moved me more even than her words, it was so very human—so very womanly. Leo, too, was strangely touched. Hitherto he had been fascinated against his better judgment, somewhat as a bird is fascinated by a snake, but now I think that all this passed away, and he knew that he really loved this strange and glorious creature, as, alas I loved her also. At any rate, I saw his eyes fill with tears as, stepping swiftly to her, he undid the gauzy veil, and taking her by the hand, gazed into her sweet face, saying—

"Ayesha, I love thee with all my heart, and so far as forgiveness is possible I forgive thee the death of Ustane. For the rest, it is between thee and thy Maker; I know nothing of it. I know only that I love thee as I never loved before, and that, be it near or far, I will cleave to thee to the end."

"Now," answered Ayesha, with proud humility—"now, when my lord doth speak thus royally pardoning with so rich a hand, it becomes me not to lag behind in gifts, and thus be beggared of my generosity. Behold!" and she took his hand and, placing it upon her shapely head, she bent herself slowly down till one knee for an instant touched the ground—"Behold! in token of submission do I bow me to my lord; Behold!" and she kissed him on the lips, "in token of my wifely love do I kiss my lord. Behold!" and she laid her hand upon his heart, "by the sin I sinned, by my lonely centuries of waiting wherewith it was wiped out, by the great love with which I love, and by the Spirit—the Eternal thing that doth beget all life, from Whom it ebbs, to Whom it must return again—I swear:—

"I swear, even in this first most holy hour of completed Womanhood, that I will cherish Good and abandon Evil. I swear that I will be ever guided by thy voice in the straightest path of duty. I swear that I will eschew Ambition, and through all my length of endless days set Wisdom over me as a ruling star to lead me unto Truth and a knowledge of the Right. I swear also that I will honour and will cherish thee, Kallikrates, who hast been swept by the wave of time back into my arms, ay, till my day of doom, come it soon or late. I swear—nay, I will swear no more, for what are words? Yet shalt thou learn that Ayesha hath no false tongue.

"So I have sworn, and thou, my Holly, art witness to the oath. Here, too, are we wed, my husband, with the gloom for bridal canopy—wed till the end of all things; here do we write our marriage vows upon the rushing winds, which shall bear them up to heaven, and round and continually round this rolling world.

"And for a bridal gift I crown thee with my beauty's starry crown, and enduring life, and wisdom without measure, and wealth that none can count. Behold! the great ones of the earth shall creep about thy feet, and its fair women shall cover up their eyes because of the shining glory of thy countenance, and its wise ones shall be abashed before thee. Thou shalt read the hearts of men as an open writing, and hither and thither shalt thou lead them as thy pleasure listeth. Like that old Sphinx of Egypt thou shalt sit aloft from age to age, and ever shall they cry to thee to solve the riddle of thy greatness, that doth not pass away, and ever shall thou mock them with thy silence!

"Behold! once more I kiss thee, and with that kiss I give to thee dominion over sea and earth, over the peasant in his hovel, over the monarch in his palace halls, and cities crowned with towers, and all who breathe therein.

Where'er the sun shakes out his spears, and the lonesome waters mirror up the moon, where'er storms roll, and Heaven's painted bows arch in the sky—from the pure North clad in snows, across the middle spaces of the world, to where the amorous South, lying like a bride upon her blue couch of seas, breathes in sighs made sweet with the odour of myrtles—there shall thy power pass and thy dominion find a home. Nor sickness, nor icy-fingered fear, nor sorrow, and pale waste of flesh and mind hovering ever o'er humanity, shall so much as shadow thee with the shadow of their wings. As a God shalt thou be, holding good and evil in the hollow of thy hand, and I, even I, humble myself before thee. Such is the power of Love, and such is the bridal gift I give unto thee, Kallikrates, my Lord and Lord of All.

"And now it is done; now for thee I loose my virgin zone; and come storm, come shine, come good, come ill, come life, come death, it never, never can be undone. For, of a truth, that which is, is and, being done, is done for aye, and cannot be changed. I have said—Let us hence, that all things may be accomplished in their order"; and, taking one of the lamps, she advanced towards the end of the chamber that was roofed in by the swaying stone, where she halted.

We followed her, and perceived that in the wall of the cone there was a stair, or, to be more accurate, that some projecting knobs of rock had been so shaped as to form a good imitation of a stair. Down these Ayesha began to climb, springing from step to step like a chamois, and after her we followed with less grace. When we had descended some fifteen or sixteen steps we found that they ended in a long rocky slope, shaped like an inverted cone or funnel.

This slope was very steep and often precipitous, but it was nowhere impassable, and by the light of the lamps we climbed down it with no great difficulty, though it was gloomy work enough travelling on thus, none of us knew whither, into the dead heart of a volcano. As we went, however, I took the precaution of noting our route as well as I could; and this was not so very difficult, owing to the extraordinary and most fantastic shapes of the rocks that were strewn about, many of which in that dim light looked more like the grim faces carven upon medieval gargoyles than ordinary boulders.

For a considerable time we travelled on thus, half an hour I should say, till, after we had descended many hundreds of feet, I perceived that we had reached the point of the inverted cone, where, at the very apex of the funnel, we found a passage, so low and narrow that we were forced to stoop as we crept along it. After some fifty yards of this creeping the passage suddenly widened into a cave, so huge that we could see neither the roof nor the sides. Indeed, we only knew that it was a cave by the echo of our tread and the perfect quiet of the heavy air. On we went for many minutes in absolute awed silence, like lost souls in the depths of Hades, Ayesha's white and ghost-like form flitting in front of us, till once more the place ended in a passage which opened into a second cavern much smaller than the first. We could clearly distinguish the arch and stony banks of this second cave, and, from their rent and jagged appearance, we judged that it had been torn in the bowels of the rock by the terrific force of some explosive gas, like that first long passage through the cliff down which we had passed before we reached the quivering spur. At length this cave ended in a third tunnel, where gleamed a faint glow of light.

I heard Ayesha utter a sigh of relief as this light dawned upon us, which flowed we knew not whence.

"It is well," she said; "prepare to enter the very womb of the Earth, wherein she doth conceive the Life that ye see brought forth in man and beast—ay, in every tree and flower. Prepare, O Men, for here ye shall be born anew!"

Swiftly she sped along, and after her we stumbled as best we might, our hearts filled like a cup with mingled dread and curiosity. What were we about to see? We passed down the tunnel; stronger and stronger grew the glow, reaching us now in great flashes like rays from a lighthouse, as one by one they are thrown wide upon the darkness of the waters. Nor was this all, for with the flashes came a soul-shaking sound like that of thunder and of crashing trees. Now we were through the passage, and—oh heavens!

We stood in a third cavern, some fifty feet in length by perhaps as great a height, and thirty wide. It was carpeted with fine white sand, and its walls have been worn smooth by the action of fire or water. This cavern was not dark like the others—it was filled with a soft glow of rose-coloured light, more beautiful to look on than anything that can be conceived. But at first we saw no flashes, and heard no more of the thunderous sound. Presently, however, as we stood in amaze, gazing at the marvellous sight, and wondering whence the rosy radiance flowed, a dread and beautiful thing happened. Across the far end of the cavern, with a grinding and crashing noise—a noise so dreadful and awe-inspiring that we all trembled, and Job actually sank to his knees—there flamed out an awful cloud or pillar of fire, like a rainbow many-coloured, and like the lightning bright. For a space, perhaps forty seconds, it flamed and roared thus, turning slowly round and round; then by degrees the terrible noise ceased, and with the fire it passed away—I know not where—leaving behind it the same rosy glow that we had first seen.

"Draw near, draw near!" cried Ayesha, with a voice of thrilling exultation. "Behold the Fountain and the Heart of Life as it beats in the bosom of this great world. Behold the Substance from which all things draw their energy, the bright Spirit of this Globe, without which it cannot live, but must grow cold and dead as the dead moon. Draw near, and wash you in those living flames, and take their virtue into your poor bodies in all its virgin strength—not as now it feebly glows within your bosoms, filtered thereto through the fine strainers of a thousand intermediate lives, but as it is here in the very fount and source of earthly Being."

We followed her through the rosy glow up to the head of the cave, till we stood before the spot where the great pulse beat and the great flame passed. And as we went we became sensible of a wild and splendid exhilaration, of the glorious sense of such a fierce intensity of Life that beside it the most buoyant moments of our strength seemed flat and tame and feeble. It was the mere effluvium of the fire, the subtle ether that it cast off as it rolled, entering into us, and making us strong as giants and swift as eagles.

We reached the head of the cave, and gazed at each other in the glorious glow, laughing aloud in the lightness of our hearts and the divine intoxication of our brains—even Job laughed, who had not smiled for a week. I know that I felt as though the mantle of all the genius whereof the human intellect is capable had descended upon me. I could have spoken in blank verse of Shakespearian beauty; inspired visions flashed through my mind; it was as though the bonds of my flesh had been loosened, and had left the spirit free to soar to the empyrean of its unguessed powers. The sensations that poured in upon me are indescribable. I seemed to live more keenly, to reach to a higher joy, to sip the goblet of a subtler thought than ever it had been my lot to taste before. I was another and most glorified self, and all the avenues of the Possible were for a while laid open to my mortal footsteps.

Then, suddenly, whilst I rejoiced in this splendid vigour of a new-found self, from far away there came the dreadful muttering noise, that grew and grew to a crash and a roar, which combined in itself all that is terrible and yet splendid in the possibilities of sound. Nearer it came, and nearer yet, till it was close upon us, rolling down like all the thunderwheels of heaven behind the horses of the lightning. On it travelled, and with it the glorious blinding cloud of many-coloured light, and stood before us for a space, slowly revolving, as it seemed to us; then, accompanied by its attendant pomp of sound, it passed away I know not whither.

So astonishing was the wondrous sight that one and all of us, save *She*, who stood up and stretched her hands towards the fire, sank down before it, and hid our faces in the sand.

When it was gone Ayesha spoke.

"At length, Kallikrates," she said, "the moment is at hand. When the great flame comes again thou must bathe in it; but throw aside the garments, for it will burn them, though thee it will not hurt. Thou must stand in the fire while thy senses will endure, and when it embraces thee suck the essence down into thy very heart, and let it leap and play around thy every limb, so that thou lose no moiety of its virtue. Hearest thou me, Kallikrates?"

"I hear thee, Ayesha," answered Leo, "but, of a truth—I am no coward—but I doubt me of that raging flame. How know I that it will not utterly destroy me, so that I lose myself and lose thee also? Nevertheless I will do it," he added.

Ayesha thought for a minute, and then said—

"It is not wonderful that thou shouldst doubt. Tell me, Kallikrates: if thou seest me stand in the flame and come forth unharmed, wilt thou enter also?"

"Yes," he answered, "I will enter even if it slay me. I have said that I will enter now."

"And that will I also," I cried.

"What, my Holly!" she laughed aloud; "methought that thou wouldst naught of length of days. Why, how is this?"

"Nay, I know not," I answered, "but there is that in my heart which calleth to me to taste of the flame, and live."

"It is well," she said. "Thou art not altogether lost in folly. See now, I will for the second time bathe me in this living bath. Fain would I add to my beauty and to my length of days, if that be possible. If it be not possible, at the least it cannot harm me.

"Also," she continued, after a momentary pause, "there is another and a deeper cause why I would once again dip me in the fire. When first I tasted of its virtue my heart was full of passion and of hatred of that Egyptian Amenartas, and therefore, despite my strivings to be rid of them, passion and hatred have been stamped upon my soul from that sad hour to this. But now it is otherwise. Now is my mood a happy mood, and I am filled with the purest part of thought, and thus I would ever be. Therefore, Kallikrates, will I once more wash and make me pure and clean, and yet more meet for thee. Therefore also, when in turn thou dost stand in the fire, empty all thy heart of evil, and let contentment hold the balance of thy mind. Shake loose thy spirit's wings, muse upon thy mother's kiss, and turn thee toward the vision of the highest good that hath ever swept on silver wings across the silence of thy dreams. For from the seed of what thou art in that dread moment shall grow the fruit of what thou shalt be for all unreckoned time.

"Now, prepare thee, prepare! even as though thy last hour were at hand, and thou wast about to cross through Death to the Land of Shadow, and not by the Gates of Glory into the realm of Life made beautiful. Prepare, I say, Kallikrates!"

The New Frontier

Just one year after the publication of *She,* with its romantic look toward the past, Edward Bellamy (1851–1898) published a book that would spur the world's interest in utopias and reinforce its belief in progress. The book was *Looking Backward, 2000–1887* (1888), and within two years Houghton, Mifflin reported the printing of 300,000 copies. Everyone was reading and talking about it, and serious attempts were underway to turn the book's vision of a better world into reality, with the formation of more than 150 Nationalist clubs, the incorporation of its programs into a political party, and the creation of two journals, *The Nationalist* and *The New Nation.*

The idealistic lectures of *Looking Backward* are barely clothed with story, but the book had sufficient suspense to induce hundreds of thousands of readers to read the lectures in order to discover what happened to the man who slept for more than a century and woke up in a new era of human decency and scientific wonders. And the book ends with Bellamy's happy inspiration to reverse the traditional disappointment of having the hero wake up to find his Utopia is only a dream: Julian West wakes up to find that he has been dreaming, but the dream that has troubled his sleep is that he awakened in the awful past.

The United States came to the utopia late. William Dean Howells (1837–1920), himself a utopian writer with *A Traveller from Altruria* (1894), believed that the frontier was responsible: It had absorbed the discontented. But as 1900 approached the frontier was ending and men's thoughts began to turn toward improving his situation where he was. Howells wrote:

> If a man got out of work, he turned his hand to something else; if a man failed in business, he started in again from some other direction; as a last resort, in both cases, he went West, pre-empted a quarter section of public land and grew up with the country. Now the country is grown up; the public land is gone; business is full on all sides, and the hand that turned itself to something else has lost its cunning. The struggle for life has changed from a free fight to an encounter of disciplined forces and the free fighters that are left get ground to pieces between organized labor and organized capital.

Political reorganization has been a part of utopian works since *The Republic,* and in this Bellamy offered nothing new. His utopia was a kind of humanitarian socialism, although it was not generally recognized as socialistic during his lifetime. What *Looking Backward* brought to the utopia was the concept of the future; instead of existing nowhere, the utopia existed in the future. That gave the vision promise for everyone and a kind of new reality. Ironically, the end of the old frontier gave humanity a new frontier— the future. And in that future was another promise, equally new, that science could help usher humanity into a new world of plenty.

English writers had gone through a similar process a few years before. Edward Bulwer-Lytton (1803–1873) published a utopian novel called *The Coming Race* (1871) about an underground race called the Vril-Ya because they use an all-penetrating electricity called Vril (which inspired the name of an English beef beverage, Bovril), who have evolved into intellectually and emotionally superior beings. But some of Bulwer-Lytton's fellow writers disagreed with him about the benefits of science.

Samuel Butler (1835–1902) located his utopia in the interior of New Zealand when he wrote *Erewhon* (1872); there an advanced civilization has discarded machinery because machinery, too, can evolve, develop consciousness, and eventually enslave man. W. H. Hudson (1841–1922) wrote *A Crystal Age* (1887), a utopia in which future Englishmen wear togas and till the soil. William Morris (1834–1896) also advocated the destruction of machinery in *News from Nowhere* (1890).

After the initial successes of his pessimistic scientific romances, H. G. Wells (1866–1946) fell under the influence of the Fabian socialists (who, he wrote, did "much to deflect me from the drift toward a successful, merely literary career into which I was manifestly falling") and turned to writing propaganda novels about utopias governed by scientists and engineers, filled with scientific marvels and mechanical plenty though often after the intervention of a terrible war, as in the classic science-fiction film he helped script, *Things to Come* (1936). In contrast, Wells's early scientific romance *When the Sleeper Wakes* (1899) not only used Bellamy's plot device but may have been written in reaction to Bellamy's vision (and incorporating its plot device, a protagonist who awakes after more than a century asleep); in the novel a future of scientific progress is marred by the tyranny of a small group of rulers who force the poor into a Labour Company.

In reaction partly to Bellamy but mostly to Wells's later propaganda novels an entire genre of anti-utopian (or dystopian, for "bad place") works developed, beginning with E. M. Forster's "The Machine Stops," continuing through Evgennii Zamiatin's *We* (1924), and reaching its high point with Aldous Huxley's *Brave New World* (1932) and George Orwell's *1984* (1949).

The utopian vision of a future in which want and privation would be eliminated by technology, and tyranny by wise laws, prevailed in the science-fiction magazines through much of the 1930s and 1940s, although frequent examples of the dystopian antithesis appeared as well. *The Space Merchants* (1953) by Frederik Pohl and Cyril Kornbluth brought the full-fledged anti-utopia into the magazines but with a unique science-fiction emphasis on plausibility. The anti-utopian view prevails today, perhaps as a direct consequence of two world wars and the U.S. trial of arms and conscience in Asia, which did much to disillusion a generation of young people and introduce new strains of dissent into society.

The utopian concepts of Bellamy still survive as at least a background philosophy in the work of a number of contemporary science fiction writers. They were particularly noticeable in the work of Mack Reynolds (1917–1983), himself a sometime labor organizer for the Socialist Labor Party for which his father was twice a presidential candidate; Reynolds acknowledged his debt to Bellamy with his own version of *Looking Backward* and an emphasis on the year 2000.

From Looking Backward, 2000–1887

BY EDWARD BELLAMY

1

I first saw the light in the city of Boston in the year 1857. "What!" you say, "eighteen fifty-seven? That is an odd slip. He means nineteen fifty-seven, of course." I beg pardon, but there is no mistake. It was about four in the afternoon of December the 26th, one day after Christmas, in the year 1857, not 1957, that I first breathed the east wind of Boston, which, I assure the reader, was at that remote period marked by the same penetrating quality characterizing it in the present year of grace, 2000.

These statements seem so absurd on their face, especially when I add that I am a young man apparently of about thirty years of age, that no person can be blamed for refusing to read another word of what promises to be a mere imposition upon his credulity. Nevertheless I earnestly assure the reader that no imposition is intended, and will undertake, if he shall follow me a few pages, to entirely convince him of this. If I may, then, provisionally assume, with the pledge of justifying the assumption, that I know better than the reader when I was born, I will go on with my narrative. As every schoolboy knows, in the latter part of the nineteenth century the civilization of today, or anything like it, did not exist, although the elements which were to develop it were already in ferment. Nothing had, however, occurred to modify the immemorial division of society into the four classes, or nations, as they may be more fitly called, since the differences between them were far greater than those between any nations nowadays, of the rich and the poor, the educated and the ignorant. I myself was rich and also educated, and possessed, therefore, all the elements of happiness enjoyed by the most fortunate in that age. Living in luxury, and occupied only with the pursuit of the pleasures and refinements of life, I derived the means of my support from the labor of others, rendering no sort of service in return. My parents and grandparents had lived in the same way, and I expected that my descendants, if I had any, would enjoy a like easy existence.

But how could I live without service to the world? you ask. Why should the world have supported in utter idleness one who was able to render service? The answer is that my great-grandfather had accumulated a sum of money on which his descendants had ever since lived. The sum, you will naturally infer, must have been very large not to have been exhausted in supporting three generations in idleness. This, however, was not the fact. The sum had been originally by no means large. It was, in fact, much larger now that three generations had been supported upon it in idleness, than it was at first. This mystery of use without consumption, of warmth without combustion, seems like magic, but was merely an ingenious application of the art now happily lost but carried to great perfection by your ancestors, of shifting the burden of one's support on the shoulders of others. The man who had accomplished this, and it was the end all sought, was said to live on the income of his investments. To explain at this point how the ancient methods of industry made this possible would delay us too much. I shall only stop now to say that interest on investments was a species of tax in perpetuity upon the product of those engaged in industry which a person possessing or inheriting money was able to levy. It must not be supposed that an arrangement which seems so unnatural and preposterous according to modern notions was never criticized by your ancestors. It had been the effort of lawgivers and prophets from the earliest ages to abolish interest, or at least to limit it to the smallest possible rate. All these efforts had, however, failed, as they necessarily must so long as the ancient social organizations prevailed. At the time of which I write, the latter part of the nineteenth century, governments had generally given up trying to regulate the subject at all.

By way of attempting to give the reader some general impression of the way people lived together in those days, and especially of the relations of the rich and poor to one another, perhaps I cannot do better than to compare society as it then was to a prodigious coach which the masses of humanity were harnessed to and dragged toilsomely along a very hilly and sandy road. The driver was hunger, and permitted no lagging, though the pace was necessarily very slow. Despite the difficulty of drawing the coach at all along so hard a road, the top was covered with passengers who never got down, even at the steepest ascents. These seats on top were very breezy and comfortable. Well up out of the dust, their occupants could enjoy the scenery at their leisure, or critically discuss the merits of the straining team. Naturally such places were in great demand and the competition for them was keen, every one seeking as the first end in life to secure a seat on the coach for himself and to leave it to his child after him. By rule of the coach a man could leave his seat to whom he wished, but on the other hand there were many accidents by which it might at any time be wholly lost. For all that they were so easy, the seats were very insecure, and at every sudden jolt of the coach persons were slipping out of them end falling to the ground, where they were instantly compelled to take hold of the rope and help to drag the coach on which they had before ridden so pleasantly. It was naturally regarded as a terrible misfortune to lose one's seat, and the apprehension that this might happen to them or their friends was a constant cloud upon the happiness of those who rode.

But did they think only of themselves? you ask. Was not their very luxury rendered intolerable to them by comparison with the lot of their brothers and sisters in the harness, and the knowledge that their own weight added to their toil? Had they no compassion for fellow beings from whom fortune only distinguished them? Oh, yes; commiseration was frequently expressed by those who rode for those who had to pull the coach, especially when the vehicle came to a bad place in the road, as it was constantly doing, or to a particularly steep hill. At such times, the desperate straining of the team, their agonized leaping and plunging under the pitiless lashing of hunger, the many who fainted at the rope and were trampled in the mire, made a very distressing spectacle, which often called forth highly creditable displays of feeling on the top of the coach. At such times the passengers would call down encouragingly to the toilers of the rope, exhorting them to patience, and holding out hopes of possible compensation in another world for the hardness of their lot, while others contributed to buy salves and liniments for the crippled and injured. It was agreed that it was a great pity that the coach should be so hard to pull, and there was a sense of general relief when the specially bad piece of road was gotten over. This relief was not, indeed, wholly on account of the team, for there was always some danger at these bad places of a general overturn in which all would lose their seats.

It must in truth be admitted that the main effect of the spectacle of the misery of the toilers at the rope was to enhance the passengers' sense of the value of their seats upon the coach, and to cause them to hold on to them more desperately than before. If the passengers could only have felt assured that neither they nor their friends would ever fall from the top, it is probable that, beyond contributing to the funds for liniments and bandages, they would have troubled themselves extremely little about those who dragged the coach.

I am well aware that this will appear to the men and women of the twentieth century as incredible inhumanity, but there are two facts, both very curious, which partly explain it. In the first place, it was firmly and sincerely believed that there was no other way in which Society could get along, except the many pulled at the rope and the few rode, and not only this, but that no very radical improvement even was possible, either in the harness, the coach, the roadway, or the distribution of the toil. It had always been as it was, and it always would be so. It was a pity, but it could not be helped, and philosophy forbade wasting compassion on what was beyond remedy.

The other fact is yet more curious, consisting in a singular hallucination which those on the top of the coach generally shared, that they were not exactly like their brothers and sisters who pulled at the rope, but of finer clay, in some way belonging to a higher order of beings who might justly expect to be drawn. This seems unaccountable, but, as I once rode on this very coach and shared that very hallucination, I ought to be believed. The strangest thing about the hallucination was that those who had but just climbed up from the ground, before they had outgrown the marks of the rope upon their hands, began to fall under its influence. As for those whose parents and grandparents before them had been so fortunate as to keep their seats on the top, the conviction they cherished of the essential difference between their sort of humanity and the common article was absolute. The effect of such a delusion in moderating fellow feeling for the sufferings of the mass of men into a distant and philosophical compassion is obvious. To it I refer as the only extenuation I can offer for the indifference which, at the period I write of, marked my own attitude toward the misery of my brothers.

In 1887 I came to my thirtieth year. Although still unmarried, I was engaged to wed Edith Bartlett. She, like myself, rode on the top of the coach. That is to say, not to encumber ourselves further with an illustration which has, I hope, served its purpose of giving the reader some general impression of how we lived then, her family was wealthy. In that age, when money alone commanded all that was agreeable and refined in life, it was enough for a woman to be rich to have suitors; but Edith Bartlett was beautiful and graceful also.

My lady readers, I am aware, will protest at this. "Handsome she might have been," I hear them saying, "but graceful never, in the costumes which were the fashion at that period, when the head covering was a dizzy structure a foot tall, and the almost incredible extension of the skirt behind by means of artificial contrivances more thoroughly dehumanized the form than any former device of dressmakers. Fancy any one graceful in such a costume!" The point is certainly well taken, and I can only reply that while the ladies of the twentieth century are lovely demonstrations of the effect of appropriate drapery in accenting feminine graces, my recollection of their great-grandmothers enables me to maintain that no deformity of costume can wholly disguise them.

Our marriage only waited on the completion of the house which I was building for our occupancy in one of the most desirable parts of the city, that is to say, a part chiefly inhabited by the rich. For it must be understood that the comparative desirability of different parts of Boston for residence depended then, not on natural features, but on the character of the neighboring population. Each class or nation lived by itself, in quarters of its own. A rich man living among the poor, an educated man among the uneducated, was like one living in isolation among a jealous and alien race. When the house had been begun, its completion by the winter of 1886 had been expected. The spring of the following year found it, however, yet incomplete, and my marriage still a thing of the future. The cause of a delay calculated to be particularly exasperating to an ardent lover was a series of strikes, that is to say, concerted refusals to work on the part of the bricklayers, masons, carpenters, painters, plumbers, and other trades concerned in house building. What the specific causes of these strikes were I do not remember. Strikes had become so common at that period that people had ceased to inquire into their particular grounds. In one department of industry or another, they had been nearly incessant ever since the great business crisis of 1873. In fact it had come to be the exceptional thing to see any class of laborers pursue their avocation steadily for more than a few months at a time.

The reader who observes the dates alluded to will of course recognize in these disturbances of industry the first and incoherent phase of the great movement which ended in the establishment of the modern industrial system with all its social consequences. This is all so plain in the retrospect that a child can understand it, but not being prophets, we of that day had no clear idea what was happening to us. What we did see was that industrially the country was in a very queer way. The relation between the workingman and the employer, between labor and capital, appeared in some unaccountable manner to have been dislocated. The working classes had quite suddenly and very generally become infected with a profound discontent with their condition, and an idea that it could be greatly bettered if they only knew how to go about it. On every side, with one accord, they preferred demands for higher pay, shorter hours, better dwellings, better educational advantages, and a share in the refinements and luxuries of life, demands which it was impossible to see the way to granting unless the world were to become a great deal richer than it then was. Though they knew something of what they wanted, they knew nothing of how to accomplish it, and the eager enthusiasm with which they thronged about any one who seemed likely to give them any light on the subject lent sudden reputation to many would-be leaders, some of whom had little enough light to give. However chimerical the aspirations of the laboring classes might be deemed, the devotion with which they supported one another in the strikes, which were their chief weapon, and the sacrifices which they underwent to carry them out left no doubt of their dead earnestness.

As to the final outcome of the labor troubles, which was the phrase by which the movement I have described was most commonly referred to, the opinions of the people of my class differed according to individual temperament. The sanguine argued very forcibly that it was in the very nature of things impossible that the new hopes of the workingmen could be satisfied, simply because the world had not the wherewithal to satisfy them. It was only because the masses worked very hard and lived on short commons that the race did not starve outright, and no considerable improvement in their condition was possible while the world, as a whole, remained so poor. It was not the capitalists whom the laboring men were contending with, these maintained, but the ironbound environment of humanity, and it was merely a question of the thickness of their skulls when they would discover the fact and make up their minds to endure what they could not cure.

The less sanguine admitted all this. Of course the workingmen's aspirations were impossible of fulfillment for natural reasons, but there were grounds to fear that they would not discover this fact until they had made a sad mess of society. They had the votes and the power to do so if they pleased, and their leaders meant they should. Some of these desponding observers went so far as to predict an impending social cataclysm. Humanity, they argued, having climbed to the top round of the ladder of civilization, was about to take a header into chaos, after which it would doubtless pick itself up, turn round, and begin to climb again. Repeated experiences of this sort in historic and prehistoric times possibly accounted for the puzzling bumps on the human cranium. Human history, like all great movements, was cyclical, and returned to the point of beginning. The idea of indefinite progress in a right line was a chimera of the imagination, with no analogue in nature. The parabola of a comet was perhaps a yet better illustration of the career of humanity. Tending upward and sunward from the aphelion of barbarism, the race attained the perihelion of civilization only to plunge downward once more to its nether goal in the regions of chaos.

This, of course, was an extreme opinion, but I remember serious men among my acquaintances who, in discussing the signs of the times, adopted a very similar tone. It was no doubt the common opinion of thoughtful men that society was approaching a critical period which might result in great changes. The labor troubles, their causes, course, and cure, took lead of all other topics in the public prints, and in serious conversation.

The nervous tension of the public mind could not have been more strikingly illustrated than it was by the alarm resulting from the talk of a small band of men who called themselves anarchists, and proposed to terrify the American people into adopting their ideas by threats of violence, as if a mighty nation which had but just put down a rebellion of half its own numbers, in order to maintain its political system, were likely to adopt a new social system out of fear.

As one of the wealthy, with a large stake in the existing order of things, I naturally shared the apprehensions of my class. The particular grievance I had against the working classes at the time of which I write, on account of the effect of their strikes in postponing my wedded bliss, no doubt lent a special animosity to my feeling toward them.

<h2 style="text-align:center">2</h2>

The thirtieth day of May, 1887, fell on a Monday. It was one of the annual holidays of the nation in the latter third of the nineteenth century, being set apart under the name of Decoration Day, for doing honor to the memory of the soldiers of the North who took part in the war for preservation of the union of the States. The survivors of the war, escorted by military and civic processions and bands of music, were wont on this occasion to visit the cemeteries and lay wreaths of flowers upon the graves of their dead comrades, the ceremony being a very solemn and touching one. The eldest brother of Edith Bartlett had fallen in the war, and on Decoration Day the family was in the habit of making a visit to Mount Auburn, where he lay.

I had asked permission to make one of the party, and, on our return to the city at nightfall, remained to dine with the family of my betrothed. In the drawing-room, after dinner, I picked up an evening paper and read of a fresh strike in the building trades, which would probably still further delay the completion of my unlucky house. I remember distinctly how exasperated I was at this, and the objurgations, as forcible as the presence of the ladies permitted, which I lavished upon workmen in general, and these strikers in particular. I had abundant sympathy from those about me, and the remarks made in the desultory conversation which followed, upon the unprincipled conduct of the labor agitators, were calculated to make those gentlemen's ears tingle. It was agreed that affairs were going from bad to worse very fast, and that there was no telling what we should come to soon. "The worst of it," I remember Mrs. Bartlett's saying, "is that the working classes all over the world seem to be going crazy at once. In Europe it is far worse even than here. I'm sure I should not dare to live there at all. I asked Mr. Bartlett the other day where we should emigrate to if all the terrible things took place which those socialists threaten. He said he did not know any place now where society could be called stable except Greenland, Patagonia, and the Chinese Empire." "Those Chinamen knew what they were about," somebody added, "when they refused to let in our western civilization. They saw it was nothing but dynamite in disguise."

After this, I remember drawing Edith apart and trying to persuade her that it would be better to be married at once without waiting for the completion of the house, spending the time in travel till our home was ready for us. She was remarkably handsome that evening, the mourning costume that she wore in recognition of the day setting off to great advantage the purity of her complexion. I can see her even now with my mind's eye just as she looked that night. When I took my leave she followed me into the hall and I kissed her good-by as usual. There were no circumstance out of the common to distinguish this parting from previous occasions when we had bade each other good-by for a night or a day. There was absolutely no premonition in my mind, or I am sure in hers, that this was more than an ordinary separation.

Ah, well!

The hour at which I had left my betrothed was a rather early one for a lover, but the fact was no reflection on my devotion. I was a confirmed sufferer from insomnia, and although otherwise perfectly well had been completely fagged out that day, from having slept scarcely at all the two previous nights. Edith knew this and had insisted on sending me home by nine o'clock, with strict orders to go to bed at once.

The house in which I lived had been occupied by three generations of the family of which I was the only living representative in the direct line. It was a large, ancient wooden mansion, very elegant in an old-fashioned way within, but situated in a quarter that had long since become undesirable for residence, from its invasion of tenement houses and manufactories. It was not a house to which I could think of bringing a bride, much less so dainty a one as Edith Bartlett. I had advertised it for sale, and meanwhile merely used it for sleeping purposes, dining at my club. One servant, a faithful colored man by the name of Sawyer, lived with me and attended to my few wants. One feature of the house I expected to miss greatly when I should leave it, and this was the sleeping chamber which I had built under the foundations. I could not have slept in the city at all, with its never ceasing nightly noises, if I had been obliged to use an upstairs chamber. But to this subterranean room no murmur from the upper world ever penetrated. When I had entered it and closed the door, I was surrounded by the silence of the tomb. In order to prevent the dampness of the subsoil from penetrating the chamber, the walls had been laid in hydraulic cement and were very thick, and the floor was likewise protected. In order that the room might serve also as a vault equally proof against violence and flames, for the storage of valuables, I had roofed it with stone slabs hermetically sealed, and the outer door was of iron with a thick coating of asbestos. A small pipe, communicating with a windmill on the top of the house, insured the renewal of air.

It might seem that the tenant of such a chamber ought to be able to command slumber, but it was rare that I slept well, even there, two nights in succession. So accustomed was I to wakefulness that I minded little the loss of one night's rest. A second night, however, spent in my reading chair instead of my bed, tired me out, and I never allowed myself to go longer than that without slumber, from fear of nervous disorder. From this statement it will be inferred that I had at my command some artificial means for inducing sleep in the last resort, and so in fact I had. If after two sleepless nights I found myself on the approach of the third without sensations of drowsiness, I called in Dr. Pillsbury.

He was a doctor by courtesy only, what was called in those days an "irregular" or "quack" doctor. He called himself a "Professor of Animal Magnetism." I had come across him in the course of some amateur investigations into the phenomena of animal magnetism. I don't think he knew anything about medicine, but he was certainly a remarkable mesmerist. It was for the purpose of being put to sleep by his manipulations that I used to send for him when I found a third night of sleeplessness impending. Let my nervous excitement or mental preoccupation be however great, Dr. Pillsbury never failed, after a short time, to leave me in a deep slumber, which continued till I was aroused by a reversal of the mesmerizing process. The process for awakening the sleeper was much simpler than that for putting him to sleep, and for convenience I had made Dr. Pillsbury teach Sawyer how to do it.

My faithful servant alone knew for what purpose Dr. Pillsbury visited me, or that he did so at all. Of course, when Edith became my wife I should have to tell her my secrets. I had not hitherto told her this, because there was unquestionably a slight risk in the mesmeric sleep, and I knew she would set her face against my practice. The risk, of course, was that it might become too profound and pass into a trance beyond the mesmerizer's power to break, ending in death. Repeated experiments had fully convinced me that the risk was next to nothing if reasonable precautions were exercised, and of this I hoped, though doubtingly, to convince Edith. I went directly home after leaving her, and at once sent Sawyer to fetch Dr. Pillsbury. Meanwhile I sought my subterranean sleeping chamber, and exchanging my costume for a comfortable dressing-gown, sat down to read the letters by the evening mail which Sawyer had laid on my reading table.

One of them was from the builder of my new house, and confirmed what I had inferred from the newspaper item. The new strikes, he said, had postponed indefinitely the completion of the contract, as neither masters nor workmen would concede the point at issue without a long struggle. Caligula wished that the Roman people had but one neck that he might cut it off, and as I read this lettɔr I am afraid that for a moment I was capable of wishing the same thing concerning the laboring classes of America. The return of Sawyer with the doctor interrupted my gloomy meditations.

It appeared that he had with difficulty been able to secure his services, as he was preparing to leave the city that very night. The doctor explained that since he had seen me last he had learned of a fine professional opening in a distant city, and decided to take prompt advantage of it. On my asking, in some panic, what I was to do for someone to put me to sleep, he gave me the names of several mesmerizers in Boston who, he averred, had quite as great powers as he.

Somewhat relieved on this point, I instructed Sawyer to rouse me at nine o'clock next morning, and, lying down on the bed in my dressing-gown, assumed a comfortable attitude, and surrendered myself to the manipulations of the mesmerizer. Owing, perhaps, to my unusually nervous state, I was slower than common in losing consciousness, but at length a delicious drowsiness stole over me.

3

"He is going to open his eyes. He had better see but one of us at first."

"Promise me, then, that you will not tell him."

The first voice was a man's, the second a woman's, and both spoke in whispers.

"I will see how he seems," replied the man.

"No, no, promise me," persisted the other.

"Let her have her way," whispered a third voice, also a woman.

"Well, well, I promise, then," answered the man. "Quick, go! He is coming out of it."

There was a rustle of garments and I opened my eyes. A fine looking man of perhaps sixty was bending over me, an expression of much benevolence mingled with great curiosity upon his features. He was an utter stranger. I raised myself on an elbow and looked around. The room was empty. I certainly had never been in it before, or one furnished like it. I looked back at my companion. He smiled.

"How do you feel?" he inquired.

"Where am I?" I demanded.

"You are in my house," was the reply.

"How came I here?"

"We will talk about that when you are stronger. Meanwhile, I beg you will feel no anxiety. You are among friends and in good hands. How do you feel?"

"A bit queerly," I replied, "but I am well, I suppose. Will you tell me how I came to be indebted to your hospitality? What has happened to me? How came I here? It was in my own house that I went to sleep."

"There will be time enough for explanations later," my unknown host replied, with a reassuring smile. "It will be better to avoid agitating talk until you are a little more yourself. Will you oblige me by taking couple of swallows, of this mixture? It will do you good. I am a physician."

I repelled the glass with my hand and sat up on the couch, although with an effort, for my head was strangely light.

"I insist upon knowing at once where I am and what you have been doing with me," I said.

"My dear sir," responded my companion, "let me beg that you will not agitate yourself. I would rather you did not insist upon explanations so soon, but if you do, I will try to satisfy you, provided you will first take this draught, which will strengthen you somewhat."

I thereupon drank what he offered me. Then he said, "It is not so simple a matter as you evidently suppose to tell you how you came here. You can tell me quite as much on that point as I can tell you. You have just been roused from a deep sleep, or, more properly, trance. So much I can tell you. You say you were in your own house when you fell into that sleep. May I ask you when that was?"

"When?" I replied, "when? Why, last evening, of course, at about ten o'clock. I left my man Sawyer orders to call me at nine o'clock. What has become of Sawyer?"

"I can't precisely tell you that," replied my companion, regarding me with a curious expression, "but I am sure that he is excusable for not being here. And now can you tell me a little more explicitly when it was that you fell into that sleep, the date, I mean?"

"Why, last night, of course; I said so, didn't I? that is, unless I have overslept an entire day. Great heavens! that cannot be possible; and yet I have an odd sensation of having slept a long time. It was Decoration Day that I went to sleep."

"Decoration Day?"

"Yes, Monday, the 30th."

"Pardon me, the 30th of what?"

"Why, of this month, of course, unless I have slept into June, but that can't be."

"This month is September."

"September! You don't mean that I've slept since May! God in heaven! Why, it is incredible."

"We shall see," replied my companion; "you say that it was May 30th when you went to sleep?"

"Yes."

"May I ask of what year?"

I stared blankly at him, incapable of speech, for some moments.

"Of what year?" I feebly echoed at last.

"Yes, of what year, if you please? After you have told me that I shall be able to tell you how long you have slept."

"It was the year 1887," I said.

My companion insisted that I should take another draught from the glass, and felt my pulse.

"My dear sir," he said, "your manner indicates that you are a man of culture, which I am aware was by no means the matter of course in your day it now is. No doubt, then, you have yourself made the observation that nothing in this world can be truly said to be more wonderful than anything else. The causes of all phenomena are equally adequate, and the results equally matters of course. That you should be startled by what I shall tell you is to be expected; but I am confident that you will not permit it to affect your equanimity unduly. Your appearance is that of a young man of barely thirty, and your bodily condition seems not greatly different from that of one just roused from a somewhat too long and profound sleep, and yet this is the tenth day of September in the year 2000, and you have slept exactly one hundred and thirteen years, three months, and eleven days."

Feeling partially dazed, I drank a cup of some sort of broth at my companion's suggestion, and, immediately afterward, becoming very drowsy, went off into a deep sleep.

When I awoke it was broad daylight in the room, which had been lighted artificially when I was awake before. My mysterious host was sitting near. He was not looking at me when I opened my eyes, and I had a good opportunity to study him and meditate upon my extraordinary situation, before he observed that I was awake. My giddiness was all gone, and my mind perfectly clear. The story that I had been asleep one hundred and thirteen years, which, in my former weak and bewildered condition, I had accepted without question, recurred to me now only to be rejected as a preposterous attempt at an imposture, the motive of which it was impossible remotely to surmise.

Something extraordinary had certainly happened to account for my waking up in this strange house with this unknown companion, but my fancy was utterly impotent to suggest more than the wildest guess as to what that something might have been. Could it be that I was the victim of some sort of conspiracy? It looked so, certainly; and yet, if human lineaments ever gave true evidence, it was certain that this man by my side, with a face so refined and ingenuous, was no party to any scheme of crime or outrage. Then it occurred to me to question if I might not be the butt of some elaborate practical joke on the part of friends who had somehow learned the secret of my underground chamber and taken this means of impressing me with the peril of mesmeric experiments. There were great difficulties in the way of this theory; Sawyer would never have betrayed me, nor had I any friends at all likely to undertake such an enterprise; nevertheless the supposition that I was the victim of a practical joke seemed on the whole the only one tenable. Half expecting to catch a glimpse of some familiar face grinning from behind a chair or curtain, I looked carefully about the room. When my eyes next rested on my companion, he was looking at me.

"You have had a fine nap of twelve hours," he said briskly, "and I can see that it has done you good. You look much better. Your color is good and your eyes are bright. How do you feel?"

"I never felt better," I said, sitting up.

"You remember your first waking, no doubt," he pursued, "and your surprise when I told you how long you had been asleep?"

"You said, I believe, that I had slept one hundred and thirteen years,"

"Exactly."

"You will admit," I said, with an ironical smile, "that the story was rather an improbable one."

"Extraordinary, I admit," he responded, "but given the proper conditions, not improbable nor inconsistent with what we know of the trance state. When complete, as in your case, the vital functions are absolutely suspended, and there is no waste of the tissues. No limit can be set to the possible duration of a trance when the external conditions protect the body from physical injury. This trance of yours is indeed the longest of which there is any positive record, but there is no known reason wherefore, had you not been discovered and had the chamber in which we found you continued intact, you might not have remained in a state of suspended animation till, at the end of indefinite ages, the gradual refrigeration of the earth had destroyed the bodily tissues and set the spirit free."

I had to admit that; if I were indeed the victim of a practical joke, its authors had chosen an admirable agent for carrying out their imposition. The impressive and even eloquent manner of this man would have lent dignity to an argument that the moon was made of cheese. The smile with which I had regarded him as he advanced his trance hypothesis did not appear to confuse him in the slightest degree.

"Perhaps," I said, "you will go on and favor me with some particulars as to the circumstances under which you discovered this chamber of which you speak, and its contents. I enjoy good fiction."

"In this case," was the grave reply, "no fiction could be so strange as the truth. You must know that these many years I have been cherishing the idea of building a laboratory in the large garden beside this house, for the purpose of chemical experiments for which I have a taste. Last Thursday the excavation for the cellar was at last begun. It was completed by that night, and Friday the masons were to have come. Thursday night we had a tremendous deluge of rain, and Friday morning I found my cellar a frogpond and the walls quite washed down. My daughter, who had come out to view the disaster with me, called my attention to a corner of masonry laid bare by the crumbling away of one of the walls. I cleared a little earth from it, and, finding that it seemed part of a large mass, determined to investigate it. The workmen I sent for unearthed an oblong vault some eight feet below the surface, and set in the corner of what had evidently been the foundation of an ancient house. A layer of ashes and charcoal on the top of the vault showed that the house above had perished by fire. The vault itself was perfectly intact, the cement being as good as when first applied. It had a door, but this we could not force, and found entrance by removing one of the flagstones which formed the roof. The air which came up was stagnant but pure, dry and not cold. Descending with a lantern, I found myself in an apartment fitted up as a bedroom in the style of the nineteenth century. On the bed lay a young man. That he was dead and must have been dead a century was of course to be taken for granted; but the extraordinary state of preservation of the body struck me and the medical colleagues whom I had summoned with amazement. That the art of such embalming as this had ever been known we should not have believed, yet here seemed conclusive testimony that our immediate ancestors had possessed it. My medical colleagues, whose curiosity was highly excited, were at once for undertaking experiments to test the nature of the process employed, but I withheld them. My motive in so doing, at least the only motive I now need speak of, was the recollection of something I once had read about the extent to which your contemporaries had cultivated the subject of animal magnetism. It had occurred to me as just conceivable that you might be in a trance, and that the secret of your bodily integrity after so long a time was not the craft of an embalmer, but life. So extremely fanciful did this idea seem, even to me, that I did not risk the ridicule of my fellow physicians by mentioning it, but gave some other reason for postponing their experiments. No sooner, however, had they left me, than I set on foot a systematic attempt at resuscitation, of which you know the result."

Had its theme been yet more incredible, the circumstantiality of this narrative, as well as the impressive manner and personality of the narrator, might have staggered a listener, and I had begun to feel very strangely, when, as he closed, I chanced to catch a glimpse of my reflection in a mirror hanging on the wall of the room. I rose and went up to it. The face I saw was the face to a hair and a line and not a day older than the one I had looked at as I tied my cravat before going to Edith that Decoration Day, which, as this man would have me believe, was celebrated one hundred and thirteen years before. At this, the colossal character of the fraud which was being attempted on me, came over me afresh. Indignation mastered my mind as I realized the outrageous liberty that had been taken.

"You are probably surprised," said my companion, "to see that, although you are a century older than when you lay down to sleep in that underground chamber, your appearance is unchanged. That should not amaze you. It is by virtue of the total arrest of the vital functions that you have survived this great period of time. If your body could have undergone any change during your trance, it would long ago have suffered dissolution."

"Sir," I replied, turning to him, "what your motive can be in reciting to me with a serious face this remarkable farrago, I am utterly unable to guess; but you are surely yourself too intelligent to suppose that anybody but an imbecile could be deceived by it. Spare me any more of this elaborate nonsense and once for all tell me whether you refuse to give me an intelligible account of where I am and how I came here. If so, I shall proceed to ascertain my whereabouts for myself, whoever may hinder."

"You do not, then, believe that this is the year 2000?"

"Do you really think it necessary to ask me that?" I returned.

Very well," replied my extraordinary host. "Since I cannot convince you, you shall convince yourself. Are you strong enough to follow me upstairs?"

"I am as strong as I ever was," I replied angrily, "as I may have to prove if this jest is carried much farther."

"I beg, sir," was my companion's response, "that you will not allow yourself to be too fully persuaded that you are the victim of a trick, lest the reaction, when you are convinced of the truth of my statements, should be too great."

The tone of concern, mingled with commiseration, with which he said this, and the entire absence of any sign of resentment at my hot words, strangely daunted me, and I followed him from the room with an extraordinary mixture of emotions. He led the way up two flights of stairs and then up a shorter one, which landed us upon a belvedere on the housetop. "Be pleased to look around you," he said, as we reached the platform, "and tell me if this is the Boston of the nineteenth century."

At my feet lay a great city. Miles of broad streets, shaded by trees and lined with fine buildings, for the most part not in continuous blocks but set in larger or smaller inclosures, stretched in every direction. Every quarter contained large open squares filled with trees, among which statues glistened and fountains flashed in the late afternoon sun. Public buildings of a colossal size and an architectural grandeur unparalleled in my day raised their stately piles on every side. Surely I had never seen this city nor one comparable to it before. Raising my eyes at last towards the horizon, I looked westward. That blue ribbon winding away to the sunset, was it not the sinuous Charles? I looked east; Boston harbor stretched before me within its headlands, not one of its green islets missing.

I knew then that I had been told the truth concerning the prodigious thing which had befallen me.

4

I did not faint, but the effort to realize my position made me very giddy, and I remember that my companion had to give me a strong arm as he conducted me from the roof to a roomy apartment on the upper floor of the house, where he insisted on my drinking a glass or two of good wine and partaking of a light repast.

"I think you are going to be all right now," he said cheerily. "I should not have taken so abrupt a means to convince you of your position if your course, while perfectly excusable under the circumstances, had not rather obliged me to do so. I confess," he added laughing, "I was a little apprehensive at one time that I should undergo what I believe you used to call a knockdown in the nineteenth century, if I did not act rather promptly. I remembered that the Bostonians of your day were famous pugilists, and thought best to lose no time. I take it you are now ready to acquit me of the charge of hoaxing you."

"If you had told me," I replied, profoundly awed, "that a thousand years instead of a hundred had elapsed since I last looked on this city, I should now believe you."

"Only a century has passed," he answered, "but many a millennium in the world's history has seen changes less extraordinary.

"And now," he added, extending his hand with an air of irresistible cordiality, "let me give you a hearty welcome to the Boston of the twentieth century and to this house. My name is Leete, Dr. Leete they call me."

"My name," I said as I shook his hand, "is Julian West."

"I am most happy in making your acquaintance, Mr. West," he responded. "Seeing that this house is built on the site of your own, I hope you will find it easy to make yourself at home in it."

After my refreshment Dr. Leete offered me a bath and a change of clothing, of which I gladly availed myself.

It did not appear that any very startling revolution in men's attire had been among the great changes my host had spoken of, for, barring a few details, my new habiliments did not puzzle me at all.

Physically, I was now myself again. But mentally, how was it with me, the reader will doubtless wonder. What were my intellectual sensations, he may wish to know, on finding myself so suddenly dropped as it were into a new world. In reply let me ask him to suppose himself suddenly, in the twinkling of an eye, transported from earth, say, to Paradise or Hades. What does he fancy would be his own experience? Would his thoughts return at once to the earth he had just left, or would he, after the first shock, well nigh forget his former life for a while, albeit to be remembered later, in the interest excited by his new surroundings? All I can say is, that if his experience were at all like mine in the transition I am describing, the latter hypothesis would prove the correct one. The impressions of amazement and curiosity which my new surroundings produced occupied my mind, after the first shock, to the exclusion of all other thoughts. For the time the memory of my former life was, as it were, in abeyance.

No sooner did I find myself physically rehabilitated through the kind offices of my host, than I became eager to return to the housetop; and presently we were comfortably established there in easy chairs, with the city beneath and around us. After Dr. Leete had responded to numerous questions on my part, as to the ancient landmarks I missed and the new ones which had replaced them, he asked me what point of the contrast between the new and the old city struck me most forcibly.

"To speak of small things before great," I responded, "I really think that the complete absence of chimneys and their smoke is the detail that first impressed me."

"Ah!" ejaculated my companion with an air of much interest, "I had forgotten the chimneys, it is so long since they went out of use. It is nearly a century since the crude method of combustion on which you depended for heat became obsolete."

"In general," I said, "what impresses me most about the city is the material prosperity on the part of the people which its magnificence implies."

"I would give a great deal for just one glimpse of the Boston of your day," replied Dr. Leete. "No doubt, as you imply, the cities of that period were rather shabby affairs. If you had the taste to make them splendid, which I would not be so rude as to question, the general poverty resulting from your extraordinary industrial system would not have given you the means. Moreover, the excessive individualism which then prevailed was inconsistent with much public spirit. What little wealth you had seems almost wholly to have been lavished in private luxury. Nowadays, on the contrary, there is no destination of the surplus wealth so popular as the adornment of the city, which all enjoy in equal degree."

The sun had been setting as we returned to the housetop, and as we talked night descended upon the city.

"It is growing dark," said Dr. Leete. "Let us descend into the house; I want to introduce my wife and daughter to you."

His words recalled to me the feminine voices which I had heard whispering about me as I was coming back to conscious life; and, most curious to learn what the ladies of the year 2000 were like, I assented with alacrity to the proposition. The apartment in which we found the wife and daughter of my host, as well as the entire interior of the house, was filled with mellow light, which I knew must be artificial, although I could not discover the source from which it was diffused. Mrs. Leete was an exceptionally fine looking and well preserved woman of about her husband's age, while the daughter, who was in the first blush of womanhood, was the most beautiful girl I had ever seen. Her face was as bewitching as deep blue eyes, delicately tinted complexion, and perfect features could make it, but even had her countenance lacked special charms, the faultless luxuriance of her figure would have given her place as a beauty among the women of the nineteenth century. Feminine softness and delicacy were in this lovely creature deliciously combined with an appearance of health and abounding physical vitality too often lacking in the maidens with whom alone I could compare her. It was a coincidence trifling in comparison with the general strangeness of the situation, but still striking, that her name should be Edith.

The evening that followed was certainly unique in the history of social intercourse, but to suppose that our conversation was peculiarly strained or difficult would be a great mistake. I believe indeed that it is under what may be called unnatural, in the sense of extraordinary, circumstances that people behave most naturally, for the reason, no doubt, that such circumstances banish artificiality. I know at any rate that my intercourse that evening with these representatives of another age and world was marked by an ingenuous sincerity and frankness such as but rarely crown long acquaintance. No doubt the exquisite tact of my entertainers had much to do with this. Of course there was nothing we could talk of but the strange experience by virtue of which I was there, but they talked of it with an interest so naive and direct in its expression as to relieve the subject to a great degree of the element of the weird and the uncanny which might so easily have been overpowering. One would have supposed that they were quite in the habit of entertaining waifs from another century, so perfect was their tact.

For my own part, never do I remember the operations of my mind to have been more alert and acute than that evening, or my intellectual sensibilities more keen. Of course I do not mean that the consciousness of my amazing situation was for a moment out of mind, but its chief effect thus far was to produce a feverish elation, a sort of mental intoxication.[1]

Edith Leete took little part in the conversation, but when several times the magnetism of her beauty drew my glance to her face, I found her eyes fixed on me with an absorbed intensity, almost like fascination. It was evident that I had excited her interest to an extraordinary degree, as was not astonishing, supposing her to be a girl of imagination. Though suppose curiosity was the chief motive of her interest, it could but affect me as it would not have done had she been less beautiful.

Dr. Leete, as well as the ladies, seemed greatly interested in my account of the circumstances under which I had gone to sleep in the underground chamber. All had suggestions to offer to account for my having been forgotten there, and the theory which we finally agreed on offers at least a plausible explanation, although whether it be in its details the true one, nobody, of course, will ever know. The layer of ashes found above the chamber indicated that the house had been burned down. Let it be supposed that the conflagration had taken place the night I fell asleep. It only remains to assume that Sawyer lost his life in the fire or by some accident connected with it, and the rest follows naturally enough. No one but he

---

1 In accounting for this state of mind it must be remembered that, except for the topic of our conversations, there was in my surroundings next to nothing to suggest what had befallen me. Within a block of my home in the old Boston I could have found social circles vastly more foreign to me. The speech of the Bostonians of the twentieth century differs even less from that of their cultured ancestors of the nineteenth than did that of the latter from the language of Washington and Franklin, while the differences between the style of dress and furniture of the two epochs are not more marked than I have known fashion to make in the time of one generation.

and Dr. Pillsbury either knew of the existence of the chamber or that I was in it, and Dr. Pillsbury, who had gone that night to New Orleans, had probably never heard of the fire at all. The conclusion of my friends, and of the public, must have been that I had perished in the flames. An excavation of the ruins, unless thorough, would not have disclosed the recess in the foundation walls connecting with my chamber. To be sure, if the site had been again built upon, at least immediately, such an excavation would have been necessary, but the troublous times and the undesirable character of the locality might well have prevented rebuilding. The size of the trees in the garden now occupying the site indicated, Dr. Leete said, that for more than half a century at least it had been open ground.

5

When in the course of the evening the ladies retired, leaving Dr. Leete and myself alone, he sounded me as to my disposition for sleep, saying that if I felt like it my bed was ready for me; but if I was inclined to wakefulness nothing would please him better than to bear me company. "I am a late bird, myself," he said, "and, without suspicion of flattery, I may say that a companion more interesting than yourself could scarcely be imagined. It is decidedly not often that one has a chance to converse with a man of the nineteenth century."

Now I had been looking forward all the evening with some dread to the time when I should be alone, on retiring for the night. Surrounded by these most friendly strangers, stimulated and supported by their sympathetic interest, I had been able to keep my mental balance. Even then, however, in pauses of the conversation I had had glimpses, vivid as lightning flashes, of the horror of strangeness that was waiting to be faced when I could no longer command diversion. I knew I could not sleep that night, and as for lying awake and thinking, it argues no cowardice, I am sure, to confess that I was afraid of it. When, in reply to my host's question, I frankly told him this, he replied that it would be strange if I did not feel just so, but that I need have no anxiety about sleeping; whenever I wanted to go to bed, he would give me a dose which would insure me a sound night's sleep without fail. Next morning, no doubt, I would awake with the feeling of an old citizen.

"Before I acquire that," I replied, "I must know a little more about the sort of Boston I have come back to. You told me when we were upon the house-top that though a century only had elapsed since I fell asleep, it had been marked by greater changes in the conditions of humanity than many a previous millennium. With the city before me I could well believe that, but I am very curious to know what some of the changes have been. To make a beginning some-where, for the subject is doubtless a large one, what solution, if any, have you found for the labor question? It was the Sphinx's riddle of the nineteenth century, and when I dropped out the Sphinx was threatening to devour society, because the answer was not forthcoming. It is well worth sleeping a hundred years to learn what the right answer was, if, indeed, you have found it yet."

"As no such thing as the labor question is known nowadays," replied Dr. Leete, "and there is no way in which it could arise, I suppose we may claim to have solved it. Society would indeed have fully deserved being devoured if it had failed to answer a riddle so entirely simple. In fact, to speak by the book, it was not necessary for society to solve the riddle at all. It may be said to have solved itself. The solution came as the result of a process of industrial evolution which could not have terminated otherwise. All that society had to do was to recognize and coöperate with that evolution, when its tendency had become unmistakable."

"I can only say," I answered, "that at the time I fell asleep no such evolution had been recognized."

"It was in 1887 that you fell into this sleep, I think you said."

"Yes, May 30th, 1887."

My companion regarded me musingly for some moments. Then he observed, "And you tell me that even then there was no general recognition of the nature of the crisis which society was nearing? Of course, I fully credit your statement. The singular blindness of your contemporaries to the signs of the times is a phenomenon commented on by many of our historians, but few facts of history are more difficult for us to realize, so obvious and unmistakable as we look back seem the indications, which must also have come under your eyes, of the transformation about to come to pass. I should be interested, Mr. West, if you would give me a little more definite idea of the view which you and men of your grade of intellect took of the state and prospects of society in 1887. You must, at least, have realized that the widespread industrial and social troubles, and the underlying dissatisfaction of all classes with the inequalities of society, and the general misery of mankind, were portents of great changes of some sort."

"We did, indeed, fully realize that," I replied. "We felt that society was dragging anchor and in danger of going adrift. Whither it would drift nobody could say, but all feared the rocks."

"Nevertheless," said Dr. Leete, "the set of the current was perfectly perceptible if you had but taken pains to observe it, and it was not toward the rocks, but toward a deeper channel."

"We had a popular proverb," I replied, "that 'hindsight is better than foresight,' the force of which I shall now, no doubt, appreciate more fully than ever. All I can say is, that the prospect was such when I went into that long sleep that I should not have been surprised had I looked down from your housetop today on a heap of charred and moss-grown ruins instead of this glorious city."

Dr. Leete had listened to me with close attention and nodded thoughtfully as I finished speaking. "What you have said," he observed, "will be regarded as a most valuable vindication of Storiot, whose account of your era has been generally thought exaggerated in its picture of the gloom and confusion of men's minds. That a period of transition like that should be full of excitement and agitation was indeed to be looked for; but seeing how plain was the tendency of the forces in operation, it was natural to believe that hope rather than fear would have been the prevailing temper of the popular mind."

"You have not yet told me what was the answer to the riddle which you found," I said. "I am impatient to know by what contradiction of natural sequence the pace and prosperity which you now seem to enjoy could have been the outcome of an era like my own."

"Excuse me," replied my host, "but do you smoke?" It was not till our cigars were lighted and drawing well that he resumed. "Since you are in the humor to talk rather than to sleep, as I certainly am, perhaps I cannot do better than to try to give you enough idea of our modern industrial system to dissipate at least the impression that there is any mystery about the process of its evolution. The Bostonians of your day had the reputation of being great askers of questions, and I am going to show my descent by asking you one to begin with. What should you name as the most prominent feature of the labor troubles of your day?"

"Why, the strikes, of course," I replied.

"Exactly: but what made the strikes so formidable?"

"The great labor organizations."

"And what was the motive of these great organizations?"

"The workmen claimed they had to organize to get their rights from the big corporations," I replied.

"That is just it," said Dr. Leete; "the organization of labor and the strikes were an effect, merely, of the concentration of capital in greater masses than had ever been known before. Before this concentration began, while as yet commerce and industry were conducted by innumerable petty concerns with small capital, instead of a small number of great concerns with vast capital, the individual workman was relatively important and independent in his relations to the employer. Moreover, when a little capital or a new idea was enough to start a man in business for himself, workingmen were constantly becoming employers and there was no hard and fast line between the two classes. Labor unions were needless then, and general strikes out of the question. But when the era of small concerns with small capital was succeeded by that of the great aggregations of capital, all this was changed. The individual laborer, who had been relatively important to the small employer, was reduced to insignificance and powerlessness over against the great corporation, while at the same time the way upward to the grade of employer was closed to him. Self-defense drove him to union with his fellows.

"The records of the period show that the outcry against the concentration of capital was furious. Men believed that it threatened society with a form of tyranny more abhorrent than it had ever endured. They believed that the great corporations were preparing for them the yoke of a baser servitude than had ever been imposed on the race, servitude not to men but to soulless machines incapable of any motive but insatiable greed. Looking back, we cannot wonder at their desperation, for certainly humanity was never confronted with a fate more sordid and hideous than would have been the era of corporate tyranny which they anticipated.

"Meanwhile, without being in the smallest degree checked by the clamor against it, the absorption of business by ever larger monopolies continued. In the United States there was not, after the beginning of the last quarter of the century, any opportunity whatever for individual enterprise in any important field of industry, unless backed by a great capital. During the last decade of the century, such small businesses as still remained were fast-failing survivals of a past epoch, or mere parasites on the great corporations, or else existed in fields too small to attract the great capitalists. Small businesses, as far as they still remained, were reduced to the condition of rats and mice, living in holes and corners, and counting on evading notice for the enjoyment of existence. The railroads had gone on combining till a few great syndicates controlled every rail in the land. In manufactories, every important staple was controlled by a syndicate. These syndicates, pools, trusts, or whatever their name, fixed prices and crushed all competition except when combinations as vast as themselves arose. Then a struggle, resulting in a still greater consolidation, ensued. The great city bazaar crushed its country rivals with branch stores, and in the city itself absorbed its smaller rivals till the business of a whole quarter was concentrated under one roof, with a hundred former proprietors of shops serving as clerks. Having no business of his own to put his money in, the small capitalist, at the same time that he took service under the corporation, found no other investment for his money but its stocks and bonds, thus becoming doubly dependent upon it.

"The fact that the desperate popular opposition to the consolidation of business in a few powerful hands had no effect to check it proves that there must have been a strong economical reason for it. The small capitalists, with their innumerable petty concerns, had in fact yielded the field to the great aggregations of capital, because they belonged to a day of small things and were totally incompetent to the demands of an age of steam and telegraphs and the gigantic scale of its enterprises. To restore the former order of things, even if possible, would have involved returning to the day of stagecoaches. Oppressive and intolerable as was the regime of the great consolidations of capital, even its victims, while they cursed it, were forced to admit the prodigious increase of efficiency which had been imparted to the national industries, the vast economies effected by concentration of management and unity of organization, and to confess that since the new system had taken the place of the old the wealth of the world had increased at a rate before undreamed of. To be sure this vast increase had gone chiefly to make the rich richer, increasing the gap between them and the poor; but the fact remained that, as a means merely of producing wealth, capital had been proved efficient in proportion to its consolidation The restoration of the old system with the subdivision of capital, if it were possible, might indeed bring back a greater equality of conditions, with more individual dignity and freedom, but it would be at the price of general poverty and the arrest of material progress.

"Was there, then, no way of commanding the services of the mighty wealth-producing principle of consolidated capital without bowing down to a plutocracy like that of Carthage? As soon as men began to ask themselves these questions, they found the answer ready for them. The movement toward the conduct of business by larger and larger aggregations of capital, the tendency toward monopolies, which had been so desperately and vainly resisted, was recognized at last, in its true significance, as a process which only needed to complete its logical evolution to open a golden future to humanity.

"Early in the last century the evolution was completed by the final consolidation of the entire capital of the nation. The industry and commerce of the country, ceasing to be conducted by a set of irresponsible corporations and syndicates of private persons at their caprice and for their profit, were instructed to a single syndicate representing the people, to be conducted in the common interest for the common profit. The nation, that is to say, organized as the one great business corporation in which all other corporations were absorbed; it became the one capitalist in the place of all other capitalists, the sole employer, the final monopoly in which all previous and lesser monopolies were swallowed up, a monopoly in the profits and economies of which all citizens shared. The epoch of trusts had ended in The Great Trust.

In a word, the people of the United States concluded to assume the conduct of their own business, just as one hundred odd years before they had assumed the conduct of their own government, organizing now for industrial purposes on precisely the same grounds that they had then organized for political purposes. At last, strangely late in the world's history, the obvious fact was perceived that no business is so essentially the public business as the industry and commerce on which the people's livelihood depends, and that to entrust it to private persons to be managed for private profit is a folly similar in kind, though vastly greater in magnitude, to that of surrendering the functions of political government to kings and nobles to be conducted for their personal glorification."

"Such a stupendous change as you describe," said I, "did not, of course, take place without great bloodshed and terrible convulsions."

"On the contrary," replied Dr. Leete, "there was absolutely no violence. The change had been long foreseen. Public opinion had become fully ripe for it, and the whole mass of the people was behind it. There was no more possibility of opposing it by force than by argument. On the other hand the popular sentiment toward the great corporations and those identified with them ceased to be one of bitterness, as they came to realize their necessity as a link, a transition phase, in the evolution of the true industrial system. The most violent foes of the great private monopolies were now forced to recognize how invaluable and indispensable had been their office in educating the people up to the point of assuming control of their own business. Fifty years before, the consolidation of the industries of the country under national control would have seemed a very daring experiment to the most sanguine. But by a series of object lessons, seen and studied by all men, the great corporations had taught the people an entirely new set of ideas on this subject. They had seen for many years syndicates handling revenues greater than those of states, and directing the labors of hundreds of thousands of men with an efficiency and economy unattainable in smaller operations. It had come to be recognized as an axiom that the larger the business the simpler the principles that can be applied to it; that, as the machine is truer than the hand, so the system, which in a great concern does the work of the master's eye in a small business, turns out more accurate results. Thus it came about that, thanks to the corporations themselves, when it was proposed that the nation should assume their functions, the suggestion implied nothing which seemed impracticable even to the timid. To be sure it was a step beyond any yet taken, a broader generalization, but the very fact that the nation would be the sole corporation in the field would, it was seen, relieve the undertaking of many difficulties with which the partial monopolies had contended."

New Magazines, New Readers,
New Writers

As the nineteenth century moved inexorably toward the twentieth, writers of all kinds turned more and more persistently to the writing of stories about science and technology, and about strange phenomena that suggested how much humanity had yet to learn about the universe. Science was providing new insights into the laws of nature such as Pasteur's work in biology, Hertz's work on the propagation of radio waves, Roentgen's discovery of X rays, and Thomson's discovery of the electron. Technology provided such inventions as motion pictures, the internal-combustion engine, the incandescent lamp, and the phonograph. But each new advance suggested how much remained to be discovered or invented; each new step into the unknown enlarged the view of what was yet to come.

New writers were coming forward. The growing middle class and the newly literate laboring class not only were demanding magazines to satisfy their curiosity about the world and their tastes in fiction, they were producing writers who would please them. The stories they liked dealt with the way people lived and behaved, and with adventures they could never experience—Wild West stories, war stories, spy stories, pirate stories, foreign intrigues, romances, explorations, and stories of invention and the future. Most of the adventure stories had been foreshadowed by the dime novels that began to be published in the 1860s, followed by boys' magazines, and then boys' novels.

New processes for the printing of newspapers and magazines had made them cheap enough to produce and sell in large quantities: the invention of the rotary printing press in 1846, the linotype and pulp paper in 1884, the halftone engraving in 1886, and such methods of distribution as the railroad, the automobile, the truck, and a nationwide distribution system, as well as the introduction of general advertising to help pay the bills.

The first general mass magazine containing fiction was published in England in 1891. It soon was followed by others in Great Britain and in the United States. The great period of the mass magazine would last for more than half a century before it succumbed to the competition of television for the advertising dollar and for the eyes of the reader. In 1896, the mass magazines would be joined by the pulp magazines, consisting entirely of fiction, and they, in turn, would give birth to the category pulps—the detective, the western, the love story, and finally, in 1926, the science-fiction magazine—before all but the science-fiction magazines expired in the fifties and sixties.

In addition to the proliferating markets for fiction, the increasing affluence of society provided opportunities for hopeful authors to make a living at their craft. Among those who made the most of their opportunities was a young, lower-middle-class Englishman named Herbert George Wells, and in the United States, Mark Twain, Jack London, and Ambrose Bierce. All of them wrote, frequently or occasionally, what would later be called science fiction.

Ambrose Bierce (1842–1914?) occasionally produced stories that contributed to the developing literature of science fiction. After serving in the Union army during the Civil War, he became a journalist in San Francisco and a major West Coast literary figure. His stories, collected in such volumes as *Tales of Soldiers and Civilians* (1891), *Can Such Things Be?* (1893), and *In the Midst of Life* (1898), exhibited a fascination with the mysterious and the macabre.

Bierce brought the techniques of realism to the service of the fantastic. He related the strangest of disappearances and the most mysterious of episodes with commonplace people using their everyday language. The tension between the realistic and the fantastic was in great part responsible for the effectiveness of the stories, a lesson in craftsmanship that would be learned by only a few until much later. Many of his stories also had psychological overtones that added to their sense of verisimilitude.

Among Bierce's fantastic stories were "A Horseman in the Sky," "An Occurrence at Owl Creek Bridge," "A Psychological Shipwreck," "Mysterious Disappearances," and his two famous works of science fiction, "Moxon's Master" (1909), one of the earliest robot stories, and "The Damned Thing" (1898).

"The Damned Thing" is typical of a kind of science-fiction story that focuses on a fantastic event that has no explanation except one that science has not yet discovered. The story has its psychological basis in the observed fact that new discoveries about the nature of the universe continue to be made, and the most profound of the discoveries are unpredictable and would have been incomprehensible to an earlier generation. As Arthur C. Clarke has pointed out, "A sufficiently advanced technology is indistinguishable from magic."

"The Damned Thing" was not the first story about an invisible creature. Fitz-James O'Brien's "What Was It? A Mystery" (1859) has already been cited; Guy de Maupassant (1850–1893) wrote a similar story, "The Horla" (1887).

Bierce, who was so fascinated by mysterious disappearances, disappeared mysteriously in Mexico in 1913. The date of his death is only a guess.

The Damned Thing

BY AMBROSE BIERCE

CHAPTER I

ONE DOES NOT ALWAYS EAT WHAT IS ON THE TABLE

By the light of a tallow candle which had been placed on one end of a rough table a man was reading something written in a book. It was an old account book, greatly worn; and the writing was not, apparently, very legible, for the man sometimes held the page close to the flame of the candle to get a stronger light on it. The shadow of the book would then throw into obscurity a half of the room, darkening a number of faces and figures; for besides the reader, eight other men were present. Seven of them sat against the rough log walls, silent, motionless, and the room being small, not very far from the table. By extending an arm any one of them could have touched the eighth man, who lay on the table, face upward, partly covered by a sheet, his arms at his sides. He was dead.

The man with the book was not reading aloud, and no one spoke; all seemed to be waiting for something to occur; the dead man only was without expectation. From the blank darkness outside came in, through the aperture that served for a window, all the ever unfamiliar noises of night in the wilderness—the long nameless note of a distant coyote; the stilly pulsing thrill of tireless insects in trees; strange cries of night birds, so different from those of the birds of day; the drone of great blundering beetles, and all that mysterious chorus of small sounds that seem always to have been but half heard when they have suddenly ceased, as if conscious of an indiscretion. But nothing of all this was noted in that company; its members were not overmuch addicted to idle interest in matters of no practical importance; that was obvious in every line of their rugged faces—obvious even in the dim light of the single candle. They were evidently men of the vicinity— farmers and woodsmen.

The person reading was a trifle different; one would have said of him that he was of the world, worldly, albeit there was that in his attire which attested a certain fellowship with the organisms of his environment. His coat would hardly have passed muster in San Francisco; his foot-gear was not of urban origin, and the hat that lay by him on the floor (he was the only one uncovered) was such that if one had considered it as an article of mere personal adornment he would have missed its meaning. In countenance the man was rather prepossessing, with just a hint of sternness; though that he may have assumed or cultivated, as appropriate to one in authority. For he was a coroner. It was by virtue of his office that he had possession of the book in which he was reading; it had been found among the dead man's effects—in his cabin, where the inquest was now taking place.

When the coroner had finished reading he put the book into his breast pocket. At that moment the door was pushed open and a young man entered. He, clearly, was not of mountain birth and breeding: he was clad as those who dwell in cities. His clothing was dusty, however, as from travel. He had, in fact, been riding hard to attend the inquest.

The coroner nodded; no one else greeted him.

"We have waited for you," said the coroner. "It is necessary to have done with this business to-night."

The young man smiled. "I am sorry to have kept you," he said. "I went away, not to evade your summons, but to post to my newspaper an account of what I suppose I am called back to relate."

The coroner smiled.

"The account that you posted to your newspaper," he said, "differs, probably, from that which you will give here under oath."

"That," replied the other, rather hotly and with a visible flush, "is as you please. I used manifold paper and have a copy of what I sent. It was not written as news, for it is incredible, but as fiction. It may go as a part of my testimony under oath."

"But you say it is incredible."

"That is nothing to you, sir, if I also swear that it is true."

The coroner was silent for a time, his eyes upon the floor. The men about the sides of the cabin talked in whispers, but seldom withdrew their gaze from the face of the corpse. Presently the coroner lifted his eyes and said: "We will resume the inquest."

The men removed their hats. The witness was sworn.

"What is your name?" the coroner asked.

"William Harker."

"Age?"

"Twenty-seven."

"You knew the deceased, Hugh Morgan?"

"Yes."

"You were with him when he died?"

"Near him."

"How did that happen—your presence, I mean?"

"I was visiting him at this place to shoot and fish. A part of my purpose, however, was to study him and his odd, solitary way of life. He seemed a good model for a character in fiction. I sometimes write stories."

"I sometimes read them."

"Thank you."

"Stories in general—not yours."

Some of the jurors laughed. Against a sombre background humour shows high lights. Soldiers in the intervals of battle laugh easily, and a jest in the death chamber conquers by surprise.

"Relate the circumstances of this man's death," said the coroner. "You may use any notes or memoranda that you please."

The witness understood. Pulling a manuscript from his breast pocket he held it near the candle and turning the leaves until he found the passage that he wanted began to read.

CHAPTER II

WHAT MAY HAPPEN IN A FIELD OF WILD OATS

". . . The sun had hardly risen when we left the house. We were looking for quail, each with a shotgun, but we had only one dog. Morgan said that our best ground was beyond a certain ridge that he pointed out, and we crossed it by a trail through the *chaparral*. On the other side was comparatively level ground, thickly covered with wild oats. As we emerged from the *chaparral* Morgan was but a few yards in advance. Suddenly we heard, at a little distance to our right and partly in front, a noise as of some animal thrashing about in the bushes, which we could see were violently agitated.

"'We've started a deer,' I said. 'I wish we had brought a rifle.'

"Morgan, who had stopped and was intently watching the agitated *chaparral*, said nothing, but had cocked both barrels of his gun and was holding it in readiness to aim. I thought him a trifle excited, which surprised me, for he had a reputation for exceptional coolness, even in moments of sudden and imminent peril.

"'Oh, come,' I said. 'You are not going to fill up a deer with quailshot, are you?'

"Still he did not reply; but catching a sight of his face as he turned it slightly toward me I was struck by the intensity of his look. Then I understood that we had serious business in hand, and my first conjecture was that we had jumped a grizzly. I advanced to Morgan's side, cocking my piece as I moved.

"The bushes were now quiet and the sounds had ceased, but Morgan was as attentive to the place as before.

"'What is it? What the devil is it?' I asked

"'That Damned Thing!' he replied, without turning his head. His voice was husky and unnatural. He trembled visibly.

"I was about to speak further, when I observed the wild oats near the place of the disturbance moving in the most inexplicable way. I can hardly describe it. It seemed as if stirred by a streak of wind, which not only bent it, but pressed it down—crushed it so that it did not rise; and this movement was slowly prolonging itself directly toward us.

"Nothing that I had ever seen had affected me so strangely as this unfamiliar and unaccountable phenomenon, yet I am unable to recall any sense of fear. I remember—and tell it here because, singularly enough, I recollected it then—that once in looking carelessly out of an open window I momentarily mistook a small tree close at hand for one of a group of larger trees at a little distance away. It looked the same size as the others, but being more distinctly and sharply defined in mass and detail seemed out of harmony with them. It was a mere falsification of the law of aerial perspective, but it startled, almost terrified me. We so rely upon the orderly operation of familiar natural laws that any seeming suspension of them is noted as a menace to our safety, a warning of unthinkable calamity. So now the apparently causeless movement of the herbage and the slow, undeviating approach of the line of disturbance were distinctly disquieting. My companion appeared actually frightened, and I could hardly credit my senses when I saw him suddenly throw his gun to his shoulder and fire both barrels at the agitated grain! Before the smoke of the discharge had cleared away I heard a loud savage cry—a scream like that of a wild animal—and flinging his gun upon the ground Morgan sprang away and ran swiftly from the spot. At the same instant I was thrown violently to the ground by the impact of something unseen in the smoke—some soft, heavy substance that seemed thrown against me with great force.

"Before I could get upon my feet and recover my gun, which seemed to have been struck from my hands, I heard Morgan crying out as if in mortal agony, and mingling with his cries were such hoarse, savage sounds as one hears from fighting dogs. Inexpressibly terrified, I struggled to my feet and looked in the direction of Morgan's retreat; and may Heaven in mercy spare me from another sight like that! At a distance of less than thirty yards was my friend, down upon one knee, his head thrown back at a frightful angle, hatless, his long hair in disorder and his whole body in violent movement from side to side, backward and forward. His right arm was lifted and seemed to lack the hand—at least, I could see none. The other arm was invisible. At times, as my memory now reports this extraordinary scene, I could discern but a part of his body; it was as if he had been partly blotted out—I cannot otherwise express it—then a shifting of his position would bring it all into view again.

"All this must have occurred within a few seconds, yet in that time Morgan assumed all the postures of a determined wrestler vanquished by superior weight and strength. I saw nothing but him, and him not always distinctly. During the entire incident his shouts and curses were heard, as if through an enveloping uproar of such sounds of rage and fury as I had never heard from the throat of man or brute!

"For a moment only I stood irresolute, then throwing down my gun I ran forward to my friend's assistance. I had a vague belief that he was suffering from a fit, or some form of convulsion. Before I could reach his side he was down and quiet. All sounds had ceased, but with a feeling of such terror as even these awful events had not inspired I now saw again the mysterious movement of the wild oats, prolonging itself from the trampled area about the prostrate man toward the edge of a wood. It was only when it had reached the wood that I was able to withdraw my eyes and look at my companion. He was dead."

CHAPTER III

A MAN THOUGH NAKED MAY BE IN RAGS

The coroner rose from his seat and stood beside the dead man. Lifting an edge of the sheet he pulled it away, exposing the entire body, altogether naked and showing in the candlelight a clay-like yellow. It had, however, broad maculations of bluish black, obviously caused by extravasated blood from contusions. The chest and sides looked as if they had been beaten with a bludgeon. There were dreadful lacerations; the skin was torn in strips and shreds.

The coroner moved round to the end of the table and undid a silk handkerchief which had been passed under the chin and knotted on the top of the head. When the handkerchief was drawn away it exposed what had been the throat. Some of the jurors who had risen to get a better view repented their curiosity and turned away their faces. Witness Harker went to the open window and leaned out across the sill, faint and sick. Dropping the handkerchief upon the dead man's neck the coroner stepped to an angle of the room and from a pile of clothing produced one garment after another, each of which he held up a moment for inspection. All were torn, and stiff with blood. The jurors did not make a closer inspection. They seemed rather uninterested. They had, in truth, seen all this before; the only thing that was new to them being Harker's testimony.

"Gentlemen," the coroner said, "we have no more evidence, I think. Your duty has been already explained to you; if there is nothing you wish to ask you may go outside and consider your verdict."

The foreman rose—a tall, bearded man of sixty, coarsely clad.

"I shall like to ask one question, Mr. Coroner," he said. "What asylum did this yer last witness escape from?"

"Mr. Harker," said the coroner gravely and tranquilly, "from what asylum did you last escape?"

Harker flushed crimson again, but said nothing, and the seven jurors rose and solemnly filed out of the cabin.

"If you have done insulting me, sir," said Harker, as soon as he and the officer were left alone with the dead man, "I suppose I am at liberty to go?"

"Yes."

Harker started to leave, but paused, with his hand on the door latch. The habit of his profession was strong in him—stronger than his sense of personal dignity. He turned about and said:

"The book that you have there—I recognize it as Morgan's diary. You seemed greatly interested in it; you read in it while I was testifying. May I see it? The public would like—"

"The book will cut no figure in this matter," replied the official, slipping it into his coat pocket; "all the entries in it were made before the writer's death."

As Harker passed out of the house the jury re-entered and stood about the table, on which the now covered corpse showed under the sheet with sharp definition. The foreman seated himself near the candle, produced from his breast pocket a pencil and scrap of paper and wrote rather laboriously the following verdict, which with various degrees of effort all signed:

"We, the jury, do find that the remains come to their death at the hands of a mountain lion, but some of us thinks, all the same, they had fits."

CHAPTER IV

AN EXPLANATION FROM THE TOMB

In the diary of the late Hugh Morgan are certain interesting entries having, possibly, a scientific value as suggestions. At the inquest upon his body the book was not put in evidence; possibly the coroner thought it not worth while to confuse the jury. The date of the first of the entries mentioned cannot be ascertained; the upper part of the leaf is torn away; the part of the entry remaining follows:

". . . would run in a half-circle, keeping his head turned always toward the centre, and again he would stand still, barking furiously. At last he ran away into the brush as fast as he could go. I thought at first that he had gone mad, but on returning to the house found no other alteration in his manner than what was obviously due to fear of punishment.

"Can a dog see with his nose? Do odours impress some cerebral centre with images of the thing that emitted them? . . .

"*Sept. 2.*—Looking at the stars last night as they rose above the crest of the ridge east of the house, I observed them successively disappear—from left to right. Each was eclipsed but an instant, and only a few at the same time, but along the entire length of the ridge all that were within a degree or two of the crest were blotted out. It was as if something had passed along between me and them; but I could not see it, and the stars were not thick enough to define its outline. Ugh! don't like this." . . .

Several weeks' entries are missing, three leaves being torn from the book.

"*Sept. 27.*—It has been about here again—I find evidences of its presence every day. I watched again all last night in the same cover, gun in hand, double-charged with buckshot. In the morning the fresh footprints were there, as before. Yet I would have sworn that I did not sleep—indeed, I hardly sleep at all. It is terrible, insupportable! If these amazing experiences are real I shall go mad; if they are fanciful I am mad already.

"*Oct. 3.*—I shall not go—it shall not drive me away. No, this is my house, *my* land. God hates a coward. . . .

"*Oct. 5.*—I can stand it no longer; I have invited Harker to pass a few weeks with me—he has a level head. I can judge from his manner if he thinks me mad.

"*Oct. 7.*—I have the solution of the mystery; it came to me last night—suddenly, as by revelation. How simple—how terribly simple!

"There are sounds that we cannot hear. At either end of the scale are notes that stir no chord of that imperfect instrument, the human ear. They are too high or too grave. I have observed a flock of blackbirds occupying an entire tree-top—the tops of several trees and all in full song. Suddenly— in a moment—at absolutely the same instant—all spring into the air and fly away. How? They could not all see one another—whole tree-tops intervened. At no point could a leader have been visible to all. There must have been a signal of warning or command, high and shrill above the din, but by me unheard. I have observed, too, the same simultaneous flight when all were silent, among not only blackbirds, but other birds—quail, for example, widely separated by bushes—even on opposite sides of a hill.

"It is known to seamen that a school of whales basking or sporting on the surface of the ocean, miles apart, with the convexity of the earth between, will sometimes dive at the same instant—all gone out of sight in a moment. The signal has been sounded—too grave for the ear of the sailor at the masthead and his comrades on the deck—who nevertheless feel its vibrations in the ship as the stones of a cathedral are stirred by the bass of the organ.

"As with sounds, so with colours. At each end of the solar spectrum the chemist can detect the presence of what are known as 'actinic' rays. They represent colours—integral colours in the composition of light—which we are unable to discern. The human eye is an imperfect instrument; its range is but a few octaves of the real 'chromatic scale.' I am not mad; there are colours that we cannot see.

"And, God help me! the Damned Thing is of such a colour!"

A Flying Start

As the twentieth century got into its first decade, the impact of technology on people's lives was becoming increasingly clear, and perceptive authors were recognizing not only the change-producing power of technology but also the fact that the process of change had just begun. But even the most perceptive sometimes overlooked the obvious.

The internal-combustion automobile had been invented by Karl Benz in 1885; it was improved by Gottlieb Daimler and manufactured in the United States in the 1890s by a variety of men, including Henry Ford. But few authors, if any, foresaw the surprising ways in which the automobile would reshape the Western world and the lives of its citizens, particularly in the United States.

The airplane was a different matter. The realization of humanity's long dream to fly like the birds was so dramatic that at least a few farsighted authors were able to perceive its impact. Oddly, they were more impressed by Ferdinand von Zeppelin's dirigible than the Wright brothers' airplane, and for seemingly good reasons.

Jules Verne, on the other hand, chose the airplane. In *Robur the Conqueror* (1886), Robur says, "The future of aviation belongs to the aeronef [airplane] and not the aerostat [airship]. Verne, however, did not foresee the improvements that would be made on the crude experiments with powered airships that had been in progress since 1784 and resulted in a manned flight in France in 1852. Robur's aeronef, incidentally, was lifted, like a helicopter, by seventy-four screws mounted on thirty-seven uprights and propelled by horizontal screws at front and rear driven by electricity.

What happened in the real world was that the dirigible not only predated the airplane by three years but it was more immediately successful. The first rigid zeppelin was flown in 1900; it was used for passenger service in Germany between 1910 and 1914, and widely employed for military purposes in the early days of World War I. The Wright brothers' flight in 1903, on the other hand, was ignored by the press, mostly because of widespread skepticism about the practicability of heavier-than-aircraft. A contract for one airplane was not signed by the U.S. government until 1908. As a consequence, the full development of the airplane was delayed until the latter part of World War I, and the airplane did not come into its own as a passenger carrier until the thirties. The dramatic end of the German zeppelin *Hindenburg* at Lakehurst, New Jersey, in 1937 also ended the dirigible as an aircraft. Ironically, the dirigible is superior to the airplane for many purposes, including the hauling of freight, and may yet regain a place in some future overall transportation system.

It is not surprising, then, that H. G. Wells, writing in 1908, should pick the dirigible as the aircraft of the future in his *The War in the Air;* what was surprising was his prophetic vision of the impact of aircraft on warfare. But Wells was not the first author to note the influence of aircraft on human existence.

Rudyard Kipling (1865–1936), born in Bombay, India, attended school in England, returned to India as a journalist as some of his books began to be printed, and finally came back to England in 1889, to win fame as a poet and fiction writer, and eventually England's first Nobel Prize for literature. His first books were *Departmental Ditties* (1886) and *Plain Tales from the Hills* (1888), which he would follow with *Barrack Room Ballads* (1890, 1892), and a series of novels and short stories that included the two *Jungle Books* (1894, 1895), *Captains Courageous* (1897), *Stalkey and Co.* (1899), *Puck of Pook's Hill* (1906), and *Kim* (1901).

Among his many short stories were several that might be classified as fantasies with an element of scientific explanation, such as "Wireless," "The Mark of the Beast," and "The Finest Story in the World." But two stories were clearly science fiction and clearly foreshadowed the science fiction of the late thirties and forties, "With the Night Mail" (1905) and "Easy as A.B.C." (1912).

Kipling saw in the dirigible the possibility of major changes in people's lives, involving the greater interconnectedness of the world once time and space were foreshortened, and the necessity to control this new method of transportation. He envisioned an Aerial Board of Control (A.B.C.) whose influence would grow to encompass almost every aspect of existence. "Easy as A.B.C." is a kind of sequel to "With the Night Mail," in which the A.B.C. goes to extreme lengths, including painful lights and sounds (which might be considered foreshadowings of lasers and supersonics), to bring rebellious districts back under control and keep communications open.

In these two stories Kipling used many of the science-fiction techniques that would slowly be rediscovered later, mostly after John W. Campbell became editor of *Astounding Stories* in 1937. They included, as Campbell put it, writing stories "that would be published in a magazine of the twenty-fifth century," that is, the use of new words, including slang, as would naturally happen in the future; the omission of explanations that would not be natural to the storyteller of that future time; and the invention of an entire new future world that would enter the story only as corroborative detail.

What Kipling did in these two stories would not be done as well again until Robert A. Heinlein began writing science fiction in 1939.

With the Night Mail

BY RUDYARD KIPLING

A STORY OF 2000 A.D.

At nine o'clock of a gusty winter night I stood on the lower stages of the G.P.O. outward mail towers. My purpose was a run to Quebec in "Postal Packet 162 or such other as may be appointed"; and the Postmaster-General himself countersigned the order. This talisman opened all doors, even those on the despatching-caisson at the foot of the tower, where they were delivering the sorted Continental mail. The bags lay packed close as herrings in the long grey underbodies which our G.P.O. still calls "coaches." Five such coaches were filled as I watched, and were shot up the guides to be locked on to their waiting packets three hundred feet nearer the stars.

From the despatching-caisson I was conducted by a courteous and wonderfully learned official — Mr. L. L. Geary, Second Despatcher of the Western Route — to the Captains' Room (this wakes an echo of old romance), where the mail captains come on for their turn of duty. He introduces me to the captain of "162" — Captain Purnall, and his relief, Captain Hodgson. The one is small and dark; the other large and red; but each has the brooding sheathed glance characteristic of eagles and aeronauts. You can see it in the pictures of our racing professionals, from L. V. Rautsch to little Ada Warrleigh — that fathomless abstraction of eyes habitually turned through naked space.

On the notice-board in the Captains' Room, the pulsing arrows of some twenty indicators register, degree by geographical degree, the progress of as many homeward-bound packets. The word "Cape" rises across the face of a dial; a gong strikes: the South African mid-weekly mail is in at the Highgate Receiving Towers. That is all. It reminds one comically of the traitorous little bell which in pigeon-fanciers' lofts notifies the return of a homer.

"Time for us to be on the move," says Captain Purnall, and we are shot up by the passenger-lift to the top of the despatch-towers. "Our coach will lock on when it is filled and the clerks are aboard."

"No. 162" waits for us in Slip E of the topmost stage. The great curve of her back shines frostily under the lights, and some minute alteration of trim makes her rock a little in her holding-down slips.

Captain Purnall frowns and dives inside. Hissing softly, "162" comes to rest as level as a rule. From her North Atlantic Winter nose-cap (worn bright as diamond with boring through uncounted leagues of hail, snow, and ice) to the inset of her three built-out propeller-shafts is some two hundred and forty feet. Her extreme diameter, carried well forward, is thirty-seven. Contrast this with the nine hundred by ninety-five of any crack liner, and you will realize the power that must drive a hull through all weathers at more than the emergency speed of the *Cyclonic!*

The eye detects no joint in her skin plating save the sweeping hair-crack of the bow-rudder—Magniac's rudder that assured us the dominion of the unstable air and left its inventor penniless and half-blind. It is calculated to Castelli's "gullwing" curve. Raise a few feet of that all but invisible plate three-eighths of an inch and she will yaw five miles to port or starboard ere she is under control again. Give her full helm and she returns on her track like a whip-lash. Cant the whole forward—a touch on the wheel will suffice—and she sweeps at your good direction up or down. Open the complete circle and she presents to the air a mushroom-head that will bring her up all standing within a half mile.

"Yes," says Captain Hodgson, answering my thought, "Castelli thought he'd discovered the secret of controlling aeroplanes when he'd only found out how to steer dirigible balloons. Magniac invented his rudder to help war-boats ram each other; and war went out of fashion and Magniac he went out of his mind because he said he couldn't serve his country any more. I wonder if any of us ever know what we're really doing."

"If you want to see the coach locked you'd better go aboard. It's due now," says Mr. Geary. I enter through the door amidships. There is nothing here for display. The inner skin of the gas-tanks comes down to within a foot or two of my head and turns over just short of the turn of the bilges. Liners and yachts disguise their tanks with decoration, but the G. P. O. serves them raw under a lick of grey official paint. The inner skin shuts off fifty feet of the bow and as much of the stern, but the bow-bulkhead is recessed for the lift-shunting apparatus as the stern is pierced for the shaft-tunnels. The engine-room lies almost amidships. Forward of it, extending to the turn of the bow tanks, is an aperture—a bottomless hatch at present—into which our coach will be locked. One looks down over the coamings three hundred feet to the despatching-caisson whence voices boom upward. The light below is obscured to a sound of thunder, as our coach rises on its guides. It enlarges rapidly from a postage-stamp to a playing-card; to a punt and last a pontoon. The two clerks, its crew, do not even look up as it comes into place. The Quebec letters fly under their fingers and leap into the docketed racks, while both captains and Mr. Geary satisfy themselves that the coach is locked home. A clerk passes the way-bill over the hatch-coaming. Captain Purnall thumbmarks and passes it to Mr. Geary. Receipt has been given and taken. "Pleasant run," says Mr. Geary, and disappears through the door which a foot-high pneumatic compressor locks after him

"A-ah!" sighs the compressor released. Our holding-down clips part with a tang. We are clear.

Captain Hodgson opens the great colloid underbody porthole through which I watch over-lighted London slide eastward as the gale gets hold of us. The first of the low winter clouds cuts off the well-known view and darkens Middlesex. On the south edge of it I can see a postal packet's light ploughing through the white fleece. For an instant she gleams like a star ere she drops toward the Highgate Receiving Towers. "The Bombay Mail," says Captain Hodgson, and looks at his watch. "She's forty minutes late."

"What's our level?" I ask.

"Four thousand. Aren't you coming up on the bridge?"

The bridge (let us ever praise the G. P. O. as a repository of ancientest tradition!) is represented by a view of Captain Hodgson's legs where he stands on the Control Platform that runs thwart-ships overhead. The bow colloid is unshuttered and Captain Purnall, one hand on the wheel, is feeling for a fair slant. The dial shows 4300 feet.

"It's steep to-night," he mutters, as tier on tier of cloud drops under. "We generally pick up an easterly draught below three thousand at this time o' the year. I hate slathering through fluff."

"So does Van Cutsem. Look at him huntin' for a slant!" says Captain Hodgson. A fog-light breaks cloud a hundred fathoms below. The Antwerp Night Mail makes her signal and rises between two racing clouds far to port, her flanks blood-red in the glare of Sheerness Double Light. The gale will have us over the North Sea in half-an-hour, but Captain Purnall lets her go composedly—nosing to every point of the compass as she rises.

"Five thousand—six, six thousand eight hundred"—the dip-dial reads ere we find the easterly drift, heralded by a flurry of snow at the thousand fathom level. Captain Purnall rings up the engines and keys down the governor on the switch before him. There is no sense in urging machinery when Æolus himself gives you good knots for nothing. We are away in earnest now—our nose notched home on our chosen star. At this level the lower clouds are laid out, all neatly combed by the dry fingers of the East. Below that again is the strong westerly blow through which we rose. Overhead, a film of southerly drifting mist draws a theatrical gauze across the firmament. The moonlight turns the lower strata to silver without a stain except where our shadow underruns us. Bristol and Cardiff Double Lights (those statelily inclined beams over Severnmouth) are dead ahead of us; for we keep the Southern Winter Route. Coventry Central, the pivot of the English system, stabs upward once in ten seconds its spear of diamond light to the north; and a point or two off our starboard bow. The Leek, the great cloud-breaker of Saint David's Head, swings its unmistakable green beam twenty-five degrees each way. There must be half a mile of fluff over it in this weather, but it does not affect The Leek.

"Our planet's overlighted if anything," says Captain Purnall at the wheel, as Cardiff-Bristol slides under. "I remember the old days of common white verticals that 'ud show two or three hundred feet up in a mist, if you knew where to look for 'em. In really fluffy weather they might as well have been under your hat. One could get lost coming home then, an' have some fun. Now, it's like driving down Piccadilly."

He points to the pillars of light where the cloud-breakers bore through the cloud-floor. We see nothing of England's outlines: only a white pavement pierced in all directions by these manholes of variously coloured fire—Holy Island's white and red—St. Bee's interrupted white, and so on as far as the eye can reach. Blessed be Sargent, Ahrens, and the Dubois brothers, who invented the cloud-breakers of the world whereby we travel in security!

"Are you going to lift from The Shamrock?" asks Captain Hodgson, Cork Light (green, fixed) enlarges as we rush to it. Captain Purnall nods. There is heavy traffic hereabouts—the cloud-bank beneath us is streaked with running fissures of flame where the Atlantic boats are hurrying Londonward just clear of the fluff. Mail-packets are supposed, under the Conference rules, to have the five-thousand-foot lanes to themselves, but the foreigner in a hurry is apt to take liberties with English air. "No. 162" lifts to a long-drawn wail of the breeze in the fore-flange of the rudder and we make Valencia (white, green, white) at a safe 7000 feet, dipping our beam to an incoming Washington packet.

There is no cloud on the Atlantic, and faint streaks of cream round Dingle Bay show where the driven seas hammer the coast. A big S. A. T. A. liner *(Société Anonyme des Transports Aériens)* is diving and lifting half a mile below us in search of some break in the solid west wind. Lower still lies a disabled Dane: she is telling the liner all about it in International. Our

General Communication dial has caught her talk and begins to eavesdrop. Captain Hodgson makes a motion to shut it off but checks himself. "Perhaps you'd like to listen," he says.

"*Argol* of St. Thomas," the Dane whimpers. "Report owners three starboard shaft collar-bearings fused. Can make Flores as we are, but impossible further. Shall we buy spares at Fayal?"

The liner acknowledges and recommends inverting the bearings. The *Argol* answers that she has already done so without effect, and begins to relieve her mind about cheap German enamels for collar-bearings. The Frenchman assents cordially, cries "*Courage, mon ami,*" and switches off.

Their lights sink under the curve of the ocean.

"That's one of Lundt & Bleamers' boats," says Captain Hodgson. "Serves 'em right for putting German-compos in their thrust-blocks. *She* won't be in Fayal to-night! By the way, wouldn't you like to look round the engine-room?"

I have been waiting eagerly for this invitation and I follow Captain Hodgson from the control-platform, stooping low to avoid the bulge of the tanks. We know that Fleury's gas can lift anything, as the world-famous trials of '89 showed, but its almost indefinite powers of expansion necessitate vast tank room. Even in this thin air the lift-shunts are busy taking out one-third of its normal lift, and still "162" must be checked by an occasional downdraw of the rudder or our flight would become a climb to the stars. Captain Purnall prefers an overlifted to an underlifted ship; but no two captains trim ship alike. "When I take the bridge," says Captain Hodgson, "you'll see me shunt forty per cent of the lift out of the gas and run her on the upper rudder. With a swoop upward instead of a swoop downward, as you say. Either way will do. It's only habit. Watch our dip-dial! Tim fetches her down once every thirty knots as regularly as breathing."

So is it shown on the dip-dial. For five or six minutes the arrow creeps from 6700 or 7300. There is the faint "szgee" of the rudder, and back slides the arrow to 6000 on a falling slant of ten or fifteen knots.

"In heavy weather you jockey her with the screws as well," says Captain Hodgson, and, unclipping the jointed bar which divides the engine-room from the bare deck, he leads me on to the floor.

Here we find Fleury's Paradox of the Bulk-headed Vacuum—which we accept now without thought—literally in full blast. The three engines are H. T. & T. assisted-vaquo Fleury turbines running from 3000 to the Limit— that is to say, up to the point when the blades make the air "bell"—cut out a vacuum for themselves precisely as overdriven marine propellers used to do. "162's" Limit is low on account of the small size of her nine screws, which, though handier than the old colloid Thelussons, "bell" sooner. The midships engine, generally used as a reinforce is not running; so the port and starboard turbine vacuum-chambers draw direct into the return-mains.

The turbines whistle reflectively. From the low-arched expansion-tanks on either side of the valves descend pillar-wise to the turbine-chests, and thence the obedient gas whirls through the spirals of blades with a force that would whip the teeth out of a powersaw. Behind, its own pressure held in leash or spurred on by the lift-shunts; before it, is the vacuum where Fleury's Ray dances in violet-green bands and whirled turbillons of flame. The jointed U-tubes of the vacuum-chamber are pressure-tempered colloid (no glass would endure the strain for an instant) and a junior engineer with tinted spectacles watches the Ray intently. It is the very heart of the machine—a mystery to this day. Even Fleury who begat it and, unlike Magniac, died a multi-millionaire, could not explain how the restless little imp shuddering in the U-tube can, in the fractional fraction of a second, strike the furious blast of gas into a chill grayish-green liquid that drains (you can hear it trickle) from the far end of the vacuum through the eduction-pipes and the mains back to the bilges. Here it returns to its gaseous, one had almost written sagacious, state and climbs to work afresh. Bilge-tank, upper tank, dorsal-tank, expansion-chamber, vacuum, main-return (as a liquid), and bilge-tank once more is the ordained cycle. Fleury's Ray sees to that; and the engineer with the tinted spectacles sees to Fleury's Ray. If a speck of oil, if even the natural grease of the human finger touch the hooded terminals, Fleury's Ray will wink and disappear and must be laboriously built up again. This means half a day's work for all hands and an expense of one hundred and seventy-odd pounds to the G. P. O. for radium-salts and such trifles.

"Now look at our thrust-collars. You won't find much German compo there. Full-jewelled, you see," says Captain Hodgson as the engineer shunts open the top of a cap. Our shaft-bearings are C.M.C. (Commercial Minerals Company) stones, ground with as much care as the lens of a telescope. They cost £37 apiece. So far we have not arrived at their term of life. These bearings came from "No. 97," which took them over from the old *Dominion of Light* which had them out of the wreck of the *Perseus* aeroplane in the years when men still flew wooden kites over oil engines!

They are a shining reproof to all low-grade German "ruby" enamels, so-called "boort" facings, and the dangerous and unsatisfactory alumina compounds which please dividend-hunting owners and turn skippers crazy.

The rudder-gear and the gas lift-shunt, seated side by side under the engine-room dials, are the only machines in visible motion. The former sighs from time to time as the oil plunger rises and falls half an inch. The latter, cased and guarded like the U-tube aft, exhibits another Fleury Ray, but inverted and more green than violet. Its function is to shunt the lift out of the gas, and this it will do without watching. That is all! A tiny pump-rod wheezing and whining to itself beside a sputtering green lamp. A hundred and fifty feet aft down the flat-topped tunnel of the tanks a violet light, restless and irresolute. Between the two, three white-painted turbine-trunks, like eel-baskets laid on their side, accentuate the empty perspectives. You can hear the trickle of the liquefied gas flowing from the vacuum into the bilge-tanks and the soft *gluck-glock* of gas-locks closing as Captain Purnall brings "162" down by the head. The hum of the turbines and the boom of the air on our skin are no more than a cotton-wool wrapping to the universal stillness. And we are running an eighteen-second mile.

I peer from the fore end of the engine-room over the hatch-coamings into the coach. The mail-clerks are sorting the Winnipeg, Calgary, and Medicine Hat bags; but there is a pack of cards ready on the table.

Suddenly a bell thrills; the engineers run to the turbine-valves and stand by; but the spectacled slave of the Ray in the U-tube never lifts his head. He must watch where he is. We are hard-braked and going astern; there is language from the Control Platform.

"Tim's sparkling badly about something," says the unruffled Captain Hodgson. "Let's look."

Captain Purnall is not the suave man we left half an hour since, but the embodied authority of the G. P. O. Ahead of us floats an ancient, aluminum-patched, twin-screw tramp of the dingiest, with no more right to the 5000 foot lane than has a horse-cart to a modern road. She carries an obsolete "barbette" conning-tower—a six-foot affair with railed platform forward—and our warning beam plays on the top of it as a policeman's lantern flashes on the area sneak. Like a sneak-thief, too, emerges a shock-headed navigator in his shirt-sleeves. Captain Purnall wrenches open the colloid to talk with him man to man. There are times when Science does not satisfy.

"What under the stars are you doing here, you sky-scraping chimney-sweep?" he shouts as we two drift side by side. "Do you know this is a Mail-lane? You call yourself a sailor, sir? You ain't fit to peddle toy balloons to an Esquimaux. Your name and number! Report and get down, and be—!"

"I've been blown up once," the shock-headed man cries, hoarsely, as a dog barking. "I don't care two flips of a contact for anything *you* can do, Postey."

"Don't you, sir? But I'll make you care. I'll have you towed stern first to Disko and broke up. You can't recover insurance if you're broke for obstruction. Do you understand *that?*"

Then the stranger bellows: "Look at my propellers! There's been a wulli-wa down below that has knocked us into umbrella-frames! We've been blown up about forty thousand feet! We're all one conjuror's watch inside! My mate's arm's broke; my engineer's head's cut open; my Ray went out when the engines smashed; and . . . and . . . for pity's sake give me my height, Captain! We doubt we're dropping."

"Six thousand eight hundred. Can you hold it?" Captain Purnall overlooks all insults, and leans half out of the colloid, staring and snuffling. The stranger leaks pungently.

"We ought to blow into St. Johns with luck. We're trying to plug the fore-tank now, but she's simply whistling it away," her captain wails.

"She's sinking like a log," says Captain Purnall in an undertone. "Call up the Banks Mark Boat, George." Our dip-dial shows that we, keeping abreast the tramp, have dropped five hundred feet the last few minutes.

Captain Purnall presses a switch and our signal beam begins to swing through the night, twizzling spokes of light across infinity.

"That'll fetch something," he says, while Captain Hodgson watches the General Communicator. He has called up the North Banks Mark Boat, a few hundred miles west, and is reporting the case.

"I'll stand by you," Captain Purnall roars to the lone figure on the conning-tower.

"Is it as bad as that?" comes the answer. "She isn't insured. She's mine."

"Might have guessed as much," mutters Hodgson. "Owner's risk is the worst of all!"

"Can't I fetch St. John's—not even with this breeze?" the voice quavers.

"Stand by to abandon ship. Haven't you *any* lift in you, fore or aft?"

"Nothing but the midship tanks, and they're none too tight. You see, my Ray gave out and—" He coughs in the reek of the escaping gas.

"You poor devil!" This does not reach our friend. "What does the Mark Boat say, George!"

"Wants to know if there's any danger to traffic. Says she's in a bit of weather herself, and can't quit station. I've turned in a General Call, so even if they don't see our beam someone's bound to help—or else we must. Shall I clear our slings? Hold on! Here we are! A Planet liner, too! She'll be up in a tick!"

"Tell her to have her slings ready," cries his brother captain. "There won't be much time to spare . . . Tie up your mate," he roars to the tramp.

"My mate's all right. It's my engineer. He's gone crazy"

"Shunt the lift out of him with a spanner. Hurry!"

"But I can make St. John's if you'll stand by."

"You'll make the deep, wet Atlantic in twenty minutes. You're less than fifty-eight hundred now. Get your papers."

A Planet liner, east bound, heaves up in a superb spiral and takes the air of us humming. Her underbody colloid is open and her transporter-slings hang down like tentacles. We shut off our beam as she adjusts herself—steering to a hair—over the tramp's conning-tower. The mate comes up, his arm strapped to his side, and stumbles into the cradle. A man with a ghastly scarlet head follows, shouting that he must go back and build up his Ray. The mate assures him that he will find a nice new Ray all ready in the liner's engine-room. The bandaged head goes up wagging excitedly. A youth and a woman follow. The liner cheers hollowly above us, and we see the passengers' faces at the saloon colloid.

"That's a pretty girl. What's the fool waiting for now?" says Captain Purnall.

The skipper comes up, still appealing to us to stand by and see him fetch St. John's. He dives below and returns—at which we little human beings in the void cheer louder than ever—with the ship's kitten. Up fly the liner's hissing slings; her underbody crashes home and she hurtles away again. The dial shows less than 3000 feet.

The Mark Boat signals we must attend to the derelict, now whistling her death-song, as she falls beneath us in long sick zigzags.

"Keep our beam on her and send out a General Warning," says Captain Purnall, following her down.

There is no need. Not a liner in air but knows the meaning of that vertical beam and gives us and our quarry a wide berth.

"But she'll drown in the water, won't she?" I ask.

"Not always," is his answer. "I've known a derelict upend and sift her engines out of herself and flicker round the Lower Lanes for three weeks on her forward tanks only. We'll run no risks. Pith her, George, and look sharp. There's weather ahead."

Captain Hodgson opens the underbody colloid, swings the heavy pithing-iron out of its rack which in liners is generally cased as a smoking-room settee, and at two hundred feet releases the catch. We hear the whir of the crescent-shaped arms opening as they descend. The derelict's forehead is punched in, starred across, and rent diagonally. She falls stern first, our beam upon her; slides like a lost soul down that pitiless ladder of light, and the Atlantic takes her.

"A filthy business," says Hodgson. "I wonder what it must have been like in the old days?"

The thought had crossed my mind, too. What if that wavering carcass had been filled with the men of the old days, each one of them taught *(that is the horror of it!)* that after death he would very possibly go for ever to unspeakable torment?

And scarcely a generation ago, we (one knows now that we are only our fathers re-enlarged upon the earth), we, I say, ripped and rammed and pithed to admiration.

Here Tim, from the Control Platform, shouts that we are to get into our inflators and to bring him his at once.

We hurry into the heavy rubber suits—the engineers are already dressed and inflate at the air-pump taps. G. P. O. inflators are thrice as thick as a racing man's "flickers," and chafe abominably under the armpits. George takes the wheel until Tim has blown himself up to the extreme of rotundity. If you kicked him off the c.p. to the deck he would bounce back. But it is "162" that will do the kicking.

"The Mark Boat's mad—stark ravin' crazy," he snorts, returning to command. "She says there's a bad blow-out ahead and wants me to pull over to Greenland. I'll see her pithed first! We wasted half an hour fussing over that dead duck down under, and now I'm expected to go rubbin' my back all around the Pole. What does she think a Postal packet's made of? Gummed silk? Tell her we're coming on straight, George."

George buckles him into the Frame and switches on the Direct Control. Now under Tim's left toe lies the port-engine Accelerator; under his left heel the Reverse, and so with the other foot. The lift-shunt stops stand out on the rim of the steering-wheel where the fingers of his left hand can play on them. At his right hand is the midships engine lever ready to be thrown into gear at a moment's notice. He leans forward in his belt, eyes glued to the colloid, and one ear cocked toward the General Communicator. Henceforth he is the strength and direction of "162," through whatever may befall.

The Banks Mark Boat is reeling out pages of A. B. C. Directions to the traffic at large. We are to secure all "loose objects"; hood up our Fleury Rays; and "on no account to attempt to clear snow from our conning-towers till the weather abates." Under-powered craft, we are told, can ascend to the limit of their lift, mail-packets to look out for them accordingly; the lower lanes westward are pitting very badly, "with frequent blow-outs, vortices, laterals, etc."

Still the clear dark holds up unblemished. The only warning is the electric skin-tension (I feel as though I were a lace-maker's pillow) and an irritability which the gibbering of the General Communicator increases almost to hysteria.

We have made eight thousand feet since we pithed the tramp and our turbines are giving us an honest two hundred and ten knots.

Very far to the west an elongated blur of red, low down, shows us the North Banks Mark Boat. There are specks of fire round her rising and falling—bewildered planets about an unstable sun—helpless shipping hanging on to her light for company's sake. No wonder she could not quit station.

She warns us to look out for the back-wash of the bad vortex in which (her beam shows it) she is even now reeling.

The pits of gloom about us begin to fill with very faintly luminous films—wreathing and uneasy shapes. One forms itself into a globe of pale flame that waits shivering with eagerness till we sweep by. It leaps monstrously across the blackness, alights on the precise tip of our nose, pirouettes there an instant, and swings off. Our roaring bow sinks as though that light were lead—sinks and recovers to lurch and stumble again beneath the next blow-out. Tim's fingers on the lift-shunt strike chords of numbers—1:4:7:—2:4:6—7:5:3, and so on; for he is running by his tanks only, lifting or lowering her against the uneasy air. All three engines are at work, for the sooner we have skated over this thin ice the better. Higher we dare not go. The whole upper vault is charged with pale krypton vapours, which our skin friction may excite to unholy manifestations. Between the upper and lower levels—5000 and 7000, hints the Mark Boat— we may perhaps bolt through if . . . Our bow clothes itself in blue flame and falls like a sword. No human skill can keep pace with the changing tensions. A vortex has us by the beak and we dive down a two-thousand-foot slant at an angle (the dip-dial and my bouncing body record it) of thirty-five. Our turbines scream shrilly; the propellers cannot bite on the thin air; Tim shunts the lift out of five tanks at once and by sheer weight drives her bullet-wise through the maelstrom till she cushions with a jar on an up-gust, three thousand feet below.

"*Now* we've done it," says George in my ear. "Our skin-friction, that last slide, has played Old Harry with the tensions! Look out for laterals, Tim; she'll want some holding."

"I've got her," is the answer. "Come *up,* old woman.'

She comes up nobly, but the laterals buffet her left and right like the pinions of angry angels. She is jolted off her course four ways at once, and cuffed into place again, only to be swung aside and dropped into a new chaos. We are never without a corposant grinning on our bows or rolling head over heels from nose to midships, and to the crackle of electricity around and within us is added once or twice the rattle of hail—hail that will never fall on any sea. Slow we must or we may break our back, pitch-poling.

"Air's a perfectly elastic fluid," roars George above the tumult. "About as elastic as a head sea off the Fastnet, ain't it?"

He is less than just to the good element. If one intrudes on the Heavens when they are balancing their volt-accounts; if one disturbs the High Gods' market-rates by hurling steel hulls at ninety knots across tremblingly adjusted electric tensions, one must not complain of any rudeness in the reception. Tim met it with an unmoved countenance, one corner of his under lip caught up on a tooth, his eyes fleeting into the blackness twenty miles ahead, and the fierce sparks flying from his knuckles at every turn of the hand. Now and again he shook his head to clear the sweat trickling from his eyebrows, and it was then that George, watching his chance, would slide down the life-rail and swab his face quickly with a big red handkerchief. I never imagined that a human being could so continuously labour and so collectedly think as did Tim through that Hell's half-hour when the flurry was at its worst. We were dragged hither and yon by warm or frozen suctions, belched up on the tops of wulli-was, spun down by vortices and clubbed aside by laterals under a dizzying rush of stars in the company of a drunken moon. I heard the rushing click of the midship-engine-lever sliding in and out, the low growl of the lift-shunts, and, louder than the yelling winds without, the scream of the bow-rudder gouging into any lull that promised hold for an instant. At last we began to claw up on a cant, bow-rudder and port-propeller together; only the nicest balancing of tanks saved us from spinning like the rifle-bullet of the old days.

"We've got to hitch to windward of that Mark Boat somehow," George cried.

'There's no windward," I protested feebly, where I swung shackled to a stanchion. "How can there be?"

He laughed—as we pitched into a thousand foot blowout—that red man laughed beneath his inflated hood!

"Look!" he said. 'We must clear those refugees with a high lift."

The Mark Boat was below and a little to the sou'west of us, fluctuating in the centre of her distraught galaxy. The air was thick with moving lights at every level. I take it most of them were trying to lie head to wind, but, not being hydras, they failed. An under-tanked Moghrabi boat had risen to the limit of her lift, and, finding no improvement, had dropped a couple of thousand. There she met a superb wulli-wa, and was blown up spinning like a dead leaf. Instead of shutting off she went astern and, naturally, rebounded as from a wall almost into the Mark Boat, whose language (our G. C. took it in) was humanly simple.

"If they'd only ride it out quietly it 'ud be better," said George in a calm, while we climbed like a bat above them all. "But some skippers *will* navigate without enough lift. What does that Tad-boat think she is doing, Tim?"

"Playin' kiss in the ring," was Tim's unmoved reply. A Trans-Asiatic Direct liner had found a smooth and butted into it full power. But there was a vortex at the tail of that smooth, so the T. A. D. was flipped out like a pea from off a finger-nail, braking madly as she fled down and all but over-ending.

"Now I hope she's satisfied," said Tim. "I'm glad I'm not a Mark Boat . . . Do I want help?" The General Communicator dial had caught his ear. "George, you may tell that gentleman with my love—love, remember, George—that I do not want help. Who *is* the officious sardine-tin?"

"A Rimouski drogher on the look-out for a tow."

"Very kind of the Rimouski drogher. This postal packet isn't being towed at present."

"Those droghers will go anywhere on a chance of salvage," George explained. "We call 'em kittiwakes."

A long-beaked, bright steel ninety-footer floated at ease for one instant within hail of us, her slings coiled ready for rescues, and a single hand in her open tower. He was smoking. Surrendered to the insurrection of the airs through which we tore our way, he lay in absolute peace. I saw the smoke of his pipe ascend untroubled ere his boat dropped, it seemed, like a stone in a well.

We had just cleared the Mark Boat and her disorderly neighbors when the storm ended as suddenly as it had begun A shooting-star to northward filled the sky with the green blink of a meteorite dissipating itself in our atmosphere.

Said George: "That may iron out all the tensions."

Even as he spoke, the conflicting winds came to rest, the levels filled; the laterals died out in long, easy swells; the airways were smoothed before us. In less than three minutes the covey round the Mark Boat had shipped their power-lights and whirred away upon their businesses.

"What's happened!" I gasped. The nerve-storm within and the volt-tingle without had passed: my inflators weighed like lead.

"God, He knows!" said Captain George soberly. "That old shooting-star's skin-friction has discharged the different levels. I've seen it happen before. Phew! What a relief!"

We dropped from ten to six thousand and got rid of our clammy suits. Tim shut off and stepped out of the Frame. The Mark Boat was coming up behind us. He opened the colloid in that heavenly stillness and mopped his face.

"Hello, Williams!" he cried. "A degree or two out o' station, ain't you?"

"May be," was the answer from the Mark Boat. "I've had some company this evening."

"So I noticed. Wasn't that quite a little draught?"

"I warned you. Why didn't you pull out north? The eastbound packets have."

"Me? Not till I'm running a Polar consumptives' sanatorium boat. I was squinting through a colloid before you were out of your cradle, my son."

"I'd be the last man to deny it," the captain of the Mark Boat replies softly. "The way you handled her just now—I'm a pretty fair judge of traffic in a volt-hurry—it was a thousand revolutions beyond anything even *I've* ever seen."

Tim's back supples visibly to this oiling. Captain George on the c.p. winks and points to the portrait of a singularly attractive maiden pinned up on Tim's telescope bracket above the steering-wheel.

I see. Wholly and entirely do I see!

There is some talk overhead of "coming round to tea on Friday," a brief report of the derelict's fate, and Tim volunteers as he descends: "For an A. B. C. man young Williams is less of a high-tension fool than some. . . . Were you thinking of taking her on, George? Then I'll just have a look round that port-thrust—seems to me it's a trifle warm—and we'll jog along."

The Mark Boat hums off joyously and hangs herself up in her appointed eyrie. Here she will stay a shutterless observatory; a life-boat station; a salvage tug; a court of ultimate appeal-cum-meteorological bureau for three hundred miles in all directions, till Wednesday next when her relief slides across the stars to take her buffeted place. Her black hull, double conning-tower, and ever-ready slings represent all that remains to the planet of that odd old world authority. She is responsible only to the Aerial Board of Control—the A. B. C. of which Tim speaks so flippantly. But that semi-elected, semi-nominated body of a few score of persons of both sexes, controls this planet. "Transportation is Civilisation," our motto runs. Theoretically, we do what we please so long as we do not interfere with the traffic *and all it implies.* Practically, the A. B. C. confirms or annuls all international arrangements and, to judge from its last report, finds our tolerant, humorous, lazy little planet only too ready to shift the whole burden of public administration on its shoulders.

I discuss this with Tim, sipping maté on the c. p. while George fans her along over the white blur of the Banks in beautiful upward curves of fifty miles each. The dip-dial translates them on the tape in flowing freehand.

Tim gathers up a skein of it and surveys the last few feet, which record "162's" path through the volt-flurry.

"I haven't had a fever-chart like this to show up in five years," he says ruefully.

A postal packet's dip-dial records every yard of every run. The tapes then go to the A. B. C., which collates and makes composite photographs of them for the instruction of captains. Tim studies his irrevocable past, shaking his head.

"Hello! Here's a fifteen-hundred-foot drop at fifty-five degrees! We must have been standing on our heads then, George."

"You don't say so," George answers. "I fancied I noticed it at the time."

George may not have Captain Purnall's catlike swiftness, but he is all an artist to the tips of the broad fingers that play on the shunt-stops. The delicious flight-curves come away on the tape with never a waver. The Mark Boat's vertical spindle of light lies down to eastward, setting in the face of the following stars. Westward, where no planet should rise, the triple verticals of Trinity Bay (we keep still to the Southern route) make a low-lifting haze. We seem the only thing at rest under all the heavens; floating at ease till the earth's revolution shall turn up our landing-towers.

And minute by minute our silent clock gives us a sixteen-second mile.

"Some fine night," says Tim, "we'll be even with that clock's Master."

"He's coming now," says George, over his shoulder. "I'm chasing the night west."

The stars ahead dim no more than if a film of mist had been drawn under unobserved, but the deep airboom on our skin changes to a joyful shout.

"The dawn-gust," says Tim. "It'll go on to meet the Sun. Look! Look! There's the dark being crammed back over our bows! Come to the after-colloid. I'll show you something."

The engine-room is hot and stuffy; the clerks in the coach are asleep, and the Slave of the Ray is ready to follow them. Tim slides open the aft colloid and reveals the curve of the world—the ocean's deepest purple—edged with fuming and intolerable gold. Then the Sun rises and through the colloid strikes out our lamps. Tim scowls in his face.

"Squirrels in a cage," he mutters. "That's all we are. Squirrels in a cage He's going twice as fast as us. Just you wait a few years, my shining friend, and we'll take steps that will amaze you. We'll Joshua you!"

Yes, that is our dream: to turn all earth into the Vale of Ajalon at our pleasure. So far, we can drag out the dawn to twice its normal length in these latitudes. But some day—even on the Equator—we shall hold the Sun level in his full stride.

Now we look down on a sea thronged with heavy traffic. A big submersible breaks water suddenly. Another and another follows with a swash and a suck and a savage bubbling of relieved pressures. The deep-sea freighters are rising to lung up after the long night, and the leisurely ocean is all patterned with peacock's eyes of foam.

"We'll lung up, too," says Tim, and when we return to the c. p. George shuts off, the colloids are opened, and the fresh air sweeps her out. There is no hurry. The old contracts (they will be revised at the end of the year) allow twelve hours for a run which any packet can put behind her in ten. So we breakfast in the arms of an easterly slant which pushes us along at a languid twenty.

To enjoy life, and tobacco, begin both on a sunny morning half a mile or so above the dappled Atlantic cloud-belts and after a volt-flurry which has cleared and tempered your nerves. While we discussed the thickening traffic with the superiority that comes of having a high level reserved to ourselves, we heard (and I for the first time) the morning hymn on a Hospital boat.

She was cloaked by a skein of ravelled fluff beneath us and we caught the chant before she rose into the sunlight. *"Oh, ye Winds of God,"* sang the unseen voices: *"bless ye the Lord! Praise Him and magnify Him for ever!"*

We slid off our caps and joined in. When our shadow fell across her great open platforms they looked up and stretched out their hands neighbourly while they sang. We could see the doctors and the nurses and the white-button-like faces of the cot-patients. She passed slowly beneath us, heading northward, her hull, wet with the dews of the night, all ablaze in the sunshine. So took she the shadow of a cloud and vanished, her song continuing. *"Oh, ye holy and humble men of heart, bless ye the Lord! Praise Him and magnify Him for ever."*

"She's a public lunger or she wouldn't have been singing the *Benedicite;* and she's a Greenlander or she wouldn't have snow-blinds over her colloids," said George at last. "She'll be bound for Frederikshavn or one of the Glacier sanatoriums for a month. If she was an accident ward she'd be hung up at the eight-thousand-foot level. Yes—consumptives."

"Funny how the new things are the old things. I've read in books," Tim answered, "that savages used to haul their sick and wounded up to the tops of hills because microbes were fewer there. We hoist 'em into sterilized air for a while. Same idea. How much do the doctors say we've added to the average life of a man?"

"Thirty years," says George with a twinkle in his eye. "Are we going to spend 'em all up here, Tim?"

"Flap ahead, then. Flap ahead. Who's hindering?" the senior captain laughed, as we went in.

We held a good lift to clear the coastwise and Continental shipping; and we had need of it. Though our route is in no sense a populated one, there is a steady trickle of traffic this way along. We met Hudson Bay furriers out of the Great Preserve, hurrying to make their departure from Bonavista with sable and black fox for the insatiable markets. We overcrossed Keewatin liners, small and cramped; but their captains, who see no land between Trepassy and Blanco, know what gold they bring back from West Africa. Trans-Asiatic Directs we met, soberly ringing the world round the Fiftieth Meridian at an honest seventy knots; and white-painted Ackroyd & Hunt fruiters out of the south fled beneath us, their ventilated hulls whistling like Chinese kites. Their market is in the North among the northern sanatoria where you can smell their grape-fruit and bananas across the cold snows. Argentine beef boats we sighted too, of enormous capacity and unlovely outline. They, too, feed the northern health stations in ice-bound ports where submersibles dare not rise.

Yellow-bellied ore-flats and Ungava petrol-tanks punted down leisurely out of the north, like strings of unfrightened wild duck. It does not pay to "fly" minerals and oil a mile farther than is necessary; but the risks of transhipping to submersibles in the ice pack off Nain or Hebron are so great that these heavy freighters fly down to Halifax direct, and scent the air as they go. They are the biggest tramps aloft except the Athabasca grain-tubs. But these last, now that the wheat is moved, are busy, over the world's shoulder, timber-lifting in Siberia.

We held to the St. Lawrence (it is astonishing how the old water-ways still pull us children of the air), and followed his broad line of black between its drifting ice-blocks, all down the Park that the wisdom of our fathers—but every one knows the Quebec run.

We dropped to the Heights Receiving Towers twenty minutes ahead of time, and there hung at ease till the Yokohama Intermediate Packet could pull out and give us our proper slip. It was curious to watch the action of the holding-down clips all along the frosty river front as the boats cleared or came to rest. A big Hamburger was leaving Pont Levis and her crew, unshipping the platform railings, began to sing "Elsinore"—the oldest of our chanteys. You know it of course:

Mother Rugen's tea-house on the Baltic—
    Forty couples waltzing on the floor!
And you can watch my Ray,
For I must go away
    And dance with Ella Sweyn at Elsinore!

Then, while they sweated home the covering-plates:

Nor-Nor-Nor-Nor-
West from Sourabaya to the Baltic—
   Ninety knot an hour to the Skaw!
Mother Rugen's tea-house on the Baltic
   And dance with Ella Sweyn at Elsinore!

The clips parted with a gesture of indignant dismissal, as though Quebec, glittering under her snows, were casting out these light and unworthy lovers. Our signal came from the Heights. Tim turned and floated up, but surely then it was with passionate appeal that the great tower arms flung open—or did I think so because on the upper staging a little hooded figure also opened her arms wide toward her father?

In ten seconds the coach with its clerks clashed down to the receiving-caisson; the hostlers displaced the engineers at the idle turbines, and Tim, prouder of this than all, introduced me to the maiden of the photograph on the shelf. "And by the way," said he to her, stepping forth in sunshine under the hat of civil life, "I saw young Williams in the Mark Boat. I've asked him to tea on Friday."

The Father of Modern Science Fiction

The accomplishments of earlier authors and the gathering scientific and social forces for change seemed to meet in the person of one small, perceptive Englishman, Herbert George Wells. He was born in Bromley, Kent, a few miles from London, in 1866, just a couple of years after Jules Verne's first science-fiction novel was published, and he died, a famous and wealthy author, in 1946, having seen science fiction become a genre and having seen the world realize several of science fiction's dreams and fears.

His father was a gardener and a part-time professional cricket player; his mother was a ladies' maid. When they were married, they bought an unsuccessful crockery shop called Atlas House, where the young Wells was born and grew up, and where his mother, concerned with seeing her children placed in some secure occupation, tried to apprentice him as a draper and as a pharmaceutical chemist.

Wells attributed his escape from his mother's conventional Victorian world to two broken legs: when he broke his own, at a youthful age, his father introduced him to the splendor of books; his father's broken leg ended his cricket-playing career and the sale of cricket equipment in the crockery shop. That was the only thing that sold, and his mother became housekeeper at Up Park. Books were available in the Up Park library for Wells to read, and money was available to send Wells on in school.

Wells had a quick mind that enabled him to master subjects easily on his own, and eventually to write on almost any subject, including science, history, and economics. His ambition to write was well timed; as he put it in his autobiography, "The habit of reading was spreading to new classes with distinctive needs and curiosities. . . . New books were being demanded and fresh authors were in request."

Wells won a scholarship to the Normal School of Science in South Kensington. He lasted three years. The first was a formative period of studying biology under the great Thomas H. Huxley, the champion of Darwinism. Darwin, whose *Origin of the Species* was published in 1859, created a great furor over the Western world with his theories, and through Huxley was a major influence on Wells. In his second and third years, Wells studied physics and geology, finally dropping out with a complaint about poor teaching. Later he won his degree in biology by examination. He worked briefly for a correspondence college and wrote a biology textbook before he turned to a full-time career in writing.

Article writing came first, a couple of metaphysical speculations in 1891; then he realized that success lay in writing about more commonplace topics. In 1894 he began writing what he called "single sitting stories" using his special knowledge of science, culminating in the publication of his novella *The Time Machine* in 1895, which he had been working at in various forms since his Normal School days. It was an immediate success. In addition to his short stories, he began producing a novel a year. They were called scientific romances and included *The Island of Dr. Moreau* (1896), *The Invisible Man* (1897), *The War of the Worlds* (1898), *When the Sleeper Wakes* (1899), and *The First Men in the Moon* (1901).

They made his reputation, *The War of the Worlds* in particular; it was reprinted around the world, often serialized in newspapers with the location for alien depredations changed to the region it was being published, as Orson Welles in his 1938 broadcast changed the location to New York and George Pal in his 1953 film version changed it to Los Angeles. With his personal success assured, Wells turned to writing other kinds of books: contemporary novels such as *Kipps* (1905), *Ton-Bungay* (1909), *Mr. Britling Sees It Through* (1915), and *Joan and Peter* (1918); and encyclopedic works such as *The Outline of History* (1919), *The Science of Life* (1930), and *The Work, Wealth, and Happiness of Mankind* (1931).

But perhaps his greatest concern was for improving the condition of humanity. He had attended meetings of the Fabian socialists while attending the Normal School; as a successful author, he became a regular member. The Fabians believed that the new affluence produced by industrialization could be distributed more efficiently so that poverty and hunger could be ended. Wells called for "an open conspiracy" among people of good will to set up a new world order, and he described it in such books as A *Modern Utopia* (1905), *The World Set Free,* (1914), *Men Like Gods* (1923), and *The Shape of Things to Come* (1934).

Wells did not think his scientific romances belonged to the Jules Verne tradition, and rejected attempts to call him "the English Jules Verne." Verne's work, he said, "dealt almost always with actual possibilities of invention and discovery. . . . But these stories of mine . . . do not pretend to deal with possible things; they are exercises of the imagination in a quite different field. They belong to a class of writing which includes the *Golden*

Ass of Apuleius, the *True Histories of Lucian, Peter Schlemil* and the story of *Frankenstein.*" His special favorite was *Gulliver's Travels.*

Wells's technique was to introduce one fantastic element, strange property, or strange world and show how ordinary people react to it. He wrote: "The thing that makes such imaginations interesting is their translation into commonplace terms and a rigid exclusion of other marvels from the story. Then it becomes human. . . . For the writer of fantastic stories to help the reader to play the game properly, he must help him in every possible unobtrusive way to *domesticate* the impossible hypothesis. He must trick him into an unwary concession to some plausible assumption and get on with his story while the illusion holds."

Ideas exploded in his stories. Some he adapted from the work of others. Most seemed original: time travel by machine, invisibility through chemicals or by speed of motion, attack by extraterrestrials, specialization through biology, superman, parallel worlds, warfare using tanks or airships, the atomic bomb, world catastrophe, alien influences on human evolution, man-eating plants, celestial bodies coming close to earth, interplanetary television, prehistoric people, conquest by ants, attack by sea creatures. . . . His particular concern was evolution: perhaps human evolution isn't over, or other creatures, such as ants or giant squids, may evolve into competitors.

By his techniques and by the number and excitement of his ideas, Wells broadened the audience for science fiction, just as Verne had done before him. Wells, with his critical mind and his superior writing skills, carried science fiction to heights it had never reached before and would seldom reach afterward.

He was the third writer Hugo Gernsback pointed to when he wanted to define what he was going to publish in his new magazine: "By 'scientifiction' I mean the Jules Verne, H. G. Wells, and Edgar Allan Poe type of story—a charming romance intermingled with scientific fact and prophetic vision."

The Star

BY H. G. WELLS

It was on the first day of the new year that the announcement was made, almost simultaneously from three observatories, that the motion of the planet Neptune, the outermost of all the planets that wheel about the sun, had become very erratic. Ogilvy had already called attention to a suspected retardation in its velocity in December. Such a piece of news was scarcely calculated to interest a world the greater portion of whose inhabitants were unaware of the existence of the planet Neptune, nor outside the astronomical profession did the subsequent discovery of a faint, remote speck of light in the region of the perturbed planet cause any very great excitement. Scientific people, however, found the intelligence remarkable enough, even before it became known that the new body was rapidly growing larger and brighter, that its motion was quite different from the orderly progress of the planets, and that the deflection of Neptune and its satellite was becoming now of an unprecedented kind.

Few people without a training in science can realise the huge isolation of the solar system. The sun with its specks of planets, its dust of planetoids, and its impalpable comets, swims in a vacant immensity that almost defeats the imagination. Beyond the orbit of Neptune there is space, vacant so far as human observation has penetrated, without warmth or light or sound, blank emptiness, for twenty million times a million miles. That is the smallest estimate of the distance to be traversed before the very nearest of the stars is attained. And, saving a few comets more unsubstantial than the thinnest flame, no matter had ever to human knowledge crossed this gulf of space, until early in the twentieth century this strange wanderer appeared. A vast mass of matter it was, bulky, heavy, rushing without warning out of the black mystery of the sky into the radiance of the sun. By the second day it was clearly visible to any decent instrument, as a speck with a barely sensible diameter, in the constellation Leo near Regulus. In a little while an opera glass could attain it.

On the third day of the new year the newspaper readers of two hemispheres were made aware for the first time of the real importance of this unusual apparition in the heavens. "A Planetary Collision," one London paper headed the news, and proclaimed Duchaine's opinion that this strange new planet would probably collide with Neptune. The leader writers enlarged upon the topic. So that in most of the capitals of the world, on January 3rd, there was an expectation, however vague, of some imminent phenomenon in the sky; and as the night followed the sunset round the globe, thousands of men turned their eyes skyward to see—the old familiar stars just as they had always been.

Until it was dawn in London and Pollux setting and the stars overhead grown pale. The winter's dawn it was, a sickly filtering accumulation of daylight, and the light of gas and candles shone yellow in the windows to show where people were astir. But the yawning policeman saw the thing, the busy crowds in the markets stopped agape, workmen going to their work betimes, milkmen, the drivers of news-carts, dissipation going home jaded and pale, homeless wanderers, sentinels on their beats, and in the country, labourers trudging afield, poachers slinking home, all over the dusky quickening country it could be seen—and out at sea by seamen watching for the day—a great white star, come suddenly into the westward sky!

Brighter it was than any star in our skies; brighter than the evening star at its brightest. It still glowed out white and large, no mere twinkling spot of light, but a small round clear shining disc, an hour after the day had come. And where science has not reached, men stared and feared, telling one another of the wars and pestilences that are foreshadowed by these fiery signs in the Heavens. Sturdy Boers, dusky Hottentots, Gold Coast negroes, Frenchmen, Spaniards, Portuguese, stood in the warmth of the sunrise watching the setting of this strange new star.

And in a hundred observatories there had been suppressed excitement, rising almost to shouting pitch, as the two remote bodies had rushed together, and a hurrying to and fro to gather photographic apparatus and spectroscope, and this appliance and that, to record this novel astonishing sight, the destruction of world. For it was a world, a sister planet of our earth, far greater than our earth indeed, that had so suddenly flashed into flaming death. Neptune it was had been struck, fairly and squarely, by the strange planet from outer space and the heat of the concussion had incontinently turned two solid globes into one vast mass of incandescence. Round the world that day, two hours before the dawn, went the pallid great white star, fading only as it sank westward and the sun mounted above it. Everywhere men marvelled at it, but of all those who saw it none could have marvelled more than those sailors, habitual watchers of the stars, who far away at sea had heard nothing of its advent and saw it now rise like a pigmy moon and climb zenithward and hang overhead and sink westward with the passing of the night.

And when next it rose over Europe everywhere were crowds of watchers on hilly slopes, on house-roofs, in open spaces, staring eastward for the rising of the great new star. It rose with a white glow in front of it, like the glare of a white fire, and those who had seen it come into existence the night before cried out at the sight of it. "It is larger," they cried. "It is brighter!" And, indeed the moon a quarter full and sinking in the west was in its apparent size beyond comparison, but scarcely in all its breadth had it as much brightness now as the little circle of the strange new star.

"It is brighter!" cried the people clustering in the streets. But in the dim observatories the watchers held their breath and peered at one another. "*It is nearer,*" they said. "*Nearer!*"

And voice after voice repeated, "It is nearer," and the clicking telegraph took that up, and it trembled along telephone wires, and in a thousand cities grimy compositors fingered the type. "It is nearer." Men writing in offices, struck with a strange realisation, flung down their pens; men talking in a thousand places suddenly came upon a grotesque possibility in those words, "It is nearer." It hurried along awakening streets, it was shouted down the frost-stilled ways of quiet villages, men who had read these things from the throbbing tape stood in yellow-lit doorways shouting the news to the passers-by. "It is nearer." Pretty women, flushed and glittering, heard the news told jestingly between the dances, and feigned an intelligent interest they did not feel. "Nearer! Indeed. How curious! How very, very clever people must be to find out things like that!"

Lonely tramps faring through the wintry night murmured those words to comfort themselves looking skyward. "It has need to be nearer, for the night's as cold as charity. Don't seem much warmth from it if it *is* nearer, all the same."

"What is a new star to me?" cried the weeping woman kneeling beside her dead.

The schoolboy, rising early for his examination work, puzzled it out for himself—with the great white star, shining broad and bright through the frost-flowers of his window. "Centrifugal, centripetal," he said, with his chin on his fist. "Stop a planet in its flight, rob it of its centrifugal force what then? Centripetal has it, and down it falls into the sun. And this—!"

"Do *we* come in the way? I wonder—"

The light of that day went the way of its brethren, and with the later watchers of the frosty darkness rose the strange star again. And it was now so bright that the waxing moon seemed but a pale yellow ghost of itself, hanging huge in the sunset. In a South African city a great man had married, and the streets were alight to welcome his return with his bride. "Even the skies have illuminated," said the flatterer. Under Capricorn, two negro lovers, daring the wild beasts and evil spirits, for love of one another, crouched together in a cane brake where the fire-flies hovered. "That is our star," they whispered, and felt strangely comforted by the sweet brilliance of its light.

The master mathematician sat in his private room and pushed the papers from him. His calculations were already finished. In a small white phial there still remained a little of the drug that had kept him awake and active for four long nights. Each day, serene, explicit, patient as ever, he had given his lecture to his students, and then had come back at once to this momentous calculation. His face was grave, a little drawn and hectic from his drugged activity. For some time he seemed lost in thought. Then he went to the window, and the blind went up with a click. Halfway up the sky, over the clustering roofs, chimneys, and steeples of the city, hung the star.

He looked at it as one might look into the eyes of a brave enemy. "You may kill me," he said after a silence. "But I can hold you—and all the universe for that matter—in the grip of this little brain. I would not change. Even now."

He looked at the little phial. "There will be no need of sleep again," he said. The next day at noon, punctual to the minute, he entered his lecture theatre, put his hat on the end of the table as his habit was, and carefully selected a large piece of chalk. It was a joke among his students that he could not lecture without that piece of chalk to fumble in his fingers, and once he had been stricken to impotence by their hiding his supply. He came and looked under his grey eyebrows at the rising tiers of young fresh faces, and spoke with his accustomed studied commonness of phrasing. "Circumstances have risen—circumstances beyond my control," he said and paused, "which will debar me from completing the course I had designed. It would seem, gentlemen, if I may put the thing clearly and briefly, that—Man has lived in vain."

The students glanced at one another. Had they heard aright? Mad? Raised eyebrows and grinning lips there were, but one or two faces remained intent upon his calm grey-fringed face. "It will be interesting," he was saying, "to devote this morning to an exposition, so far as I can make it clear to you, of the calculations that have led me to this conclusion. Let us assume.—"

He turned towards the blackboard, meditating a diagram in the way that was usual to him. "What was that about 'lived in vain'?" whispered one student to another. "Listen," said the other, nodding towards the lecturer.

And presently they began to understand.

That night the star rose later, for its proper eastward motion had carried it some way across Leo towards Virgo, and its brightness was so great that the sky became a luminous blue as it rose, and every star was hidden in its turn, save only Jupiter near the zenith, Capella, Aldebaran, Sirius, and the pointers of the Bear. It was very white and beautiful. In many parts of the world that night a pallid halo encircled it about. It was perceptibly larger; in the clear refractive sky of the tropics it seemed as if it were nearly a quarter the size of the moon. The frost was still on the ground in England, but the world was as brightly lit as if it were mid-summer moonlight. One could see to read quite ordinary print by that cold clear light, and in the cities the lamps burnt yellow and wan.

And everywhere the world was awake that night, and throughout Christendom a sombre murmur hung in the keen air over the countryside like the belling of bees in the heather, and this murmurous tumult grew to a clangour in the cities. It was the tolling of the bells in a million belfry towers and steeples, summoning the people to sleep no more, to sin no more, but to gather in their churches and pray. And overhead, growing larger and brighter as the earth rolled on its way and the night passed, rose the dazzling star.

And the streets and houses were alight in all the cities, the shipyards glared, and whatever roads led to high country were lit and crowded all night long. And in all the seas about the civilised lands, ships with throbbing engines, and ships with belling sails, crowded with men and living creatures, were standing out to ocean and the north. For already the warning of the master mathematician had been telegraphed all over the world, and translated into a hundred tongues. The new planet and Neptune, locked in a fiery embrace, were whirling headlong, ever faster and faster towards the sun. Already every second this blazing mass flew a hundred miles, and every second its terrific velocity increased. As it flew now, indeed, it must pass a hundred million of miles wide of the earth and scarcely affect it. But near its destined path, as yet only slightly perturbed, spun the mighty planet Jupiter and his moons sweeping splendid round the sun. Every moment now the attraction between the fiery star and the greatest of the planets grew stronger. And the result of that attraction? Inevitably Jupiter would be deflected from his orbit into an elliptical path, and the burning star, swung by his attraction wide of its sunward rush, would "describe a curved path" and perhaps collide with, and certainly pass very close to, our earth. "Earthquakes, volcanic outbreaks, cyclones, sea waves, floods, and a steady rise in temperature to I know not what limit"—so prophesied the master mathematician.

And overhead, to carry out his words, lonely and cold and livid, blazed the star of the coming doom.

To many who stared at it that night until their eyes ached, it seemed that it was visibly approaching. And that night, too, the weather changed, and the frost that had gripped all Central Europe and France and England softened towards a thaw.

But you must not imagine because I have spoken of people praying through the night and people going aboard ships and people fleeing towards mountainous country that the whole world was already in a terror because of the star. As a matter of fact, use and wont still ruled the world, and save for the talk of idle moments and the splendour of the night, nine human beings out of ten were still busy at their common occupations. In all the cities the shops, save one here and there, opened and closed at their proper hours, the doctor and the undertaker plied their trades, the workers gathered in the factories, soldiers drilled, scholars studied, lovers sought one another, thieves lurked and fled, politicians planned their schemes. The presses of the newspapers roared through the nights, and many a priest of this church and that would not open his holy building to further what he considered a foolish panic. The newspapers insisted on the lesson of the year 1000—for then, too, people had anticipated the end. The star was no star—mere gas—a comet; and were it a star it could not possibly strike the earth. There was no precedent for such a thing. Common sense was sturdy everywhere, scornful, jesting, a little inclined to persecute the obdurate fearful. That night, at seven-fifteen by Greenwich time, the star would be at its nearest to Jupiter. Then the world would see the turn things would take. The master mathematician's grim warnings were treated by many as so much mere elaborate self-advertisement. Common sense at last, a little heated by argument, signified its unalterable convictions by going to bed. So, too, barbarism and savagery, already tired of the novelty, went about their mighty business, and save for a howling dog here and there, the beast world left the star unheeded.

And yet, when at last the watchers in the European States saw the star rise, an hour later it is true, but no larger than it had been the night before, there were still plenty awake to laugh at the master mathematician—to take the danger as if it had passed.

But hereafter the laughter ceased. The star grew—it grew with a terrible steadiness hour after hour, a little larger each hour, a little nearer the midnight zenith, and brighter and brighter, until it had turned night into a second day. Had it come straight to the earth instead of in a curved path, had it lost no velocity to Jupiter, it must have leapt the intervening gulf in a day, but as it was it took five days altogether to come by our planet. The next night it had become a third the size of the moon before it set to English eyes, and the thaw was assured. It rose over America near the size of the moon, but blinding white to look at, and *hot;* and a breath of hot wind blew now with its rising and gathering strength, and in Virginia, and Brazil, and down the St. Lawrence valley, it shone intermittently through a driving reek of thunder-clouds, flickering violet lightning and hail unprecedented. In Manitoba was a thaw and devastating floods.

And upon all the mountains of the earth the snow and ice began to melt that night, and all the rivers coming out of high country flowed thick and turbid, and soon—in their upper reaches—with swirling trees and the bodies of beasts and men. They rose steadily, steadily in the ghostly brilliance, and came trickling over their banks at last, behind the flying population of their valleys.

And along the coast of Argentina and up the South Atlantic the tides were higher than had ever been in the memory of man, and the storms drove the waters in many cases scores of miles inland, drowning whole cities. And so great grew the heat during the night that the rising of the sun was like the coming of a shadow. The earthquakes began and grew until all down America from the Arctic Circle to Cape Horn, hillsides were sliding, fissures were opening, and houses and walls crumbling to destruction. The whole side of Cotopaxi slipped out in one vast convulsion, and a tumult of lava poured out so high and broad and swift and liquid that in one day it reached the sea.

So the star, with the wan moon in its wake, marched across the Pacific, trailed the thunderstorms like the hem of a robe, and the growing tidal wave that toiled behind it, frothing and eager, poured over island and island and swept them clear of men. Until that wave came at last—in a blinding light and with the breath of a furnace, swift and terrible it came—a wall of water, fifty feet high, roaring hungrily, upon the long coasts of Asia, and swept inland across the plains of China. For a space the star, hotter now and larger and brighter than the sun in its strength, showed with pitiless brilliance the wide and populous country; towns and villages with their pagodas and trees, roads, wide, cultivated fields, millions of sleepless people staring in helpless terror at the incandescent sky; and then, low and growing, came the murmur of the flood. And thus it was with millions of men that night—a flight nowhither, with limbs heavy with heat and breath fierce and scant, and the flood like a wall swift and white behind. And then death.

China was lit glowing white, but over Japan and Java and all the islands of East Asia the great star was a ball of dull red fire because of the steam and smoke and ashes the volcanoes were spouting forth to salute its coming. Above was the lava, hot gases and ash, and below the seething floods, and the whole earth swayed and rumbled with the earthquake shocks. Soon the immemorial snows of Thibet and the Himalaya were melting and pouring down by ten million deepening converging channels upon the plains of Burmah and Hindostan. The tangled summits of the Indian jungles were aflame in a thousand places, and below the hurrying waters around the stems were dark objects that still struggled feebly and reflected the blood-red tongues of fire. And in a rudderless confusion a multitude of men and women fled down the broad riverways to that one last hope of men—the open sea.

Larger grew the star, and larger, hotter, and brighter with a terrible swiftness now. The tropical ocean had lost its phosphorescence, and the whirling steam rose in ghostly wreaths from the black waves that plunged incessantly, speckled with storm-tossed ships.

And then came a wonder. It seemed to those who in Europe watched for the rising of the star that the world must have ceased its rotation. In a thousand open spaces of down and upland the people who had fled thither from the floods and the falling houses and sliding slopes of hill watched for that rising in vain. Hour followed hour through a terrible suspense, and the star rose not. Once again men set their eyes upon the old constellations they had counted lost to them for ever. In England it was hot and clear overhead, though the ground quivered perpetually, but in the tropics, Sirius and Capella and Aldebaran showed through a veil of steam. And when at last the great star rose near ten hours late, the sun rose close upon it, and in the centre of its white heart was a disc of black.

Over Asia it was the star had begun to fall behind the movement of the sky, and then suddenly, as it hung over India, its light had been veiled. All the plain of India from the mouth of the Indus to the mouths of the Ganges was a shallow waste of shining water that night, out of which rose temples and palaces, mounds and hills, black with people. Every minaret was a clustering mass of people, who fell one by one into the turbid waters, as heat and terror overcame them. The whole land seemed a-wailing, and suddenly there swept a shadow across that furnace of despair, and a breath of cold wind, and a gathering of clouds, out of the cooling air. Men looking up, near blinded, at the star, saw that a black disc was creeping across the light. It was the moon, coming between the star and the earth. And even as men cried to God at this respite, out of the East with a strange inexplicable swiftness sprang the sun. And then star, sun, and moon rushed together across the heavens.

So it was that presently, to the European watchers, star and sun rose close upon each other, drove headlong for a space and then slower, and at last came to rest, star and sun merged into one glare of flame at the zenith of the sky. The moon no longer eclipsed the star but was lost to sight in the brilliance of the sky. And though those who were still alive regarded it for the most part with that dull stupidity that hunger, fatigue, heat, and despair engender, there were still men who could perceive the meaning of these signs. Star and earth had been at their nearest, had swung about one another, and the star had passed. Already it was receding, swifter and swifter, in the last stage of its headlong journey downward into the sun.

And then the clouds gathered, blotting out the vision of the sky, the thunder and lightning wove a garment round the world; all over the earth was such a downpour of rain as men had never before seen, and where the volcanoes flared red against the cloud canopy there descended torrents of mud. Everywhere the waters were pouring off the land, leaving mud-silted ruins, and the earth littered like a storm-worn beach with all that had floated, and the dead bodies of the men and brutes, its children. For days the water streamed off the land, sweeping away soil and trees and houses in the way, and piling huge dykes and scooping out Titanic gullies over the countryside. Those were the days of darkness that followed the star and the heat. All through them, and for many weeks and months, the earthquakes continued.

But the star had passed, and men, hunger-driven and gathering courage only slowly, might creep back to their ruined cities, buried granaries, and sodden fields. Such few ships as had escaped the storms of that time came stunned and shattered and sounding their way cautiously through the new marks and shoals of once-familiar ports. And as the storms subsided men perceived that everywhere the days were hotter than of yore, and the sun larger, and the moon, shrunk to a third of its former size, took now four-score days between its new and new.

But of the new brotherhood that grew presently among men, of the saving of laws and books and machines, of the strange change that had come over Iceland and Greenland and the shores of Baffin's Bay, so that the sailors coming there presently found them green and gracious, and could scarce believe their eyes, this story does not tell. Nor of the movement of mankind now that the earth was hotter, northward and southward towards the poles of the earth. It concerns itself only with the coming and the passing of the star.

The Martian astronomers—for there are astronomers on Mars, although they are very different beings from men—were naturally profoundly interested by these things. They saw them from their own standpoint, of course. "Considering the mass and temperature of the missile that was flung through our solar system into the sun," one wrote, "it is astonishing what a little damage the earth, which it missed so narrowly, has sustained. All the familiar continental markings and the masses of the seas remain intact, and indeed the only difference seems to be a shrinkage of the white discoloration (supposed to be frozen water) round either pole." Which only shows how small the vastest of human catastrophes may seem, at a distance of a few million miles.

About the Editor

James Gunn, born in Kansas City, Missouri, in 1923, served in World War II as a U.S. Navy ensign and earned two degrees from the University of Kansas: a bachelor's degree in journalism in 1947 and a master's degree in English in 1951. He worked as an editor for a paperback publisher but spent much of his career at the University of Kansas, first as editor of the alumni magazine and then as administrative assistant to the Chancellor for University Relations. In 1970 he returned to teaching, specializing in the teaching of fiction writing and science fiction, was promoted to full professor in 1974, and retired in 1993 to return to full-time writing. Among his best-known novels are: *The Joy Makers*, *The Immortals* (which was adapted as a television movie and then a series, *The Immortal*), *The Listeners*, *Kampus*, and *The Dreamers*. He also became a well-known scholar and winner of the SFRA Pilgrim Award with such books as *Alternate Worlds: The Illustrated History of Science Fiction*, *Isaac Asimov: The Foundations of Science Fiction* (which won a Hugo Award for nonfiction), and the six-volume *The Road to Science Fiction*. He served as president of the Science Fiction Writers of America and as president of the Science Fiction Research Association and founded the Center for the Study of Science Fiction.